**DURHAM COUNTY COUNCIL**
Arts, Libraries and Museums Department

Please return or renew this item by the last date shown.
Fines will be charged if the book is kept after this date.
Thank you for using *your* library.

 100% recycled paper.

292 Kennington Road, London SE11 4LD

Copyright © 1999 Alasdair Lamont

All rights reserved. No part of this publication may be reproduced in any form, except for the purposes of review, without prior written permission from the copyright owner.

British Library Cataloguing in Publication Data.
A catalogue record for this book is available from the British Library.

Printed and bound by Watkiss Studios Ltd.
Biggleswade, Beds.
Issued by New Millennium*
Set in 12 point Times New Roman Typeface
ISBN 1 85845 226 0
*An imprint of The Professional Authors' & Publishers' Association

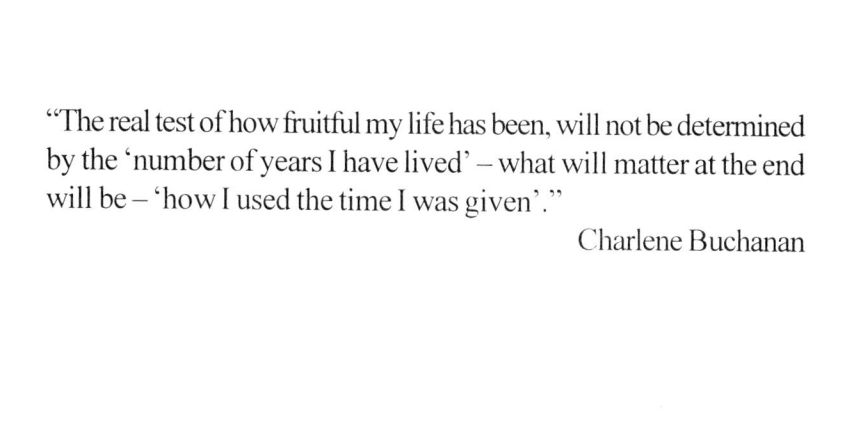

"The real test of how fruitful my life has been, will not be determined by the 'number of years I have lived' – what will matter at the end will be – 'how I used the time I was given'."
Charlene Buchanan

This story is lovingly dedicated to my late wife Rena.

# Chapter 1

Roger and Charlene were climbing up the steep rocky path, through natural woodland of pine, oak and birch, when suddenly the way ahead expanded on to the open hill, and to a tingling view of the sharp, eminence of Ben Calder.

"I think I must be out of condition;" said Charlene. "It's been a long time since my last climb." She looked apprehensively at the three-hundred-foot high rocky cone ahead.

Roger nodded. "I know how you feel. It was the same for me when I joined the club three months ago. Since then I've been walking every Sunday. You'll soon get used to it."

Charlene stopped and took several deep breaths. "Get a move on, girl," she said quietly, to herself.

The Kelvin Hiking Club had come to the Trossachs from Glasgow; intending to see the breathtaking view from the summit of one of the lower peaks in a group of mountains dominated by Ben Lomond, known as the 'bristly country'. This rough mixture of rock, crag and scrub had once served as a hideout for Rob Roy.

The rocky track gave way to irregular patches of bracken, rush and bog myrtle.

"Look!" said Charlene. "There's a red squirrel climbing up that Scotch pine. That's a rare sight nowadays. Its grey cousin has almost taken over."

"That's what I like about walking in the hills," said Roger. "You get a lot of opportunities to see nature in the wild."

He had just finished speaking when two red stags darted from cover and ran across their path. Awed, Roger and Charlene stood motionless as they watched them disappear among the trees.

Roger went ahead and turned to help Charlene to clamber up the boulder-strewn track. Suddenly the unexpected sight of a long twisting loch opened out before them. The transition from the wild plateau on the summit to the loch and wooded countryside was delightful in its simple beauty. Had it not been for the small, floating clouds moving slowly across the horizon it would have been difficult to separate the sky from the loch? Beyond it and towering above the pine-covered shore of Loch Arden, Ben Lomond squatted like an enormous pachyderm.

Roger led his companion to a small ledge overlooking a steep cliff face. "You get the best view of all from here," he said.

"That must be the village of Arden." Charlene pointed to a group of cottages clustered round a church spire. "Isn't it lovely?"

Below them rocks and knolls were covered with trees and luxuriant heather giving the whole a purple tinge.

"You can imagine Wordsworth and Dorothy wandering about the village, can't you?" said Charlene.

"It's surprising what you learn," said Roger. "I hadn't thought of it like that exactly."

"They were looking for Rob Roy's grave, and then they walked the fourteen miles from here to their hotel. And that's not all - they were up at eight o'clock next morning to continue their journey."

"Look over there," said Roger, "at the paddle steamer returning from the end of the loch." A tiny plume of black smoke was being carried upwards to Ben Lomond as the steamer moved towards the tiny wooden pier at Arden.

Charlene glanced at her watch. "We've been here for some time. I hope the others haven't abandoned us."

"The Kelvin wouldn't do that. That's what we have a leader in the party for, to keep us all safely together."

They crawled back to the summit plateau but there was no sign of the rest of the party.

\* \* \* \* \*

Roger had met Charlene on an earlier part of the climb. She was a new member and immediately she had interested him. She was tall, slim and agile, dressed in brown corduroy trousers with flared bottoms and in a pale blue anorak; but she was not so fashionably dressed as to suggest a benevolent father or a wealthy husband. He estimated she was about his own age; which placed Charlene in her early forties. Her forehead was made unnaturally high by a brown, woollen hat which had not been pulled down far enough, and a few tell-tale wisps of slightly auburn hair, streaked with grey, had escaped from the bonnet and were blowing in strands across her eyes in the cold wind. Because Roger had wanted to reflect on his marital problems, he had spent only a few, brief moments with her before moving up ahead, leaving her in the company of the other women. This was not unusual, for it was the constant change of walking companion which gave the club members most pleasure, as they were able to talk to different people about different topics.

He had noticed the absence of engagement and wedding rings, but had not enquired if she were married. If he had, she would surely have asked him then about his own marital state and that was very uncertain at present.

\* \* \* \* \*

Isolated as they were at that moment from the rest of the party, they perched side by side on an adjacent rock and waited.

"What have you two been up to?" They heard Myra's teasing voice; she was known as the club gossip. They looked round to see the others had suddenly appeared and joined them. Myra saw every eligible man as a possible husband and had been interested in Roger since he had first joined the club.

"Nothing that would be of interest to you, Myra," said Roger. "I suppose you've met Charlene?" He waved a hand feebly by way of a belated introduction. "We were just admiring the view."

Myra laughed loudly. "Do you really expect me to believe that?" She had not managed to seduce anyone in all her years as a member of the group.

"Let's get a move on," called Walter. "We've got a long way to go and it'll be dark before we get back if we don't move off soon."

Roger and Charlene separated, taking up different positions in the snake, as the single file line of walkers was fondly called.

The party managed to stay together as they walked down the slope leading to the small green loch. When they came to a maze of chopped off trees, Roger was forced to make his way slowly from one stump to another to avoid causing pain to his big toe. Consequently a large gap built up between him and the leading group as they neared the car park.

It was not enough that he was emotionally low, but the constant, thumping pain on the damaged toe was slowing him down. He felt he might stop altogether at this rate. He saw a few stragglers coming down behind him and decided to go behind a tree to "admire the view", as relieving oneself was euphemistically called.

Just as he was emerging from his hiding place he walked again into Charlene who happened to be bringing up the rear of the stragglers. She had been hoping to resume their conversation.

"Hello again," she said with a broad smile.

"Hello, yourself."

The two of them walked on until they came to a level green shoulder where the terrain became less painful for Roger and less tiring for Charlene.

"Would you like to know about Black Holes?" he asked out of the blue. "It just happens a physicist friend of mine gave me a book about them."

Charlene smiled and nodded.

"It seems all the energy around them is taken in by these dark patches in the sky." He had only a very hazy idea of the facts, but tried to explain as well as he could.

"Isn't there a danger that everything will go into the hole and the whole universe disappear?" Charlene was quite alarmed by her new knowledge. "And where does it all go anyway?"

"I'm afraid I don't know. I'm a lawyer, not a scientist, but I'll ask my friend for the answers if you'd like to know."

"No. Stop before I get worried more than need be!"

"Don't you think sometimes we shouldn't try to delve too deeply into God's creation? Let's just enjoy it while we're here."

"You seem to do a lot of reading. Have you ever read *The Little Prince*?"

"Not that I remember. Anyway I gave up reading fairy tales when I was ten."

Charlene had been reading St Exupery's classic to her class of young children, and had been inspired spiritually by it. She offered to bring it with her next Sunday.

"You strike me as someone with a philosophical approach to life. If you read the story with a child's eye you might learn more than you would as an adult."

Roger felt there might be something special about her. The other women members of the group spent their time talking about their work, or gossiping about the latest club romances. Her fair-haired companion intrigued Charlene in her turn. She was going to enjoy her walks now that she'd found a kindred spirit. Her regret was that although she was wearing low-heeled shoes she was almost as tall as he was. Even at that he was about six feet, rugged and clean-shaven with fair complexion and light wavy hair; an athletic type who liked climbing mountains as opposed to walking on them.

They were nearly over the brow of Ben Calder when Roger said casually, "You're a rare bird, Charlene."

She stopped and gripped his arm. "Do you mean that? You don't know how much it means to me."

"Well, I certainly think you're unique among the women in this club, and I have no doubt you're unique elsewhere as well."

"You've made my day. You'll never know how much I needed someone to boost my ego," she said engagingly.

"One would never know you've got problems by looking at your smiling face. Not like me: my face gives me away all the time."

"I realised early on you might be in a difficult situation because, as you say, you showed it in your eyes." She pointed a black mitten at him. "Did you know your eyes reflected the sky?"

"What's that about eyes reflecting the sky?" called a voice from just below the breast of the hill. "We've been waiting for you two to come down before we left." Walter, whose voice it was, shook his finger at them aggressively, like a referee reprimanding an offending player during a football match.

"I'm sorry," said Roger. "I wasn't aware of the time. My bad foot was forcing me to walk rather slowly."

"If you have foot trouble," came the unsympathetic retort, "you should consider whether you ought to be walking on the hills at all. Anyway, let's get back to the cars right away. It'll be dark very soon."

Roger and Charlene separated, realising that they needed to avoid gossip, and walked with other club members to the car park.

When the Kelvin Hiking Club had left the city centre, those members without transportation had been allocated to the cars of the five drivers going to Ben Calder. Roger wished he had known Charlene then; she could have come with him instead of travelling with Walter. His passengers, Bill and Beverley took their unfinished flasks and biscuits and went over to a bench. This would give him a few minutes resting time. It was a pity he had finished his flask; he could have done with something to revive him.

"I've brought two flasks with me," said a sweet voice, which he instantly recognised. "One has coffee and the other tea. Which do you prefer?"

"You'll have the others gossiping now, Charlene," he warned mischievously.

She ignored the comment and asked again which flask he preferred.

"I think I'd like the tea. Do you have sugar and milk?"

"Of course. Do you have a mug?"

Roger opened a pocket on his rucksack and produced one, badly chipped.

"If I were you I'd get rid of it and treat myself to a new one," she reproved mildly. "Do you take the milk first?"

He nodded and watched as she poured the tea.

"By the way," she called out as she returned to Walter's car, "I take it you'll be going on next week's walk ... whatever the weather?"

"I haven't missed one yet," he shouted back.

\* \* \* \* \*

When Roger arrived home from the Ben Calder climb, his wife Edith was sitting on the sofa in the living room reading the Sunday paper. Had it not been for his failed marriage, he reflected, he would not have found Charlene. He looked at the clock; Edith still had half an hour to go until her Sunday night meeting with her elderly lover, William Porter.

"You look very happy with yourself," Edith observed as he came into the front room, still wearing his hiking gear. "Have you found my replacement already?"

Roger knew that the less he said, the less he provided her with incriminating evidence. He dropped his small blue rucksack on the floor beside his favourite fireside chair, and started to remove his heavy anorak. "It was a nice walk," he said.

He would need to watch out what he said in future. There was a time when he would have wanted to tell everyone about the wonderful woman that he'd met that day. Maybe Edith was right. They both needed a change of partners.

"What are you thinking about?" his wife asked suspiciously. She was certain that Roger was keeping something from her.

He took off his anorak and threw it on the floor beside the rucksack without answering, not wanting to provoke an acrimonious row at a time when he was beginning to understand the reasons for the breakdown of his marriage.

"I know my behaviour has tended to be uncaring, but it wasn't always like that. We were very happy once." A wistful look crossed his face as he recalled how often Edith had refused his engagement ring.

She grunted and continued to read the Sunday paper. She wasn't very much interested in the past any more; only in her future with Willie Porter.

"It was all that study of the law. I was concentrating on my course and that was what was responsible for my neglect of you." He didn't like to admit, even to himself, that he had been in the wrong but he continued after a pause. "And then, after that it was my all-consuming interest in my profession."

"We've been over that before," she said heatedly. "I gave you so many chances to put things right, but the situation just got worse. No, Roger Buchanan! I may not have found someone with such a good brain as yours, but he does love me and he shows it. He's not like you and he makes me happy."

Edith had been nursing her grievances for a long time. Did he think she was going to give up a man who had shown her more care and understanding in the past few months than he has done since they were married? Willie might only be a window cleaner, but he knew much more than Roger about her needs.

"Maybe if we were prepared to try again, if you were to give me another chance, maybe we could go back to the days when ... "

"I don't think you've heard a word I've said," Edith interjected in exasperation. She had found happiness and was angry with him for trying to make her feel guilty by his pleading. "We've been over all that before. When it comes to love you can't repair what's been broken," she said, rejecting his offer. "You can't go back to the past. The only way for us lies ahead, in the future. I've found Willie Porter and I intend to go on seeing him. Our marriage is finished."

He mustn't let her upset him, he thought. It was far too easy to let anger reveal things, which were better left unsaid.

"Is it that Jane Faulds, then, that's getting you in this happy frame of mind?" she said, trying to entice further information from him.

He had made a mistake telling her so much about the club members, particularly about the women; they outnumbered the men at least two to one. He had only done it to get her interested in coming with him to the club meetings and hopefully, loosen Willie Porter's grip on her. Now she thought she was entitled to know everything. He hadn't told her about the women to provide ammunition with which she could shoot him down. She must have noticed how affectionately he had spoken of Jane, he thought ruefully.

"Has the cat got your tongue?" Edith said scathingly. "I'm surprised you ever won a case. You don't take so long to say what's needed in court."

"It's not that at all. I would like to say more, but I've decided it's not the sensible to do so. I'm trying to bring about a reconciliation with you, Edith. If you would only give me another chance."

Edith had become so embittered that any solution would have been acceptable to her, other than the reconciliation Roger wanted.

He could see that the life style she intended to adopt was full of contradictions. William Porter was proposing to seek work on the oil rigs, while she would look for a job as a domestic servant or waitress. He didn't think the happiness she was seeking would come from her association with this man. Perhaps William was a more adequate experienced lover than he was? But intercourse without other common interests would eventually lead to the breakdown of the relationship. Roger's legal experience had included so many similar cases but there would be no point in his mentioning them to her. For the time being, anyway, Edith was happy.

Why was he was taking so long to answer her, Edith thought. Plainly he was preparing a suitable defence. Maybe Jane was making herself available? She wondered if Jane knew the true situation. And if she did ... she might hold the key to a divorce. Did he realise that he'd be paying maintenance for a long time to come? She and Willie wanted to be with each other; nothing more than that, but he didn't want to divorce his wife, who would be happy to have him back from time to time.

"I asked you if you were interested in Jane Faulds and you

haven't answered me." Edith was determined to know what was going on.

"Edith, I don't know why my being interested in another woman should be causing you so much concern. I would have thought your own conscience would be troubling you. But, if you are determined to know, I'll tell you."

He had no intention of mentioning Charlene Graham. "It's true I've been paying a little attention to Jane Faulds. She rather reminds me of you. Maybe that's why I'm interested. She knows I'm unhappy, but not the reason. She invited me to the St. Valentine Day's dance when it was organised by her church and I have to admit I had a pretty good time there. I think she likes me, but I'm not sure. And I want you to know there is no sex between us."

"That's not what I heard. It so happens I met a friend who's in the Kelvin Club. She asked me why I didn't come along with you, and I replied that we were in the process of splitting up."

"Who was that?" challenged Roger.

When Edith didn't answer, he continued, "It must have been Maureen Harrison. She's a frustrated single who's determined to damn anyone who looks as though they're enjoying themselves. It's not fair to expect me to live like a hermit. Of course I enjoy the company of some of the women in the club. There would need to be something not quite right about me not to. But there's never been any sex. Just talking, walking and sometimes dancing."

Edith hesitated. Maybe he really was trying to work something out. She wondered if she should risk giving up Willie Porter. But what would happen to her the next time she and Roger had a row? She was not without some sense. She realised that life with Willie - a married man, with whom she shared only two interests, was not an ideal one; particularly since he was an older man who insisted on looking after his estranged wife, in spite of his interest in Edith.

"Edith." Roger's voice broke through her reverie. "Now that you've assumed you can have your freedom, I would like our marriage to end at an early date. You can have the house and an allowance."

And she had been considering taking him back, she thought. That would have been a mistake for a start. Clearly he'd got plans for Jane Faulds.

"In that case we'll both get in touch with our lawyers and try to work something out. I suppose you'll need to ask your partner to act for you. I've left something on the cooker for your evening meal. I'm away out to see you-know-who. I'll be back some time, probably late."

Roger, who had now come to terms with his wife's defection, sat at the kitchen table and reflected on his future as he ate his evening meal. The soup was first class and his wife made the finest brown bread he'd ever eaten. He was going to miss it when they separated. He quickly finished the remaining soup and sandwiches and took the dirty dishes over to the sink to wash them. As usual, Edith, who was not keen on tidying up after her, had left her own used dishes and two dirty pots in the sink.

He hoped she wouldn't be too greedy though, expecting him to keep her and her man in the style to which she had became accustomed. It was true she had worked while he had studied at the university and so she was entitled to more than would otherwise have been the case.

It looked as if he were getting himself involved with three women, he thought. You'd think Edith would be enough to handle. He was too quick in getting himself involved with Jane. She was a pleasant enough wee lassie, who rather reminded him of Edith. Maybe that's why he was attracted to her in the first place.

They say a rejected husband is usually looking for a visually compatible replacement, one who can give him the happiness which has gone from his marriage. Jane was a kindly caring girl, who would no doubt have replaced Edith as a sexual partner. But did he have much else in common with her? They both enjoyed walking of course. Unlike Charlene Graham, however, she did not have wide-ranging interests, and her conversation was not nearly as interesting.

He went through to the sitting room and stretched himself out in front of the fire. There didn't seem to be much television worth viewing. Roger threw the Sunday paper on the settee and took the club programme from his wallet.

During the winter session, when the daylight hours were short, the Wednesday evening meeting of the hikers took place indoors. The entertainment committee had arranged a wide-ranging programme of activities. There were dances, talks by well-known speakers, quiz nights, Anniversary nights like the Burns' Night Supper and the inevitable Christmas Party.

He wondered what was on next Wednesday and scanned the list of events until he came to the appropriate date. "Ugh! A Beetle Drive," he grunted. It might not be very exciting, but at least it might give him the chance to meet his kindred spirit again, he thought.

Roger had just dozed off in the warmth of the fire when the phone rang.

"Er ... who? ... Sorry I don't know." He had not heard the opening remarks of his caller nor had he recognised the voice. "Who's calling?"

"It's Charlene Graham. Did I get you at an awkward time?"

"Oh! It's you Charlene. Forgive me for not recognising you immediately," he replied cautiously. Roger had not expected his new companion to contact him at home. What would have happened if Edith had answered the phone?

"I hope you won't be angry with me," said Charlene. "I just wanted to make sure you had arrived home all right. I was worried when I saw how tired you were looking. You still had that long drive ahead of you."

Evidently Charlene did not suspect that he was married. Should he take the chance of losing her friendship by telling her right away, he wondered, but he decided not to do so because he felt a compulsive need of her company?

"Oh! I'm fine. I've been dozing before the fire. It's marvellous what a whisky can do for you."

"It wouldn't do anything for me Roger. I never drink alcohol."

That was foolish of him. He thought he should leave the subject of his wife for the time being. Two black marks in two minutes wouldn't go down well.

"I don't drink a lot of it myself," Roger said, trying to minimise the damage. "Just the occasional one. Sometimes I like a glass of wine with my meals. I think it adds a lot to the experience."

Charlene came from a home where her late father had insisted on a policy of no alcohol. She had tasted a glass of French wine when she was on holiday, but had been so unimpressed she had decided to leave "this dubious pleasure" alone.

"I don't mind other people doing what they feel is essential, so long as they don't expect me to follow their example or use it as an excuse for their bad behaviour," she replied. "But then I'm sure your manners are without reproach."

"Charlene," he said gently. "How did you get my phone number? I don't remember telling you where I was living."

"Maureen Harrison lives near me. We went home together in the bus and she talked about you."

Roger replied immediately, on the principle that the best defence is attack. "I don't know her very well at all. In fact I've hardly even talked with her during the walks. I'd be very surprised if she could even tell you my surname."

"Maureen knows everything about everybody," replied Charlene. "And if she doesn't, she does her best to find out. She's already opened a dossier on me. She keeps a mental file on everyone. Even you."

Roger thought it would be better to make an indirect reference to being married and admit that his wife was still living with him.

"I've lost someone I loved very much," he said without going into details.

Charlene responded immediately. "I'm aware you have a wife and that you are very unhappy. Maureen made a special point of telling me so. I had intended to leave it to you to tell me about when you felt the time was suitable. I know you are a decent man, Roger, whom I can trust, and that's all I need to know right now. She also told me I had no "chance with you", since you were already going out with Jane Faulds."

Roger, who was astounded at the harmful tittle-tattle of women in the club imagined what Maureen had been thinking. If I'm not to have him then I'll make sure someone else doesn't want him. He had known Maureen was a foolish woman, who gossiped, often maliciously, at the slightest excuse. But he would have been less forthcoming when he spoke to her had he known the destructive results of her prattle.

"I'm sorry you had to learn about my problem at second hand," Roger said, apologising for not having told her sooner. "My wife and I resolved our position when I came home tonight. We'll see our lawyers and set the wheels in motion for a divorce."

He heard Charlene's gasp at the other end of the phone. "Then it's true. You are married," she sounded disappointed.

"Will this make any difference to our friendship?" Roger asked timidly. "I enjoyed talking to you this morning so much. There are a great many things we have to discuss. I was just thinking it would take us a long time to cover all our mutual interests."

"Do you think I'd have phoned you if I didn't want to continue our friendship? So long as you want to share your thoughts with me as you did today, I'll be there. You should know, however, that I believe husband and wife are partners until separated by death, as the Bible tells us. I'm sure we can continue to be good friends, despite people like Maureen Harrison."

"Charlene. I'm so glad to hear that." Roger was relieved to know he still had her friendship.

"Will you be coming next Wednesday to the Beetle Drive?" she asked. "If you are, I'll bring my copy of The Little Prince with me."

"There aren't many club nights I miss. She - I mean my wife, Edith - goes out with Willie Porter on a Wednesday and I don't like being at home thinking what is happening to the woman I love - or, rather loved once. A beetle drive is not my cup of tea. But it does provide me with an opportunity to meet other people."

"I'll see you there then," she said chirpily and put the phone down briskly.

It was strange how some things worked out. She was not proposing a love pact, but he was glad she was still interested in being friends.

His musing was brought to an abrupt halt when Edith's voice boomed out. "Who was that on the phone?"

"No one you'd know."

"I'm well aware of that," she replied coldly. "But I asked you who it was? If you can't answer that simple question, I'm surprised any of your clients succeeded in their court cases."

"I don't think it's your business to know who's speaking to me. You lost the right to know what I was doing when you decided to give me up." Edith seemed to be upset about something. Did he have a fight on his hands? He risked a question. "You're home earlier than usual. Is anything wrong?" Roger looked more closely at her face and saw her tearful eyes for the first time.

"Willie Porter doesn't want to leave his wife. He doesn't mind living with me somewhere else, so long as he's in easy touch with her," she said, distressed.

"It sounds to me as if you've found someone who wants to have his cake and eat it. Are you sure you're doing the right thing?"

"I don't think there's much chance for us, though I know he loves me. He shows it in so many ways you don't." She took off her imitation sable coat and threw it over the settee before sitting down opposite him. "This is going to make no difference to our relationship. You can have a divorce or a separation, the choice is yours. But, as far as, I'm concerned, I'd prefer a separation."

"That's no solution at all," said Roger, getting up and pouring himself another whisky. "You're behaving like Willie Porter. You want the best of both worlds, and I'm to be piggy in the middle."

She shook her head angrily. "A separation would leave you free to play around with Jane Faulds. Maureen tells me she's pretty good in bed," said Edith, hoping to appeal to Roger's one weakness.

He had given up the idea of continuing his association with Jane Faulds now he had met such an interesting friend in Charlene and this factor more than outweighed any other.

"I'm sorry, Edith. I've moved away from you too, but there's no one waiting to take your place. We should just go ahead, as we agreed, and ask our lawyers to set a divorce in motion."

Edith would have preferred to keep Roger in a kind of limbo, just in case her relationship with Willie Porter turned sour. "If that's what you want, Roger, then we'll do it your way."

She went over and switched on the television to a programme Roger positively disliked. He got up.

"I think I'll just go to bed. Good night, Edith."

"Good night, Roger. It's nice to know when you're not wanted."

Roger climbed the narrow stairs leading to the spare bedroom, and wondered if he were doing the right thing. Was it possible he was beginning to look on a divorce as an opportunity to begin a new life with Charlene?

Edith was glad to be alone for a while. The new phase in her relationship with Willie Porter had made her emotionally distraught and, feeling sorry for herself, she started sobbing quietly.

## Chapter 2

James Robertson took copious notes as he listened attentively to his partner explaining the events, which had led him to seek a divorce from Edith.

"Roger, clearly she's the one in the wrong. You'll have to divorce her to ensure she doesn't take everything you've got."

"No. No. No. That won't do at all," interjected Roger. "The settlement needs to be arranged without blame on either side. There are many reasons. Most importantly, she helped me get where I am by being the breadwinner while I studied. I've already said I'll give her the family home and a reasonable monthly allowance. She's still able to work you know."

"In that case well try for the two year period of breakdown and agree a settlement. Who's acting for her?"

"I don't know yet. Probably the local firm, Cooper. I've no doubt we'll get a letter from them soon enough."

"The only other thing we need to deal with now is the matter of the family goods."

"I don't think there should be any trouble there. Apart from a few belongings I'll need to set me up somewhere else, and my own personal things, she can have the rest."

"Let's hope she will accept that. She may very well dispute ownership," he warned.

"I'm pretty sure she won't be arguing about the things I want."

"I know you've a daughter studying in Aberdeen. How does she feel about your divorce? Will she be needing an allowance as well?"

"Naturally she's on her mother's side, but she'll be expecting financial help till she's graduated."

A knock on the door announced Roger's secretary. "Excuse me," she said politely. "There's a woman on the phone. She wants to know if she can have a few words with you. She says it's urgent."

It can't be Edith, thought Roger. His secretary would have said his wife was on the phone. If it were Charlene, he didn't want James to know about her, not just yet.

"That'll be all right Sheila. Tell her I'll be with her in a minute."

Roger turned to his partner. "I hope you haven't spent too much time on conveyance work. I think you've enough details now to go ahead with the divorce."

When Roger returned to his office, his secretary was filling in time talking to the unknown caller.

"Thank you," he said. "I'll take it from here. Will you come back when I've finished?" He waited until she had closed the door behind her.

"Roger Buchanan here. How can I help you?"

"You don't have to be so formal," answered Jane Faulds. "Roger, I wanted to know if you were going to the Beetle Drive tonight?"

"Oh!" Roger hoped Jane wouldn't notice his disappointment. "I was thinking of going," he replied casually. "Has it been cancelled?"

"No. It's still on. But there's been some changes to the rules." Jane giggled as if this was an explanation for her phone call.

Why was she phoning him then? Surely the alterations affected the other members as well and could be dealt with by an announcement before the Beetle Drive began. She might be paying for the call, but he had other things to do and wanted to get on with them.

"I thought a lawyer like you knew all the questions and the answers as well. The Beetle Drive is on tonight all right. The point is I've just been having morning coffee in town with one of the organisers. She tells me club members will be paired together for the evening. I'd like you to be my partner."

Damn the woman. He wanted to be with Charlene. Why otherwise would he go to such a boring evening?

"Are you still there?" enquired Jane urgently.

"I'm still here. I've just been looking at my diary." He flicked the pages loudly. "It looks as if I might not be able to go," he lied, as he looked at the blank page. "I've got an early evening appointment with a client. One never knows how long these meetings will last. Even if I have a meal in town instead of going home, it might still not be possible."

Jane Faulds had begun to look on Roger as someone special. The other women in the club had withdrawn from the competition, assuming he had chosen her for the time being; it certainly looked that way. But Sunday had been different. Jane had made a special point of ignoring him and his depression.

"Are you doing this to me because I walked with the others on Sunday, and didn't want to hear about your problems?"

"It has nothing to do with that. Although, I have to say I could have done with a bit sympathy. I was feeling very low after a sleepless night."

"Is it that new member Charlene Graham who's got to you? Are you taking her to the Beetle Drive and don't want me to know?"

Roger was beginning to feel angry. She had no right to phone his office in the first place and, in the second, he had never given her the impression that she could call herself his girlfriend.

"Jane, I don't think who I go with has anything to do with you. If I have a mind to ask Charlene to be my partner then that's up to me."

"And your wife!" she shouted angrily over the phone. "You didn't think I knew about her, did you?"

"If you didn't I knew it wouldn't be long before you found out. I made the error of confiding in what I believed was a kindly ear. No doubt Maureen Harrison got to you with her gossip."

"No she didn't. I heard it over coffee today from someone else. But you'll notice I didn't say anything because I'm fond of you, Roger, and I want to be your friend."

"I want all the pretty girls to be my friends," Roger replied playfully, in a Don Juanish manner. "It's likely to be some time before I can ask anyone to be my special friend. As far as tonight is concerned, I'll have to leave the partnering until then. At this stage I can't say what my position will be. Anyway, enjoy yourself. I'll have to go. My secretary has just come in for some dictation. Goodbye for now." He put the phone down just as she was beginning to demand an explanation for his changed attitude towards her.

His secretary, an attractive woman for her years, sat in her usual place with her notepad open. She knew about his intention to begin divorce proceedings and vaguely wondered if he had any thoughts in her direction.

"I'm ready," she said, as she smiled and crossed legs to expose her pretty knees and a fair amount of thigh.

The phone rang again, just as Roger was about to dictate a letter.

"What d'you want?" he shouted angrily, thinking it might be Jane back to continue where she left off.

"There's no need to speak to me like that." Edith was hurt by his abrupt manner. "I thought you would like to know I've engaged Cooper to handle my side of the divorce."

"Forgive me Edith. I had a fool on the phone a little while ago. I thought it was them phoning back again." Roger was angry with himself for having been so short with Edith. This was not the time to upset her unnecessarily. "Is there something I can do for you?"

"As a matter of fact there is. My lawyer has asked me to talk over certain things with you. I thought the sooner the better. How about tonight in La Boromeo?"

Her call was both a nuisance and a blessing at the same time. If he went with Edith, it would avoid a partnership conflict at the Beetle Drive.

Even if he and Charlene began at the same table, there would be no possibility for them to stay together as the game progressed, since the winners and losers moved in different directions after each round. The chances were they wouldn't be doing much talking to each other until the tea and biscuits at the close of the evening. However, it would be nice. He would have to stop using that word so often if he were going to make an impression on Charlene.

"Are you still there Roger? I presume you're checking your diary?" Edith knew that this was his night out at the walking club.

"Yes, yes, that's what I was doing. I've nothing that can't be left till another time. Tonight will be okay. You know which day of the week this is? Don't you?" It was Wednesday, her usual night out with Willie Porter.

"Yes, I know. We sometimes have to make sacrifices. Will you come home earlier tonight? I know you like me to be gone when you come home on Wednesdays. But tonight there's no pressure on you."

"I'll be there," he said, and put the phone down.

He turned to his secretary. "It's time we started earning our wages," he said. The lawyer was just about to begin his dictation when the phone rang again.

"Roger Buchanan here. How can I help you?" Despite his anger at being interrupted for a third time his voice was gentle.

"It's me, Charlene. Roger, are you still going to the Beetle Drive? I've been told its partners."

"Miss Graham. It's nice to hear your voice."

"Roger. You'll need to be more careful. You've said that forbidden word," she chided him gently. He registered Charlene's point and went on. "Anyway, I'm glad you phoned Charlene. I have an appointment tonight, so I'll not be able to go to the club."

"I don't fancy a Beetle Drive either, but I suppose I'd better turn up or everybody's going to think we've gone somewhere together, bother it. Will you be on the Sunday walk?"

"You know what I said last time. I haven't missed many since I joined the club."

"I'll bring The Little Prince with me. I'm longing to hear your views about it."

"I hope you won't be disenchanted. Goodbye for now."

"Goodbye, Roger," she said, and put the phone down.

"Where were we?" Roger lifted his notes and turned to his secretary.

"Trying to earn our living," she sneakily replied.

\* \* \* \* \*

La Boromeo was a small Italian restaurant, which appealed to a clientele looking for well-cooked Italian pasta served in a warm, pleasant and smoke-free atmosphere. Edith looked around approvingly.

"I wonder why we never thought of coming here before? It's only a short drive from home." She lifted the menu and studied it until she came to the page offering an all-inclusive meal at an attractive price.

Roger looked at her. "I see you're looking at the gourmet package. Sounds a reasonably priced meal to me, particularly since it includes wine and coffee. I think we should go for that one. Don't you?" he asked cautiously.

Edith shrugged her shoulders. "If that's what you want Roger, go ahead. There's very little I really want. But then I know you've always fancied the Italians. Isn't that why we went there so often on holiday?"

Roger had agreed to come here to ensure an amicable severing of their marriage. It looked as if Edith were trying to sabotage that from the start.

"We can't get a gourmet meal for one with you selecting from a` la Carte," he pointed out. "If you look carefully at the Gourmet Menu you will see most of the items from the main menu are there. Some of them just require a small extra payment, that's all." He called the waiter over. "We'll both have the Gourmet meal."

"Very good, Signor. Have you chosen what you want?" The owner, who was taking the order, had been born in Scotland but his accent had been strongly influenced by his Italian-speaking parents.

"Gnocchi alla Romano for me," said Roger.

The waiter immediately wrote it down and turned to Edith.

"And for the signorina?"

Edith did not like to be hurried. As a matter of principle she would have asked him to wait till she was ready, but there were other matters to deal with and she did not want to waste time eating.

"I don't know. I'm not feeling too hungry tonight. If I must, I'll have that." She pointed to an item at the bottom of the page.

"I'm sorry, signorina. You can have that if you wish, but you can't eat it."

"That's stupid for a start. I'm sorry we came in here," she said angrily.

"Signorina! Please!" said the disheartened little Italian. "It's not something for to eat. It's to wish you a good appetite. Bon appetito is not to be eaten."

Roger, who had read the name of the nearest item, came to her rescue. "My wife would like spaghetti bolognese. Wouldn't you dear?" he said, smiling to his wife and nodding his own agreement to the choice.

"Yes. That's what I want," said Edith, extricating herself from her silly mistake.

"Forgive me signora. I did not understand."

"Will you be wanting vino bianco o rosso?" he said, turning to

Roger. The Italian was aware that his guest had read the greeting at the end of the menu.

"We both like white wine. Vino bianco per favore."

"Bene. I'll be with you in a momento," and made his way into the kitchen.

"I have to admit that the meal was positively first class. All four courses." She had taken several glasses of wine and was in a distinctly merry frame of mind as she praised the food.

"Would you like a liqueur with your coffee to finish?" the waiter asked Roger.

"Tia Maria for my wife and a Drambuie for me," said Roger. He was imbued with rashness brought on by a liberal intake of alcohol. He was not drunk but he had taken enough to loosen his tongue.

"Did you really enjoy "vitello alla Romano"?" he asked his wife.

"Yes. Very much. It had veal, cheese and ham," she replied. "And did you like your scampi alla Liv ... Oh dammit. The stuff you had."

"Livornese," he corrected gently. "I certainly did. It's supposed to make you want to do it."

Edith, who had warmed to Roger during the meal, looked him straight in the face. "But not with me, big boy. Our days of sex are finished."

"I didn't think they had revived," he growled. "Anyway there are other fish in the sea."

"I think you've said enough. Pay the bill and let's get out of here. I want to talk to you." She rose impatiently and walked towards the cloakroom.

They had to go round a large pond on the way home. It was one of those evenings when the heavenly artist emptied his paintbox, tinting the western sky with every hue from red through to blue as the sun set.

"That's very impressive," said Roger attracting his wife's attention to the radiant sky. "Maybe we should stop here in the car park and have our talk, looking at this wonderful spectacle."

Edith was fascinated by the wealth of colour dazzling her eyes. It had been a long time since either of them had seen such a spectacular sunset. "I wish I had my camera with me. It's worth a photograph."

"Unless you've got a fast film, you haven't much chance of getting a picture that will do this sunset justice," said Roger.

"He's going back to his wife," she said without warning. "That's what I wanted to tell you. He says she's not able to look after herself and, besides, his daughter is very upset with me."

"That's the best news I've heard for a long while," retorted Roger. "So the divorce is off and we can try to repair our marriage."

"That's not what I said. He's going back to his wife to look after her, but we'll be seeing each other from time to time."

"Like Wednesdays and Sundays. The position hasn't changed. You still want this man to be your lover. What's wrong with me? I thought I'd done well enough in that department."

Edith looked into his deep blue eyes. "Roger, when I fell in love with you it was because you reminded me of my red Indian brave come to life, the one in my school reader. I never imagined anyone could be so fortunate that day when I got back from London. I would have gone anywhere with you."

"And it looks as if you still react the same way. Did Willie Porter look like your Indian as well?"

"He gave me the kindness and understanding which you used to show me. I was so very depressed until he came along."

"Now, you're telling me nothing has changed. You still intend to keep on seeing him and you expect me to foot the bill for your extramarital adventures." Roger was angry. He had thought that Edith's increased warmth had been the beginning of reconciliation.

"I don't really want a divorce. Just a separation. You can see who you want, and I can meet Willie when I want," she said, making him an offer, one that he definitely intended to refuse.

He switched on the engine and depressed the clutch. "I would much rather have a clean break. That way I can possibly meet someone and begin afresh with them. I think I need to start a new life." He turned the ignition switch.

"I'll never marry again," she said, as the engine roared into life. It's always the men who come out best in the end. By the way, don't think I don't know about Charlene Graham. She seems to be very interested in you from what I hear."

By now Roger had gone round the end of the pond and was waiting to join the main traffic.

"Charlene just loves to talk," he said. "We could become very good friends."

"And how long before she marries you?"

"Not until you die, Edith," he said without sinister overtones. "She's a devout Christian and believes that marriage is for life. But she does seem to enjoy my company. I know I find her very interesting and exhilarating."

"Roger, I don't believe your little white-as-snow Christian is all that altruistic. I'm certain she'll accept an offer of marriage as soon as you've been divorced. But I'm not going to make it easy for you."

"I didn't really think you'd behave as badly as that, Edith. You're not that sort of person."

"How do you know what sort of person I am?" she retorted. "Have you ever really tried to find out?"

"I've admitted I neglected you, even though I thought there was an excuse," he said as he turned into the main street and headed for home. "You decided to end our marriage when you left with that man. Let's agree to a clean break with no acrimony on either side," and he put his foot down on the accelerator.

\* \* \* \* \*

Sometimes the Sunday climb, like today's ascent of Ben Lomond, was so popular that a coach had to be hired to accommodate everybody who wanted to participate.

The special bus rushed merrily along the narrow winding road on the northern shore of the loch with its crowd of chattering passengers. There was one notable exception to the general air of animation.

"Roger, you don't have very much to say for yourself today. It's usually very difficult for anybody to get a word in edgeways," Jane Faulds said crossly.

Roger had been wondering why he had been given the seat next to her. After all, Charlene had put her name under his on the bus list. Could it be that Robin Carson, the club secretary and leader of today's climb, had been influenced by the gossips when allocating places on the coach?

"I'm sorry Jane. Things are not going very well for me personally just now, and there's been a lot going on in Court." Roger was jerked forward awkwardly when the coach pulled up suddenly.

"We've arrived," he said as he looked over Jane's shoulder, and watched the coach move slowly into the small car park of the pub where the path began.

Being at the front of the coach, Charlene got off first and went over to a wooden bench to change into her boots.

By the time Roger and Jane got off the coach, an impatient group, including Charlene, had moved off into the small forest at the base of the mountain. Roger was disappointed she had not waited for him. Was she annoyed with him because he sat with Jane?

He began the slow process of changing from soft-shoes into his climbing boots.

"I don't like being at the tail-end," said the dark-haired Jane perkily. "It takes you so long to change with that toe of yours and I'm ready. I'll just get on and catch up with the others."

"All right. Have a nice climb," said Roger and sat on a nearby log. He wished Charlene had waited. They could have walked together now that Jane had gone ahead.

Being last to change, Roger ran uphill and took up his position at the rear of the long snake of walkers; but he had only reached the tail-end when everyone stopped. The early birds, it appeared, had come to a fork in the path and wisely had waited for the leader. Then Roger caught a glimpse of Charlene in her blue anorak and brown corduroy trousers farther along the line. Several members were looking at something in her hand. "Charlene!" he shouted and pushed his way through the tall, brown bracken to join her.

"That's a Sticky Willie!" said Charlene, as if she were addressing her class of toddlers. She waved a wild flower with sticky seed heads like a pointer. "Look at this." Her voice commanded attention, as she threw one seed after another on Roger's pullover.

"So it sticks," Robin Carson replied curtly.

"Ah, but why does it? That's the point." Charlene was behaving like a teacher. Unfortunately, she was oblivious to the fact that the others were really not interested.

Roger had observed that club members rarely stopped to observe the plant or animal life, which he found so fascinating. As far as the others were concerned, they were satisfied with gossip and getting to the top of the mountain as quickly as possible.

"That's very interesting. Come and tell me." He took Charlene's arm and guided her away from the others. "I thought you were annoyed at my sitting with Jane Faulds," he said once they were alone. "And I assumed that was the reason why you didn't wait for me."

"No. I wasn't angry at all. I wanted to get to the shelter of the forest and adjust a wrinkle in my tights," she smiled.

"It's so simple when you know how, as the conjurer said."

Charlene always hesitated before speaking her mind, especially when she felt she was intruding. "I notice you seem to be having a lot of trouble with your foot."

Roger lifted his left boot and shook it. "My big toe hurts when I've been walking for a while. It feels as if I've got a pebble in my boot."

Charlene smiled sympathetically. "Why don't you ask your doctor for help?"

"I consulted my doctor a long time ago but he told me not to let anyone operate on it. I've had to suffer it ever since."

"At least see your doctor, and ask him to send you to the Chiropody Hospital," Charlene persisted. "Will you do that for me?"

"Just to please you, I'll make an appointment."

The party had reached the long gentle slope about halfway up Ben Lomond when Robin shouted, "Time for a break."

There was a rush to sit on one of the flat-topped stones, which were plentiful in the area.

Jane had found a new man to concentrate on, and, for the time being, had lost interest in Roger and his companion.

"She won't bother us now," said Roger. "In fact she probably won't even be looking our way. It's strange how one can hide in a crowd." He brought a heavy pullover from his rucksack and spread it on one of the stones. "I'll not be wearing this today. You can sit here."

Charlene thanked him. "Don't you think we should share your flask of tea and keep mine for later on?"

"That's a good idea. The tea keeps hotter when the flask is full." Roger brought out a red plastic flask from his rucksack.

Charlene unscrewed the top of the flask. "Let me see the replacement."

"Tarra!" he shouted and brought out his new mug. "Is that acceptable?"

Charlene smiled and baptised it with its first filling of boiling hot tea. "You remembered what I said about being poisoned, didn't you? Drink it while it's still hot."

"I'll be moving into a council flat in New Town," Roger said suddenly. Charlene nodded her head. She had been uncomfortable, knowing that Roger was returning to his wife after being with her. She would feel very much happier in future now that he was on his own.

Edith had been indifferent to his announcement when he told her, that his partner Robertson had advised him to leave the family home. It would have been difficult to show a complete breakdown in the marriage, otherwise. He had been allocated a ground floor flat, consisting of living room, bedroom, kitchen and bathroom, which would be ready for occupation next week.

"Is your wife going to live permanently in your former home?"

"It just so happens that my daughter, Marjorie ..." He had begun to reply, when Charlene interrupted.

"You have a daughter as well? How many other little secrets have you got hidden away?" She laughed. "What does she think of your divorce?"

"I was about to say that my daughter will soon be finishing her course at the Aberdeen Commercial College and will be staying in the family home with her mother," Roger went on. "My daughter takes the view that her mother needs her and has chosen to take her side."

"We've had long enough," Robin broke in. "We'll need to get a move on."

"How about a toilet stop?" called out one of the ladies.

"If you didn't have one before we started, you'll have to hold on until we get back to the forest. But, if you're desperate, we'll form a circle about you to give you a bit of privacy."

"I'm not that desperate. I was thinking of the others, especially the men." She trembled with embarrassment.

"Is everybody all right?" The leader stared at each member in turn. "Let's get a move on then."

They had reached the precipitous slopes before the final summit, which usually sorted out the men from the boys when Charlene said, "I'll need to stop again, I'm right out of breath."

"And training," shouted a mischievous club member.

Roger suggested they should have a short break. "How about something to drink? There's still your flask."

Charlene agreed at once. "I'd like that. If the others start going down before we get to the top we can join them."

"Shall I put a spoonful of sugar in your tea this time?" Roger was ready with a heaped spoon.

"In coffee yes. But tea no, not usually. All right, maybe I need more energy," she said breathing heavily in between. "Oh that's good," she purred. "It's heating my hands up as well. I've got a poor central heating system. My body runs cold when I'm cold. I'm just contrary, like Mary."

Charlene was looking towards Ptarmigan, a smaller peak in the Ben Lomond chain, when she began to speculate on its name. "It doesn't look like a bird to me. Could it be that they used to nest there?"

"I don't know, either." Roger emptied the dregs of his mug on the path. "There was one occasion when I saw it casting a shadow and I thought I could see a large bird in flight."

"How perspicacious of you, Roger. There's a little drink left for you," she said emptying the remains of her tea on a small clump of grass.

"If I hadn't been a lawyer and was used to big words like that, I might not know what the school teacher meant," said Roger putting flask and mug back in his rucksack. "Don't let's be the only people who didn't finish the climb." He stood up and offered her his hand. "Easy does it." He tugged gently by her arm.

"What a smashing view you get from here." The exhilarated Charlene shouted, as she spun round and round.

"Careful, don't go falling over the edge," said Roger, taking hold of her anorak.

The rest of the party had left the summit and were on their way back down when Roger and Charlene arrived at the cairn-like sign post.

"Where's my favourite hill?"

Roger put his finger on the brass plate and searched through the names, whilst Charlene pulled her knitted, brown hat well down over her ears. "I'm beginning to feel cold again, now that we've stopped walking."

Roger pushed a gloved finger along the direction line until he was pointing at Ben Arthur. "Some people call it the Cobbler."

Charlene gasped at the beautiful panorama and forgot about the chilling wind. She had never seen the Loch Lomond hills stand out so clearly before. "They look so close one can almost touch them," she said enraptured.

"It's got to do with refraction," Roger announced. "It makes things look deceptively close."

"Oh, Roger! Look down there. Look at all those islands."

"That's the Highland Boundary fault." It was Roger's turn to do a bit of teaching.

"Do you see that cone-shaped mountain over there?" He pointed to the hills on her left.

Charlene scanned the area without success. "They all look very much alike to me." She was about to admit defeat and ask for further help. "Oh yes! I can see it now." It was quite small compared to Ben Lomond.

"That's the Conic Hill. It's part of that same fault."

"I'd like to go up they're some time," suggested Charlene, slapping her hands round her body to keep warm. "Let's get down from here, Roger. I can't take much more of this wind."

"Just as you wish. I think there's an outing to the Conic on the club programme. So you should get a chance to climb it then. It's a lot easier than walking up "The Ben"."

"We're really late now." Charlene was getting worried. "Has anyone ever been left behind?"

"They wouldn't do that. We'll just get a slight ribbing and be told its not considered good manners to keep other people waiting."

They climbed over a fence and almost stood on a young boy who was crying.

Charlene immediately took a hold of his hand. "Are you looking for your mummy?" she asked the child softly, at the same time patting him reassuringly on the shoulder. The small boy immediately stopped weeping but said nothing in reply. "Was she here the last time you saw her?" The boy anxiously nodded. "In that case you've nothing to worry about. Your mummy will come back here for you when she notices you're missing." She wiped the tears from his eyes with a tissue and searched in her pocket for a sweet. "Would you like this?" The little boy nodded. "Here you are then. Remember. Be a good boy and wait till mummy comes back. Don't you go up the hill now," she warned him gently.

Charlene had just finished soothing the child when his mother appeared from the forest. "I was desperate," she said. "I went away without telling him."

"So long as he's found you that's all that matters," said Charlene, as she and Roger went down the path that led to the car park and arrived with plenty of time to spare before the coach came to pick them up.

"My mother will have everything ready. I usually have a light meal and then we go to the evening service." Charlene settled herself in the seat next to the window.

"It's a dance next week. I suppose I can expect to see you there," Roger said hopefully.

"Of course. I love dancing, especially the older dances."

"Me too," agreed Roger, realising that they would not be together much longer.

"Time flies so quickly when one is enjoying life," he said as they got off the coach.

"I've parked my car over there," Charlene said pointing to a rather battered Morris Minor.

"I'll see you across the road. I'm parked a few cars along from you. I've had a wonderful time today and it almost made me forget my problem." Roger gazed into her eyes. He took her slim hand in his and patted it. It was too early to embrace or kiss her farewell, he thought.

"Well, cheerio, Charlene. See you on Wednesday."

"Not if I see you first." She extricated her hand and opened the car door. "I have something for you," she said handing him The Little Prince. "Cheerio for now."

When Charlene got home, Mrs Graham had everything ready, as her daughter had expected.

"Charlene, you've got that look in your eyes again. Have you met someone else?" Her mother knew that her daughter was lonely, after she and her friend, Ryan O"Donnell, had parted company.

"I don't have much time to explain just now mother, except to say I've met a man called Roger Buchanan. He's a lawyer and ... he's divorcing his wife."

Kate Graham gasped. "You can't be serious. You're not seeing a married man!"

"Trust me mother. You'll approve when I tell you all about him. At the moment I need to get myself ready."

Charlene dropped her small rucksack on the hall floor and went into the front room, which also served as her bedroom. She lit the gas fire to take the chill off the air.

She liked Roger very much, she thought, as she began to remove her hiking gear and put on a blouse and skirt. She wondered if he really liked her. Wouldn't it be nice ... then she stopped. She criticised others for speculating about this kind of thing and knew she must avoid doing so herself. It was, though, all right to think about the future. Wouldn't it be marvellous, if they could become very good friends?

"Charlene, the tea's out," called her mother from the kitchen, where they normally ate their meals. "We haven't much time to get to church."

"Coming, mother," called out her daughter. "I'm having a lick and a promise as the cat said." She was looking forward to hearing the new minister, Tony Drinkwater.

## CHAPTER 3

On the day after the walk, Roger consulted his new GP and learned that his problem toe could not be eased with simple chiropody.

"I'll make an appointment for you to see a specialist. From what I've been able to establish there's the likelihood you'll need surgery," said Dr Marshall.

Roger's face expressed concern at his prognosis.

"Is there something wrong?" asked the big man.

"You just mentioned surgery. Another doctor told me that I was never to let anyone perform surgery on my foot. It was as if he were saying that I would be crippled at the best, and lose my foot at the worst."

"I think you should ignore that advice and see my friend, Mr Fleming, at the Central General Hospital. I'm absolutely certain he'll advise you to have the small bone removed, the one, which is giving you all the trouble. It's just as if you were walking on a small stone all the time, and that must be very painful for you." Roger was still not convinced. "Why don't you go home and talk it over with your wife?"

"That's not possible." The doctor shrugged his shoulders. "What do you want me to do then?"

"I think you'd best make an appointment." He didn't want to appear cowardly to his friend. He was sure she'd approve his decision.

Roger thanked him and left immediately. He'd phone Charlene and ask for her opinion. He could always cancel the appointment.

\* \* \* \* \*

The Kelvin Hiking Club met every Wednesday in the large public hall of the local library. This evening's meeting would be very popular; dances were always well attended.

"Why didn't you come to Beetle Drive last week? Asked Maureen Harrison, as Roger handed over his money.

"I had a meeting with a client," he almost lied. His private business had nothing to do with Maureen. He noted that a large crowd was already waiting in the dance hall.

"Are you going to give me a dance?" she asked.

"What have you done to deserve it?" he challenged, looking the club gossip in the eyes. He could have said what has she done not to deserve it, but that would have been a bit cruel. So long as you were aware of such people you could take steps to counteract some of the consequences of their tiresome behaviour, he thought.

"What's taking you so long to make up your mind, Roger? You know I'm one of the best dancers in the club."

"Maybe, Maureen. It depends on who's coming," he told her. "I can't dance with everybody, and I've already promised some of the girls I'd dance with them."

"Are you trying to take my boyfriend away from me?" said Jane, who had just arrived. "He won't have time for anyone else now that I'm here." She wanted to embarrass her friend.

Maureen did not like to be put in second place. "Who said you were Roger's girlfriend anyway?" She tapped her foot vigorously on the floor to restrain herself from hitting Jane on the head with her shoulder bag.

"Ladies!" shouted Roger. "A little decorum if you please. I'll decide who's going to be my girlfriend, if you don't mind. In any case, I thought you said a new member was coming tonight, Jane. Why isn't he here with you?"

"He was only spending the weekend with his brother. He heard about the trip up the Ben and insisted on coming in his own car. I didn't even get a chance to be with him on the way back; he wasn't going in my direction."

Roger looked at his watch. Charlene was late. She had said she'd meet him in the hall entrance at seven-thirty, and it was now nearly eight o'clock. He hoped nothing had happened to her.

The three-piece band had finished setting up their equipment and they were now ready to begin.

"Ladies and gentlemen, we'll open the evening with a quickstep," said a slim man with long hair and a beaky nose.

"Your partner seems to have stood you up," Jane Faulds said sarcastically, as Roger was standing disconsolately near the door, still waiting for Charlene. "How about you and me doing this one?"

Although he was still feeling hurt by her malicious remark about him "having a wife", he wanted to be part of the group and this meant joining in their activities.

"I'm a free agent," said Roger, not wanting to give the impression there was anything more between himself and Charlene than just being good friends. "OK then, I hope you're wearing your armour-plated shoes."

They had been dancing for a couple of minutes when Jane tapped him on the shoulder. "You haven't said a thing since we started."

Roger's mind was filled with his missing friend. "I'm sorry Jane. It's rude of me to dance with you without giving you my full attention. What were you saying?"

Jane didn't quite know how to answer. Should she ask him why he had suddenly gone cold on her? Roger had been very interested when they first joined the club, at the same time one Wednesday evening. Come to think of it, there was a dance that night as well.

"Who's being quiet now?" said Roger, giving his attention to the dancing.

"I was just thinking. We met at a dance. You accepted my invitation to the church dance, and here we are, dancing once again in each other's arms. What happened in between?"

"As you know, Jane, I joined the club because my wife and I had split up. It wasn't something I wanted, but it happened and I had to make the best of it." He spun her round and went on. "It's true I gave you a bit more attention than the others, and I'm fond of you, but we're not in love. You must remember I had been badly hurt when my wife told me she wanted to end our marriage. No man's ego is helped when he fails to hold on to his wife, especially when he loses her to an older man. You were the first one around when I needed a woman's comforting hand. I must have a while to think over my position. It's too soon to ask anyone to share my shattered life."

There was a resounding clash from the band, bringing the dance to a halt. "There aren't enough people on the floor. I want you'se all to pick another partner," the drummer announced.

"We could keep on dancing. Nobody will notice." Jane was anxious to keep Roger for herself.

"You and I both know that wouldn't be fair to the others." Roger released his hold on her and walked towards a group of women, who were waiting for a partner to ask them to dance.

Jane then saw Fred Cowan, the club president coming into the hall, and immediately dashed across to claim him as her partner. At least she could enjoy being held in his strong arms even if there was no chance of her going to the altar - after all, married men were out of bounds, however good-looking they might be.

"I'm here," said the quiet voice of Charlene Graham, who had been standing behind Roger when the music stopped. "Sorry I'm late."

Roger spun round and saw the princess, as he thought of her. "Good. Now that you're here I'll not need to fight off the Amazons."

"My sister Shirley turned up with her family and stayed for an evening meal. I had a lot of extra work to do, especially the washing-up." Charlene explained, as the music started up again.

"Nevertheless, you still managed to get here." Roger's vibrant voice showed his pleasure at her presence.

"I had a letter from the hospital about my foot. They want me to go in on Friday." Roger's voice sounded sad.

"Isn't that a bit soon?" said Charlene.

"No. Apparently Mr Forsythe has to allocate some time to the men otherwise he'd only be working on women's feet."

"What is the matter with your foot?"

"I need an operation to remove a small bone. After that I won't be going on Sunday walks for a while."

"I'll be missing them as well, since I'll be visiting you in hospital. But I won't come alone, in case you have family visitors."

"I'd like that very much. They know I'm on my own, so I'll probably be in for a week."

"Did you manage to read the book?" she said, changing the subject.

"The book?" Roger asked quizzically.

"Yes, The Little Prince." Charlene had not appreciated Roger was teasing her.

"Seriously though, I'm very impressed. It may appear to have been written for children, but its philosophy is aimed at adults. When I was reading it, I wondered if this is what Jesus meant when he asked little children to come unto him. Was He really meaning that His listeners should hear Him with the uncluttered mind of the innocent child?"

Charlene was about to make a comment, but it was cut short by another clash on the cymbals, and an announcement that the dancers should now change partners again.

"See you later," they both said, as each chose another partner.

"Remember me?" Maureen Harrison had come in close to prevent Roger choosing someone else. "My turn now." Her voice imitated a young child's.

"Maureen, I'm going to be quite frank with you ..." He stopped speaking as the music started up again but continued as it became softer, "I'm going to be frank with you. It's come to my ears that you've been spreading the story of my marriage breakdown. I would never have told you, if I'd known you would not respect my confidence."

"That's a lie," said Maureen aggressively. "I never..." Roger interrupted her before she could get any further. "Don't blacken your soul any more. You were the only person who could have told Jane and Charlene, for you were the only person who knew the story."

"I felt it was my duty to tell them." She tried to sound sincere. "You had no right to let women think you were unattached. When you told me, I decided to tell the two people in most danger. And another thing, we girls don't like men coming here and playing around with our affections." Her dark eyes flashed angrily. "I think you treated Jane abominably by not partnering her to the Beetle Drive ... "

"How could I? I was seeing a client."

"None-the-less Charlene ought to be ashamed stealing someone else's man."

Once again the music stopped before Roger had a chance to reply. But this time he did not mind, for he had stopped beside Charlene. "My favourite partner," he declared, as he approached her and took her in his arms.

"That was an interesting point you were making about Jesus expecting us to listen with the mind of a child. I've never thought about that interpretation." Charlene wriggled her elbows until Roger's left hand felt more comfortable.

"The first page is a wonderful example of the differences between child and adult thinking," said Roger agreeing with what his partner was saying. "The bit about the children guessing correctly that the drawing is not a hat but an elephant inside a snake. The whole book is full of that kind of symbolism. I not only enjoyed reading it, but I felt there was something spiritual about what the author was saying."

Once again the cymbals sounded and the drummer asked the dancers to change partners again. Roger hated this kind of dance, but he could see the need for it in a club where the women outnumbered the men. He walked over to a group of women, who included the eighty-five-year-old widow, Mrs Flanagan.

"You're my partner," he announced. The octogenarian shuffled uneasily towards him.

Geriatric night at the Palais thought Roger unkindly.

"I hope we have our tea soon," she said, licking her lips in anticipation. "I do like my cup of tea. Don't you think we should get something a bit more substantial than a biscuit?"

"We should have a three course meal included for our fifty pence," he agreed, mischievously. "But the dance has only just started. It will be a while before you get your cuppa."

When it came to the time for another change, Roger found himself standing beside Maureen Harrison again.

"This is going to be the last interruption," she said as she came up and offered herself to him. "We'll be allowed to stay together to the end of the quickstep." Roger wished he could have been more fortunate and have had Charlene as his partner.

"Maureen, I don't want to hear any more gossip about me. Do you understand?" He behaved as if he were questioning an obstinate witness. "What I do in my private life is my business, and mine alone. If I want the news of what I'm doing to be broadcast, I'll do it myself."

Maureen was not easily put off. "No one wants to gossip about you, if that's what you think. We only want to warn some of the more vulnerable girls about people like you." She stopped and looked Roger squarely in the face. "And another thing, we don't like a woman who comes fresh into the club and take the men who are already committed. We've got too few to go round."

Roger knew there would be no reasoning with this small-minded woman, so he decided to say no more and they danced in silence till the end of the quickstep.

Since he had been brought up to have good manners, which she herself did not seem to possess, he said, as he offered her his hand, "May I escort you to your chair."

"If you want to," she said noncommittally and walked beside him to the top of the room without his support.

"Thank you for the dance," he said politely and went back to stand with the group of men.

By contrast the next item was a leisurely Highland Waltz. Roger liked this dance, and as soon the band started playing, he made straight for Charlene, who had already moved a few paces towards him.

"I'm sure you'll know this old time waltz. It's danced to that lovely tune, Mairi's Wedding." Roger took Charlene in his arms and was thrilled to have the excuse of dancing to hold her so closely.

"Oh, good," said Charlene obviously enjoying herself.

The music began again and the two happy people danced off as if they were in the dream sequence of a Hollywood spectacular. "This is our first real dance together." Charlene stared into her partner's eyes for some sign that he cared for her. "I know your marriage has broken up and that you joined the club to get away from your unhappiness. Is that the end of the story?"

Roger agreed he had come to the club to try and forget. "When we know one other better I'll tell you the whole story. For the moment, let's dance."

"I'd like to tell you about myself," she insisted. "I'm here because I had a break-up with my boy friend, Ryan O"Donnell. We had been together for several years, without marriage ever being mentioned until a few weeks ago, when he told me our relationship must come to an end. It seems he had reached the conclusion I was trying to trap him into marrying me."

"And were you?" Roger asked quietly.

"Of course not. Nothing improper ever happened," she said firmly. "The upshot was that we decided to end our affair. I, too, have been very unhappy, but that's all over. I've met a friend and I'm enjoying his company."

"And I've met my princess at last." Charlene smiled. No one had ever called her that before. When the dance ended, Roger whispered that it might be better for her reputation if he went and stood with the men again. "Maureen Harrison and her like are just looking for the opportunity to blacken your character."

"They'll find no blemish on my reputation," said Charlene defiantly. "But if it makes you feel better we'll move around tonight."

Roger squeezed her hand as they parted. "We'll need to dance again, Charlene," he said loudly, for the benefit of Maureen and her friends.

Fred Cowan, who had been the club president for as long as any of the present members could remember, stepped out to the middle of the floor, waving his hand to warn the drummer not to go on to the next dance.

"Ladies and gentlemen. I hope you're all enjoying yourselves. I know I am." He spoke, uneasily as he searched for the right words. "I've been asked by the excursion secretary to remind you that if not enough people put their names on the bus list by next weekend for the climb up the Cobbler, the bus will be cancelled."

There were a number cries of "Oh no!" from members.

"Well, if you want us to run buses without having to subsidise them from club funds, more of you will need to put your names down." He took a note from his pocket and read it. "There's another thing I should tell you in case you don't know. The street where we usually meet is blocked by road works, so those of you who want to go to Luss on Sunday should make for the Buchanan Street bus station instead. Then we can all take the bus and go to Luss."

Fred gave a tight smile, as he listened to the rhyming end of his announcement, and nodded to the drummer that he could now go ahead with the next dance.

The few eligible men of the Kelvin Hiking Club were expected to share their favours with the unaccompanied lady members. This unwritten rule had obliged Roger to partner many of the other women rather than Charlene, with whom he would have preferred to dance. Deciding it was about time for him to have another dance with her, Roger manoeuvred himself into a position where they could see each other.

"Would you'se take your partners?" The bandleader announced without remembering to say what it was. "And we want to see you'se all on the floor this time."

Roger waited until the music had begun, before making his way across the hall to Charlene.

When he had finished speaking, Fred Cowan had gone to the side where the ladies usually assembled. "May I have this dance?" he said skilfully interposing himself between Roger and Charlene.

"Er. I ... " Charlene did not know what to say and looked to Roger for help.

"Has somebody else asked you?" Fred enquired when she hesitated.

"No. No." She looked towards Roger, who indicated that she should go ahead. "Thank you for asking me."

Roger walked over to someone who had been smiling pleasantly at him. "Would you like to dance?"

The red-haired woman in the dark blue dress stepped forward, without replying, and stood beside him waiting for the music to begin. "I see you already know my school friend, Charlene. I'm Irene Carter."

"Really? She didn't say anything to me. Maybe she hasn't seen you yet." The band began to play a tango. "I don't particularly favour these modern dances." Roger's competence was matched by his partner's, who had been a ballroom champion at one time. "But there's nothing quite so good as the dances our parents enjoyed," he said, gliding smoothly to the music.

He wondered what the president was saying to "his" Charlene. He was feeling jealous as he watched the two of them laughing at some remark. What was he saying to make her laugh like that? He was a married man, after all. Why was his wife not there with him? He should be dancing with her. But wasn't he a married man too? Shouldn't he be dancing with Edith?

"I could be dancing with a tailor's dummy for all I know," Irene interrupted his daydreams.

Roger apologised at once. "I've been very rude, Miss Carter. Please forgive me."

"I'm Mrs Carter. My husband's the club secretary. That's Robin dancing with Maureen Harrison." She pointed to a small man in a dark blue suit, which matched her dress.

"So he's the person I spoke to when I phoned to find out about the club."

"Since there are only two of us at home, and you didn't speak to me you must be right, I suppose."

Roger, who had not given up his surveillance of Charlene and her partner, watched as the president began a very energetic sequence of gyrations. I couldn't match that, thought Roger. At his time of life he ought to be more careful.

When Irene saw her partner watching the antics of the Charlene's partner she observed, "Fred likes to show off to all the new girls. I should have warned her."

Suddenly the president stopped. He spun round, clutching his heart and stumbled towards the platform.

"I think something's wrong." Roger stopped dancing and rushed to give him aid.

Fred suffered a number of involuntary spasms and fell to the floor. The bandleader, reaching him first, took off his jacket, rolled it into a pillow and put it under the prostrate man's head.

"Would you'se all stand back, please?"

Jean Ross, who was a nurse, guessed the nature of the convulsions and went over to help. She was joined by a number of senior club members.

"It looks as if Fred has had a massive heart attack," she whispered after a preliminary examination. "I'll call an ambulance, but I think we'll find that Fred Cowan's dead."

Being the next most senior member of the club Robin Carter announced that Fred was seriously ill, and that the committee had decided to cancel the rest of the evening's activities.

"What about my tea?" Mrs Flanagan asked Roger who happened to be standing near her.

"I don't know about that, my dear," he said softly just as the secretary was about to make another announcement.

"The committee have also decided that many of you have come a long way tonight and need a cup of tea before you make the return journey."

But Charlene had been so shocked by the sudden death of her partner, she decided to go home at once.

"I'm coming with you," Roger insisted. "You're still shaking, and no wonder after that."

Once they were out in the street, he took her by the arm and walked smartly to the other side where her car was parked. The battered old Morris was looking older than its owner was. "I know what you're thinking, Roger. How could a sensible person like me allow herself to be palmed off with this heap of trouble?" She stopped to open the door and threw her coat on the passenger seat. "My sister's husband helped me with it."

"He must know practically nothing about second-hand cars if he guided you into paying good money for this heap."

Roger quickly looked inside and noticed a hole in the floor.

"Is that where your feet go?"

"My sister sold it to me when she bought a new one. I could see that it had some defects, but I didn't want to upset her."

"You didn't want to upset your sister?" said Roger ironically. "From what you told me about how much you paid her for it, you must have paid most of her new car. Your next car is going to be a new one. I guarantee that."

"I'll be thinking of you and praying for you on Friday," she said, as she started up the engine. "Bye, bye," she called, and drove off.

## Chapter 4

Roger's divorce was going to take a long time whichever way one looked at it. Two years, at least.

During the months that followed their first meeting Charlene and Roger saw each other in the library on Wednesday nights, sometimes at an evening concert or opera and, after his foot had recovered, they went on the easier Sunday hikes. He had come to accept that his marriage had ended and that he would have to wait in a kind of no-woman's-land, as it were, until his divorce came through and he could pass on to the next stage.

Jane had given up making life awkward for him and had turned her attention to some of the confirmed bachelors and the occasional new male member. All the women members, except for those she had known before joining the club, had little to do with Charlene. She had broken the unwritten rule about leaving another woman's man alone.

Fortunately Charlene was like the three wise monkeys; she saw no evil in anyone's behaviour, heard no evil and spoke no evil. She was extremely happy that she had a friend in Roger. They could enjoy each other's company in public, where no one could accuse either of them of behaving improperly. She had been raised to have high standards by parents who had themselves lived a faultless married life.

As was usual in the winter, the Wednesday night meeting at the end of the session was a kind of self-entertainment evening. Roger and Charlene always arrived separately to avoid speculation and gossip and, invariably, Roger was first. In fact he had come so early that he was the only member in the library's large public room.

"Is this where the Hiking Club meets?" said a petite brunette with brown eyes, wearing a deep purple costume. Roger had never seen her on any of the club outings.

"Yes. You've come to the right place, but you're far too early," he replied, as he welcomed her. "I'm Roger Buchanan."

"I'm Helen ..." She stopped and looked at him incredulously. "Did you say Buchanan?"

"Yes. Why do you ask?"

"What a coincidence. I'm Helen Buchanan." She put her large executive case on the table and opened it. "I've been doing my family history in the library. One branch of the family is missing." She brought out a file marked Duncan Buchanan. "I haven't come up against any of them so far. This is the line I'm talking about. My grandfather had several brothers and a sister. I've located them all, except for Duncan Buchanan, who had two sons and a daughter. One of the sons, Roger, was killed in the War. The other son, Robert, left home, and nothing more was heard of him."

"You don't need to go any further. He married my mother, Edna O'Brian, and had a son, Roger - that's me. I was called Roger after my uncle, who was killed in the war. Isn't it a small world? I used to wonder if my father had any relations on his side of the family."

"That means you and I are first cousins once removed," she said.

"Hello there cousin," said Roger, smiling, as he invited her to sit with him and wait for the others.

"My father's sister, that's my Aunt, Mary Buchanan, is living on her own over in Partick. I'm sure she would like to meet Robert's son. Would you like to come and see her next Saturday?"

"I'd like that very much. I believe your grandfather, Hector, was a trader in Africa. That was as much as my father knew. I'd like to hear more about him. May I bring a friend with me?"

"Certainly. Why don't you come for afternoon tea?"

"I can't speak for my friend, Charlene, though I think she'll confirm the arrangement when she comes in."

"Good. I'll be looking forward to your visit. I have to admit my motive is a wee bit ulterior. I'm hoping you'll fill in some of the gaps for me."

"Hello Roger," said Maureen as she came in the door. "Is this Charlene's replacement?"

"Don't be so silly. This is Helen Buchanan. She's a kind of cousin of mine. She's interested in joining the club."

"Oh really," said Maureen disdainfully. Another single woman added to the competition for eligible men, she thought. "You know it's a hiking club you're wanting to join, don't you?" she said, hoping this would scare off Helen.

"I love walking very much. That's why I want to join. All this looking at dusty old files I do every day must be compensated for by exercise when I can get it."

Roger caught sight of Charlene coming through the door. He had been keeping an eye open for her.

"Charlene, over here please! I want you to meet my cousin. Well ... sort of cousin."

The two women greeted each other. "I've been asking Roger to come and visit my Aunt Mary next Saturday for tea. He asked if he could bring a friend. Do you think you can manage?"

"I'd been thinking of spending this Saturday tidying up my allotment, but I can postpone it till Sunday. Roger and I feel we aren't ready for really tough mountaineering yet. He had a foot operation, and although it was successful, he's not really ready for a hike yet. I'd love to come and meet your Aunt Mary."

By now most of the club members had arrived, and Robin Carson, the secretary, said. "I want you to divide yourselves into groups of ten. And try to do it so that there are about equal numbers men and women in each group."

This was the opportunity the unattached females were waiting for. They each grabbed a couple of men and approached any other women who had been able to do likewise, asking them to join them and form a group. Inevitably, the more experienced of the ladies made up groups with four or more men whilst the others ended up with no men at all.

"Now, now, ladies. We have this problem every time. We just can't allow three or four groups to have all the men in them." He went to Maureen Harrison, who had acquired five men. "No more than three men," he advised her.

Maureen protested. "If you exchange a man for a woman, we'll have equal numbers."

Robin Carson ignored her. "Those of you who've been here at this time of the year before know what to expect. But for the benefit of newcomers, I'd like to say that each group has to entertain the others for at least ten minutes. So the first thing you have to do is think out how you're going to entertain the others."

"I see there's a piano. I'll volunteer to provide the music," said Charlene, standing up to look at it from the distance.

"I can do press-ups," said Sidney Armstrong. "I'll challenge anyone to beat me by doing more."

"There's to be a prize for the best entertainment as judged by the committee," Roger reminded the others.

"Why don't we do a one-act play?" suggested Helen, who did not realise they would also have to write it as well.

"How about the Can-Can?" Irene Carson suggested naughtily. "The men can pretend to be women, by rolling up their trouser legs."

Since no one supported Irene's suggestion, she was prompted to ask. "What will we do then? Some of the others seem to be rehearsing already."

Charlene, who had been trying to think of something, said, "How about a choir? There's bound to be a couple of good voices. I'll play the piano and sing as well."

"If there's nothing else, we should go for that," agreed Irene.

"I sing in our church choir," said Helen.

"Then you should be all right," said Charlene. "We should be able to sing three old Scottish songs in the time."

"I like it. We'll introduce ourselves as the Kelvin Choir," chuckled Roger.

When all six groups had performed, the committee selected two - to go through to the final - Maureen Harrison's, concert party and Roger's, Kelvin Choir. Both groups were given an outstanding ovation at the end of their repeat performance.

Robin Carson then called on the audience to pick the winning group by the loudness of their cheering. The concert party was judged to be the winner.

Robin praised the all-round quality of the entertainment and handed Maureen a large box of mixed sweets. Once he had finished his speech he signalled to the women in charge of the purvey. In a short while they emerged from a side room with trays of scones, sandwiches and cakes and large kettles of tea and coffee.

"That was a most enjoyable evening," said Helen, as she finished her cup of coffee. "It's pity we didn't win the prize. I thought we were more entertaining than the other group."

"There's no justice," said Irene. "An impartial jury would surely have given it to us." She began to button her coat. "Well what are we going to do on Wednesday evenings, now that we're getting to the summer?"

Roger helped Charlene on with her coat and then put on his heavy anorak. "Maybe we should meet informally in Queen Street station on Wednesday nights and visit interesting places in and around the city. I'd like to see some of our Roman remains; like Rough Castle," he said.

"What a good idea." Helen Buchanan clapped her hands.

"I'll pass the word round that you're starting a Wednesday night walking group," said Irene.

"Does everybody want to take up my idea?" asked Roger.

"Yes!" shouted a chorus of voices around him.

"All right, then, we'll meet at Queen Street station. Will seven-thirty suit everybody?"

The crowd shouted their agreement and started to leave.

Helen gave Roger a piece of paper with her own and her Aunt's address on it. "If you've any problems about Saturday's visit get in touch." She kissed him goodnight and left with Irene.

Roger put the paper in his wallet and left the library with Charlene. They had both begun to realise that their friendship was taking off in another direction. Roger had reached that stage when being separated from Charlene for any length of time had become unbearable. Charlene knew that her affections were deepening from fondness into something more.

"The operation on your big toe was successful. There's no need to limp. Just put your foot firmly on the ground. You won't feel any pain ... any more," chided Charlene gently.

"It's just the habit of a lifetime." Roger stamped his foot to show there was no pain. "You know what they say. You can't teach an old dog."

"Nonsense," said Charlene. "Forget about that and get on with walking. We'll need to go on some of the harder climbs or the members will think we've hung up our boots, as they say."

By the time Roger and Charlene had returned to their cars, the library was in darkness and everyone had left. He opened his car door and invited her to sit inside while they talked.

Charlene was looking a bit uncomfortable. "I don't believe in divorce, Roger. Marriage should be for life."

"There are hundreds of people divorcing and remarrying every day. Are they all breaking God's law?" he asked.

"I believe they are. Marriage is till death as the vow says. I wanted to know what our minister thought about my position with you, so I went to see him in the vestry."

"Did he give you any words of comfort and joy?"

"As far as he was concerned, he was prepared to marry those of his parishioners who wished to be married to someone else after divorce. I asked him if he felt that a divorced person could be given the blessing of a marriage ceremony and he said he could see nothing wrong, since it was a new beginning."

"That is my view as well," said Roger, feeling largely relieved. "But in the case of young children, every step should be taken to prevent them being hurt by the separation."

"Oh Roger!" Charlene put her arms round his neck and kissed him on the lips. "What are we going to do?" She held him tightly, and went on. "I think I've fallen in love with you and you're a married man."

"And you don't believe in divorce! What a dilemma for you, princess!" Roger hoped he did not sound unsympathetic. Although he did not share Charlene's views, he respected them.

"I'm sorry, Roger," Charlene said defiantly. "I must hold on to my belief. It's all I have. I can't accept Mr Drinkwater's view of a new beginning. This can only be true when one or other partner in a marriage dies."

Roger told her he loved her. "We can still be very good friends, Charlene. There's no law, which says we can't go about with each other and do things together we both enjoy. Even in Italy, where there is no divorce, couples split up and live with other partners as man and wife, without the blessing of the Church. But I wouldn't ask you to do that."

"Would you like to meet my mother?" Charlene asked. "I've told her all about you."

"I believe that would be the proper thing to do. Your mother should see what kind of person her daughter is associating with, don't you think?"

"Come and have dinner with us tomorrow. I'll meet you at the church gate which is only a short distance from my home."

They had been sitting in Roger's car so long that a police car, which had passed them on a number of occasions, stopped beside them.

"Is anything wrong?" asked the plain-clothes officer, thinking that Charlene might have been detained against her will.

"No, officer. My friend and I are just talking. We've found each other at last."

The policeman saw the sparkle in Charlene's eyes and realised he had intruded on two lovers at the beginning of their journey.

"Sorry for interrupting you, sir." The officer winked at his colleague and drove away.

\* \* \* \* \*

Two churches, one of which had formerly housed the Free Church congregation, had been built near Elmwood Gardens where Charlene's parents had gone to live soon after their marriage. They had joined the congregation in the old Free Church building and had regularly worshipped as parishioners there, until Mr Graham's death and subsequently, Charlene, who had been baptised by Anthony Drinkwater's predecessor, and her mother attended Sunday service whenever possible and always on the four special Communion Sundays.

Roger, who was standing at the side gate of Elmwood Parish Church waiting for Charlene, looked at the smoke-stained gargoyles on the red sandstone building and wondered how many members of the congregation were aware of this decoration and its purpose. Sometimes tradition was a fine thing, he reflected. But these ugly heads did little to enhance the structure. They gave the impression of having been a random afterthought, and they were certainly out of place nowadays. He would have thought people didn't need to chase the devil away any more ... or do they?

"Penny for your thoughts." Charlene had come up and was now standing quietly behind him as he gazed at the front of the church building.

Roger was slightly startled by her sudden appearance. "Oh! I was just thinking about the gargoyles."

"The gargoyles?" Charlene repeated, as if she didn't understand.

Roger pointed to the heads above the door. "Those things." He stabbed his finger at each in turn.

"I've been coming to this church for a long time and I've never really noticed them before." Charlene walked into the small church garden to get a closer look.

"They used to drive the devil away," said Roger. "Presumably they've been put above the door to prevent him from entering and interfering with the church services."

Charlene looked wistfully at the trees and the small borders on either side of the entrance gate. "My father used to look after the garden. Those labels ... he made them himself ... are beginning to bite into the bark. I'll need to do something about them before they damage the trees." Then she went over and snapped the string of a label, which had been overtaken by the tree's growth.

Roger looked around. "Isn't it strange. There isn't an elm tree anywhere. We should be seeing them all around us in a place called Elmwood Gardens."

"It may have something to with Dutch Elm disease," suggested Charlene. "What's in the plastic bag?"

"Brown bread - don't you remember?" he said.

"I thought you were kidding about baking your own bread." Roger handed over the bag with two loaves and hoped she'd enjoy them.

As they began to walk the short distance between the church and Elmwood Gardens, she said, "Mother's a bit nervous about meeting you."

"How do you think I feel?" Roger felt more and more edgy as they approached Charlene's home.

Charlene and her mother, Katie, shared a two bed-roomed flat in a tenement building, which had seen better days. Mrs Graham, who had been widowed for five years, had been able to take care of herself until recently, but now her bronchitis had reached a critical point.

"When my parents came here, you had to be somebody to rent a house in this neighbourhood. There are still a lot of respectable people around, but not nearly as many as there were. The factor spends very little on repairs." Charlene spoke sadly.

"It probably has something to do with profit margins," Roger suggested politely.

Charlene opened the glass-fronted door and beckoned Roger to follow her into the hall.

"Give me a minute to prepare mother first." She opened another door leading to the kitchen. "Mother I'm back," she called. "Roger's here to meet you."

"Where is he?" asked Katie Graham, as her arthritic limbs made her walk with a shuffle from the small pantry, where she was preparing the evening meal.

"I left him in the hall."

"Well bring him in. Don't keep him standing out there!"

Charlene opened the kitchen door and saw that Roger was standing shyly behind it.

"Roger, this is Mother." Charlene took her mother's hand and clapped it gently in her own.

Kate Graham was a very private person, and not used to meeting her daughter's friends. In fact very few of Charlene's male acquaintances had ever been given the honour of being introduced and being asked to a meal with Charlene and her mother.

"It's a pleasure to meet you, Mrs Graham." Roger went over and shook her hand. "This is for you." He handed her a box of sweets.

Mrs Graham smiled as she accepted his gift. "You didn't need to bring anything with you, except your appetite."

Roger saw at once that Mrs Graham was an older version of her daughter. She still had a lot of charm. If Charlene grew old as gracefully.

"Mother. Roger baked this," said Charlene as she handed her one of the brown loaves.

"Have you always made your own bread?" asked Mrs Graham.

"No. I was forced to have a go when the local bakery closed down." He omitted to say his estranged wife had been the baker.

"If it tastes as good as it looks, then Charlene and I will enjoy it very much. We both like brown bread. Do you like fillet steak?"

"Yes. I do."

"The meal's nearly ready then. The bathroom's next door if you want to wash your hands."

"That lentil soup was simply delicious. Reminds me of the sort my mother used to make. She used ham bones."

"The soup was made from the stock after mother boiled a piece of ham," said Charlene. "Would you like another helping?"

Roger, who had a passion for soup, was pleased at the offer. "If you don't think I'm being too greedy. But don't leave yourself short."

"Don't worry about that. Mother always makes a large pot. There's plenty for tomorrow and the day after."

As soon as Roger had finished his second helping, Charlene began to clear the kitchen table. "I think your mother's a wonderful woman, Charlene. Now I know where you get your kindly disposition from."

"I had a wonderful father as well." Charlene's eyes were glistening as she remembered.

"Charlene! Come and collect Roger's plate," her mother called from the kitchen.

She returned with a fillet steak and disappeared into the pantry to collect the plates of vegetables.

"Help yourself, Roger"

"From what I've seen so far you're a first class cook, Mrs Graham. Can Charlene cook as well?"

"Charlene can cook anything you need. You can be sure of that."

He smiled. "She's had a good teacher."

After the meal, Charlene said. "If you go into the front room you'll find a copy of the Herald. I know you like doing the crossword. When we've finished the washing up, I'll bring through coffee and biscuits."

"Are you sure I can't help?" Roger asked.

"No, no. Just wait for us in the front room," Charlene replied.

"That suits me fine," Roger said as he left them to it.

"Don't you think Roger's out of this world," said Charlene when she joined her mother in the pantry.

Kate Graham had noticed certain qualities in her daughter's friend, which had reminded her of her late husband. "I think he's fond of you," she said.

"More than that, Mother. The way he looks after me is just the way father cared for us. I'm sure he loves me."

"I hope you're not disappointed, Charlene. You've been enthusiastic before."

"I know Roger's the right one for me," said Charlene and left for the front room.

"Haven't you forgotten something?" asked Charlene as soon as she came in.

"No ... I have the Herald and a pen."

"That's not what I meant, and you know it."

He smiled as he took her in his arms and kissed her firmly on the lips.

"That'll do to be going on with," she said, closing the door of the front room behind her.

## Chapter 5

Helen's elderly Aunt Mary, whose ancestors had come to Partick at the time of the Clearances, lived alone in a council house. In front was a tiny garden, which had once been tended lovingly by Mary's parents and their family, but was now overgrown with weeds. Although there was not much ground between the pavement and the front door, it had clearly supported a profusion of plants of all kinds in the past.

Mary Buchanan was the name etched on the small brass plate.

"We're here." Roger pressed the bell push but heard nothing. "I'll fix it for her," he promised himself and rattled the letter-box.

"That's Helen at the window," said Charlene who was standing on Roger's left beside it.

Helen opened the door. "We didn't hear you ring the bell, and we thought some children were rattling the letter box for fun. Auntie's waiting inside. She isn't too well nowadays."

Aunt Mary, tall and slim, walked unsteadily towards Helen's cousin, holding on to chairs and other pieces of furniture to keep her balance. "I apologise for the state of the place. I try my best, but I only get the home help twice a week, and all she wants to do is to go shopping at the Co-op."

Roger embraced her and kissed her on the cheek. "I'm so happy to meet you, Miss Buchanan. My late father never told me about you."

"We used to go to the same school. He lived across the road. I heard he went to Edinburgh and got married. And by the way, none of your Miss Buchanan nonsense. Call me Aunt Mary."

"All right, Aunt Mary. If you have a screwdriver I'll fix that door bell for you later." He broke off saying, "This is my friend, Charlene Graham. We met at the walking club."

"Why don't we all sit down?" said Mary. "I don't expect you'll be ready for tea right away." She made them comfortable and continued proudly: "My father, Hector, and his brother, George, were doing missionary work in Nyasaland about eighteen-eighty after David Livingstone died. George, the older brother, had gone to work as a missionary in Livingstonia and had survived malaria to train as a doctor in Glasgow and Edinburgh. On the other hand, Hector was sent there as a young man ten years later by the Moir Brothers to trade in ivory and other goods. My father kept a diary in which he tells how he sailed upriver trading with the natives. It was very brave of him, for many of the men who went to this part of Africa died there."

She opened the drawer of the table beside her chair and brought out a small black cloth-bound notebook, which had pencilled notes written in it.

"He tells how his bedroom was broken into while he was still sleeping, and how his umbrella and bag were stolen," she said, eagerly searching the pages for the entry. "Here it is." She put on her glasses. "He writes that he saw the chief's son walking past the window of my father's office using his umbrella like a sunshade. He strutted up and down several times, as though he were inviting my father to come out and question him about it. But he remained where he was. It would not have been good for trade if he had accused the chief's son of committing the serious offence of stealing. Tribal laws were very severe. Whole families had been killed when the chief had found them guilty of an offence."

"Your father was a very brave man," said Roger. "Did he actually tell you about his days in Africa?"

"Unfortunately he died when I was very young. I didn't really get a chance to know him, which is something I've regretted all my life." Aunt Mary removed a faded print from the diary. "Here's a photograph of him. Such a handsome man he was. And here's one of my Mothers. Such a pretty woman."

Roger compared the photograph of her mother to Mary, sitting in front of him, and thought how much she looked like her.

"You never got married? Did you never miss having a family?"

"No. Never," she replied somewhat shortly. "I had my two sisters and - brother, you see."

Helen, who was now anxious to get back to her flat, said. "I'll put on the kettle and heat the sausage rolls. Everything else is ready."

"I'll see what I can do about the bell," said Roger.

He quickly discovered that a broken wire was the reason for its silence. He joined the two pieces together and merrily pressed the bell push.

"Brrrrrrr." The bell sounded and frightened Aunt Mary.

"Why did you do that, without warning me?" she complained. "I could have had a heart attack."

"I hope people don't ring your doorbell then, Auntie. You could be in great danger," said Roger teasing her.

Helen came in with the tea trolley. "Here we are. Tea's up."

"That was a lovely tea," said Charlene as Roger drove her home. "Your Aunt is such a splendid person."

"I'd like to read her father's diary sometime. It sounds very interesting," he said.

"Roger, would you like to visit my allotment? It's not far from here and it's on our way home."

"Yes, I'd like to."

"That's the entrance over there," said Charlene, pointing to the remnants of an ornamental gate with a family crest on it. Roger turned the car in to a minor road which had formerly been a private one leading to the estate house. "We're here," said Charlene suddenly, indicating a place to park. A large wooden gate secured entry to the allotments. Beyond it a wide path, up which a car could be driven if necessary, went through the middle of the Association's ground from the gate up to a small forest. A maze of smaller paths on either side of the main path enabled the allotment-holders to reach their plots.

Roger saw that almost every garden had its shed or greenhouse, made from old window frames dumped there by double glazing firms and any bits and pieces, which could be salvaged for the purpose.

Charlene's plot sported a greenhouse and a shed, now falling into ruin.

"This is it," she said as proudly as if she were showing him round the grounds of Windsor Castle. "This is where I do my gardening."

"That's a lot for you to look after by yourself. I hope you'll let me change that. I'd like to work it with you if you'll let me."

"It's a long time since a man worked this allotment. No one since my father's death, in fact. I'd be honoured to have your help. And I'll share the produce with you."

Roger gave her a hug. "You've got a man to help you now. We

should come here regularly on Saturday afternoons. Your allotment has fallen behind and I think I know why."

"I hope we're not too tired for the Sunday walks," said Charlene with a smile.

* * * * *

Like many other couples whose courtship lasted a long time, Roger and Charlene had developed a routine, in much the same way as married couples do, but with much more freedom for their personal preferences than would be likely if they were married. Roger was working longer hours with his partner in their legal practice, and Charlene was busily engaged on new schemes of work: she was now employed as Assistant Head Teacher in the infant department of Green Street School.

They went on walks together as often as they could, sometimes without the club, and gardened at the allotment in the summer. Roger also kept the Graham home in working order, decorating the kitchen and pantry and generally carrying out every maintenance needed. Charlene and Roger went to concerts in the winter and Roger sometimes had meals with Charlene and her mother in Mrs Graham's home.

"I think the thing I most enjoy about coming here ... after you dear princess ... is your mother's fish and chips," said Roger as they sat in the front room drinking coffee.

"That was not my mother's cooking you had today. It was mine."

He kissed her hand, intending to compliment her in the continental fashion.

"I wish I was doing as well in all my departments," she said despondently, as she lifted her coffee mug and held it between her hands. "For the first time in my teaching career the job is beginning to get on top of me. I've been under pressure now that a new head teacher has been appointed. She wants to change everything overnight, and at the same time, expects me and her other assistant heads to work full-time while changes are made. I just can't do it. It's getting to be too much."

"We'll need to do something about it." Roger assured her. "The problem is ... what? One thing you need to do is to tell Mrs High-and-Mighty you aren't four people. You can only do one job at a time. I know it's hard. You don't like confrontation; nobody does, Charlene. Most of us are prepared to stand our ground and tell the other person where to get off. You'd find things would improve if you took that kind of action."

"I'm not a fighter," protested Charlene. "I get scratched, and immediately retreat into a corner to lick my wounds. You didn't know I was a coward did you, Roger?" She looked at him as though she were a child needing her father's help.

"You're most certainly not a coward just because you don't like standing up to a bully." Roger told her as he took her hand in his and squeezed it gently. "David toppled Goliath with a small stone, because he knew just where to aim it. That's what you have to do. Look for your boss's weaknesses and attack them. She'll soon leave you alone."

"How about a short-term solution to give me the strength?"

Roger picked up the Rambling Club's summer brochure he had brought along with him and slapped his hand with it. "The solution is here, Charlene. For various reasons we've been unable to have a holiday together. We ought to put that right as soon as possible."

"That's it," said Charlene, delighted at the idea. "I need to get away from it all."

"I was going to suggest we go to the Rambling Club guest house in the Lake District. That way, nobody can criticise us for improper behaviour." He opened the brochure and thumbed through it until he came to the appropriate page.

Charlene hesitated. It was not because she was worried about the possible impropriety. They would be occupying separate rooms and anyway they'd probably have to share with others of the same sex.

"Do you think I'll get enough rest? The Rambling Club believes in a strenuous mountain climbing programme."

"It doesn't say you have to go on any of the walks, or take part in any of the entertainment, unless you want to," he said throwing down the brochure on the carpet at his feet.

"Oh well, in that case I have no objections. If the weather is very good, I could be tempted to do the middle-grade walks."

"And if you're in a lazy frame of mind you could do the lowest grade where they take the bus instead of walking," Roger teased.

He got to his feet and helped Charlene from the settee. "That's it, we've settled on the guest house at Grasmere for the October holiday. I'll fill in the application form when I get home and post it right away. The sooner we apply, the better our chances will be. Now then, since we've settled the holiday, let's get down to the plot and do some work."

As soon as they arrived at the allotment they could see that something was wrong. The padlock from the greenhouse door was lying on the ground. Someone had broken in. Charlene pushed the door open apprehensively.

They've stolen my father's heater. The one he got when he retired," said Charlene, surveying the interior of the greenhouse. "It's a good job I didn't leave his stainless steel spade last Saturday. I would have been very upset if that had been taken as well."

Roger examined the hasp to see if he would be able to screw it back on. "I wonder who could have done this? Could it be someone on the allotment? The heater suggests the person has a greenhouse. I'll take a walk round and squint inside your neighbours' huts."

Charlene was idly looking through the greenhouse window, and said in dismay, "They've been at the onions as well. That's the tops lying on the path. It's things like this that make you wonder if it's all worthwhile."

"I don't believe in violence. But it makes my blood boil and I want to get back at the people who did this. It's so upsetting to lose something which belonged to your father," said Roger.

"It could have happened at any time since last Saturday. The trail's cold now, as the police would say." Charlene had always been a realist.

"If it's been discarded at the rubbish tip, it might still be there," Roger said encouragingly.

"While you take a quick look round, I'll get the flask out."

Roger returned empty-handed. If Charlene's greenhouse heater was hereabouts, it must have been very well hidden.

"Let's forget about it for now and enjoy our tea." She handed him soap and towel to wash his hands in the water barrel.

While they were drinking their tea the Association secretary, an elderly man of eighty-five whose son looked after his allotment, walked past.

"Those biscuits look nice," he said.

"Would you like one?" Charlene offered him the open box.

"No thank you, lassie. I've been out already for a wee refreshment." By this he meant a glass of whisky in the local pub. "I hear you had visitors."

"News seems to travel fast. I've only just found out myself," she said.

"Your neighbour in the next plot left early. Said he saw your padlock on the ground. He didn't want to touch it in case he got his fingerprints on it. Have you any idea who might have done it?" said the old man.

"That's what I was going to ask you," said Roger. "You know all the plot-holders."

"That might have been true at one time. I don't get around much nowadays. My son does most of the gardening now. But if I hear anything about your greenhouse heater, I'll let you know. A wee word of advice. Do the small jobs first, or they'll be pushed out the way by the big ones and never get done."

"That's a sound bit of advice. And it's something I always do," said Charlene.

"By the way, I'm getting a cart load of manure from the local stables. Would you like some?" asked the old man.

Charlene looked to Roger for confirmation.

"I think we could do with a load, particularly for the onion bed," said Roger. "We might as well grow the best onions we can. We don't want our thief to put up with inferior quality, do we?"

"I'll away and let you finish your tea." The secretary lit his pipe, and moved on to have a word with another plot-holder.

"Is that the application to the Rambling Club?" Charlene asked, when Roger handed her an open envelope.

"Look and see." It was a reply confirming Roger's booking for the autumn school break. "I had already come to the conclusion that you needed a break away from everything. I hope Shirley appreciates how much you do for your mother when she has to take over your role."

\* \* \* \* \*

"That's everything," said Charlene, putting the bag containing their picnic in the boot. "Did you remember to bring the envelope with the confirmation of our booking?" she asked.

"Yes, it's in the glove compartment," Roger replied.

"Then we're all set to go," said Charlene. She looked up at the front room window and waved to her mother. "Come and wave goodbye to Mother." Charlene had become emotional when she realised that this might possibly be her mother's last farewell.

Roger, who had been checking the oil and water waved a lump of cotton waste and immediately started to rub his hands with it?

It was not long before Roger's red Rover had joined the Motorway for Carlisle. He had brought a collection of tapes, mainly classical music, and had been playing these during the earlier part of the journey. However, as they neared the Lake District Charlene suggested that they discuss the programme and which of the activities they should support.

"This is supposed to be a resting holiday," Roger reminded Charlene. "So it'll be C grade climbs."

"But taking the C walk usually means going by bus and having tea in the nearest café," protested Charlene.

"In that case, we'd take the B walk. That looks like a good spot for a picnic," said Roger driving in to an empty lay-by.

As soon as the brake was on, Charlene turned towards Roger and gazed lovingly at him. He took her in his arms and kissed her passionately on the lips as he held her intimately close to him. It was two years since that wonderful day on Ben Calder when Roger and Charlene had spoken to one another for the first time. He put his hand under her skirt and started to massage her thigh.

"Not yet, Roger," she said, putting her hand on his to restrain him. "I know how frustrating it must be for you; to have the apple and not to be allowed to eat." She had kept herself for the one man in her life. Now that she had found him, she would wait until she was married.

Roger agreed, reminding her that the two solicitors had finalised the arrangements for the divorce. When Edith signed the documents he would be a free man. He might be able to persuade her to listen to the Reverend Drinkwater's advice.

They were still entwined in each other's arms when a heavy goods lorry rumbled to a halt near them. "Don't mind me," shouted the jovial driver as he lit a cigarette and listened to his radio.

Charlene hastily rearranged her clothing and got out. "We'll have our picnic over there at that table," she said, standing beside the boot waiting to collect the picnic bag.

Roger was wondering if he would have enough room for afternoon tea, the catering highlight of the holiday, when he saw the sign Grasmere. Soon afterwards he spotted an old grey, limestone building. "That's it," he said pointing to the name of the Ramblers Club.

He then turned into the driveway of what had once been the home of a Manchester industrialist; it had been converted by the Ramblers into a guesthouse catering for about fifty people.

Some of the rooms were intended to hold three or four, but the majority were meant to be occupied by two; often married couples who didn't want to be separated. The food was plain but well cooked, and there was plenty of it.

Charlene was sharing a room with two others in the main guesthouse and Roger was sharing a room in the annexe with Sidney Armstrong, also from the Kelvin Club, who was unexpectedly taking his holiday at the same time.

Once they had settled in they made their way to the dining room for afternoon tea. A small crowd had gathered round the dining room door to read a notice, which had been pinned to it. It read - Silver Wedding Celebration. The leader, Peter Carlton and his wife, Sheila, who are celebrating their Silver Wedding, have decided to share the occasion with the Ramblers' guests. A party has been organised for this evening after dinner.

They left immediately after reading the notice. It would be better if they took a walk instead, if they were to manage dinner and a party.

When the evening meal had been served, the lights were dimmed and a beautifully iced cake, displaying a number twenty-five in silver figures, was brought in from the kitchen by the cook. She placed it on the table and waited for the arrival of the manager and his wife. There was an air of expectancy as the guests stood in the flickering light. Then the dining room door opened and Peter and Sheila came into the room. She looked stunning with her dark hair and red dress. They smiled and waved as the guests cheered them on their way over to the candlelit cake.

"For they are jolly good fellows ... " someone started singing, the others joined in. "For they are jolly good fellows ... "

The cook handed over a large bouquet of flowers to Sheila. "These are for you," she said, shuffling awkwardly. "The staff and guests all put together and bought it. We want to wish you many more years of happiness." She quickly withdrew to spare herself embarrassment.

Roger whispered to Charlene, "I hope we too can have a Silver Wedding." She squeezed his hand and smiled.

The middle-aged couple thanked everyone for their kindness and good wishes. Peter then announced that the concert would take place next door. There was the usual scramble to get the best seats. Roger and Charlene did not particularly want to sit in front in case they were asked to perform. They were quite happy to occupy two in an unlit corner.

"Do you really think we'll ever have a silver anniversary?" asked Charlene hesitantly.

"If we don't get run over by a bus," said Roger soberly.

"We could get there quicker by counting each year of the marriage as two years. A more reasonable twelve and a half years, and then on to our gold as well."

Sitting next to them was an older couple, both in there sixties. They gave the impression of being teenagers who had just discovered that thing called love. He had his arm wrapped round her shoulder and had clearly been cuddling her before Roger and Charlene sat down beside them.

"We're newly married," said the small woman; she had obviously once been a very pretty blonde. "Does it show?"

"I'm afraid so," replied Roger. "But don't let us interfere with your honeymoon." He looked at Charlene. "My friend and I hope you'll both be very happy."

"I couldn't help overhearing what you said about a silver wedding anniversary," said the man with the greying hair. "We might get up to silver ourselves, if we're lucky."

The entertainment followed the usual pattern, with singing groups, jokes, dancing and - appropriately for Grasmere - readings from Wordsworth. Just as the evening was coming to an end, the man who shared his room with Roger came out to stand in front of the audience, his arms folded.

The group leader stood beside him. "This gentleman is well-named. He's Mr Sidney Armstrong from Glasgow. And he claims to be able to do more press-ups than anyone else is in the guesthouse. He would like some of the men, or the women if they like, to come out and challenge him to a contest."

Roger felt well qualified. He had been doing press-ups with weights slung round his neck. "I'll try."

Everyone clapped as he took up his position, crouching on the floor beside his room-mate.

"One!" the crowd called out, followed in succession by "Two!" and "Three!", and so on, until they had reached fifty, at that point the audience began to lose interest.

I can easily keep this up all night, thought Roger. And it looks as if Sidney could as well. But Roger finally collapsed on the floor. "I've had enough," he moaned.

Sidney Armstrong continued for a few more press-ups until the leader announced he had won the challenge.

"I presume you gave in to avoid embarrassing Sidney," observed Charlene as they left for their rooms.

"There was another reason," said Roger. "I wanted him to speak to me for the remainder of the week."

Next morning after breakfast, they collected their packed lunches and flasks of hot water from the dining room before leaving for the day's walk.

Roger put the lunch in his rucksack. "It's quite an easy one for us. We're touring by coach round the various sites associated with Wordsworth. It'll save a bit of time if I pay for all our trips now."

They walked hand in hand to the small room, which served as an office. "Will it be all right if I pay by cheque?" Roger asked Sheila, squeezing Charlene's hand. She had never been happier.

"You can pay us with anything. Soap coupons if you like," laughed Peter.

"I'd like to pay for both of us. My friend will pay me afterwards," he added quickly.

The manager handed him the account. "That's what's due for the week" And then as an afterthought "That's for the two of you."

Roger wrote out a cheque and handed it to Sheila. "I suppose you look after the money in your family," he said.

She looked at the cheque and instantly her smile vanished.

"Have I made a mistake?" Roger was puzzled.

"Depends on how you look at it," she replied sourly. "My husband and I have a joint bank account, just as you seem to have with your wife." She hesitated for a moment, "Mr Buchanan."

## Chapter 6

That smells lovely, thought Roger, as he tapped the baking tin on the worktop to ease out the brown loaf. Very soon six, small, wholemeal loaves had been placed on the wire tray. He'd give Charlene and her mother two, keep one out for himself and put the rest in the deep freezer.

He had been reading *The Little Prince* and was thinking about the young man's visit to the various planets and the strange characters who lived on them when it occurred to him that the little prince had never visited a lawyer. Roger wondered what weaknesses he would have found in his profession.

He picked up a small notebook and began to scribble down his idea for a story.

"Good morning," said the little prince.

"Ah! Good morning," said the lawyer.

"Have you come to play with me?"

The lawyer sat in a high chair, behind a huge desk, which had almost been covered with heaps of coloured papers.

But the little prince, who never answered questions even when they were put to him by a lawyer, asked

"Why do have you so many papers on your desk?"

"I need them for my game," replied the lawyer, as though he had said something of great importance.

Roger's train of thought was interrupted by the sound of the doorbell ringing, and, as he walked up the small passage to open the door he wondered if Charlene had changed her mind and decided to visit.

"Hello big boy." Edith was the last person he had expected to see.

"Aren't you going to ask me in?" She stood there clutching her umbrella as if she expected to use it as a cosh. "I don't think you'd want to discuss your private business out here?"

"Not at all," said Roger opening the door wider. "It's just that your visit has taken me by surprise. Come in. I've nothing to hide!"

"I'm aware of that. Your sweet and lovely Charlene Graham will be waiting for you at her home. She makes a point of not being alone with you here."

Roger thought how embarrassing it would have been for Charlene if she had broken her rule.

Edith walked ahead of her husband down the passage into the living room of his two-roomed flat and promptly sat in his green leather chair.

"You've done very well for yourself. It must be very nice to relax in this when you home come from the office."

Edith bounced on the cushion, before she pushed back to bring out the footrest. "Very comfortable. There's nothing as good as this in my home!" She snuggled towards the back of Roger's chair to savour it to the full. "I fancy one like this. Must have cost you a month's salary. Maybe you'd like to give it to me in the settlement."

"Would you like a tea or a coffee?" Roger asked.

"Nothing, thank you." Edith was feeling pains in her abdomen and wanted "to avoid anything with acid", as she would have said. "I've come to talk about the settlement."

From the beginning Charlene had said that she didn't want anything from his former life. He was to give Edith the house and everything in it. She wanted to start off fresh when the time came. It was true that Edith had supported him while he was training. Yet surely he should have been left with something more than his earnings. And there was the possibility that Charlene might be contributing to her support as well.

Roger protested it was unfair to seek further changes when an agreement had already been reached through their lawyers.

"I haven't been feeling well for the past few months," she said rubbing her stomach. "The doc thinks it might be connected with the operation I had a few years ago."

This was the first time Edith had spoken about her illness. Could she have been infected by Willie Porter and didn't want to say so, he thought?

"I wanted a part-time job, but that's out now. I'll need a reasonable allowance to pay the mortgage on the house." She said, shaking her head as if her mouth were filled with excess acid.

"The amount of the mortgage is nominal now," said Roger. "In any case, if you were to sell it, you'd get a capital sum on which the interest would be much more than any allowance a court might award you."

"Then I'd have nowhere to live," she said angrily.

"That makes two of us. When I gave you the house, I had to look for somewhere to stay. I was fortunate to find a flat in New Town."

"Yes, big boy. You always seem to land on your feet." Her voice was unpleasant. "I want a quarter of what's left from your monthly income after deduction of tax," she said bluntly. "I'll need that much to be able to stay in your former home."

"The advantage of being a lawyer is that I know what the court might award you for maintenance. I could insist we sell the house and I'll take my share."

"That won't happen. I want it for my daughter, and the only way to be sure of that is to stay in it myself."

"As you know, my legal partner is looking after my interests here. I'll have to refer this to him with your views on the matter."

She looked belligerently at him. "I intend to have my way, Roger." She clutched at her abdomen.

"Are you in pain?" Roger asked sympathetically.

Edith's eyes were near to tears but she did not want his sympathy. "It's the smells from your kitchen making my eyes water," she lied.

"You said you were unwell?"

"Yes! It has something to do with that op. I had years ago. The doc sent me for some tests."

Roger remembered it well. Edith had blamed him for her condition when "half her inside", as she put it, had been removed "You never mentioned this before. Surely it didn't begin when we separated? Can I do anything to help?"

"It'll pass. How about this settlement? If you force me, I'll go to court and accuse Charlene of being co-respondent."

"There's never been any adultery with Charlene. It's most unkind of you even to suggest it." Roger was angry. He would have to protect Charlene. "Since you might be tempted, I'll talk to my partner on Monday morning, and have him send you a new agreement," said Roger. "I trust you will sign the divorce papers when that is done and end the uncertainty of my position."

Edith confirmed that she would and got up. "I could do with ... a chair ... " She stopped after a few steps and held her middle. "Be grateful I'm letting you keep ... this one."

"Are you sure you'll be all right? I'm concerned. Is there something I can do?"

Edith rubbed her stomach. "I think it's indigestion, but the doctor doesn't agree."

Roger walked with her until she reached the outer door. "I'd be prepared to give Charlene up if you wanted me to come home and look after you."

"That might have been possible a long time ago. Willie Porter knew my problem. He gave me support and love when I needed it. Thanks for the offer. It has come too late. I have to go. Someone's waiting for me."

Edith stepped over the doorstep and walked towards the main exit without looking back.

Now that Edith had left, Roger quickly wrote the rest of his short story and called it *"The Missing Journey of the Little Prince."*

Where had he put the pot lid? Roger began to panic. Edith's visit had kept him late and upset him more than he had realised. He lifted the plastic bag with the loaves. There it was underneath. The lid looked quite modern with its plastic knob. Mrs Graham need not burn her fingers any more.

He put the various surprise items, the ones Charlene valued so much, into the plastic bag and set out for Elmwood Gardens a little later than he expected.

Since Charlene had been watching at the window for Roger's car he did not need to knock when he reached the second floor; she had the door open ready to greet him. As soon as the door had been closed, the two of them embraced one another and indulged a long lingering kiss.

"I needed that," said Roger. "I had an unexpected visitor. Edith called just before I left. She wants a bigger allowance as well as the house."

"That's up to you Roger. At the moment you're a free agent. While your wife is still alive, we can only be good friends. So you can decide this matter in any way you like."

"She threatened to name you as co-respondent," he said. "I had no alternative but to accept her demands. She also told me she would be getting special treatment for her illness."

"Roger. You do what you think is for the best. I've never done anything to hurt anyone. I've nothing to fear from your wife. There isn't any possibility of proving what she's saying about me."

"I don't want your reputation damaged."

"Let's get on to something else, Roger. It feels like such a long time since Wednesday."

"And for me, too," said Roger. "Maybe one day we'll be together all the time and then you'll change your mind and want me to go somewhere and give you a break." Roger handed her the two loaves. "There's one for each of you."

"Oh, good. It doesn't last very long."

"Here's the lid for your mother's pot."

"Oh, how lovely. Mother will be pleased." She looked inside the bag. "Is that all?" she said pretending to be disappointed. Roger usually had one or two surprise items for her.

"There is … one thing more. Let's go through to the front room and sit down." He took her by the elbow and directed her along in front of him. Once they were inside, he opened a small, brown notebook and read his story about the little prince's new journey.

"That was very interesting," she said patting Roger on the back. "But isn't that what we're all doing? Shifting bundles. I've got several in the hall waiting to go to the allotment." She got up and opened the door. "And then we'll be shifting bundles from the allotment to here. And, if you're lucky," she smiled, "you'll be shifting bundles from here to your flat."

"Yes. That's what life seems to be all about," said Roger. "Shifting bundles. We'd better get a move on. Remember I was late in getting here, and we're going to the concert tonight after we do our stint on the plot."

When they reached the quiet of the allotments, Roger said he would like to discuss their future. Edith's visit had brought out some areas for their consideration.

Roger carried two small folding chairs to the far end to avoid being overheard by those neighbours working near them.

"Charlene, now that my divorce has been finalised, don't you think you should review your rule?"

"No, Roger. If every commandment were subject to amendment as soon as it was thought to be unsuitable, it would not be long before it would be 'Thou shalt kill', 'Thou shalt steal', and 'Thou shalt commit adultery'. There's no ending."

"It's a bit hard on me as well as yourself," wheedled Roger.

"My belief is that Edith will still be married to you in the sight of God. I would be committing a sin if I married you. We're not able to make a promise to each other."

"Charlene, it's you I want. There are a few ministers who hold your view, but most of them have accepted the New Beginning philosophy. Why haven't you?"

"All I can say, is what I have said before. I make no claim on you. If you want to break up our liaison then I won't stand in your way,"

"You know very well, I don't want that. My love for you is not something for switching on and off. Each had a need of the other, and this ripened into love that night after the club. To separate us from each other now would be like paper without a pen."

"I know it's very frustrating for you, Roger. You've denied yourself a woman for so long. And the one you want so much, shakes her head, saying we must wait a little longer."

"God works in mysterious ways. I think he allowed us to meet, as part of some greater plan. We'll know what that is some day. I'm sure of it." He glanced at his watch. "We'd better get a move on, if we are to able to do any work before we leave."

\* \* \* \* \*

"I had to take the only seats that were left," said Charlene as she and Roger occupied two seats behind a pillar.

"Who's conducting?" asked Roger.

"Frederico Bertellini," she replied, as a heavy Italian with a bald head raised his baton.

Da, da, de, daa - da, da, de, daa. The start of the first movement did not augur well; the timing was too fast. It was as if Beethoven's score mattered very little. Roger glanced at the programme. It was supposed to be the Fifth. Why doesn't the orchestra, especially the leader, ignore his baton and get on with it thought Roger? He tried to catch Charlene's eye but she smiled a message of love and closed them.

After a while Roger stopped listening and was grateful when the dreadful performance ended. The whole audience, including Charlene, began cheering their approval as a bewildered Roger stared in surprise.

During the interval, which followed immediately, Roger told Charlene this was the poorest conducting he had ever witnessed.

"I'm sure you can't be right, Roger. All these people aren't wrong, and even if you were correct, they're applauding the composer."

"How do you know Beethoven isn't fuming at this moment along with me? You can't get away from it, that performance was the worst ever. Did you not see the Gazette's critic? He didn't applaud. I'm sure his column on Monday will agree with my opinion."

\* \* \* \* \*

Charlene and Roger had been friendly for a while now; yet their widowed mothers had never met. However, that would soon be put right; Roger had arranged for them to meet and was now on his way to Troon where his mother lived with his sister Netta.

"It's some time since I was taken to the seaside," said Kate Graham to Roger, as he drove along the scenic route beside the firth. "I'm finding it harder to get about on my own nowadays. My last visit to Troon was when my two girls were very small. We had a picnic on the sand." She sighed. "My husband, God bless him, was alive then."

They were almost at their destination when Roger saw Mrs Graham looking towards the Isle of Arran. "Would you like to get a bit closer?" he asked.

"No, thank you," said Mrs Graham, "I'd rather meet your mother."

"We're almost there," said Roger, turning into a side street and bringing the Rover to a halt at the main gate of a large bungalow.

"We've arrived and I can prove it," he joked to the two women.

Mrs Graham straightened her coat and hat, as she stood on the kerb waiting for Roger to lock the car doors. "This way," he said, opening the gate.

Charlene took her mother's arm as they walked up the gravel

path to a glass-fronted door. It opened, without anyone having knocked, and Roger's sister, came out to greet them.

"This is Annette ... we call her Netta," he said giving her a kiss and then turning quickly to her visitors. "This is my friend Charlene and her mother, Kate Graham."

"I'm pleased to meet you," said Netta. They greeted each other so warmly. "Roger has been saying so many nice things about you. Come inside, There's a cool breeze from the sea." She then looked at Roger. "Although mother is not feeling well today, she's looking forward to meeting you."

There had been a local scandal when the former Edna O'Brian had run off with the late Robert Buchanan, Roger's father, and married him in Edinburgh. She was sitting now with her legs up on the settee; her back propped up by two pillows. Roger went over to his mother and kissed her affectionately.

"Mum, this is Mrs Graham, Charlene's mother," he said.

The two elderly ladies embraced and kissed each other on the cheek.

"And this is my friend, Charlene." Roger took her hand and brought her out from behind her mother.

Charlene embraced the frail Edna and gave her a kiss. "I'm very happy to meet you. Roger's told me so many wonderful things about you."

"I'm glad to see my son has met a nice girl like you." Charlene winced. There were so many better words than nice.

Edna pushed her son's shoulder. "Help Mrs Graham with her coat."

Annette had already set the small table with sandwiches, biscuits, cakes and scones. "I made the scones and pancakes myself. I hope you like them."

"I'm sure we shall. Roger shared the pancakes you gave him on his last visit with mother and me."

"My mother was born in Dumbarton, not far from your village," said Roger.

"Then it's possible we might have seen one another when we were out walking in the Kilpatrick Hills behind Dumbarton," said Kate. "In those days my sister and I went there after church on Sunday."

"I didn't get much time for play or exercise," replied Edna. "I come from a large family. We all had jobs to do and our mother kept us all very busy."

They talked to each other for half an hour, recalling places and people they had known when they were young.

"I remember watching the red-headed A J Cronin walking to school," said Edna. "He was such a handsome boy. Roger tells me the house where he was brought up is still there."

"Did you see Dr Finlay's Casebook on the television?" asked Mrs Graham.

"Yes, I did and I liked it very much."

"Mother, would you like to take a trip down to the shore? It's so lovely outside," said Roger. "It's so clear you can see the Sleeping Warrior."

"You don't need to look over to Arran's hills for that. Just look at me. I feel like the Sleeping Warrior myself."

"I think we'll have to leave now, if we're going to be on time for church" said Charlene as she helped Kate from her chair. "My mother is feeling tired." She looked at Roger. "Where did you put her coat?"

"On the hall stand. I'll get it."

Kate Graham came over to the settee. "I've enjoyed my visit. It was good meeting you," she said, looking at Roger's mother.

"Do come back and see me another Sunday," said Edna Buchanan. "I like having visitors, now that I have to rest so much."

"Goodbye Mrs Buchanan," said Charlene.

"Goodbye mother." Roger held her hand as he kissed her.

## Chapter 7

Roger's daughter, Marjorie, had been unable to find employment in Scotland after she qualified at Aberdeen College.

"If I'm to get a good start, I'll need to go to London. That's where all the jobs are," she told her mother.

"I thought people didn't need to work in the big city. There's so much gold lying around for the taking," her mother teased.

Marjorie took the dirty tea cups from the small table in the living room and carried them into the kitchen. "If I can only get started, then I'll have the experience I'll need when I apply for posts in the North."

"How long do you think you'll be down there?" asked Edith.

"At least three months."

"Oh ... that long," said her mother. "I was going to suggest coming with you."

This was something Marjorie hadn't considered when she had made her plans.

"I think you'd better stay here until you find out how your treatment is going. Dr Ferguson has been attending you for a long time and he's got a better knowledge of your condition."

"Perhaps ... that would be better," said Edith.

"I'm glad you've changed your mind."

Edith detected a note of relief in her daughter's voice "Have you already got a flat for yourself?" she said with a slight emphasis on the last word.

This was the moment of truth. Marjorie had never lied to her mother. She'd better tell her about Stephen.

"I thought you might be upset if I told you I was going to live in a friend's flat for a while," said Marjorie.

Edith stared at her daughter. "Does your friend wear trousers?"

"I could say no and leave it at that, and still be telling you the truth. He wears a kilt. I met Stephen at the College and we got to know each other rather well."

"How well?"

"Very well, mum," her daughter replied. "We intend to live in his flat, as partners, to see if we are good for each other."

"That's what we used to call "living in ..." Edith suddenly stopped speaking and screwed her eyes in pain.

"Mum, sometimes I think you're a bit old-fashioned. If we don't suit each other there'll be no costly divorce like the one you and my father have gone through."

Edith rubbed her abdomen as if she was trying to break wind. "I've been having some pain recently." She popped an indigestion tablet in her mouth. "This'll help." Edith was feeling a lot worse than she was admitting. Some tests had been taken at the Central General Hospital and she was waiting for the results. "The pain's going away now." Her mother was not speaking the truth.

"Mum, you've been doing too much cleaning. All that bending can't be good for you." She took her mother's arm and helped her to the chair by the fire. "How about a nice cup of tea? I'd like one myself." She popped into the small kitchen and put on the kettle.

"There's nothing wrong with a trial marriage," her mother said quietly.

"What was that?" said Marjorie bringing through a pot of tea

"Nothing," replied her mother a little more loudly. Edith could have had a wealthy suitor but she had wanted to marry for love. "It seems modern youngsters want to make up their own minds. Are you leaving tomorrow morning?"

"Yes, Mum. Will you be able to see me off?"

"What do you think?"

Marjorie arrived very late at Euston Station and wondered if this was why Stephen hadn't turned up.

"Are you needing a porter, miss?" an Irish voice asked.

Marjorie turned round. "Stephen Ralston! You can't trick me with that imitation of an Irish porter."

He lifted her holdalls, one in each hand. "Just my little joke."

"What's happened to your kilt?"

"I only put it on for the highland dances now-a-days."

"That's a pity. Do I have to wait before I get a kiss?" she asked. "It's been a long time since Aberdeen. Maybe you've forgotten how to?"

"Not at all. And I haven't forgotten how to do the other thing either," Stephen answered back happily.

"What can you possibly mean?" said Marjorie pretending ignorance.

"We'll come back to that later on. How about something to eat?"

There had been no restaurant car on the train and Marjorie was starving. "Let's buy fish suppers and eat them in the flat."

"What a good idea, Marjorie."

When they arrived at the apartment building, Stephen parked his car in the tenants' parking bay and took Marjorie's holdalls while she carried the fish suppers.

"I haven't seen anything like this," she said as he opened the glass entrance door to the modern block of flats, which had been built in place of an original building which the developers had called, a Victorian monstrosity.

"If you forget your keys, just press the button. It rings a bell in the flat, and I can open the door from inside. More people are doing this to keep strangers out."

They took the lift to the eighth floor.

"We're here." Stephen practically threw the holdalls out of the lift. "Quickly Marjorie, you don't get much time before the gate closes." Another glass door separated the doors of the two flats on the eighth floor from the top of the stairs. "It helps to keep the flat warmer," he explained.

"What a lovely place you have, Stephen? Which room is mine?"

He pointed to the door on his left. "We don't have separate rooms. We're sharing," he said.

"We didn't agree to share a room," Marjorie said angrily.

"I'm only pretending." Stephen laughed, trying to extricate himself from near disaster. "That's your room on the right. The bathroom and kitchen are straight ahead ... beyond the sitting room."

"I'll take the food through to the kitchen if you'll deal with my things. I take it you have all the usual equipment in your kitchen?"

"You'll find everything you need close to hand."

Although the flat had central heating, the living area also had a gas fire. Stephen turned it on to assist the central heating. Then he set out two small tables with plates, cups and saucers, and fetched a bottle of Liebfraumilch from the fridge.

"I thought we'd celebrate with a bottle of white wine," he said, pulling the cork with a resounding plop and pouring out two glasses. He raised his glass. "To us. May we become very good friends and live a life of happiness together." The two of them clinked glasses. "Does that wine suit your taste?"

"It's lovely." She gave him a lingering kiss on the lips. "I'll have some more later," she said, putting her glass on the table.

"I'll be happy to oblige," said Stephen, thinking she meant a kiss.

Marjorie returned from the kitchen with the two suppers and asked, "Would you like tomato sauce on yours?"

"Yes, I would."

"In that case, Stephen, you'd better go and fetch it!"

They sat cross-legged on cushions in front of the fire and ate the fish. Stephen leaned over and cleared some tomato sauce from her lips with a kiss.

"Stephen Ralston, you seem to think you're on to a good thing."

"I just wanted to show my appreciation."

"Your appreciation for what?"

"For putting the suppers on the plates and making the tea."

"There's nothing special about that."

"But you did it with love. That's what made the difference when I ate it. That's what I appreciated."

Marjorie finished the last chip. "That was most enjoyable, I must have been very hungry. Normally I could only have eaten half of it." She licked her fingers.

He lifted the tray of dirty dishes and took them through to the kitchen. "I'll soak them in water until you're ready to wash up."

"My father's a lawyer. He told me about people like you. You could convince a blind man he'd be all right when someone switched on the light."

"There's some more wine left in the bottle," he said topping up their glasses. "Here's to us and our partnership. Would you like one of these?" He enquired offering Marjorie what looked like a cigarette.

"No thank you, Stephen, I don't smoke." She waved her hand in front of her face to disperse an imaginary, unpleasant smell.

"They're not cigarettes." Stephen said.

"Are you offering me marijuana? I never saw you smoking that stuff at the College."

"I was too busy studying. I only picked up the habit when I came to London. There are a lot worse things than a bit of pot."

"I'm not happy about it. As far as I'm concerned, it's not for me. If you want to indulge, I'll go to my room. You did say it was the one to the right of the door."

"I don't know why you're so upset." He inhaled deeply on the paper tube. "It's no worse than smoking cigarettes." She got up as if to go her room.

"All right," said Stephen, stubbing out the joint on an ashtray. "I don't want to spoil our first night together. We haven't been with each other since I visited your digs behind Union Street."

Marjorie looked at the clock and yawned. "It's after eleven o'clock, Stephen, and I've had a long day. I'll just have to go to my room. If you meant it about the dishes, I'll do them in the morning. There are a few conditions, like washing up, we'll need to discuss."

"Okay Marjorie. We don't want to spoil things. You go ahead and rest." He gave her a peck on the cheek. "I'll stick the dirty dishes in the sink and watch the late night film. You can have a long lie in as well since tomorrow's Saturday. Would you like breakfast in bed?"

Marjorie yawned again. "No, thank you. I never eat breakfast in bed. I like to get up as soon as I'm awake," she said. "I think I'll just make it to the bedroom before I collapse. But first, a phone call to mum to find out how she is." Marjorie tried several times without getting a reply. "I should have phoned earlier, mother's probably gone to bed. I'll try again tomorrow."

Next morning Marjorie washed up as she promised and set out the shining cutlery and clean dishes on the table for breakfast.

"Stephen!" she called in the direction of the bathroom. "Do you want corn flakes or rice crisps?"

"Corn flakes."

"Is it to be tea or coffee?"

"Tea. You know it's always tea in the morning," he shouted, as he finished drying himself.

"You could have changed your mind," she said, putting a cup and saucer beside his plate of corn flakes. "Be ready in a couple of minutes then," she yelled.

"You might as well share my bed from now on." Stephen used a large mouthful of tea to swallow a well-chewed piece of toast. "I don't think there's any doubt about our being physically suitable for each other after your performance last night."

"You make it sound as if it was all my idea." Marjorie felt embarrassed in the light of day.

"We do need another room, where either of us can go when we need to be on our own. A place for our thinking time, you might say," she reasoned. "If I came in with you we'd need a bigger bed, and then we could sell the single beds and get new furniture for the spare room." She raced on.

"Hold on Marjorie. One thing at a time." He needed space to consider what she had just said. "Firstly we'd have to make a commitment to each other, by becoming engaged. I'm sure you'd agree to that."

"Of course, I'd like to become engaged to you." She rushed round the table and hugged him as they kissed each other.

"We don't want to start anything now. I'm just recovering from last night," he said quickly.

"Surely I can kiss you to show how happy you've made me, can't I?" She laughed. "When will we buy the ring?"

"I think I heard the postman." Stephen got up and put on his dressing gown, and went down to the front door. He returned with a handful of mail.

"The usual junk letters," he said throwing them carelessly on the table. "There's something for me though. It might be an answer to my job application."

"Open it then," said Marjorie. "You've been on tenterhooks waiting for it."

He carefully slit the envelope. "I'm afraid there's nothing very much." He looked gloomily at her. "They've written to tell me ..."

"Come on!" cried Marjorie, who was sitting uneasily in her chair. "Don't keep me waiting. Are you getting the job?"

"They've written to tell me ... " He hesitated deliberately, to prolong the agony, "that I've been given a United Nations contract to work for the Zimbabwe government." Although his work would take him all over the country, he would be based in Harare and given accommodation according to his marital status.

Marjorie hugged him tightly as she kissed him over and over again. "Will I be going with you?" she asked exuberantly.

"I would hope so. I'm likely to be there for a long time. If we get married before I go, then we'll get married quarters."

"And I could find employment in Harare," said Marjorie. But then she remembered her mother. "What's going to happen to Mum? It's difficult enough keeping in touch with her from London. It'll be nearly impossible from Africa."

"Are you upset?" He noticed the melancholy look in her eyes.

"No, it's nothing you've done. I was just remembering Mother's illness. I can't leave her at this time. After Father left, she told me she'd a pain in her stomach. It seems it had something to do with her operation a number of years ago."

"I hope her illness proves to be nothing serious," said Stephen optimistically. "We can always take her with us; there's a good medical service there. I'm certain we'll have room galore where we're going. But if she doesn't want to leave her home, then you'll want to stay with her I expect."

"That settles it," said Marjorie. "I'll phone her right away." She was just about to lift the handset when the phone rang. "That'll be Mother," she said excited.

"Hello. Is that Marjorie Buchanan?" said an officious voice.

"Yes."

"I'm Penelope Clark, a social worker with the Central General Hospital. I'm sorry I have bad news for you."

"Mother's not ..." she gasped.

"No, but she's very ill. I'd advise you to come right away."

"I'll be there as quickly as I can arrange." Stephen deftly caught the handset, which she had let fall.

Marjorie was shattered. This was not the kind of news she had been expecting. She took a tissue from the box lying on the table, and wiped her eyes, but there were no tears to dry.

"Why does life treat us like this? One minute I'm made happy by becoming engaged, only to be hear this terrible news about mother at the same time."

Stephen took her in his arms. "It might not be as bad as the social worker says." He stroked her fair hair with his comforting fingers.

"I should have known Mother wouldn't tell me the truth, not if she thought it would prevent me getting on with my life."

"There can't be any doubt what your decision must be," said Stephen. "We must leave as soon as possible. Put some things in your holdall while I phone for a taxi."

Marjorie walked to her room as if in a dream. She couldn't believe this was happening to her. She pulled a holdall from beneath the bed and threw some spare clothes inside, without folding them, as she would have done at any other time.

When the taxi arrived, Stephen lifted the holdalls and went quickly to the lift.

"We should be in time for the afternoon flight to Glasgow," said Stephen, as he kissed Marjorie in the lift. "The social worker may be taking too serious a view of things."

The ward sister met Marjorie and Stephen at the entrance. "Your mother had her uterus among other things removed ten years ago. This gave her a few more years."

Marjorie was devastated. "She never told anyone. She was always taking indigestion tablets."

"They weren't doing her any good. Mrs Buchanan lived a lot longer than anyone expected."

"How long does my mother have?" she asked.

The sister hesitated. "We've been told not very long. Days possibly? I'd advise you to stay here tonight."

Marjorie was too concerned to cry.

"Your mother keeps asking for Roger."

"Roger's my father, but I haven't heard from him for years."

"You should let him know about her terminal illness." She put Edith's records in the office and asked Marjorie to follow her to the ward where she left them alone with Edith.

Edith Buchanan was at that stage in her illness when she was hardly able to speak. This will probably be my last chance; she thought when she saw her daughter coming into the ward. I'll need to make a special effort if I'm to see Roger again.

"Hello Mother." Marjorie tried to sound cheerful, as she bent over and lovingly kissed her mother on the forehead.

Edith said nothing. She wanted to conserve her energy.

"Is the pain any easier?"

Instead of nodding her head, Edith blinked her eyes, to let her daughter know she was comfortable.

"Do you need anything? You're still all right for paper hankies. But you haven't touched any of that lovely orange juice."

I'd better say it now, thought Edith.

"I want to see my husband," her voice was thin and hoarse, but distinct enough for Marjorie to hear her plea.

"Mother, you don't have a husband," her daughter replied.

"I want to see Roger." Edith frustrated tried to raise herself up in her desperation.

"Roger," she repeated despondently, and relaxed once again as if she had accepted the fact that her request was useless.

The nurse, who was aware that her patient was deteriorating rapidly, and wanted to be on hand at the end, had been listening to Edith. She beckoned Marjorie over.

"Your mother is likely to last for a while yet. Who is Roger?" she asked.

"Roger Buchanan is my father, Mother's former husband," said Marjorie.

"I would advise you to contact him and ask him to come to the hospital. If you don't ... you're going to feel very guilty when your mother dies." The nurse lifted the phone and handed it over.

Marjorie had not spoken to her father since he and Edith had agreed to a divorce. She would have preferred to have seen her parents separated, with the possibility of reconciliation.

"Mother is going to die soon," Marjorie said to her father, without any preliminaries. "She wants to see you. That's why I'm phoning."

Roger was devastated. The last thing he wanted was Edith's early death.

"Isn't there anything that can be done?" he asked.

"Nothing," said Marjorie angrily. "Mother has terminal cancer. That's how serious it is."

"I was getting ready to go out, but I'll be with you in about twenty minutes."

Roger phoned Charlene.

"I'm just unable to believe this is happening," she said. "I almost feel responsible. You must get there as quickly as you can. Your daughter's going to need you. Call me when you can," Charlene said and put the phone down.

"Who was that?" asked her mother who had been preparing the evening meal. "Edith Buchanan is dying from cancer and has asked to see Roger. He won't be eating with us tonight."

Roger went quickly to the Central General Hospital, wanting to see Edith almost as much as she wanted to see him. Since it was not visiting hour a nurse stopped him when he was about to enter. "Can I help you sir?"

"I've come to see my ... Edith Buchanan." His voice faltered.

Knowing that Mrs Buchanan was terminally ill; the nurse delayed him no longer. "She's in the little room beside the entrance."

Marjorie and Stephen were standing on either side of the bed, looking on helplessly when he arrived.

"Come over here Stephen," said Marjorie, so that her father could stand beside the bed.

"I've come to see you." Roger bent over and gently kissed Edith on the lips. "I didn't know you were in hospital. If I had ... I would have come sooner. You know ..." His throat tightened. "I'm still fond of you."

Edith's lips tried to form words, but she had no breath and they remained unsaid. The effort was too great. Then she tried speaking with her eyes.

"I think I know what you're trying to say Edith. Otherwise why would you ask for me?"

He could see from her response that she was happy. He understood that she still loved him.

"I love, you too," he said brokenly, and kissed her on lips, which were no longer able to speak.

What a moment for reconciliation, thought Roger. We both went wrong somewhere. But where? My love for Edith is as strong at this moment, as it ever was, and now it is too late. Edith looked for the last time at her three visitors and then slipped lifelessly to one side.

Marjorie, who had been under a great strain for the past few months, immediately burst into tears and hugged her mother for some time before she would allow her father to show his last respects.

When the ward sister heard the loud sobbing, she came in and checked her patient's pulse. "I'm afraid Mrs Buchanan has gone." She closed Edith's eyes as if to confirm her death. "I'll get her things together for you to take away and arrange for the death certificate before you go. "Would you like a cup of tea?" the sister asked gently.

"I would," said Marjorie. "How about the men?"

Roger and Stephen nodded in agreement.

They went into the corridor and walked slowly to the patient's recreation room near the ward office.

"If you wait here, I'll bring the tea," said the sister.

"Father, I'll make all the arrangements for mother's cremation. I won't be needing your help," Marjorie said with a touch of bitterness in her voice. There was no one else to be angry about just then. "You may come to the cremation, but, if you do, you mustn't join the family. I'm broken-hearted by mother's death."

"That's not fair Marjorie. Your mother made it clear that our marriage was over and that she wanted to live with Willie Porter. Incidentally why was he not here tonight?"

"Mother hasn't been seeing Mr Porter for a long time."

"She gave me the impression she was still with him when she came about the divorce arrangements. Marjorie, I want you to love me like you once did," he said.

"I find it hard to forgive you, Father. Maybe some time later ... Stephen and I will be getting married and leaving for Zimbabwe in the near future."

Roger looked from his daughter to the man standing by her side. "Presumably this gentleman is your fiancé?"

"Yes Mr Buchanan," said Stephen. "We became engaged recently in London."

"You've got Stephen here. He'll look after you," said Roger. "I think I'll go home and grieve in private. Remember, if you want to see me before you leave all you need do is phone."

Dr Ferguson was waiting in his small office when Marjorie arrived. "I'm sorry there was nothing we could do to save your mother. I was a young doctor the last time Mrs Graham was here. We knew a lot less then than we do now. When your mother had that operation a number of years ago, the surgeon removed most of her reproductive organs to try and eliminate all the cancer. Somehow it had managed to get to the stomach."

He signed the death certificate in the sombre silence, which followed. "There you are," he said handing it to Marjorie. "What can I say?"

"Would it have helped if mother had come sooner?" asked Marjorie.

"Grieving relatives seem to find comfort in the knowledge that all that could be done was done and that the patient's death did not result from any delay in the medication." Dr Ferguson stared gently into her eyes. "Would you have it any other way?"

"I suppose you're right, doctor. I withdraw my question."

\* \* \* \* \*

Edith had been cremated and her ashes scattered in the Garden of Remembrance as she had wished and Marjorie had returned to London without saying goodbye or attempting reconciliation with her father. There would be little time to make an appointment with the Registrar.

Neither of them had spent any money on new outfits for the special day. Stephen wore his best office suit, and Marjorie, a pretty two-piece costume in light blue. Her only concession was a spray of flowers carried on her matching blue bag.

"It's such a pity neither your parents nor mine will be able to attend, though I do think you should have sent your father an invitation. It would then have been up to him."

Marjorie's face darkened. "I couldn't stand being anywhere near him, when I remember what he did to my mother."

Stephen took her hand and held it in his. "Your father had nothing to do with her death if that's what you're thinking. The cancer was a silent intruder. You can't blame your father for that."

Marjorie became tearful. "I miss her very much," she muttered. "How I wish she was here with me today. We often talked of when I would get married, and what she would wear, and all the little details, which you recall long after the ceremony is over. And now she's gone."

But Stephen felt it was wrong to alienate them from Roger. "At least send him a card to let him know what's happening. After all, he is your father."

"Maybe I'm being unreasonable. I'll send him a card when we leave for Africa telling him I'm married and where we are going to live," she agreed. "I hope Doreen and Albert haven't forgotten where they are to meet us."

After the registry office wedding ceremony Stephen and Marjorie went back to a local hotel for a simple celebration meal with their two friends ...

"Wasn't that registrar a queer old coot?" said Marjorie.

"You should be careful what you're saying. He might object to being called queer," warned Stephen. "You would've thought he was marrying the Queen in Westminster Abbey the way he went on." As far as Stephen was concerned; he had been happy with the registrar's special attention.

The wine waiter interrupted them and asked, "Would you like the wine list now, sir?"

"I expect we should have a bottle to launch our marriage," Stephen glanced at the wine list and handed it back. "Let me have a bottle of your best house wine ... white, I think," he said looking at the others.

As soon as the waiter had gone, Stephen revealed that many hotels simply filled a bottle with the house wine and stick on a false label. "I'm not paying for a name, which hasn't anything to do with the wine in the bottle in the first place."

\* \* \* \* \*

"What kept you?" Marjorie said angrily, as Stephen came in carrying several parcels. He had left her to do the packing while he did some last-minute shopping.

"I'm sorry dear, I got held up in the traffic." He put his parcels on the bed and gave her a kiss. His late return had left them only three hours to finish their packing and make the check-in at Heathrow.

"Look at the mess you left me with," she said waving her hand about the small hotel bedroom. They had moved here when Stephen sold his flat. It was piled high with everything, other than his furniture, which had already been forwarded to their bungalow in Harare.

"What was so important that it couldn't wait?" She continued to fill her holdall with her personal luggage. Marjorie had a number of family photographs, her mother's rings and few pieces porcelain, family heirlooms, which were too important to consign to the cargo bay.

"Mosquito nets," he said opening one of the packages and pulling out a fine, white, net curtain. "We don't want to get malaria, do we!"

"No! But we do want to catch a plane and there's not much time. Those things could have waited."

"But this could not." He handed her a tiny parcel.

"Oh, you've kept your word." She had guessed at once the nature of his gift. It was an engagement ring - the one with a big blue stone she admired the other day. Marjorie put it on and held it at arm's length. "It looks a bit like Mothers. Thank you, Stephen," she said giving him a kiss. "Now let's get this lot packed. The taxi will be here in an hour."

"Perhaps these will be useful," he said consigning the mosquito nets to one of the heaps on the floor. He had not been truthful with her. Having heard about an opportunity to make a lot of money working for an emerging African State he had gone to make enquiries. It turned out that, as a former soldier, he would be engaged as a mercenary at twice his government pay. The proposition was not quite what he had in mind.

Marjorie and Stephen managed to get everything packed before the receptionist phoned to say that the taxi had arrived.

"I hope we'll be able to take our holdalls on the plane," said Marjorie, after they had booked in. She had once travelled with lockers so small that her holdall would not fit and had had to travel with it under her feet for the whole of the flight.

"Our plane can cope with these," he replied pointing to the holdalls. "But first I think we should have a snack in the departure lounge. Aircraft meals never seem to give you that full-up feeling."

After they had eaten they paid a visit to the duty free. Proprietary goods from abroad were always more expensive and sometimes unobtainable in Harare. Stephen lingered over the cigars and malt whiskies while Marjorie indulged herself at the perfume counter

"If they ask at the customs, tell them you smoke cigars, " he warned Marjorie as they settled in their seats.

"Then, you'd better put this bottle of Chanel number five in your bag. If they ask you, tell them you can't do without it."

It was extremely warm when Stephen and Marjorie arrived at Harare airport. They had worn clothes more appropriate to Britain's climate. "I'll be glad to change into tee shirt and shorts," said Marjorie waving the in-flight magazine like a fan.

As soon as they had passed through customs and immigration porters surrounded them. Stephen pointed to a small man with big teeth and within seconds the man had loaded his trolley. "Follow me, Sir," he said, smiling broadly as he overtook the queue on his way to the concourse.

"Here you get taxi," he said and hesitated for his tip. Stephen was remembering the advice "never be over-generous" when he realised he had no local currency. He took a spare pound note in his pocket and handed it over. Clearly the man was displeased. Some thoughtless tourists often gave the porter gift coupons. He had not recognised the Scottish banknote. Stephen realised what was wrong and pointed to the bureau de change. When the man came back he was grinning all over. He rarely got a tip this big.

Stephen had been told that someone would meet them at the airport; but there was no sign of an expatriate.

"You Mr Ralston," said a thin, black man with greying hair. "I am Andrew, your man." Stephen had not expected their servant to come.

"Where's your truck?" Marjorie asked apprehensively as she surveyed the heap of luggage at her feet.

"Friend must go to car park to wait. He comes soon." Then Marjorie saw a safari type vehicle making its way over to the front entrance.

On the way to their bungalow, some five miles from the airport, Andrew talked incessantly about his duties, and his single-roomed hut at the back of the house. Not only was he to be paid a reasonable wage, but also he had other perks like lighting, heating and mealies.

"Mealies?" enquired Marjorie.

"Yes Mistress," he repeated, thinking she was objecting.

"What is it?" she asked.

"You'd call it corn cob," said Stephen, boasting knowledge he'd overheard in the airport.

The electric gate opened and Andrew's friend drove them up the path to the bungalow. "This is sure some place," said Stephen looking round the magnificent estate.

"Hello there," called an Englishman in a light-coloured suit. "I see you've arrived."

He joined them at once. "I'm Dr Sinclair. I was supposed to meet you but there was an emergency at the hospital."

The doctor was living alone in a bungalow not far away from them and had been glad to act as the unofficial welcoming committee. However, there was bad news; the Ralstons furniture had not arrived from South Africa. They had a choice. They could stay in one of his spare rooms or at the prestigious Hilton.

"We'll take up your offer Dr Sinclair," said Stephen.

"That was a wise choice," said the doctor. "It would have been a long time before your expenses were refunded."

# Chapter 8

Charlene was hoeing the onion bed when Roger made his decision. He took the hoe from her hand and let it fall to the ground. "I've something to say," he said with an air of mystery. "It's almost three month's since Edith died and I think it's time for us to be formally engaged." He hugged her in his arms, expecting her to respond with a quick "Yes", but Charlene was still upset by the sudden and painful death of his former wife.

"But it's so soon," she said. "People will think we're being insensitive."

"You can't say we haven't waited. It's more than three years since that day on Ben Calder," Roger reminded her.

She hesitated, beginning to realise that marrying Roger was now a real possibility. But was marriage what she really wanted? Could she not be equally happy if they continued as at present, and remained just good friends?

"I would have thought you'd have jumped at the chance to become Mrs Buchanan."

"I've been single for a long time, Roger. It was much easier to make plans for a married future when no decisions had to be made. You'll have to bear with me. It's a bit unnerving to be asked to change the habits of a lifetime." She brushed his hair with her fingers.

"Is the sexual side of marriage worrying you?" Roger knew that Charlene was a virgin. "Have some of your married girlfriends frightened you with honeymoon horror stories? If that's the reason for your hesitation, put it out of your mind. I've never made any demands of you in this department, because I knew you wanted to wait until after we were married before you gave yourself to me."

"I suppose there is some truth in what you're saying, Roger. I've only a superficial knowledge of what's expected from me. " She embraced him and kissed his brow. "I'm worried that the experience will be very painful."

Roger kissed Charlene firmly on her lips. "It should be as pleasant as a kiss. When we embrace, as we are doing now, I feel a strong desire for you. You must be aware of this."

"I've noticed how easily you are aroused when you're close to me," she confided.

"But I repressed my feelings for your sake, knowing how you felt about premarital sex."

"There's another important point. I've always been able to make my own decisions. I'm wondering what it will be like leaving these to my husband. I attach a great deal of importance to the man being the head of the house deciding what is best."

"You've no need to worry on that score either." Roger embraced her once again and gently renewed his kisses. "If there's to be little or no sex in our marriage it won't be a hardship for me, since we've many other interests to keep us occupied."

"You make me feel so happy," she said returning his embrace.

"As far as being the boss is concerned, any decision I take will always be taken in your interest too. I hope I'll never make you unhappy because of anything I say or do."

"In that case Roger, I'll be happy to marry you." Charlene picked up the hoe again, and vigorously chopped some flowering groundsel. "From the sublime to the ..." she smiled.

\* \* \* \* \*

On the following Monday morning, little Brian Watson listened with disbelief as Charlene told the class she had become engaged to Mr Buchanan. He held up his hand and, uncharacteristically, waited until she asked him to speak. She wondered what the precocious five-year-old was going to say this time.

"Please, Miss, you can't marry two people. I'm going to marry you when I grow up. So Mr Buchanan can't."

She had come across this kind of strong affection for her, from pupils like Brian, on many occasions, and knew how to deal with it.

"I'm fond of all my little boys and girls, Brian. You're all like my own family." She looked round the class and thought that this is probably the only family I'm likely to have.

"Roger - that's my friend's first name - will be able to marry me very soon, Brian. Whereas I'd have to wait a very long until you were a big man before you would be allowed to marry me. You wouldn't like that to happen, and have me wait until I was very old, would you?"

"No, Miss Graham. I want you to be happy. You can marry Mr Buchanan."

"That's what I wanted to hear, Brian. We can still be good friends and one day, when you meet someone special you can ask me to your wedding."

"I'm never going to marry anyone else," said Brian, sitting down dejectedly.

Later that day, after Charlene had driven into New Town to meet Roger at the jeweller's, they only touched hands briefly on meeting. Both were well-known in the town and wanted to keep the news of their engagement quiet until they had told the members of the Kelvin Hiking Club.

"Roger, go in and ask if there's a private room where we can view the rings." She could see that prospective buyers were visible to everyone looking in from the pavement. "We're both well-known in the community. I want to keep our engagement a secret for a while."

"My fiancée will be in here shortly," explained Roger once the proprietor had taken him into the back room. "I asked her to wait, before following me in." Roger explained as he sat down in the private room.

A little later, Charlene was shown in.

"Are you nervous, my dear?" he asked, standing up to greet her. "It won't be long now before that finger has got something on it."

"Have you been shown anything yet?"

"Not yet. He's asked one of the assistants to make a selection for us."

When the jeweller re-appeared a young assistant who was holding a tray of about twenty rings accompanied him. There were some with single large diamonds and others with three or more smaller diamonds in rows or circles, and some had coloured stones.

Roger set his sights on the diamond solitaire, without revealing his choice to Charlene.

She tried on one ring after another, holding her hand up to the light each time, as if trying to judge the ring's suitability by its sparkle. The jeweller looked on enigmatically. He had seen it all before. His experience told him that each woman had an ideal ring and any attempt by him to divert her from that purpose might end up with a lost sale.

"It's between these two," Charlene said eventually, pointing to the solitaire, which she had returned to the tray? "That one and the one I'm wearing on my hand. What do you think Roger?" Charlene wiggled her fingers in front of his face.

"You make your own choice, Charlene, and then I'll say what I think."

She tried on the solitaire again.

Shaking her head up and down approvingly, as she tried the sparkle test, she said. "I think I like this one." She looked into his eyes. "Is it to be this one?"

"Great minds think alike," he said at once. "That's the one I picked as soon as I saw it on the tray."

"That's a very good choice, Madam," the jeweller said with conviction. "There's a slightly blue tinge to it, don't you think? It's usual to purchase the wedding ring at the same time, so that you can match them." He brought out a tray of gold bands and selected one. "This should do well with your engagement ring. You can have them engraved later."

The assistant took the tray of rejected rings back to the safe, while the proprietor fetched a small red box from a drawer. "When you're not wearing it, you can keep it in here." The wedding ring was put disdainfully in a plain brown envelope.

\* \* \* \* \*

"As I told you on a previous occasion, Miss Graham it's a New Beginning," affirmed the Reverend Anthony Drinkwater, minister of Elmwood Parish Church. "That's the way the church looks at it nowadays."

He opened his diary and scanned the entries. "The nearest Saturday which fits in with Charlene's school holidays is the one before Easter Monday. I don't usually perform weddings that day but if it will help, I'll fit you in at two o'clock." He glanced over his spectacles as he awaited the couple's confirmation.

Roger intervened, speaking to Charlene. "If we leave it till the following Saturday, then you'll be returning to your work immediately from your honeymoon. I think we'd be better taking up Mr Drinkwater's offer." As he spoke the minister was writing some figures on a piece of paper.

"You're right, Roger." She nodded her head in agreement.

The minister pushed a folded piece of paper towards Roger, who took a quick look and put it in his pocket. On it was written: Church officer £10 Organist £10 Minister? It was clearly an account for the wedding ceremony. Perhaps, because he wasn't a member of the congregation he was expected to pay! He would never have thought of giving the minister a gratuity. Maybe he didn't drink water, he thought with a grin.

"That's settled then," declared the minister, "I'll put you down for the Saturday before Easter Monday. That was a New Beginning too."

\* \* \* \* \*

There was no need to pretend to be free agents now. Following the club custom they would have the president announce their engagement during the tea interval at the Wednesday evening meeting of the club. The official notice would be inserted in the next day's morning newspaper.

Eileen Montgomery, who had been appointed to take over from the late Fred Cowan, had agreed to make the announcement just before the tea break. Charlene would keep her ring hidden beneath her glove beforehand and would then display her treasure for the admiration of all. She could hardly listen to the speaker who was showing the slides of a climbing holiday in Zermatt. Halfway through the talk Miss Montgomery stood up. "I think this is a good time for tea in our Hörnli hut," she said interrupting the speaker with a broad smile. "We'll come back to Mr Murray after the tea break. But before you go and queue up, I have a very pleasant duty to perform. A little bird told me that two of our members have become engaged." She waited to see the response.

There was hardly a murmur for, what was supposed to be a secret, that had become common gossip among the women before the start of the meeting. Charlene had made the mistake of taking a club member into her confidence, and of course the news had been passed on.

"I suppose you're all keen to know who it is? Well, you can stop guessing. Charlene Graham and Roger Buchanan are engaged to be married. I would like them to have the congratulations of all of us." Several people, who had not been in on the secret, looked back to where Charlene was sitting and smiled to her. "We'll return to Zermatt after the tea break."

Apart from Jane Faulds, Irene Carson, and two of the men, the rest of the members rushed up to the tea queue. They had no intention of missing their tea just to see Charlene's trophy. The two women admired Charlene's choice.

"It's a lovely ring," said Jane. "I wonder if I'll get a stone like that some day?"

"There wasn't much enthusiasm, was there, Roger?" Charlene said, with a touch of disappointment as they walked over to the Beresford at the end of the meeting. "It lacked all the jollity I had with my colleagues at school on Monday. It was lovely to watch them trying on the ring. Most of the women here are just not interested."

"Maybe they're waiting till we all meet in the bar at the Beresford before they make a fuss," suggested Roger.

The Beresford had an immense lounge but only one large table and this had been taken over by the usual crowd from the club by the time Charlene and Roger had arrived.

"Hello, everybody!" Roger called out, as he approached the congested table.

"Sorry. We're full up here," called Maureen Harrison.

"There's no more room," declared another.

"You'll need to sit somewhere else," said a third woman.

There was no attempt to include them by squeezing in another two chairs.

Roger saw a comfortable table near the fire. "That will do us just fine, Charlene. The warmth will help to dispel the cold shoulder that we've just been given!"

He tried to avoid her eyes. He knew she was close to tears. She didn't deserve to be treated this way, he thought.

"Have a lime and lemonade," he said, trying to cheer her up, and was about to go to the bar to order drinks, when Jane Faulds came over with Sidney Armstrong.

"Do you mind if we join you?" she asked amiably. "The table up there is too full."

"We'd be glad to have your company," said Roger offering Jane a chair.

Sidney brought out his wallet. "What will you have to drink? The treat's on me tonight, this being your engagement."

Wasn't it strange that Jane, who was supposed to be the centre of the row, was the only one among them with a heart, reflected Roger?

Sidney fetched the drinks. "I'm going to propose a toast." They all raised their glasses and waited for him to begin. "To Roger and Charlene. May they live long, be healthy and have a very happy marriage."

The four of them clinked their glasses and laughed together.

"I'm sure we're the centre of the discussion now," said Jane glancing back at the other table.

Roger began to speculate on their continued membership of the club. He and Charlene would forgive, these unkind people, but even if Charlene could ignore the way she had been hurt, he would find it impossible to be friendly with them in future. There were two exceptions - Jane and Sydney.

"We're not going to have much time to go walking," said Roger. "We'll be too busy putting a home together." Charlene smiled.

"I take your point," said Sydney reading between the lines. "However if you and Charlene would to like go on a short walk sometime; just give me a call."

Jane could see that Roger wanted to talk privately with Charlene. "I'm going to the ladies room Sydney, would you be a dear and get another round of drinks? I'll pay this time." As soon as they were alone Roger had a hurried consultation with Charlene.

Sydney came back with the drinks and Jane rejoined them soon after. "We'd be very happy to go out walking with you sometime," said Roger. "Jane could make a foursome." She smiled. "And another thing, Charlene and I are planning to get married at Easter."

"That's awfy soon after your engagement. Don't tell me you two have to - " Roger interrupted and said, "Don't be silly Sydney. The date suits us both. What I want to know is ... will you be my best man?"

"Of course I will. Presumably it's to be a Saturday. What date's that?"

"Saturday the thirteenth, I'm afraid," said Roger.

"Always the best man never the groom," quipped Sydney. Jane stared at him. What was wrong with her?

"You can bring a partner with you," Charlene said looking at Jane.

Sydney was not certain how he felt about Jane. They had been dating from time to time; usually when she had tickets for one thing or another. "Would you like to be my partner?" he asked.

"Will we make it a double wedding then?" she smiled, flashing Charlene's solitaire, which she had borrowed temporarily.

"Maybe I'll think about it," he said and finished his whisky.

\* \* \* \* \*

Now that Roger and Charlene were officially engaged, they began the search for a home of their own. Charlene and her mother saw at least one house a day, during the next two months, and rejected most of them for one reason or another, until Roger saw a newspaper advertisement which offered the kind of home for which they had been looking and in the right area.

It was a bungalow in a quiet district, where the prices were generally high. The late owner had taken ownership on the day it was completed and had left it, near enough as the architect had designed it. They had rejected other houses because Roger was reluctant to tear out someone else's fantasy kitchen or wall-to-wall-bedroom furniture. Fortunately a buyer's market, coupled with the fact that they could close the deal immediately, gave them an edge over the competition. Roger had estimated the value to just a thousand pounds above the best offer by the closing date and, since the lawyer had been anxious to close the deal, he had phoned Roger with the good news. It was fortunate that the law of Scotland made all offers binding on acceptance.

\* \* \* \* \*

The Allotment Association had written several times to Charlene, in the course of the past few years, about the condition of her plot and paths. It had not helped the situation when she began using every spare hour to get things ready for her wedding day

"It's quite blunt," said Charlene, showing the letter to Roger. "I've been told to get my plot tidied up, or give it up." The letter reminded her of the terms of her let.

"Let's be practical," said Roger. "There's no way we can keep it going and do all the other things which need our attention. We've both got our full-time work and you won't want to neglect your mother just because you've got a home of your own. And then, there's me and our own garden to look after."

Charlene was torn between maintaining her father's memory, by retaining his allotment, and fulfilling her new life.

"Life's constantly changing Charlene, and we have to get on with it. Hopefully there will be an improvement." Roger looked round the allotment, and thought of all the hard work the Graham family had given to this tiny plot of land.

"It's a bit bigger than our own back garden, but if we stop growing vegetables, there'll be enough ground in Burleigh Avenue to accommodate most of the things we really must take with us. I can't guarantee to transplant everything, without thinking about the possibility of failure," said Roger. "Isn't it fortunate we've already prepared the soil for the transfer of your favourite plants."

"If I want to change my life style, I suppose I'll need to make some sacrifices," said Charlene. "But there's one thing I must grow."

"Emperor scarlet runner beans!" he called out like a contestant seeking the top prize in a TV Quiz Show.

"They were my father's favourite. You don't see fresh beans in the greengrocer's very often. If we grow our own I'll be happy just with that."

"The letter said we had up till today to move our things out of the plot," said Roger. "If we don't, when the new man comes in tomorrow he'll either dig them up or refuse to allow us to take them away."

"We'll be able to transfer all the plants you want except those that are overgrown like the Black Knight buddleia, honeysuckle and spiraea Billardii. We'll buy new bushes and take cuttings from the others with sentimental value." Roger promised her.

At that moment the elderly club secretary, who usually made his rounds on Saturday mornings, came along the path and stopped beside them.

"They'll all strike very well," he confirmed having overheard what was being said. "It's sad for me to see my friend's daughter giving up her plot. I used to enjoy talking to your father a great deal. He was very knowledgeable about plants, especially tomatoes. He never seemed to go on holiday. Everybody depended on him to water their plants when they were away."

He pulled out his briar pipe and began to fill it with a cheap tobacco from a yellow packet.

"You don't need to tell me the fine man my father was." Charlene screwed up her eyes, to avoid the smoke. "There was no one like him. Always ready to help others when they needed it. He died a long time ago, as you know, but I still miss him very much."

"Doesn't Roger compensate a little for his loss?" The old man puffed vigorously and produced a cloud of smoke.

"Of course he helped. But I still miss my father. I would have been happier to have had them both."

The secretary struck another match. "This damn tobacco is always far too wet when it's fresh." He puffed away until he was sure his pipe was properly alight.

"You know that the new plot holder is taking over tomorrow," he reminded Charlene. "Do you think you're going to be able to finish by tonight?"

"We're working as hard as we can," said Roger. "But we intend to be through long before it gets dark."

Roger had demolished and burnt the old shed, but the greenhouse was still in quite good condition.

"He was asking what you wanted for your greenhouse," said the secretary, giving a couple of quick puffs on his pipe.

"How about a coat of paint?" Roger laughed.

"Ha, ha. I presume you don't intend to risk taking it to pieces? The wood doesn't look as if it could stand it."

Charlene interjected. "I don't mind if you give my successor the greenhouse."

"Give it for nothing?" said the surprised secretary.

"Of course," she said. "But, if you feel it would be better to make a charge, then ask for a nominal sum and put it in the Allotment Holders' account."

"I think that would be best. The other plot owners would be worried if people started giving their greenhouses away for nothing." He puffed on until his head was enveloped in a dense pall of smoke.

"I'll get on my way now; I have other people to speak to. If you want to come and see me any time, ask one of the plot owners to let you in. Which reminds me, would you leave your key in the box on the hut at the door?" He went on his way.

Roger waved his hands rapidly to clear the smoke. "That was some session. We could have done a lot in the time we've wasted."

"It was hardly wasted, Roger. My father's friend was saying goodbye in his own way."

"I suppose so. He doesn't look the type to go in for tearful farewells. How about a cup of tea?" said Roger, taking a flask from the shopper.

The small shrubs were packed in plastic bags with soil, which had been made fertile by many years' application of horse manure. The ripe crops were lifted and packed in cardboard boxes and wooden trays.

Charlene looked at the heap of bags and boxes. "There's enough stuff here for us to make two trips."

They wasted no time dumping the things from their first delivery in the back garden of the house, and returned immediately to the plot to fetch the remaining load.

"That's it, Roger." Charlene put the key in the box beside the gate. "This is me saying farewell from the Graham family. It started a long time ago with my father. The plants come and go ... and so do the people."

They pulled the heavy wooden door shut, closing off the side entrance to the allotment.

"That's one door closed both physically and metaphorically speaking." Charlene's voice was sad. "I feel like crying."

Roger tenderly squeezed her hand. "Why don't you?"

## Chapter 9

"Good morning," said Marion, gleefully shaking her Aunt to make sure she was really awake. "This is the big day."

Charlene stretched her arms out, as she always did when she woke, and said nervously, "I wish it would all hurry up and get itself over and done with."

"Auntie, you don't want to say that. Your wedding-day's not going to last very long. You want to savour every second. It's something special. You don't want to miss any part of it." Marion, who was Charlene's bridesmaid, had married a couple of years earlier and was regretting having not taken her own advice.

"You're right. I want to enjoy every minute of this special day." Though she wondered if she'd enjoy everything. She'd never been to bed with a man before.

"I've brought you a cup of tea." Marion interrupted her thoughts. "Remember, you've an early appointment. I'll do your make-up when you come back."

"You're so good to me, Marion. I feel you might be my own daughter the way you think about things. Is there any toast?"

By the time Charlene had finished her breakfast she had consumed three large pieces of toast generously spread with butter and marmalade.

\* \* \* \* \*

Roger needed no alarm clock this morning. He slept well and always woke up very early. "I've got the breakfast ready, Sydney! Come and get it. You can wash afterwards," Roger called. He had asked Sidney Armstrong, his friend and best man, to stay overnight in Burleigh Avenue.

"Be with you in a minute," Sydney yawned back.

"It's scrambled eggs and bacon, come and get it!"

Sidney got into his dressing gown, and sat in the kitchen, waiting to be served.

"What did your last servant die from?" said Roger mischievously. "You can help yourself from the pan. Here's a warm plate!"

Sydney filled his plate and joined Roger at the table.

"I'd like to leave my car at the Elmwood Court Hotel," said Roger, spreading his toast thickly with black cherry jam. "I need to leave it there to take us on our honeymoon - a hire car is taking us from the church."

"You'll be wanting the both of us to drive to the hotel after breakfast, leave your car there and come back in mine."

"That's what I had in mind," said Roger.

\* \* \* \* \*

When Charlene arrived back from the hairdresser her mother was wringing her hands with worry. "What are we going to do? The flowers haven't come yet."

"The florist isn't to blame," said Marion. "The market is very early. If all else fails, we can always go to your friends in the allotment association."

"Just imagine going down the aisle with a bunch of cowslips, dead nettles and bindweed." Charlene was laughing nervously when the doorbell rang.

The florist apologised and wished Charlene a happy day. The soft-hued bouquet consisted of gypsophila, maiden fern, osteospurnum, pale-orange gazanias and six yellow roses chosen to match her cream dress.

Marion helped lift her Aunt's dress over her hair, which was piled high, without disturbing it. "Something new? That'll be your dress," said Marion. "Now, something old?"

"Me," her Aunt chirped. "My thermal underwear is old."

"Something borrowed."

"Your grandma's woollen shawl."

"And ... something blue."

Charlene lifted the hem of her slip to reveal an ornate blue garter. "That should give Roger a little surprise"

"And now for the final touch," said Marion, putting the wisp of a veil on Charlene's hair.

Peter Anderson, Shirley's husband, had been allowed to come into the front room now that Charlene was ready. He was carrying a bottle of champagne and a tray of glasses "This is your wedding-day," he said, filling the glasses. Charlene shook her head. "For heaven's sake," said Peter, "aren't you going indulge a bit today?"

"You're wasting your time, father," said Marion. "Not as much as a glass of wine at Christmas."

They all clinked their glasses together and wished Charlene a happy day. Charlene responded by taking a token sip.

"The next time I see you, you'll be Mrs Buchanan." Her mother hugged her daughter tearfully.

Charlene wiped her mother's tears. "You're not losing me, Mother. Roger and I will keep in touch. We'll all do our shopping on Fridays as we've always done. You know the old saying is true. Just think of it. You're gaining a son."

"Yes, I expect things will work out," Mrs Graham remarked pensively. "Now I really know how my own mother felt and I feel sorry for her."

Since the church was only a short distance from Charlene's home, Mrs Graham, Shirley and Marion decided to walk the few hundred yards, on a day, which had been made deceptively warm by the bright sunshine. Tradition required that the bride arrive by car.

"You look just like my father," she said, as she surveyed his elegant attire. "That's just what he would have worn, Peter. I'm happy to have you stand in for him, but I do wish he'd been here with me today. I miss him very much."

Charlene was verging on tears. Peter patted her soothingly on the shoulder. "Roger will be looking after you now," he reassured her. "Just think about him."

"I'll do that Peter," she replied sweetly, and wiped her eyes with a tiny handkerchief which was already moist with her mother's tears.

Hearing the sound of a car, Peter went over to window and saw the lemon-coloured limousine. "The hire car's here. Let's lock the door and go."

The congregation consisted largely of Charlene's friends and colleagues and a few of the minister's parishioners who had come to enjoy the free spectacle on one of the rare occasions when there was no collection.

The driver of the limousine brought it lazily to a halt outside the Parish Church. Peter alighted and helped Charlene to the pavement and they posed for a photograph.

"I'll be back and waiting for you when you come out. The police won't let me block the traffic on a Saturday," and he drove off.

Roger, Sidney and Marion were already standing in front of the minister, waiting for Charlene.

For the third time since his arrival, the minister asked Sidney about the ring. Confidently he took it from his pocket and held it up, grinning all over.

Then, on a signal from the church officer that the bride had arrived, the Reverend Anthony Drinkwater nodded towards the organist. Immediately the strains of "Here comes the bride" filled the church, and Charlene, supported by Peter, started her slow walk down the side aisle towards the minister and her future husband. When they drew level with the front pew, Peter handed his charge into Roger's care and joined the rest of his family.

This was a magic moment for Charlene. The years of waiting and frustration were over. At last she was about to become Mrs Roger Buchanan.

Roger and Charlene looked at one another and smiled happily in anticipation of the moment when they would become one.

Charlene had chosen their favourite hymns and no one could fault the singing of the congregation, which was of a very high standard.

"A ring is given and a ring is received," the minister intoned, as Roger put the plain gold band on Charlene's finger. He could feel her trembling as the excitement mounted.

He was marrying the most beautiful woman in the world, thought Roger, as he gazed into her eyes. His train of thought was interrupted by the minister giving the final blessing, after which the organist played a pleasant tune allowing the happy couple and senior relatives to gather at the communion table. Mr Drinkwater preferred the signing to be witnessed by the whole congregation.

More photographs were taken, including the inevitable one of the couple's signing of the register.

"Remember, the next time you sign your name, you'll be Mrs Buchanan." The minister quipped. Sidney giggled and everyone laughed a little. It helped to ease the tension.

It was a strange feeling to see all those eyes watching, Charlene thought, as she went out by the central aisle to the music of the Trumpet Voluntary. She wondered if it were true, the congregation only looked at the bride. But then it was her day, after all. Why shouldn't it be?

The yellow limousine was waiting at the kerb for the newly married couple.

There were two surprises waiting for Charlene and Roger. Her class of toddlers had been placed in a line down the path leading to the gate; like a guard of honour.

Delores Gray and Billy Boston, who were at the head of the line, came forward holding a silver horse-shoe. "This is for you Miss," they said together as the other slightly embarrassed youngsters threw handfuls of confetti.

Charlene bent down and patted them on the head. "Thank you all very much," she said, handing the trinket to Roger. Then she gave Billy her best professional stare. "When I come back to school, you'll need to call me Mrs Buchanan now."

"Yes miss," he said and shuffled back in line.

"Good luck," shouted some members from the Kelvin Hiking Club who had come along to show their support. "Good luck," shouted Jane and Helen as they covered Charlene's hair with pink and white confetti. As one could have expected Maureen Harrison did not attend.

"Do you have any money for the scramble?" Sydney asked.

"Do they still carry on that old custom?"

"Some do," said Peter. "Don't tell me you haven't any small change?"

Roger admitted that he had not seen the need for it.

"It's a good job I raided the till this morning. It's the kind of thing the groom is liable to forget." He gave Roger a handful of small coins.

"Charlene," screamed a number of women, who were following her to the car. Charlene knew what was expected; but would like to have kept her bouquet. She pulled out a single orange gazania and cast the bouquet over her head. It fell straight into the hands of Jane Faulds. "You're next," said Helen, patting her jealously on the shoulder.

The chauffeur opened the door for Charlene as Roger was throwing the good luck money to the large crowd of small children. Then the driver put the car in gear and drove off just as the traffic lights were changing to green.

Elmwood Court Hotel, the former home of a wealthy Glasgow business- man, was particularly attractive at this time of the year with extensive drifts of daffodils and early-flowering shrubs like azaleas. The photographer had decided a long session in the cold hotel garden was better than flashlight photos in the reception room. The result was the guests went inside to the warmth, while the main participants quickly cooled down outside.

Charlene's wedding outfit gave her no protection against the east wind, which had strengthened since they had left the church. Mercifully the photographer said the magic word 'cake' and they went inside.

Being teetotal, Charlene and her mother had made arrangements for the toasts to be drunk in non-alcoholic drinks.

"I need a drink," said Shirley, once the photographer had moved inside. He had one more picture to take - the cutting of the cake - and that would be the end of his assignment.

One of the waitresses came over and offered her an orange juice cocktail in a glass whose edge had been dipped in sugar.

"That's not what I want!" Shirley angrily dismissed the waitress. "Bring me a whisky."

Once the cake had been cut, the manager ushered the guests into the dining room. "The bride and groom," his voice boomed out, as the pair walked arm in arm to the main table and sat down, to loud applause.

The minister said Grace and the staff began to serve soup. Charlene was glad she had not chosen something cold like a cucumber salad.

Sydney had ordered several bottles of wine for the top table. There was no reason why the majority should be denied wine with their meal.

"Are you still going to spend tonight at home?" whispered Charlene's mother.

"Yes. We would like to call in and see Roger's mother on our way south, and take her a piece of the wedding cake," said her daughter.

The minister, who had seen Sydney drinking heavily, suggested that it would better if he took over as master of ceremonies. One dreary speech followed another. Why was it that wedding speeches were so dull and full of maudlin sentimentality? He thought.

Sydney insisted on making the toast to the Bride and Groom, but not before he had told some risqué jokes.

Although Roger had found little difficulty speaking in open court on behalf of his clients, he winced as he looked on the sea of faces. "My wife and I ... " He was forced to stop when the guests stamped their feet and cheered loudly. Then he continued, searching for some words to take his oratory out of the banal. He was conscious of Charlene glancing at him and this made it worse. He knew she was expecting the best from her man. It had been so easy to talk brilliantly as they walked over the hills. "I would like to take this opportunity of thanking you all for coming to our wedding."

"Firstly, I want to thank the Reverend Drinkwater for performing a wonderful wedding ceremony."

Then followed the usual long list of people, who were due to be thanked for helping the marriage to its successful conclusion, right down to the manager and his staff.

"I never had a chance to meet Charlene's father; from all accounts he was, like his daughter, a very special person." He took a quick look at Charlene and her mother. Their eyes expressed a mixture of joy and sadness. "We miss his presence here today, very much." There was a murmur of approval. "I am the most fortunate man in the world to have been accepted by his daughter. I want to propose the toast - "To my dear wife Charlene"."

"Immediately Roger raised his glass, the guests shuffled to their feet and raised their glasses. "To Charlene!"

The minister, prompted by the manager, told the guests to wait outside while the staff prepared the dining room for the dancing. The only places to wait were in the bars. The hotel made most of its profits during this time.

The three-piece-band began to set up their speakers and amplifiers while Charlene and Roger, who chosen to watch, were congratulated by some late arrivals.

"Charlene doesn't drink alcohol," said Roger to William and Mary Drumhills, when offered a drink.

111

"Didn't everything go well today?" said Mary, happy at her colleague's eventual marriage. "I remember the day when I saw Roger at the school show. I thought then that something was in the air. I saw Charlene get into his car. Now we know why?"

"And we want to offer our congratulations as well," said William, who had just returned with a whisky for Roger. He warmly shook their hands. "You deserve to be together."

"When you get settled, we'll be in touch and have you along for dinner," said Mary as they moved into the bar.

"There you are," said a voice behind Marion and the inebriated Sydney slumped into a gold covered armchair near her table. "Roger and I have been friends for a long time." She looked at him with a smile as he absent-mindedly helped himself to her sherry. "Isn't it a wonderful wedding?" His voice was slightly slurred.

"Is it true that some of you are threatening to throw Roger in the pool?"

"Of course. Won't it be fun." Sydney giggled at the thought.

"You'll have to excuse me. I see my husband. Haven't had a chance to speak to Alexander all day." As soon as she had warned Roger and Charlene about Sydney's intention, the newly married couple went off to the small rest room.

"I don't want my husband to come home soaked to the skin on our wedding night." She shivered at the thought.

"Forewarned is forearmed," said Roger. "We can't leave before the dance is under way."

Roger took her in his arms. And then his mouth took possession of hers, hungrily searching for a passionate response to match his.

Charlene drew herself away. "Not here Roger. It won't be long now."

"I expect you're right. And we've still to say farewell to Mother. How do you think she'll take being on her own?"

"She's been on her own before - when we went to Grasmere. Anyway Shirley is taking her home for a few days."

The bandleader announced the opening waltz. Roger and Charlene felt like contestants in the popular television programme as the guests clapped them round. Then Marion and Sydney who was just managing to stand and keep time to the music joined them. Within a minute all of the guests had joined the happy couple on their first dance as husband and wife.

Charlene could feel Roger's aroused body close to her. Her inner glow was slowly changing to a feeling of panic. Roger had assured her that the experience was pleasant; but she had heard stories, which made her less certain.

Since they intended to leave without prior notice, they went round the tables saying farewell to their guests. Finally, after they had said a special farewell to Mrs Graham they slipped out of the hotel and drove back to Burleigh Avenue.

"I'm glad we had a chance to say goodbye to mother before we rushed off," said Roger, as he carried Charlene, in her wedding dress, over the threshold. They had decided to spend the first night as a married couple in their own home and had not bothered to change in the hotel. Charlene also wanted to let her mother-in-law see her in her wedding dress

"We've got an early start tomorrow - remember," said Roger.

Charlene, standing by their large double bed and looking every bit a princess, wondered if Roger was putting off their first physical encounter. She removed the flimsy veil she had called a hat, and laid it on the bed.

He placed his arm lazily on her shoulder, "You are beautiful, princess," he said with emphasis. "Do you know that?" His gentle voice made her pulse thump alarmingly.

"You'll need to take over from Mother. She helped me into my dress this morning."

Nervously Roger unhitched each of the fifteen fasteners on the back of her dress and revealed the smooth, creamy skin beneath.

"Have you finished?"

"Not yet, there's one other thing." He put his fingers under the straps of her slip, and pushed them down over her shoulders. Trancelike, he held them for a moment, before letting it fall to the floor to join the dress, which was already there. Charlene watched Roger in the mirror, but did nothing to stop him.

She smiled and unbuttoned his shirt. Roger stared in fascination on her tiny, young bosom for the very first time and wrapped his arms about her as she pressed herself close to him. Moving her hands upwards to his broad shoulders she caressed his muscles, her body curving into him, interlocking like a piece in a jigsaw She felt his hairy chest stimulating her firm nipples. The kiss, which had been exploring the soft contours of her mouth, exploded like a firework penetrating her whole being.

"Tonight our love sees the culmination of a long period of waiting." His hands began to explore her nudity as she stroked his hair and kissed him passionately on the chest.

"Shall I take off the rest of the wrapping?" He was like a child desperate to see his Christmas present.

Charlene looked down at her naked breasts and nodded. As soon as her underskirt, pants and blue garter had joined the rest of her clothes, Roger began to explore the forbidden erotic zones with his fingers. It was a pleasure for which he had waited a very long time.

"Don't go too quickly Roger," she pleaded, becoming a little apprehensive. "Remember I'm still like a young child in these matters. You don't want to scare me, do you?"

He looked into Charlene's face and said, "Only as quickly as you want me to, dear."

"I never thought I'd see the day when I'd be parading about like Lady Godiva," Charlene said, using a joke to cover her anxiety

"But she had long hair to hide her modesty," said Roger.

Charlene pulled the bed cover back and lifted her light blue night-dress from under the pillow. Meanwhile, Roger collected her azure dressing gown from the hook on the back of the door, and helped her to put it on. "Is this your blue mood tonight?"

"I'm certainly not downhearted. This is the happiest night in my life." She stepped out into the unlit hall.

"I won't be long," she said.

When Roger returned, ready to go to bed, he proudly displayed his muscular chest and removed his pyjama trousers, standing completely naked beside her.

There was no reply. Charlene had closed her eyes and fallen soundly asleep, just like the proverbial baby.

They'd never believe it, he mused, as he put out the reading lamp and slipped in under the bedclothes. It wouldn't be fair to wake her. She had had a lot to do before the wedding. Her sister could have done more to help.

Soon Roger was asleep as well. The strain of the past five years had caught up with him at last.

# Chapter 10

"Brrrrrr." Charlene's travelling alarm clock began to ring. "Is it that time already?" she said, rubbing her eyes and turning round to give Roger a cuddle.

"Oh! I'm tired." Roger kissed his wife of a day.

"Did anything happen last night?"

"You were asleep when I came back from the bathroom. I didn't have the heart to waken you."

"We'll try again tonight." Charlene beamed with anticipation. "I'm afraid my tranquilliser did more than I expected."

"Tranquilliser," he repeated.

"Yes, I asked Shirley what I should do. I told her how worried I was about letting you down. She asked Peter to give me tranquillisers."

Roger saw a white box with the label Peter Anderson, M.P.S. on it. Shirley had put one over on him again. "This is a tranquilliser of sorts but it's usually prescribed as a sleeping tablet."

"That explains it then. I took one just before we left the hotel."

He hugged her and was immediately stimulated to erotic intimacy by the throbbing of her warm thighs. His hands were moving all over, searching for hidden crevices in the smooth soft curves of her abdomen and bottom. His fingertips were throbbing in time with the beating of her heart.

"I like what you're doing," she said, taking his hand in hers and kissing it. But I bruise easily," she reminded him. "You don't want the world to think you beat me on our wedding night, do you?"

"Forgive me Charlene. I'm feeling frustrated and need to do something about it. If I hadn't said we'd call on my mother, I'd have asked you to stay in bed with me."

Charlene smiled with relief. The unknown had been postponed once again.

"Was the toast to your liking? Not too much marmalade?" Roger asked when he came back to collect the tray.

"Just lovely."

"The tea wasn't too strong?"

"The tea was just the way I like, with just a little milk."

"I'm glad of that, because that's the way I want my breakfast from now on." He laughed.

"I'd better get ready, if we're leaving for Troon." She handed Roger the tray, and pushed the bedclothes back.

"I know it looks silly, but I'll be wearing my wedding dress until your mother sees it. Will you fasten me up?"

"You can always change into your other things afterwards and leave the dress with her." Roger suggested. "And any way, before we go, I'd also like a photo of the two of us in the garden in our wedding clothes."

Roger set the camera on a tripod, and was busily focusing it when their elderly spinster neighbour shouted across to them. "Can I be of help?"

Before Roger could reply, the sprightly eighty-year-old was climbing over the fence, and crossing their lawn. "I've taken lots of pictures in my time. Just show me what to press and what to look through." He pointed to the viewfinder. "Look through here and press this." Lizzie unscrewed the camera from the tripod and said she preferred to hold the camera to her eye. With shaky hands Lizzie took a picture of Roger and Charlene standing awkwardly in their wedding outfits against the garage wall.

"Would you take another please?" Roger asked and she happily obliged.

"Thank you, Miss Ross," they said in unison.

"It was nothing. By the way, everybody calls me Lizzie. If you hold on a bit, I've got something for you." She scrambled back over the fence, with the same agility as before.

Roger put the camera on the tripod again and took a couple of pictures of them both with the self-timer before Lizzie Ross returned.

"I heard Mr Buchanan was getting married so I bought you a little present." She handed over a parcel, which clearly contained a book.

Charlene opened it to reveal a cookery book by Delia Smith.

"Just what I wanted." Charlene was delighted. "Nobody gave me anything like this as a wedding present. I'll always treasure it Miss ... I was going to do it again ... Lizzie."

"I don't suppose it's any use asking where you're going?"

"I don't mind telling you. We're going to Galloway," said Roger.

"I hope the weather is good to you." Miss Ross walked quickly to the fence, hopped over and went into her kitchen without looking back.

Roger picked up the tripod. "Do you think we reminded her of a lost love? Perhaps her boyfriend was killed in the Great War."

\* \* \* \* \*

Edna Buchanan was lying on the sofa and watching the television as she usually did at this time, when they arrived, and Netta, who happened to be at the window when her brother's car drew up, went to the door to greet them. Roger kissed her and she kissed Charlene.

"Mother's not been very well this morning, but please don't say anything unless she does."

"Have you been in touch with the doctor yet?" Roger was worried that the illness, which had prevented his mother from being at his wedding, was getting worse.

"Doctor Henderson usually calls to see her about this time every week. If she doesn't come this morning, I'll give her a call."

"Tell me all about the wedding." Roger's mother sat upright and switched on her hearing aid when they went into the front room. "How do you think I'm looking?"

"Much the same as usual, Mother," Roger said uncertainly.

Mrs Buchanan stared at Charlene's wedding dress. "That's the most beautiful thing I've ever seen." In her younger days Edna O'Brian had spent a lot of time choosing her clothes and had a good idea of quality.

Charlene opened a plastic bag and brought out a small bunch of flowers. "These are from the top table," she said, handing the small bouquet to her mother-in-law.

"Oh, they are nice." Charlene winced at the word. "Netta will put them in water for me."

Charlene delved into the bag again and produced a small box with a piece of the wedding and a small favour from it. Her mother-in-law took the silver slipper and said, without realising the significance of her words, "It should have been worn by a princess." Roger smiled inwardly.

After sharing tea with Netta and her mother, Roger and Charlene excused themselves saying that the time was coming up to five o'clock and they had to find a suitable bed and breakfast.

\* \* \* \* \*

"We're a couple of fools. This is the Easter weekend. No wonder everywhere is full up," said Roger, cross with himself.

"We'll just have to drive back home again. "We should have realised the school holiday would be shared by a whole mass of people," said Charlene philosophically.

"This is as far as we're going," said Roger when they arrived in the long main street of a small village. "If all else fails we can at least have a supper. There's a fish and chip shop over there." But all the likely houses had "no vacancy" signs prominently displayed.

Roger knew that if he told his colleagues they'd spent their honeymoon at home they would roar with laughter. Charlene, discouraged by the long search, suddenly realised that she had just seen a vacancy sign. "Stop and go back a bit Roger. I think I saw a place."

The house was on the busy road, without even a garden to distance it from the traffic.

"Maybe the room will be noisy, and that's why no one has taken it. But even so we can stay one night and then move on tomorrow and search for somewhere better." He rang the doorbell.

A well-spoken Englishman with impeccable manners opened the door. "Are you looking for a room?"

"We hadn't realised it would be the Easter weekend. Everywhere is full up. My wife and I are getting desperate."

"We only arrived a few days ago and we're still getting ourselves sorted out," he explained. "I've told others we're not open for business yet but, if you can put up with a little discomfort, you can have one of the rooms we've just managed to get ready upstairs. Would you like to come in and have a look?"

Beggars can't be choosers, thought Roger, as he and Charlene followed the man past a heap of bits and pieces in the hall, waiting to be put away.

"Pauline, this couple needs a room for tonight." It seemed as if his wife had final approval. She came and examined them. "Aw right then, we'll take them." Her thick Irish accent contrasted sharply with the man's Oxford English. "My husband will show you the room." She was not to know that Roger and Charlene would have slept in a barn if it had been offered.

Their host showed them what turned out to be a well-furnished room with a double bed.

"Will this be satisfactory?" he asked.

The newly-weds nodded. "Can you do an evening meal?" Roger asked hopefully. "We'll just get a fish supper if it's inconvenient."

Gordon looked at them for a few seconds. "I'm very fond of cooking. If you'll just take the same meal as we're having ourselves, then we would be happy to have you eat with us."

Roger and Charlene gratefully accepted, before their host or his wife could change their minds.

"That's the first time I've had chestnut soup," said Charlene, always ready to try out new eating experiences.

"You'd hardly notice the flavour of the chestnuts," said Roger who was particularly fond of them.

"I've never had it either, until tonight," said Pauline in her Irish accent. "Gordon's an adventurous cook. He likes trying new dishes, like the one we're having next. It's something from Spain. What's it called, Gordon?"

"Bacalao Andaluz." He pronounced the name like a native Spaniard. "Otherwise known as Andalusian salt cod steaks."

Roger had gone off cod as a child, so he was not thrilled at the prospect of renewing its acquaintance. Charlene did like cod, and was looking forward to tasting this new dish. There was nothing spectacular about its presentation as Gordon served directly from the cooker pan.

"What, no chips?" Roger said, only partly joking. "I have to confess that cod is not my favourite fish." But his empty plate belied what he had just said. "However this was cooked so well that I enjoyed it very much."

"It's good of you to say so," smiled his host. "We've gone to Greece for the sweet. It's Loukoumades next."

Roger looked at Charlene. "That name sounds familiar to me, but I don't remember where I heard it before."

"You ought to. It was when we went out eating together for the very first time. You remember the tiny Greek restaurant near my mother's home. We had Loukoumades that time."

"Sorry, you'll have to tell me."

"It's the Greek name for honey balls."

"Yes. I remember it now. I thought they tasted like very sweet doughnuts."

Gordon came in with a dish of small sugar-coated balls. "Loukoumades," he called out. "I brought the coffee with me. Shall I pour you a mug, Mrs Buchanan?"

"Not for me, thanks. It would keep me awake." That wouldn't be a bad thing, thought Roger, considering what had happened last night. He was hoping for a more intimate night.

"You can watch the television in the lounge if you want. Pauline and I will join you when we've tidied up," said Gordon.

Later, after some idle trivia talk, Pauline said suddenly, "Are you newly-weds?" she faltered.

Charlene was startled. She had said nothing, which could have given her a clue. "How did you know?"

"That's easy. Your rings are far too new. The engagement ring is the latest style. And you've both got that look. Gordon and I noticed you've been staring at one another for the whole evening."

"Have you known this all along?" asked Roger.

"Of course! Why do you think we offered you the room with the double bed?" Gordon winked at him.

"It's been a lovely evening; very much better than we expected. We were on the point of going home since we couldn't find a room."

"I'm glad we were able to come to your rescue. Breakfast will be ready when you come down," said Gordon. "I expect you'll want to be going up to your room." Roger and Charlene thanked their host and hostess, said good-night and climbed the tight, circular staircase.

Pauline must have remembered about Charlene's faulty thermostat for she had connected an electric blanket to take the chill off the bed.

Roger pulled her close to him and kissed her with a passion that made every nerve fibre tingle. While he kissed her, one hand undid the buttons of her blouse while the other released the clip of her silky bra. He bent slightly and kissed the firm tiny nipple. One hand explored with tactile efficiency every part of her body while the other cupped her breast. She felt her tummy tighten when his rough finger stroked the remaining nipple. By now Charlene was breathing heavily and excited up to the point of satisfaction. He lifted her into the bed.

"I'm ready now," she said turning towards him. "The bed's lovely and warm" Roger quickly discarded his pyjamas and lay beside her wondering. Charlene began to run her fingers all over his skin. "When are you going to make love?" she asked.

The two them were facing each other. Roger held her firmly about the waist and separated her legs with his. She felt his hand exploring her thighs and manipulated himself until they were in intimate contact.

Within a few seconds, Charlene cried out, "Oh! That's painful."

"I'm sorry dear, I didn't mean to hurt you."

He unwound himself from her thighs and held her about the waist, kissing her gently to make her feel more at ease. Charlene had not only been very tense, but it also seemed as if nature had not prepared her for this kind of union.

"Charlene. You're far too resistant. The problem is similar to the hypodermic needle - the muscles tighten to prevent penetration and that causes pain. I'll call at the chemist tomorrow for a tube of cream. For the present we can enjoy each other by just lying in close contact letting the sensitivity of our skin convey its stimulating titillation."

Very soon Charlene complained that her arms were getting tired. They kissed each other passionately and said goodnight.

After breakfast next day, the newly-weds-said farewell to Pauline and Gordon and continued their journey until they came to a charming hotel just outside Galloway. Although it boasted of being in existence since 1759, the owners displayed photographs showing that the rooms were modern and well-furnished, each with their own private facilities.

The receptionist said that there had been a cancellation. They could have a room for the rest of the holiday week. "That suits us fine. We'll be leaving on Sunday. My wife," he hesitated for just a fraction, "has to start work on Monday next." They arranged for dinner, bed and breakfast.

Roger asked Charlene to wait in the garden while he took their luggage to the room. Meanwhile Charlene, wanting to explore the grounds, went through a prepared gap in the hedge to the garden beyond which, looked as if it had been designed at the same time as the house. The whole area was paved with old slabs, having gaps here and there for small trees and shrubs. The borders were filled with multi-coloured foliage and miscellaneous flowering bulbs.

Charlene sat at a table looking at a map of the district while Roger dealt with the booking. She had a man in her life now and these were the things taken care of by the man of the house.

When he returned, he noted the time and suggested they have a coffee. Calling the waitress from the restaurant where she was setting the table for the evening meal he ordered coffee and biscuits for two.

Charlene reached across the table and grasped Roger's hand. They gazed at one another for several minutes before Roger broke the spell. "Princess, I love you more than anything in this world. I don't know what I'd do if I lost you?"

"And I - you," she replied. "We must always try to make the fullest use of the time we've been given."

"How about a short trip round the village before dinner?" said Roger.

"So long as you feel up to it. I don't want us to tire ourselves. I'm just as anxious as you are, to consummate my unfulfilled desires," she said.

"Charlene, if it should happen that your body cannot accept me," he became serious. "I want you to know it'll not make any difference to my love for you. I want to reassure you that our relationship does not depend on intercourse for us to enjoy each others company"

She smiled at Roger and said, "I'd much rather have an orgasm if it's possible."

"Let's hope that we can. But don't think I'd neglect you if there wasn't." Charlene put her arms around his neck and kissed him. This was the confirmation that justified that day on Ben Calder. She was determined that things would happen tonight.

"How about that walk now?" said Roger. They took hands and walked through the village like teenage lovers.

Roger and Charlene had been trying for most of the week to have satisfactory intercourse. But it had always ended in the same way with Charlene becoming tense, feeling pain and asking Roger not to go any farther.

Tonight would be the last opportunity in their honeymoon for things to go well. Roger had noticed that almost every item chosen by Charlene at dinner contained alcohol. There had been a wine sauce with the fish, sherry in the trifle and a generous portion of whisky in the Gaelic coffee. He wondered if she had taken a conscious decision to fortify herself on this last attempt. She was undoubtedly quite merry and a great deal more relaxed when they retired after dinner.

Charlene tightened the towelling belt of her robe and opened the door of the shower. "I've used a lot of the cream," she said, shivering slightly as she recalled the icy contact of the lubricant with her sensitive skin.

"Just pop into bed and warm it up for us," he said, as he took his turn in the shower. "And leave the light on. I want to see what's happening tonight."

When he had finished drying himself, Roger did not bother with his pyjamas and, naked, he walked smartly over to the bed. Charlene had pulled the bedclothes back, but was still wearing her blue towelling robe to keep her warm. Roger gripped one end of it and pulled it out from underneath her. She was lying face up and, still a little shy, had hidden her pubic hair with her hand. Roger lay beside her for a little while massaging her thighs to give her time to get used to things. Then he gripped her face in his broad hands and kissed her all over, then he finished with a lingering kiss on the corner of her mouth. Charlene gazed at him with enquiring eyes and waited for his next move. He slipped one arm round her back and then eased himself on top of her. As his hand moved up and down her spine, she shivered with animal pleasure and invitingly opened her legs. Roger had never seen her so relaxed before.

"Roger I want you more than anything just now. I'm sure everything will be fine tonight."

He put his hand between her legs exploring every possibility. But he stopped for a moment when her breathing became erratic; he feared she was about to have an orgasm. "Are you ready?" he asked kissing her mouth with a coaxing kiss.

"Yes," she said, sure of one thing. She wanted Roger more than anything tonight and, if even there was pain, the experience would be worth while. Roger moved his hand between her legs in explicit demand. He could hear her gasp. She was not quite ready yet. She restrained his hand, briefly, before guiding him in. He slid comfortably past the "gates of hymen". Her body had received him quite easily in the end. Now that they had achieved this first stage, things would gradually get better.

Charlene wanted to become the aggressor now. She eased herself from below Roger and climbed on top, arching her back and vibrating her body over him, enjoying to the full her newly-discovered pleasure. Her pulsating torso was slow and measured at first; gradually became faster as she gained confidence until she could go no faster or deeper. Somewhere she found a new source of energy, which almost sent her out of control as she accelerated faster and faster. Then this violent spell ended with a groan and delirious trembling of her thighs. She had achieved her first orgasm. Roger asked her to remain as they were; to continue to enjoy the intimate contact. And although he had not reached a climax, he was happy to know that the future looked bright for them both.

"Have I done any better tonight?" asked Charlene.

"Of course! Ten out of ten," said Roger. She touched him as he came out of her. "Are all men like this?" she asked.

"No, some are bigger. Many are smaller. Remember a baby is a good deal bigger. So it must be possible for all men."

"Yes. I expect that must be the case."

Charlene got out bed completely unconscious of her nudity and suggested they shower together. Then we'll have a cup of tea and a biscuit.

Next morning Roger paid the bill and loaded the car for their journey home. Charlene had a triumphant look on her face as they sped on their way. "You didn't know I had it in me," she said. A puzzled look followed when Roger laughed at the double entendre. He was certain that their love life had taken a turn for the better.

It was evening when they returned to Burleigh Avenue. "How about a fish supper," said Charlene, singing happily as she set the table. She was in a sparkling mood; her body having been overwhelmed by a new experience.

# Chapter 11

"I don't know whether it's because I'm getting older, or the job's becoming harder," Charlene said to Mary Drumhills as they sat in the School staff room, having their morning tea. "I haven't got the energy I used to have. Roger says I'd do better to leave now and enjoy an early retirement."

"Everybody seems to be saying the same thing nowadays. I used to think it was just me." Charlene was surprised to find that Mary felt the same way she did.

Charlene had a class of thirty children and was also responsible for the teaching by the five teachers in her department. Her role as Assistant Head would have entitled her to a lot of non-teaching time had the school been allocated the staff it needed. But there was a deficit, which had to be made good, largely by Charlene.

The secretary came into the staff room carrying some letters from the head to some members of the staff.

"Here's your post, girls." She smiled, as she handed the letters around.

"I've been waiting a while for this," said Mary Drumhills, opening a large manilla envelope. She took out a folded chart illustrating the story of chocolate. "That's all there is," she said to Charlene. She had been hoping for some samples as well.

"You'll all be interested in the jobs list I expect," the secretary said, putting it on the staffroom table.

All the teaching vacancies had been gathered together in a single list, which was then circulated to the Staff, presently employed in schools controlled by the local authority. The Director of Education had repeated last month's notice offering early retirement to Deputy and Assistant Head Teachers.

Dora Thomson, who had no intention of applying for any of the vacancies herself, scooped the large sheet of paper up. "I'll take this to my room and have a quick look. I won't have a chance at lunchtime."

Charlene was prepared to wait until the end of the school day to see what was on offer. Perhaps she could find a post with a more sympathetic head teacher

"Many people don't live very long after retirement," said Mary. "It makes one think they should be lowering the retirement age. Would you take early retirement if it were offered?"

"I've been feeling much more tired than I used to. The doctor gave me a tonic and said that should help. But it hasn't done me much good. I'm still exhausted when I get home. Roger has told me he would retire when I did. But even if I were tempted, it would be a very difficult decision for me to take. On the one hand I'd have more time with Roger and I'd be able to pay more attention to my mother. Then again, I'd lose my little children. I would miss them so very much. They're the only family I've got or ever likely to have."

"There was an announcement in last month's list of vacancies that Assistant Head Teachers in your age group could take early retirement. From what I could see, looking at the severance pay, it's a very attractive prospect. Don't you think this is a good time to get out?" said her friend.

"I'd need to discuss it with Roger. When I've had a chance to look at the list, I'll take it home and find out what he thinks." The ringing of the bell brought an end to the break.

"Please, Miss, can I go to the toilet," said Forbes Johnstone, as soon as he came into the classroom.

Charlene stood with her head up and arms folded, so that she towered over him. "Why do you think you had a break?" she reprimanded him.

"So that we can play football, miss."

"Not only that. You go to the toilet and then you can play football."

"That's what I said, Miss," argued the child.

"You missed the bit about going to the toilet."

"But I didn't need to go to the toilet, so I played football," he replied innocently.

"I'll let you go this time, but remember in future to go the toilet before you play football."

"Please, Miss." A girl in a pretty frock, with pink flowers, raised her hand.

Charlene sighed as she asked. "What is it ... Delores?"

"Billy Boston ate my sandwich, Miss."

This was a problem Charlene had with many pupils.

"Why did you eat her sandwich?" Charlene questioned Billy.

"I was showing her a trick," he replied promptly as though that was sufficient explanation.

"Tell me what happened, Delores."

"He said he would make it disappear," said the girl in the pink frock.

"But you said Billy Boston ate your sandwich."

"Yes, he did. And when I told him I wanted it back, he said he couldn't because he'd made it disappear." Delores was ready to cry.

"Billy Boston, don't you ever do that again. What you did is the same as stealing and that's something I won't allow in this school." Charlene looked at him as sternly as she could. "Tomorrow, as a punishment, you will bring Delores a sandwich from your mother to replace the one you stole and you've to tell your mother the reason you're being punished."

Immediately Delores heard this judgement on Billy, she stopped crying, and began to talk animatedly to her friends, just as if the incident had never happened.

"We haven't filled in our chart today." Charlene addressed the class. "What day is today?" She turned to the footballer who had now returned from the toilet.

"Sweetie day, Miss," said Forbes, confident that it was the correct answer.

"It's true that the class usually gets a sweet from me at the end of the week, but there are some people who don't deserve any." She squinted at the footballer and looked over at Billy Boston. It was a threat she never intended to carry out. Delores was anxious to please, having been the centre of attraction over her sandwich. "Please Miss, this is Friday."

"That's correct Delores. I want you to write Friday at the top of the sheet. Now what's the weather like today?"

One pupil called out. "It's dry." Another said it was windy, whilst a third said it was cold.

"That means today is a cold, dry, windy day." Then Charlene pointed to the girl in the pink dress again. "Delores, would you write down what I just said?"

There was a knock at the door and the janitor came in. "Sorry to interrupt you, Mrs Buchanan. I've been to Mrs Drumhills room investigating a broken window. They told me Billy Boston was responsible. Can I take him to the head teacher? She wants to deal with it herself. She says she'll need to make an example. Too many windows are being broken."

"Of course you can have him. But you may have a problem proving it. He was probably busy eating a sandwich belonging to Delores when it happened. I think the head will have to look to some of the others who were playing outside at the time." She looked accusingly at the boy who had just been to the toilet.

"It wasn't me," he said, protesting his innocence. "It must have been someone else."

Charlene felt so tired she made an appointment to see her GP on the way home at four-thirty. "The last time you came to see me, I gave you an iron tonic," said Dr Preston. "How did that help?"

"Not much."

The doctor looked at his file. "You're a schoolteacher, Mrs Buchanan. That's a very different job from when I was at school. The tension is on the teacher now and not the pupil. I hear the same story from all my teacher patients. It looks as if you're all under a lot of strain. If it's getting too much, you might have to try another job; but I can't advise you on that."

"There is something I can do."

"And what is that Mrs Buchanan?"

"Take early retirement. There's a good chance my application would be successful."

"That sounds good to me. You'll be able to pace yourself better, and have a rest when you need it."

"Then you don't see anything against my retiring early?"

"Provided you don't opt from outside interests altogether. It's how we use our time that matters. As I said, get the pacing right and you'll be fine. There'll be no need for a prescription."

Charlene had established the routine that, during the week, she and Roger had sandwiches for their lunch and a two course meal in the evening, which consisted of a main dish and either soup or a sweet.

"That's a marvellous smell," called Roger, as he hung his anorak up on a hook in the hall. "It's my favourite. Fried haddock and chips with tomato sauce."

"You timed it to perfection." Charlene called back. "I had trouble with Billy Boston today. He stole a sandwich from a pupil and ate it. He pretended to her that he would make it disappear, and he did so - by eating it."

"Sounds as though con-man Billy will be asking me to defend him in court some day."

"There was something else," she said seriously. "The list of vacancies repeated last month's announcement asking Assistant Heads surplus to requirements to take early retirement. My post and age group is mentioned. What do you think I should do?"

"You know my view, Charlene. We're not getting any younger. We started our married life nearer to –the finishing line. I think you should take it. There are many advantages. In any case, you've been complaining about a lack of energy."

Charlene brought the list from her bag. "I've marked the item in pencil."

Like most lawyers Roger took a long time to peruse the paragraph, which occupied almost the whole of one column.

"Hm." He grunted. "That's a very good offer. As the Mafia says, "It's an offer you can't refuse." It's very good if you consider that you won't be paying National Insurance or Superannuation and there'll also be less tax on a reduced income. You will, for the time being anyway, be as well off as when you were teaching for your money."

"I've been able to work the finances out for myself. That's not the sticking point for me. I love the job and I'm going to miss the children terribly. Is that too big a price to pay for my freedom?"

"Think of your health. Think of me and think of your mother. They're the additional reasons for wanting to get out."

"I was very close to asking for an application form when I left. On the whole I think I've a lot to gain."

"I'm sure the one thing you might feel sorry about is the children." He pushed his empty plate aside. "We didn't have soup tonight so that must mean we're having a dessert. But there are no spoons, so that is a mystery to be solved."

"There's no mystery about it, Roger," Charlene said with a sudden sharpness. "I didn't have time to put them out. Would you mind getting them, please? I'm always busier and more forgetful on Friday. You'll also find the ice-cream in the fridge."

*   *   *   *

Charlene's application for early retirement had been granted to take effect from the end of the term. But it had not come alone. She was now complaining regularly, about a full stomach. It was as if she had eaten too much, too quickly. But, whenever she mentioned her condition to Roger, he always gave her the same answer. "I'm not a physician, dear, but I think you should see one and insist on being sent to a consultant."

However, despite his glib reply, Roger was not uncaring. He had noticed that something was wrong when she began to talk about not having enough energy to do things. This was most unusual, since she had always been very active.

Charlene, however, had taken her complaint to Dr Preston on a number of occasions recently and he had examined her and been unable to find anything wrong, other than possible indigestion. Like most people, when they are ill, Charlene wanted reassurance that she was only suffering from a minor complaint, which would soon, clear up. So she telephoned her sister.

"Shirley, I've been having a lot of discomfort lately." She winced as she felt a throbbing pain in her abdomen. "I told Roger about it and all he does is tell me to see the doctor, but when I go to Dr Preston he tells me he can't find anything wrong."

Shirley made some grunting sounds, as if she were comparing Charlene's pains with her own experience.

"I've had discomfort, like you. It happened once when I ate something on holiday in Turkey. Peter thought it might have been mild food poisoning. He fetched me something from a local pharmacist and that seemed to settle things."

"You can't be suggesting my cooking is so poor I'm getting food poisoning all the time! In any case Roger never has any trouble."

"You could be having diverticulitis. That's quite painful. It's a colonic problem. It's a wonder your doctor didn't suggest it. I'll get Peter to drop in with an indigestion remedy of his own prescription. It's very good. I've suggested he put it on the market, but he does nothing about it. Have you tried a hot water bottle?"

"Strangely enough, Roger did suggest heat treatment but it only gives me temporary relief."

"When I see Peter, I'll tell him all this, and see what he recommends," said Shirley. "I'll get back to you later."

"Who were you speaking to?" enquired Roger. He had overheard a part of the conversation, but not enough to guess who was speaking on the other end of the phone.

"Since you don't want to help me," said Charlene petulantly, "I've had to ask someone else. My sister's always ready to give me her advice."

"Provided her advice is based on knowledge, that would be no bad thing. The trouble with her is that, because her husband is a chemist she thinks that makes them both experts."

Charlene did not like to hear Roger criticise her sister. She had hoped they would become good friends, but they sniped at each other whenever they met and this was making Charlene very unhappy. Eventually she managed to get Roger to promise he would not try to upset Shirley.

"I can tell you it's going to be a very difficult promise to keep," he muttered.

"Even if you can't agree with her, say nothing. All I ask is that you'll try to keep your temper."

\* \* \* \* \*

Charlene was very excited; today would be her last day at Green Street School. The end of term gave a suitable opportunity to celebrate the retirement of the popular Assistant Head.

She went first to the new head teacher, Wilton McKenzie, to say her goodbye and thank him for all his help during her service as head of the infant department.

"I'm losing a very valuable member of my staff. I don't know what we're going to do without you."

"Mrs Drumhills has been taking a special interest in recent months. I'm certain you'll be able to depend on her. And there are other dedicated teachers as well," said Charlene.

If you do decide to return to teaching, even part-time, I would be happy to have you working here with us. Perhaps we can call on you from time to time to help during an absence."

"Yes. I'd like that." She was beginning to feel emotional when she thought not about seeing "her family" any more.

The secretary knocked on the door and entered. "Mr McKenzie, the pupils and staff are waiting for you and Mrs Buchanan in the assembly hall.

"Thank you Hilda. We'll be along shortly." He turned to Charlene and shook her hand. "I really meant it when I said I'd miss you." He donned his black gown and led the way to the hall.

The platform had been decorated with paper streamers and balloons and the music teacher was sitting by the piano. As soon as Mr McKenzie and Charlene entered the hall the children rose to their feet and cheered to the prompting of their teachers. Charlene smiled at everyone and waved back to her class, which had been given the privilege of sitting on the front seats.

The school chaplain said a prayer asking for a long life and happy retirement for Mrs Buchanan and the head spent more than ten minutes extolling her virtues while she squirmed with embarrassment. Then Mary Drumhills took over and announced a short concert to celebrate her colleague's retirement.

Choirs of pupils from Charlene's own class had been rehearsing secretly in Mary's room at the close of school for the past week. They sang "Amazing Grace" one of Charlene's favourite tunes. Her eyes were drawn to a group of well-behaved pupils. Billy Boston and his pal Forbes Johnstone had never behaved so well before. And Brian Watson kept looking at her; his glistening eyes told the story.

There were further items of singing and instrument playing before Mrs Drumhills reached the important point in the celebration. The children had all brought their contributions to buy Charlene a present.

Dolores Gray, wearing a pale blue frock, had been chosen to make the presentation. She was holding a slim package about a foot square.

"Mrs Buchanan, we want you to have this to remember us." She stopped and looked at her note before continuing, "and would like you to enjoy a happy ... " She looked at the paper again, "retirement."

Charlene was smiling but underneath the mask she was very close to tears. "Thank you, Delores ... and all of you for this lovely present." She carefully unwrapped the brown paper. The children had given her a watercolour picture by a local artist. . "This is just the most wonderful present anyone ever gave me. Thank you all very much. I think Mrs Drumhills must have been behind this. I've always wanted a painting of our village and now I've got one. It will hang on my front room wall and when I look at it, it will remind me of my little boys and girls." She wiped a tear and went on. "Of course you will never grow up - I'll always see you the way you are just now."

Mr McKenzie then stepped forward and announced that there would be a long interval.

Charlene thought it was Christmas all over again. All of the pupils in her class had brought their own small present and all the members of staff had added their good wishes, with a present from them over tea and cakes supplied by the head teacher.

The dining staff and the cleaners, who did not normally come into the teaching staff room, were there today. They wanted to give Charlene a gift as well. "We know you like gardening, Mrs Buchanan, so we got together and bought you a plant." Mrs Jones then produced a large mock orange already in flower. Charlene thanked them for their kindness and told them she had a place for it in the front garden. They would always be able to see it growing when they passed her home.

Mr McKenzie looked at his watch and noted that the festivities had taken them through to lunchtime when the school was being closed for the vacation. As soon as he announced the closure, the children cheered and rushed towards the exits, while the staff ambled slowly past Charlene saying their last farewells.

# Chapter 12

Charlene's retirement coincided with their wedding anniversary. There was a double reason to celebrate so Roger made a point of going somewhere special. They had heard good reports about the Cladach Hotel, located, as its Gaelic name implied, near the shore of the River Clyde, at Cardross.

"My mother used to play in the grounds here as a child when it was a field," said Roger. "By the way, who told you this place served first class food?"

"I heard about it from my colleague, Angela Howard. I've always wanted to come here and taste for myself." Charlene was driving as usual on these occasions. "The staff told me to get rid of some of my wealth. So you can blame them if everything is not up to standard."

While they were waiting inside the bar, the headwaiter, wearing white gloves handed each of them a rolled-up menu sealed with a red and gold medallion. "Would you like a drink while you're waiting?"

Roger said they would and ordered a glass of white wine for himself and lemonade with ginger beer for Charlene. By the time they had chosen their main dishes the barman had come over with their drinks. He was followed shortly after by the headwaiter who took their orders and suggested that they go through to the dining room and finish their drinks. The Cladach was very quiet - Roger hoped this was not a bad sign.

"You want Guacamole and duck a l'orange," the waiter confirmed as he exchanged some pieces of cutlery for others which were more appropriate to their choice.

"My God!" exclaimed Roger, who had volunteered to be the first to try the Guacamole when it arrived. "My mouth will be red and raw after that. Just eat the toast dear, unless you want to lose the lining of your mouth." Roger was convinced that the popularity of the dish could only be due to the fact that no one ever ate it.

The restaurant was beginning to fill up, and as it did so, there was a constant toing and froing of staff from the kitchen, much to the annoyance of Roger and Charlene. The fish course consisted of the tiniest piece of sole in a white sauce with two halves of a grape on top.

"If the fish had been any smaller it would have disappeared behind the grapes," Roger remarked as the waiter removed their plates and served the duck.

"You don't usually get a whole duck," said Charlene.

"But it's a very small duck," said Roger as he waited for the vegetables.

The waiter returned and served two very small potatoes and one tiny spear of broccoli.

"That's it," said Charlene philosophically, inwardly shaking with laughter.

Roger removed the skin and tried to carve a slice of duck meat. After a few slivers he searched the carcass, only to find it was almost entirely bones. "That's a fiasco, but there's still the orange," he said devouring several slices.

"The potato's too hard", complained Charlene. "I can hardly cut it with my knife."

"Neither can I."

At the end, when the waiter asked how they had enjoyed the meal, Roger said "Frankly, not all!" and went on to complain in detail.

"I'll pass your complaint to the chef, sir. You shouldn't have eaten the duck, if you were dissatisfied. I could have exchanged it for something else. I'm sorry about the vegetables, I'll bring you some more from the kitchen." He disappeared through the swing doors with the duck carcass.

"I'm convinced this must be the chef's night off," Roger said irritably, as he pushed his plate away. He was sure he would explode and wreck the restaurant if he gave vent to his feelings.

They finished up by filling themselves from the well-stocked cheese and sweet table until they could eat no more.

"It's a good job we didn't have much to eat beforehand," said Roger cynically.

Charlene collected her coat and they were about to leave when they ran into Angela Howard.

"I see you're living the good life," remarked her friend. "My husband and I come here often."

Charlene recalled this was where she had given the wonderful account of the Cladach Restaurant.

"We've had just about the worst meal we've ever had out," said Charlene.

"We've just had duck a" l'orange and it was simply delicious," said Angela, smiling at her husband. "Anyway if you're enjoying the company the food is not important."

"It looks as if you and I are out of step with the world, Roger," said Charlene as they left the restaurant. "However, not eating my meal seems to have done me some good, or maybe its Peter's remedy. It's an experience like this, which makes you lose confidence in places recommended by your friends. But perhaps we got the chef on a bad day."

On the way home Charlene suggested they should go for a walk the next day.

"Have you any place in mind?" he replied, bringing the car to a halt at a red traffic light.

"I was thinking we've never been up Ben Calder since our first meeting. Let's go there," she said.

"I wonder why we never got round to it. It was such an important stage in our lives."

The lights changed to amber. Roger put the car into gear, and started to move off.

"I suppose the answer is, we became very busy doing other things, like gardening and setting up home together."

"And looking after your mother," added Roger.

Charlene smiled at him. "And looking after Mother," she repeated. "You've been so good to her. One would think she was your own mother, the things you do for her."

"I promised you that she wouldn't suffer when I took her daughter away from her. I think you could say I've kept my promise."

"You couldn't have been a better son-in-law. I know mother appreciates everything you've done for her."

"You're making me blush with all this praise." Roger brought the car to a halt at the next traffic lights, not far from their home. "If it's a good day tomorrow, I'll be looking forward to our climb up Ben Calder."

Then Charlene remembered the concert; they had been allocated tickets for the opening concert in its new hall. But Roger had not forgotten; they would have to allow sufficient time to climb the peak and still leave time to attend the concert.

* * * * *

The next day was perfect for rambling. There was a clear blue sky and the sun was shining, much the same as it had been on that momentous day when Roger and Charlene had first noticed each other. The temperature was low enough to permit comfortable hill walking.

Roger opened the boot and brought out their climbing gear, and the rucksacks with their food and drink.

"Roger," she sounded apprehensive. "It's such a long time since we climbed anything bigger than the steep road behind the house to look over at Ben Calder. I hope it doesn't prove to be too much for us."

"It's not like you to expect to fail."

The climb proved more tiring than they had imagined. Although Roger and Charlene had an animated conversation during the earlier stages of the climb, when the slope was at an accommodatingly low angle, as the Ben became steeper their conversation gradually dwindled and stopped. The last very steep slope required having frequent resting periods, if it was to be climbed.

"Now I know how you felt that day, Roger, when I spoke to you here on the summit. You must have been totally exhausted," said Charlene.

"I was tired, depressed, frustrated and unloved. That combination just caused me to give up when I reached the top."

"Do you recall how I spoke to you?" said Charlene with a big grin on her face. "You must have thought me the cheekiest person imaginable."

"Far from it. You were the only walker that day that took the time to make me feel less unhappy. I'll never forget you sharing your tea with me when you saw how exhausted I was."

"You weren't the only one to be uplifted that day," she countered. "You helped me when you described me as a rare bird. I had just broken up with my boyfriend and I was upset too."

"You managed to conceal your unhappiness. You thought about the need of others."

Roger hugged her tightly. "I'm the happiest man in the world to have found a person like you, Charlene. I couldn't have asked for anything more."

"I think I did very well too when you became my friend, Roger. You were always considerate of me and my mother, always thinking of ways to make both of us happy."

Charlene's mother had admitted that Roger reminded her of her late husband. The two women had found the inspiration they needed; the person inside Roger.

"I've never regretted my marriage to you Charlene. I think I got the best of the bargain."

"I believe our marriage was truly made in Heaven," said Charlene. "We have been able to work well in promoting a real understanding for each other, to be caring for each other at all times, committed in love to one another and to our Maker."

"Whenever I need a reference in future, I'm coming to you."

"I can't complain about our marriage. It's been everything I expected except ... " Charlene stopped and poured another cup of tea. "Except I do have two regrets. I was upset when I couldn't have your child and that you hadn't become reconciled with your daughter."

Back at the car they had tea and biscuits and a lingering kiss before setting off for home. "Hope we haven't left it too late," said Charlene. They were still quite a distance from Burleigh Avenue and they had to eat, wash and dress for the concert. Charlene, however, had already prepared the meal, placed in the slow oven so that it would be ready to serve.

Charlene asked Roger to get ready while she gave her mother a call. "How were things?" he asked on her return.

"She's keeping well. She's expecting a visit from Shirley and her family and much looking forward to it."

Despite a busy day Charlene and Roger arrived at the New Concert Hall in plenty of time.

\* \* \* \* \*

Stephen and Marjorie were sitting by the floodlit pool in their Harare bungalow, drinking large whiskies with soda.

"How is the project up in Wangie going?" Marjorie sipped liberally from her glass.

"Do you mean the water irrigation scheme, the coal mining or the development of the National Park?" Stephen had been away for several weeks in the North, advising the government and seeing which of a number of essential economic developments needed money most urgently.

"I mean the coal you're digging near the National Park," she said crossly.

"For a start, I'm not digging any coal at all, I'm merely making it possible."

"But you're spoiling the land with a horrible heap of waste as high as a mountain." Marjorie was always concerned when she saw humans interfering with Nature. "It'll soon be covered with vegetation and look like any other mountain. It's humans who pollute the environment with their buildings."

"I don't regret what I'm doing. The people there have schools, shops and a hospital. It all comes from the coal."

"Would you rather that the black Africans were forced to use the Tribal Trust Lands in order to stay alive?" Stephen had been angry when he saw trees being cut down for cooking and warmth.

"These people have so little, you can't blame them for using their natural resources," his wife replied, as she lifted her whisky and took another quick sip.

She began to stare into the distance, as if she were looking towards her former home in Glasgow, and thinking of better times with her late mother.

"It's been a long while since mother died. Yet I can't get her out of my mind. I think about her every day and always for long spells at a time. Will I ever be free from the despair and frustration I feel at her loss?"

Stephen topped up their glasses, before replying. "You'll never be free from those memories. You could be, but you won't. They're your only tangible link with her."

"I wish I hadn't been so cruel to my father. It must have hurt him very badly at mother's cremation, when I told him he no longer had any rights to her body. And then to follow that up with a refusal to let him take his place with the family, it's a wonder he ever wanted to keep in touch with me."

"Did you ever send a card telling him we were married?" Stephen enquired.

"I never got round to it. I didn't know what to say. Well not ... what to say exactly, but ... how to say it."

She took another big swallow.

"That was a big mistake. He's still your father and we're told to honour our parents. It doesn't look as if you are keeping that particular commandment."

"Rubbish!" she replied at once. "My father needs to earn my respect and he hasn't done so yet."

"It's useful to reverse the roles, and try to see the other person's point of view."

"My mother and I forgave my father over and over again, but he did nothing to change his ways. He had no intention of reforming his bad habits."

"The trouble with an argument is that each side is so certain they're in the right. When people behave like that they have little or no chance of coming together and debating the rights and wrongs of the situation. You've heard the oft-repeated advice, meet the opposition halfway to show your desire for a solution to the problem." He sipped his whisky and waited for her response. "Don't you think it's about time you phoned your father, at least, to let him know we're married?" he said quietly. "Try and make it up with him. Phone him now and tell him your news."

"All right then. That's what I'll do." Made bold by three large whiskies, Marjorie lifted the phone.

At first she dialled her father's number without making contact. "Must be my friend Millie on the exchange today," she said playfully. Eventually she heard the phone ringing. "I think I'm through now."

"Brrrr. Brrrr." The phone rang, annoyingly, for what seemed liked an hour, but was in fact only a few seconds.

"Who's there?" called a voice she didn't recognise.

Marjorie who was feeling guilty at not having been in touch with her father, took the opportunity to avoid a confrontation and immediately put the phone down.

"I'm sorry, Stephen. You married a coward. I just can't do it, at least not for the time being."

"I'd like you to promise you'll try again some other time," he said.

She thought for a while, and then said, "You know he wasn't very happy at my having a Registry Office wedding. Perhaps it would be better to phone him later, when we get the church's blessing. I know we would have been married by a minister in London, if things hadn't been done in such a rush."

"Promise me you'll phone your father soon." Stephen insisted.

Marjorie patted him on the head. "I will," she promised.

\* \* \* \* \*

The multi-million-pound concert hall was fully-booked for it's opening concert by the Glasgow Symphony Orchestra. It was so popular, that tickets had been shared between a comprehensive guest list, and subscribers, like Charlene and Roger, who had been allocated a pair of tickets in the ballot. An overwhelming crowd of patrons advanced on the new hall for the first concert of the season.

"I hope we'll be able to leave the car park just as easily as we got in," said Roger, troubled by the cars parked outside on the double yellow lines. "Those car owners don't want to be trapped in the official car park."

"You'd think we'd meet someone we know in this crowd," said Charlene as they went into the hall.

"There's somebody you do know," said Roger, pointing to a woman in a red costume. "That's the Provost - her ticket's one of the many little perks of office."

The team of designers had used their talents to produce a concert hall that was not only aesthetically pleasing but with superb acoustics. Fitted carpets gave a soft warmth on cold days and the walls were made attractive by a collection of paintings on loan from the Glasgow Art Gallery.

The Provost was standing before a pair of canvases on permanent display, quizzically examining them for their hidden message. The more she looked, however, the more she became puzzled. "She knows how much we paid for them. No wonder she's surprised," whispered Roger. But when he went closer to look for himself, he shouted out, "Good God! What is this supposed to be telling the human race?" He looked at the much-talked-about paintings and could only see patterns - there were certainly no earth-shattering messages.

"Are these the ones causing all the stir?" asked Charlene.

"I'm very much afraid so," replied Roger. "Although I'm disappointed, I'm not sure what I'd have in their place."

They bought a programme and proceeded to their seats. "That must be about the largest framed painting ever," said an astonished Charlene as they stood before a Victorian painting of the Council at the turn of the century.

"Great-uncle George was on the council about that time," said Roger examining the date of the painting. "Far too many Victorian gentlemen look alike. He could be anyone in the picture," he said jabbing his finger at various men with moustaches.

"Hello. I never expected to see you here," said Charlene's former colleague, Mary Drumhills. There were embraces all round. "I saw you on your way to the hills this morning and thought you would be too tired to come to the concert." She laughed.

William Drumhills now appeared, carrying two cups of coffee. "If I'd known you were here, I'd have bought two more."

"Don't worry about me," said Roger. "I'm having something at the interval. In any case I don't fancy having to leave my seat during the performance."

"You must take it Charlene." William insisted.

"Thank you," she replied gratefully.

Roger took his chance and opened his programme while the women were chatting. A slip of paper fell to the floor.

"What's this?" said Roger.

"Haven't you heard? Oh, of course, you've been away all day and missed the news," said William.

"What news?" repeated Charlene.

"Haven't you heard," said Mary, "Sir Benjamin died this afternoon."

By now Roger had time to look at the slip announcing the change of conductor.

"Good gracious," he called out. "The management have been fortunate to obtain the services of Fredrico Bertellini at the last minute. He is well-known for his sensitive interpretation of the Beethoven Symphonies."

Then the hurry bell sounded before Roger had a chance to say, "Let's get out of here." and everyone moved towards the hall, as though they were being carried on a tidal wave.

Some of the keener members of the orchestra were already practising. Roger wondered if this was done from the musician's dedication or quite simply the fear of making a mistake.

By now the leader appeared to a round of gentle applause. More practising from the violins this time with the leader adjusting a string and playing a couple of notes. Eventually the rotund figure of Frederico Bartellini appeared carrying an armful of batons. "He's come armed with missiles this time in case the audience turn on him," whispered Roger, as the audience began clapping loudly. He bowed and smiled to every part of the hall and especially to Her Royal Highness who had come to open the Concert Hall.

After a few moments of silence Frederico raised his baton, flicked it to one side and the orchestra began to play Beethoven's Fifth symphony.

Da da de dah ... da da de dah. However, this time the conductor lived up to his reputation as an exponent of Beethoven. It ranked high on the list of performances, mostly on record, which Roger had had a chance to hear.

By the time the interval came, Roger had a feeling of contentment and was looking forward to a coffee. "I wish they'd let us order tea and coffee as they do for alcohol," said Roger. "And before you say it Charlene, I don't think they'd be cold being poured out in advance."

"How'd you like Frederico tonight," said William. He had heard about the conductor's previous visit.

"I can't find fault with his conducting tonight," replied Roger.

The concert was ending earlier than usual tonight to allow the important people that did not include the Buchanans or Drumhills, to have a celebration gourmet meal.

"They don't know quality," quipped William. "How about coming back with us for a drink, a bite of supper and chat after the concert."

"What a lovely idea," said Charlene hugging Roger closer to her and laughing happily.

# Chapter 13

Charlene was weeding the Spring border, when Roger asked how she was feeling. He had become worried because she was looking more tired than usual.

"To tell you the truth Roger, I've not been feeling well for the past few days. That nasty full feeling in my abdomen is back again." She pressed her right side to indicate where she felt the pain.

"What do think's causing it?" Roger felt uneasy.

"I phoned my sister a couple of days ago and asked her what she thought."

"Why do that? She isn't a doctor; hasn't even got a first aid certificate."

"Peter keeps up with all the latest developments," said Charlene, as if this was sufficient explanation. "I could get some indigestion tablets from the local chemist; but if they didn't work he'd make up something himself."

Roger was unhappy at Charlene placing such trust in her brother-in-law. "Did you take his advice?"

"I haven't had time. Doing my own housework and looking after Mother; it's about all I can manage at the moment."

"This isn't good enough. I want you to call Dr Preston and make another appointment. The sooner you see him the better."

He left Charlene and went outside to cut the grass. The electric lawn mower, left by the previous owner, was so badly worn that it mutilated the tiny grass lawn at the back of the house. It would have to be replaced, he thought as he glanced over at the porch window. Charlene was setting the table; the meal would be ready soon. "When's your appointment?" Roger called out as he passed her on his way to the bathroom.

"I haven't made one." She admitted, lowering her eyes

"You haven't made one? Well who were you phoning then?"

"I discussed things with Shirley."

"Oh!" exclaimed Roger. He knew how easily her sister influenced his wife. "And ... what did she say?" he asked.

"We decided I didn't need an appointment. In any case I don't want to bother the doctor if nothing's wrong with me."

147

Roger could hardly believe what he was hearing. "You're taking the word of your unqualified sister, instead of consulting the doctor! I've never heard such a load of rubbish in all my life!"

"You're more concerned with getting angry with my sister than you are about me." Charlene was near to tears.

"And well I might be. I'm very concerned about your health. That's why I'm angry. I want you to phone the surgery right away and make an early appointment. Tell the receptionist it's urgent." Roger gently took her arm and guided her over to the telephone.

"I don't want to be told there's nothing wrong with me," she protested.

"That's precisely what you do want the doctor to tell you, or to confirm that you're only suffering from a minor illness."

"I still don't want to do it," said Charlene petulantly.

"In that case, my dear, if you won't phone, I will. You have a choice. Phone and make the appointment yourself or lose face by having me do it for you." He handed her the phone.

Reluctantly she took it and dialled the surgery.

"I'd like to make an appointment to see Dr Preston," she said to the receptionist. "Ten o'clock tomorrow morning?" She repeated for Roger's benefit. "Thank you very much." And put the phone down. "I've done as you demanded." For the first time in their marriage Charlene raised her voice. "If I'd waited a bit longer it would have gone away. It always does."

"Are you telling me you've had these pains before, and said nothing?"

"I didn't do nothing about them. I always phoned Shirley for her advice and Peter would give me something to ease the pain."

"Charlene, I'm appalled by what you've told me. I'm glad you're getting a medical opinion tomorrow."

"It suits me fine; after I've seen the doctor, I'll take mother shopping. She needs a pair of shoes, anyway."

"It's nearly time for the gardening programme," Roger called out as Charlene was finishing the washing up. "If you don't come soon you'll miss the start of it."

"You can switch it on. I won't be long." She put the pots in the cupboard and wiped the worktop. That would have to do. Roger got so edgy if she weren't sitting with him.

As she came into the front room the titles were ending and the presenter was starting to speak.

"It's very easy to take your own cuttings," the well-known gardener was saying as he walked over to the shrub border. He snipped off suitable pieces from a number of plants and put them in plastic bags. "That will keep them moist until we get back to the greenhouse."

"We've seen all this many times before," complained Roger. "I wish he'd get on to making the garden pond."

"Don't be in such a hurry, Roger." Charlene said as she waved her hand at him not to interrupt.

"Now this plant's a bit tricky." The presenter was holding a piece of witch hazel.

"That plant's so much better looking than ours. I'd like a cutting from it," interjected Charlene.

The gardener warned his viewers; "Anybody who's ever tried to root a cutting of witch hazel will know how difficult it is. You might be lucky, but if you really want to be successful then this is the way to do it." He took one of the lower branches and fixed it to the ground with a wire peg.

"That's why I've never been able to root a cutting from Shirley's witch hazel!" Charlene exclaimed, happy to find an explanation for her failures.

"I wish he'd hurry up and get to the pond. That's what I'm interested in."

Charlene reminded him that a lot of gardeners were just starting out and they had to be catered for as well.

A young woman with a high-pitched voice started to pontificate about the proper way to grow seedlings. "That woman irritates me," said Roger testily. "I wish they'd deal with the pond."

"Since neither of us are to be allowed to watch the programme, perhaps I can tell you how worried I am about Mother being on her own. She was lying behind the door the last time I called. She'd tripped over the carpet in the hall. I just managed to squeeze past and get into the house. We'll really have to do something about her."

"Just because we've taken early retirement your sister seems to think we've got plenty of time on our hands. That way she avoids the responsibility, as well as the feeling of guilt - if she is capable of feeling anything, anyway."

"That's not fair Roger. Shirley loves Mother just as much as I do. She has a lot of other responsibilities. It's very difficult being a housewife and raising a family."

"This has always been the problem, dear. You make too many excuses. Anyhow her family are grown up. - Quiet, a minute dear." Roger had heard the word pond.

The presenter was speaking. "We've come to the end of this week's programme. I'm sorry we didn't have time to include our item on building a pond owing to our visit to the Gardening Show. But don't worry, it'll be in next week's programme."

Roger got up and switched off the TV in disgust.

Next day Charlene left to keep her appointment with the doctor. But first she'd call on her mother. In the past, when Mrs Graham needed shopping from the small general store hear her home, she had been able to climb the two flights of stairs on her return. But she could no longer do this without assistance. It was clear she would be housebound if she were to be left on her own. And in addition there were the complications caused by her broken wrist and her tendency to fall.

Charlene opened the door of her mother's flat in Elmwood gardens and walked through the large hall into the kitchen. Katie Graham was sitting in what had been her husband's easy chair, with her back to the window reading the local paper and was warming her legs by the gas fire, which she had turned up to full setting.

"That's far too high," Charlene reproved, turning the knob down to its midpoint. "That's better."

"I hope I'll not be too cold. I had trouble turning the gas on in the first place."

"You should be using the hand warmer Roger and I gave you at Christmas. It would help to loosen your fingers. And you want to take a teaspoon of cod liver oil every day. That's said to be good for arthritis." Charlene emptied her shopping bag on to the table. "There are some things for your lunch and tea, today and tomorrow. I'll put them in the fridge."

She had been so busy thinking about the fire that she hadn't noticed the bruise just above her mother's right eyebrow until now. "How did you get that mark on your forehead?" she said giving her mother the good morning kiss she had almost forgotten. Katie Graham did not answer. "Did you hear what I said Mother?"

"I heard what you said, Charlene. I don't want to say. You just get upset when I tell you."

"Does that mean you've had another fall?"

"Yes. I fell and knocked my head against the door handle but I managed to get up after a while and go to bed." Katie spoke as though this was a normal event. Charlene had become quite concerned. "You've had several unexplained dizzy spells. You're not getting up from your chair too quickly are you?" She did not wait for an answer. "Maybe you should come to the doctor with me." But she changed her mind when she recalled the rule; one patient for each appointment.

When Charlene joined the small queue in the waiting room at Dr Preston's surgery, the room was noticeably colder than it had been at home.

"Mrs Buchanan!" called the receptionist. Charlene got up at once from her seat. "Dr Preston will see you now." The young woman pointed to a door in the corner.

"Come in, Mrs Buchanan. What can I do for you?" said Dr Preston glancing at her record as she sat down. "I've a note here saying you've been having abdominal discomfort. Don't we all," he quipped.

Charlene had already removed her coat and was beginning to undress when the doctor said, "I think it would be easier if you lay on the couch." She quickly rearranged her clothing and did as he suggested.

"How long has this been going on?" Dr Preston rephrased his question in a more helpful form. "I mean, when were you first aware of the discomfort?"

"I'm not sure, but I know I've had it for some time. My brother-in-law is a pharmacist. He seems to think I've got indigestion."

Dr Preston listened courteously, but made no comment as he carefully probed the right side of her abdomen with his fingers.

"I haven't been able to find anything out of the ordinary," he said when he had finished his examination. "Maybe your brother-in-law is right."

Charlene sorted her clothing and sat down on the seat again. "Shall I take something for it?"

Dr Preston was already writing a prescription. "I'm giving you a hydroxide suspension. It should give you some relief."

He handed her the prescription, "Is there anything else?"

"May I ask about my mother? She had a fall last night and injured her head, though not seriously."

"I'm afraid this is all too common. It comes with getting old. If it happens again bring her in to see me."

At her next stop, the shoe shop, she was told her mother needed a special shoe. "We don't get much call for this type nowadays," said the sales assistant. "I'll have to order it specially."

She told him to go ahead and order two pairs. "When can I expect delivery?" she asked.

"In about a fortnight, but if you leave your phone number, I'll give you a call when they come in."

Roger, who had been gardening during Charlene's absence, was in between jobs when he heard the red Rover in the driveway. Hoping she had good news for him, he threw his trowel in the border and rushed over to meet her as she came into the back garden. He hugged and kissed her as if she had been away for a week instead of a few hours. "What did the doc say?" he asked with a slight tremor in his voice.

Charlene smiled reassuringly, "It's just as my sister said, indigestion. Dr Preston has given me a prescription which he thinks will help."

"Even if your sister is right, it's good to have professional advice," he said happily.

Charlene was putting the shopping away when the phone rang. "Would you answer it, dear," she said. Roger rushed into the front room, lifted the handset, and was reflecting on the telephone's inconvenient position when he heard his daughter's voice. "This is Marjorie, Dad. I'm phoning from Zimbabwe."

Roger was astonished. "Good Lord," he said. Marjorie's rejection after the divorce still hurt him. He hoped this would lead to a new beginning and was relieved that she had not replaced the phone as she had done on another occasion. "You've gone all quiet. Is anything wrong?"

"No. Nothing's wrong. In fact everything's right again." Marjorie had tried several times already to make this call, but had always stopped when she heard her father's voice during her previous attempts. This time she had been determined to go through with it, and had begun to talk as soon as she heard him speaking. "It's very difficult for me." Her voice revealed the strain she was under. "We said a lot of unkind things to each other the last time, and I'm afraid it was my action in banging down the phone which caused the breach between Mother and you to widen even more. When I think about what happened that day, I think it may have been my behaviour which persuaded her to go ahead with the divorce. She had been thinking of asking you for a reconciliation. I know this is true, for she said so many times later on, even when she was dying, that she really loved you very much and wished she had shown it when you most needed it." The tension became too much and she burst into tears.

"Are you all right, Marjorie?" Roger asked with some concern. His daughter had stopped speaking but she had not put the phone down. He could hear a gentle sobbing in the background. "Please answer me, Marjorie. I don't want to lose you again."

"Nothing's wrong." She tried to stifle her tears. "It's just that I'm overcome with emotion when I think back to those unhappy days. How I wish we could put the clock back and start all over again! I know what I should have done and, although it's too late to change what happened, I want to make amends."

"You've nothing to be sorry for." He tried to comfort her. "We all make mistakes. People carry around their own judge and jury. We punish ourselves for our wrongdoing with greater severity than any court. Isn't that the reason you're phoning now? Your conscience is worrying you and you're hoping to put things right through a reconciliation."

"You're speaking like a lawyer," she said. "I thought you'd taken early retirement anyway. But I do know what you're trying to tell me. You're saying we all punish ourselves for our own misdemeanours."

"Hold on a second," he said, as soon as he heard Charlene coming into the front room.

"Is anything wrong?" she asked.

"Nothing," he said giving her a quick kiss on the cheek. "Marjorie's on the phone. Come and speak to her."

"I don't think I can," she protested, as he took her hand and pulled her towards the phone.

"Are you still there, Marjorie?" he asked.

"I'm still here. I heard a woman's voice. If it's Charlene I'd like to speak to her."

He handed over the phone. "Marjorie would like to have a word," he said.

Charlene was still reluctant to speak to Marjorie, or even to listen to her. She was easily bruised, physically and metaphorically. But she was determined not to widen the rift between father and daughter and said, "This is Charlene."

"Hello Charlene. This is your favourite step-daughter speaking," said Marjorie, adopting a light-hearted approach. "I'm so sorry we haven't met. But I want to make amends now and ask you to begin a new relationship with me. I want you to forgive me if any action of mine has hurt you, and to tell you I realise how badly I behaved towards you. I hope we can be friends."

This was something for which Charlene had often prayed.

"Marjorie, you've not only made your father happy by phoning, but I'm also happy to know you want my friendship. Of course I want to be your friend, and I'm sure we'll become very close as time goes by. It's such a pity you're so far away. Perhaps your husband will be posted to the UK."

"Judging by your voice, I can tell you're a kind person. That makes me feel even more wretched about my behaviour."

"If there's anything to forgive, then consider it forgiven and the matter is at an end."

"That makes me feel very much better." Marjorie was beginning to feel more relaxed. "Now that we're friends, how about visiting Zimbabwe? It would be nice if you could stay for a month, but I don't suppose you'll both have such a long holiday."

"Oh yes we do." Charlene's voice was happy. "We've both taken early retirement, so that would be no problem."

"If you can come soon you'll have the benefit of our winter. There are so many things I want to talk to you about and to show you and my dad. Please say you'll come."

"I'll pass you over to your father to make the arrangements. Bye for now." Charlene handed the phone to Roger and said she would start the lunch.

"I've just invited Charlene and you to Harare. Can you come?" said Marjorie. "That's a splendid idea, my dear," he responded warmly. " I'll try and book a flight for next month and I'll write. One of us had better stay out of the bankruptcy court, so we must stop this call now. Give my regards to Stephen. Goodbye, my dear." He called Charlene from the kitchen. "Say farewell to your daughter."

They were relaxing in the porch after lunch when Roger asked Charlene if she had remembered to add the magic ingredient to the meal.

She was a very practical woman; magic had no part in her philosophy. "I didn't put anything in your meal today that anyone else couldn't just as easily have used. Magic ingredient indeed!"

"You've forgotten about love," Roger said softly. "You cook my meals with love and that makes all the difference to them."

"I only do what I think will make us both happy. Maybe that's your magic ingredient."

"If you love what you're doing then that transfers itself to the end product."

"Put that way it sounds more acceptable," Charlene admitted. "However, it doesn't get me taken out for a meal. It looks as if I'm never going to taste the haute cuisine of 'Beverley House'."

"Is that so, Mrs Buchanan?" He waited for her reaction. "What day is Thursday?"

Charlene was mystified. "What's so special about Thursday? Is it my birthday you mean?" As soon as she had said the word birthday, Charlene realised what Roger was talking about. "You're taking me there for a birthday meal," she asked hopefully.

"Yes dear, that's just what I meant. I was hoping to include the invitation in your birthday card, but I've just had the booking confirmed."

She stretched across the table and gave him a kiss. "You're always thinking of nice ways to surprise me." Her eyes sparkled, enhancing her smile. "But it will cost too much. I would probably choke when I thought how much each spoonful of soup was costing."

"That's why we usually end up eating at home. However, I've made the booking and I don't intend to cancel."

"What if I say I don't want to go? You wouldn't want to eat on your own would you?"

"There's no fear of that. I could always ask Jane Faulds, if she's free."

"Roger, that's unkind," said Charlene. "You know how much it hurts me. Although I forgave Jane long ago for saying I'd stolen you from her, I can't forget it."

"There, there, princess, I didn't mean to upset you. I thought I was being funny. But clearly the wound is still there." He put his arm around Charlene and patted her on the shoulder. "No more nonsense then. We'll be having a birthday party in Beverley House next Thursday." He kissed her on the forehead, as he often did as a preliminary to a longer and more passionate kiss on the lips. "I do love you so very much."

This cheered Charlene. "And I love you too Roger." She gave him a brief kiss on the point of his nose. The two held each other tightly for a few minutes, as if to make sure the other did not vanish like a ghost. Suddenly, Charlene groaned. "It's that discomfort again." She pressed her hand firmly over the right side of her abdomen and started to rub the area in the hope that the slight pain would go away.

"Is the pain the same as the last time?"

"Yes, exactly the same. But don't worry darling, I'm sure it will go away as it did the last time." She continued to press on her abdomen. "I can't feel anything. Must be something wrong with the gastric juices. I'll phone Shirley. She'll know what to do."

When Charlene returned to the kitchen, Roger had put the kettle on. "Are you feeling better now?" he asked.

"I'm feeling fine now. I got rid of some wind on my way to the phone." Then she became serious. "Shirley had a call from Mother's neighbour. It seems they had to break in and take Mother to the hospital."

Roger took Charlene's hand. "I do hope it isn't anything serious."

"I'm afraid it is. Shirley told me Mother was overtaken with a fit of coughing on her way to the bathroom and tripped and fell on the hall rug."

Roger screwed up his face, as if he too were experiencing the fall. "Where is she?"

"In the Central General. She tried to save herself, but fell heavily on her side and broke her hip. But that wasn't the worst of it. She couldn't get herself up from the floor, so she had to lie there close to the phone, without being able to use it."

"This must have happened soon after you left."

"There's more to come. The hospital doctor suggested Mother might have had a slight stroke."

"That's very distressing," said Roger. "It looks to me as if she needs full-time care."

"I'm so glad you're with me Roger. When I asked Dr Preston, he warned me that the attacks would happen more frequently. The doctor at the Central General has suggested either we put her in the Old Folks' Home or look after her ourselves. That would mean bringing her here."

Roger, who had not quite expected this latest development, thought for a while about the various consequences of further action?

"If your mother isn't requiring medical attention on a daily basis, then I think the family have to take on the responsibility of looking after her."

"She'll be resting in hospital for a few days. It would have been longer if she were living alone, but since she'll be coming here; we can collect her whenever we want. I do hope you're happy about this." Charlene hoped he would agree to have her mother in their home.

"Hold on a minute Charlene." Roger put in quickly. "When I said family I meant Shirley as well as us. Clearly the job will have to be shared. We can't look after her by ourselves without having regular breaks away. We can only manage if we share the responsibility. Say a break of a week or a month, whatever is the more convenient."

"Roger, Mother may not have long to live. I'd feel so guilty if I'd been selfish and thought only of my own comfort."

Roger felt the words were aimed at him. She must have thought he would raise objections to her plan.

"I know how you feel. You want to give her the attention you can't trust your sister to provide. You've convinced yourself that only you can provide for your mother. Let me remind you that you could be doing this for a very long time. What do you think this could do to your own health? Remember you've just been complaining about abdominal pain and we haven't got that sorted out yet. On top of which, I would like to take up Marjorie's offer of a month's visit. We've got to try and cement good relations with my daughter, now that she's in touch with us again."

"The only problem with Shirley is she only does what she wants," said Charlene with emphasis. She had always found her sister a hard opponent. "However, I'll phone her now and tell her what's happened. And ask if she's prepared to take her turn. But I'd like to do it on my own, Roger."

"Not at all, so long as she's willing to co-operate."

Charlene left the front room door a little open, so that Roger could overhear, if he wished.

"I've been discussing Mother's condition with Roger. He agrees with me that we must do something to ensure this doesn't happen again."

"I agree very much," said Shirley. "Mother would be better in sheltered accommodation where she'll be looked after twenty-four hours a day."

"That's not what Roger and I have in mind. I thought we might talk it over when you visit the hospital. I'll be going there tonight. Will you?"

"That's over on your side of Glasgow," Shirley complained. "It'll take me at least an hour in the heavy traffic to visit her unless we can have her transferred to my local hospital." Shirley had not considered the reverse argument, that it would probably take Charlene even longer to reach the proposed hospital. "I don't suppose it will be possible to change things for a few days, anyway. If you let me know the ward, I'll go and visit her in the morning. That's my best time."

"I was hoping to go myself in the morning. I can't manage tomorrow evening and I'd like Mother to have a visitor both times."

"Sorry, just can't manage it. It's my bridge club and I'm playing in the championships. If I don't turn up, my name will be withdrawn." Shirley's tone of voice gave no possible hope she would change her mind. "You'll just have to visit Mother yourself in the evening."

Charlene had always given in to Shirley. She did no shopping or cleaning for her mother, or any of the dozen or so of the other jobs Mrs Graham needed. It was all left to Charlene, who was expected to accept the situation without further argument. However there was a more important matter to talk about so she'd let Shirley have her way once again. In future she'd ensure decisions affecting Roger and her would be by mutual agreement.

"You say there's something important to talk about? You've aroused my curiosity," said Shirley.

"The doctor advised me Mother was going to need closer attention than she's been getting." Charlene's voice was sharp. "We'll share the responsibility and bring her home and look after her."

"What about the other possibility I mentioned? That Old Folks' Home near you. We could put her in there. It would be a problem travelling every day, but I'm prepared to do that rather than have Mother here. There's the children."

"Shirley, no one would consider putting a loving parent in a place like that. I wouldn't do it. I want you to agree to take a turn having her at your home and we'll do our share, having her over here."

There was a long silence at the other end, as Shirley searched around for a way out. "This is something I'll have to discuss with Peter, and he's not home yet. He must be dispensing prescriptions for the doctors' late night patients. I'll phone you in the morning when I've had a talk with him."

Having secured a respite, Shirley said goodbye and put the phone down.

"Well, what did she say?" asked Roger when he came into the front room.

There was no immediate answer from Charlene. "You don't need to tell me. She said she would have to talk it over with Peter. It's not unreasonable that she should, Charlene. After all the decision she takes will affect him as well."

Charlene may well be a caring daughter but she needs a bit more backbone in dealing with her sister, thought Roger. "I'd better go over to Elmwood gardens and secure the door," said Roger as he put on his anorak.

"There's no need for that, the joiner fixed the door before he left. I'll ring the hospital later on to find out about mother. Now I could do with a cup of tea," she said and switched the kettle on once again.

# Chapter 14

Charlene had waited all day for her sister to phone and let her know what if anything she proposed to do about their mother. She had even waited until after her own evening visit to the hospital, in case Shirley planned to meet her there. She had always found her sister's response quite unpredictable and often hesitated some time before phoning Shirley; her enquiries were usually treated as though they came from a fool about a matter that had an obvious solution.

Eventually she put through a call. "Shirley, you promised to phone me after you had spoken to Peter," she reminded her

"You can't expect me to be at your beck and call," her sister replied indignantly. "Running this home and looking after my husband and family are my first priorities."

"But Shirl, you said you'd to talk to Peter and let me know the outcome."

"I can't help it if he was too tired to discuss it when he came home from work. Remember, we have still to earn a living, not like some people I could mention not a million miles away from here."

"Stop being silly, Shirley. If you don't want to take your share of looking after mother, just say so. If your social life is more important, then nothing I can say will make you change your mind."

"It's not that at all. I have too many responsibilities on my plate. Peter's got a most important job and he needs my backing to do it well." She paused, looking for arguments to support her case for opting out. "Then there's the children. I can't neglect them."

"They seem to be able to manage well enough when you go out to play bridge," said Charlene sharply, her attitude to her sister hardening.

"The fact of the matter is ... Peter and I discussed Mother's problem fully last night and we came to the conclusion there was no need for us to lose any sleep over it. She can go into the Old Folks' Home and we'll visit her as frequently as we can, and maybe take her out for a drive now and then."

Roger, who was standing supportively nearby, understood what was happening from Charlene's occasional repetition of Shirley's replies.

"Charlene, give me the phone please," he said, taking it from her unprotesting hand.

"Hello, Shirley? This is Roger. I've been listening with no great surprise to your very selfish attitude. You seem to think it's all right for me and Charlene to look after Mother while you get on with your social life."

"You and Charlene don't have jobs to keep you occupied. Peter has his work and I have the children to look after. You can be more generous with your time than we can."

Roger repeated her last words for Charlene's benefit.

She shook her head as though saying that she could have told him so. "Tell her you'll phone back when she's had time to reconsider," she whispered.

Roger waved his hand at her indicating that he intended to go on as he had planned.

"If that's how you feel, Charlene and I will look after Mother without your help. You'll always be welcome to visit her and I'd hope you'd do it as often as possible. I've still to talk the details over with Charlene but I would think your mother would probably wish to live in her own home with all its memories. I don't need to hear anything more from you on the matter. Good bye."

He replaced the phone and turned to Charlene, saying "I think you'll be much happier taking care of Mother than having her put in a home. After all, she gave me as much kindness as you did when I needed it at the time when Edith left me. The least I can do now is to see that she doesn't suffer during her remaining years."

Charlene began to weep. "I don't know whether I'm crying with relief at not having to ask Shirley to help or because I know now that I made the right choice when I married you, Roger."

"There you are, Charlene." Roger put his arms about her. "We were meant for each other. It's as if we're different halves of the same person. I really don't know how to explain what I mean, but I do know that I love you and I'll do anything to make you happy. Didn't I tell you, that day on Ben Calder, that you were a rare bird? I meant it. You are unique among women."

Charlene stopped crying and began to look a little embarrassed. "I don't deserve such praise Roger. I only do what I think any decent human being should do."

"That may be so. But you do it when others only pay lip service. That's what matters, Charlene my dear." Roger kissed her and escorted her to the smaller of their two bedrooms.

"Mother can stay here for a while, until she's fit enough to decide what to do. And, if she wants to, she can return to her own home and we'll work out the details about what arrangements will best suit her."

Charlene wrapped her arms about him and in playful fashion. "I'm going to give you a great big hug for being such a wonderful husband."

She had just gone into the spare room when the phone rang. "Would you answer it dear? My hands are full at the moment."

He went through to the front room. "This is ward twelve sister in the Central General Hospital. Am I speaking to Mr Buchanan?"

"Yes," said Roger, fearing he was about to learn some bad news about Mrs Graham.

"Then could you please tell your wife that her mother is not too well. We think she should come as soon as she can."

"Who was that?" asked Charlene, carrying some fresh sheets to the bedroom.

"It's bad news from the hospital."

"Mother isn't..." She stopped. She did not want to mention the dreaded word.

"The sister said your mother was not too well and asked if you could come right away. Just leave that and get yourself ready, and I'll phone Shirley and let her know."

Roger had to ring for some time before Peter answered.

"Shirley's mum is not too good, Peter. Charlene has been asked to go to the hospital as soon as she can. I think you should take Shirley there to meet her."

"If you hold on, I'll go and see what she says."

After a few minutes, Peter picked up the phone again. "Shirley thinks it can't be too serious. She's asked me to take her to the hospital at the end of the episode. She never misses Coronation Street."

"Well, I can only say I'm surprised. You'd think at a time like this her mother would be more important than a soap opera," said Roger in disgust and put down the phone.

"I'm ready, Roger," called Charlene as she walked to the front door, putting on her coat.

"I'm afraid Shirley wants to finish watching her programme. She doesn't think the hospital call is urgent." Roger put on his heavy anorak and they went out to the car.

Roger drove as quickly as the heavy traffic allowed. Charlene was worried at his speed and told him so, but agreed there was a need to hurry. Soon they had arrived in the hospital grounds.

"You know where to park the car. I'll be closer if I get off here. Join me when you can," said Charlene and ran all the way until she came to the entrance of the building where her mother had been taken. Instead of waiting for the lift she walked up the three flights of stairs.

When she eventually reached the top, a nurse was waiting by a side room near ward twelve where Mrs Graham had been taken.

"Are you Mrs Buchanan?" the nurse asked quietly.

Charlene nodded. "I got here as soon as I could."

"I'm afraid your mother is dead." The nurse said sympathetically. "She died shortly before I phoned. But I didn't want to upset you by telling you on the phone."

Roger joined his wife just as the ward sister finished her explanation. "I'm sorry we didn't get a chance to see her before she died," he said sadly. "There's something anticlimactic when it happens that way. It would have been better if we had been with her at the end. I hope that, whichever one of us goes first, will be held in the comforting arms of the other at the end."

"I couldn't agree more. God grant that we will be blessed in that way," confirmed Charlene and turned to the nurse. "Can we see my mother now?"

The sister opened the door of the small room and showed them over to a curtained bed. She drew the curtain to one side and pulled a white linen sheet down from the patient's face. "Your mother didn't suffer any pain. She was talking to one of the nurses and was looking forward to your visit just a moment before she died. We didn't have her with us for very long but we were able to see that she was a very gentle soul and was so careful not to make extra work for us. I'll leave you with her. Please see me before you go. There are your mother's things to be collected."

Charlene went close to the bed. Roger was surprised how calmly she was taking her mother's death. The tears would come later, he thought.

"Mother looks so peaceful lying there," she said leaning over and kissing her on the forehead. "You're with father now, after all those lonely years, Mother. I wonder what it's like?"

Roger felt a little like an intruder at this very personal moment. "I think I should warn your sister before she leaves the house, if possible. I'll call from the phone in the café."

"She ought to be told," agreed Charlene, sitting down next to the bed.

Roger was crossing over to the phone, when he caught sight of Shirley sitting at a table with Peter. Both of them were drinking coffee.

"I was going to give you a call," he told them.

"Why would you want to do that?" Shirley looked at him curiously, saying, "Your earlier call made it clear you were leaving me to get on with my own life. And that's what I'm doing. I'll be with Mother, presumably, for a while, so I'm having some nourishment beforehand."

"There's no hurry Shirley. Your mother is dead. Your visit no longer matters."

"She can't be dead. I wasn't told there was any likelihood of that when you phoned," Shirley said resentfully.

"And now my wife's too late. I blame you for this." said Peter in defence of Shirley, as he and his wife left their half-empty mugs on the table and hurried out of the café.

When they came out of the lift, Shirley rushed along the passage to Ward 12. Peter had decided to let his wife see her mother by herself.

"Your mother isn't here, Mrs Anderson," said the ward sister intercepting Shirley on the way in.

"I know that my mother's already dead. That's why I'm here."

"She's not in the ward," she said, pointing to the small room with the frosted glass door marked private. "Your mother's in there with your sister,"

Shirley and Charlene embraced and both began to cry for the

first time. Then Charlene took her sister's arm and guided her to the bed in which their mother lay. She pulled back the curtain and lifted the sheet from her mother's face. "See how peaceful she looks."

Shirley took a handkerchief from her pocket and wiped her eyes before kissing the still pale face. "If I had known how near the end she was, I would have done anything to help, Charlene. Honestly, I would." Shirley was genuinely upset.

"We'll bury her with father," said Charlene. "There are still two empty graves left."

Shirley was examining her mother's hands when the sister arrived with a plastic bundle, which she handed to Charlene.

"Where are my mother's rings?" Shirley demanded. "She had them on her hands when she was brought in here."

"There's no need to worry. We removed them for safe keeping," explained the nurse. "They are among her effects, which I have just given to your sister. Would you please check them, Mrs Buchanan, and sign this slip?"

Charlene quickly emptied the things on a nearby table and noted that her mother's clothes were intact. She then tore open a brown envelope which had "engagement and wedding rings" written on it.

"Everything's all right. These are my mother's rings and clothes," she confirmed.

"This booklet tells the bereaved relatives what to do when someone dies. You'll find it very helpful, and it also tells you where you may find help to cope with your loss." She put the booklet in Charlene's hands. "I'll leave you now, but if there's anything you want to know before you leave, just come along and see me."

As soon as the ward sister had left, Shirley turned to Charlene. "I'm the older daughter. Mother's rings belong to me now," she challenged.

"Since your mother's estate is a small one, it will be shared equally by you and your sister and, unless you can agree how to divide her things, they must be sold and the money divided between you," said Roger, who had come to join them.

Charlene was unhappy at the thought of arguing over her mother's property. Mrs Graham had written a will in her own hand when she knew she might die at any time. "There's a will in the bureau, Shirley. Mother wanted her things to be shared. She left her rings to me, thinking I would have a need for them. We are to share the contents of the house in Elmwood gardens and her shares and savings. But all I really want is mother's engagement ring. You can have everything else Shirley, if you'll let me keep it."

Shirley realised her mother's savings and shares were of considerably greater value than the ring and accepted the suggestion.

"I'll wear it beside your ring if I may, Roger," she said turning to him.

"By all means. It will always be there as a reminder of her," he said, feeling Charlene had been too generous in accepting the engagement ring as her share of the inheritance, but said nothing.

\* \* \* \* \*

Several weeks had passed since Katie Graham had been buried in the small cemetery near her daughter's home.

"I know you're still grieving for your mother." Charlene was staring at a photograph of her parents, when Roger returned from the library. "But I do think we should take up Marjorie's offer of a holiday with her in Zimbabwe."

He put six African travel books on the small table beside her. "That's your compulsory reading for this week." He joked. "There are books on Malawi and Zimbabwe."

"If your daughter lives in Zimbabwe why did you bring a book about Malawi?"

"Some ancestors of mine went exploring there. I thought we might visit it." He picked up a book, which dealt with three central African countries, including Zimbabwe, and turned the pages until he came to a description and photograph of Victoria Falls.

"There you are." He handed her the open book. "The Falls are not too far from Harare. It's always been an ambition of mine to fly over them in a small plane."

"It's very impressive. Do you really think we can afford it?" she asked tremulously. "And then there's malaria to be considered."

"If you start worrying about what can happen, you'll never go anywhere," he admonished her. "I made enquiries about a flight and the cost is reasonable but we'd have to go in two weeks time."

Charlene thumbed through the pages of the book. "If we don't do it now, we're not likely to do it later. You go ahead and make your booking. Of course, we'll need new clothes. I don't have many things that would be suitable for Zimbabwe."

"We'll have to have some inoculations. We should have been taking malaria tablets three weeks before departure. I'll make an appointment with the doctor and you can ask him about your indigestion at the same time."

They visited Dr Preston and afterwards went into Glasgow City centre where they had a gleeful buying spree. Every store seemed to be having a sale. "The only thing we don't have is a mosquito net," said Charlene. "But a friend of mine has said she'll loan me hers."

"Charlene, I don't think you'll need a net where we're going. But if it makes you any happier, we'll pack it with our other things. We'll need to get some pudding rice for Marjorie. She says it's very hard to come by over there. The only other thing is to pick up our prescription from Boots. The assistant said it would be ready for collection in an hour."

When they collected the malaria tablets Roger asked her if the doctor had given her something for her indigestion.

She shook her head. "He couldn't find anything to account for my feelings of discomfort. He said there was no change, since I had been to see him some months ago, and that he would give me something stronger to take with me."

\* \* \* \* \*

They had taken their cases to their neighbours' house to avoid the news that they were going on holiday being passed on to the burglarising fraternity.

"We've had a burglar alarm installed. That should deter any intruders," he advised his neighbour, who had been given a spare set of keys and asked to keep a watchful eye on the house.

As soon as the taxi arrived, the luggage was quickly loaded in the boot and they left for the airport.

"Bye bye," Roger and Charlene shouted to their neighbours,

giving the taxi driver the impression they had been living with them. They soon arrived at the airport.

"That'll be four pounds fifty, sir," said the driver as he opened the boot and took out the cases.

Roger handed the driver a five-pound note. "Keep the change. That was a safe journey. You got us here in plenty of time. Thank you very much."

The driver mumbled an embarrassed thanks, closed the door and sped off back to Glasgow.

They had just been given their seat numbers by the booking desk, when Shirley arrived on the scene. She went over and kissed her sister. Ignoring Roger, she told her she had come to see her off and to give her something for her indigestion. "This is Peter's special prescription. It never fails," she said. I don't suppose it succeeds either, Roger thought.

"We don't have much time to get through to the passenger lounge." Charlene was becoming agitated now that the flight time had been put back.

"Have you made your wills?" Peter reminded them solicitously. "If you haven't, you can always make out an emergency one here in the airport."

But Roger and Charlene had already made wills in each other's favour, and Charlene explained, "If we both go at the same time, then what we leave will be shared out between Roger's daughter and your children. So you don't have to worry about my not leaving you anything."

"What about mother's engagement ring? Are you taking it with you? Don't you think it would be safer leaving it with me?"

"Shirley, I'll be wearing my mother's ring as long as I'm able to do so." Charlene wondered if her sister were more interested in her property than in wishing her a wonderful holiday.

Peter and Shirley waved good bye and the travellers started on the first stage of their journey. "I'll send you a card as soon as I arrive," Charlene called to her sister as they made their way to the departure lounge.

Roger and Charlene managed to sleep for most of the flight to Zimbabwe, so they did not suffer badly from jet lag.

"Your luggage sir?" said the grinning porter, pointing to the cases, which they had just taken from the carousel.

"Yes, those are our cases," said Roger. "You take them for us."

Although it was summer in Britain, the evening temperature back home had been low enough for them to wear heavy clothing for the journey.

"Isn't the heat intense?" said Charlene as they walked through the customs and emerged into the airport hall. "How's that?" he said fanning Charlene's glistening forehead.

"Oh lovely! Give me more of that." she said happily.

"And to think this is Zimbabwe's winter!" The heat had surprised Roger.

"What must it be like in the summer?" Charlene said, using her own hand to take up where Roger had left off.

A group of about twenty Japanese travellers hurried behind their coloured guide towards their impatiently revving coach. Inevitably one of them stopped near Roger. "You take photo please?" he said smiling broadly and handed him the latest in Japanese technology.

Roger needed no further instruction and clicked the shutter as requested. "Thank you. Thank you," said the man and his wife as they bowed respectfully to Roger, thanking him for his help.

"So far, it's little different from Glasgow Airport," said Charlene, quietly to Roger.

"There's a seat over there," said Roger, taking Charlene's hand and leading her to a nearby ventilation shaft.

"Oh fine." She flopped on the bare bench as Roger tipped the porter.

Nearby was a group of about twenty students of mixed race gathered round a middle-aged white man.

"I'd like to welcome you to Zim and the Church Foundation," he said. "Our transport has just arrived. Please follow me." The young men and women quickly lifted their simple belongings and went excitedly to the coach.

Roger and Charlene took it turns, to look round the airport and its shops. While the other watched the luggage.

"I didn't come to Africa to buy a newspaper," said Roger on

his return from the money exchange. He glanced at his watch. "Marjorie's late. She must know we've arrived by now."

Charlene decided it was her turn for a stroll and went to the door of the main terminal. She looked towards the car park and saw the large Japanese group getting into a van which was obviously built for safari work.

Although Charlene had only seen photographs of Marjorie when she was a child she felt certain the young woman in the dark blouse coming towards her was Roger's daughter.

"Yoo hoo!" shouted Charlene and waved in her direction. Then she looked to where Roger was sitting and waved him over.

"You must be Charlene," Marjorie said softly. "Father has told me so much about you. I think I already know you."

She did not explain that her father had written a long letter extolling Charlene's virtues when he had invited her to the wedding. I hope she likes me, thought Charlene. But she needn't have worried. Her charming smile was sufficient to dispel any last-minute reservations Marjorie might have had. They embraced and said how pleased they were to be meeting each other at last. By the time Roger arrived at the entrance with a porter and their luggage Charlene and Marjorie were old friends.

Marjorie grasped her father round the waist and hugged him so tightly one might have thought she was afraid to let him go now that she had found him again. She gave him a kiss, holding him yet a while longer before releasing.

"Have the porter bring your things over to the car park. I'll collect the car and meet you there," said Marjorie. It was about five miles between the airport and Marjorie's bungalow; but she made the route more interesting by taking a diversion to include some of the sights in the former Salisbury.

She had left instructions for her servant to set out tea things in the front room and have water boiling for a pot of tea. "This is Walter," she said indicating an old, black man who smiled a greeting at them. "He came with the house but he's hoping to go back to his village soon."

After tea, Marjorie showed them to their room and asked them to return to the lounge to discuss their holiday plans.

As soon as they came in she got down to details. "It's quite a long drive to the Main Camp Lodge at Wangie, so we'll have an early start tomorrow morning." Charlene could feel a wave of exhaustion. From the way her daughter-in-law spoke the schedule indicated an intensive safari in several National Parks.

* * * * *

As Marjorie drove into the Main Camp just an hour before sunset, she explained that Stephen had some work to do in Wangie. So that would give them a few days on their own in the National Park.

The lodge was substantially built of stone with all the usual apartments. Charlene thought the so-called camp was better than her former home in Elmwood gardens.

"Watch out for the baboons," said Marjorie. "Apart from being vicious creatures, they steal any food left unattended."

"I can't get used to the dark at six on an August evening," said Roger, throwing a few more logs on the fire. "Nor the cold."

"It's the altitude that does it," said his daughter.

Charlene was happily enjoying the warmth as she reflected how well things had turned out. She'd been to many exotic places, but she'd never experienced anything quite as exciting as the bush. There was something overwhelming in its quiet simplicity. The missionaries had spoken about the Water of Life. Without the waterholes there would be no life. Now they attracted all kinds of wild life and the tourists. Marjorie had driven along dried-up river-beds, past giant ant hills and baobab trees with their roots seemingly growing in the air, to get to the waterholes. There was nothing on television that could compare with the real thing. And all the while it was deceptively safe. Roger had had a close call when he went to film some impala at the edge of a water hole. Fortunately he'd seen the crocodile basking in the shallows before he reached the danger point.

"You've been sitting quietly for a while," said Roger, to his daughter as they drove on.

"I've been thinking we live in a really wonderful world," she replied. "Civilisation has given us a lot but it's taken a lot as well. I was just thinking how important the waterhole is to all life."

"That's one for civilisation. I wouldn't fancy walking to Loch Arden for a drink of water," said Roger, reminding Marjorie how the reservoir was thirty miles from their home.

"We're looking on an area of the hunter and the hunted," said Marjorie. "This place might look safer than Argyle Street on a Saturday night, Charlene, but it isn't."

"When are we going to see lions?" said Roger disappointedly. "We've seen elephants, Cape buffalo and giraffe, but no lions."

"I've been here many times and only seen lions once - and then by accident. I'd left the safety of the car to investigate what I thought was a partly eaten animal carcass ..."

"So your lion was a dead one then," said Charlene.

"Most certainly not. It had been a Cape buffalo."

"So you saw the kill. Where were the lions?" asked her father.

"The pride was about twenty yards away from me. They could hardly be seen against the foliage. There were six lionesses in all. They couldn't have cared less for me. With full bellies, lions become extremely lazy," she explained. "But I didn't know that at the time. I must have run the fastest twenty yards ever."

Marjorie had arranged to spend two days at each seven lodges in Wangie and other National Parks. At the end of the fortnight she had done a mini tour of Zimbabwe exhausting both herself and her guests. Naturally enough by the time she arrived home she had had enough of visitors to last her for a while. Roger could see that his daughter had become irritable, easily finding anger for the slightest slip on his part. Later that evening, after they had returned from the safari, Roger suggested to Charlene that should try and book a holiday in Malawi. Charlene thought that was a wise plan.

# Chapter 15

Several days had elapsed since Marjorie, Roger and Charlene had returned from their safari to the Wangie National Park.

"What's the matter, my dear?" Roger asked his daughter, one evening when she was in a particularly sulky and irritated mood.

"Can't you do anything for yourselves?" came the answer.

"You have to remember we don't know our way around," he replied.

"I am used to getting some time to myself during the day, but now."

"You can't blame us for using your knowledge and experience while we're here," he said gently trying to ease the situation

"But now that you've returned to Harare, you wait for me to make the decisions." Clearly Marjorie was finding it difficult to cope with two more people in her life

"I brought my driving licence with me hoping to drive around Harare a bit on our own. But five hundred pounds a week for car hire is a bit steep." Roger hoped she would see they were in a trap just as much as she was.

"It hasn't been costing you anything to live here. Don't you think you could've spent that to give me a week off?" Marjorie said angrily. "I'm getting browned off by it all. You seem to have forgotten that it's you and not me who's on holiday. Don't you think you should do something by yourselves?"

"If Mrs Graham had been alive, we wouldn't be here," he reminded her. "We had very little time to prepare. That means we don't know where to go."

"Why don't you find out then, Dad? You aren't a child any longer. Why can't you go off and do something which doesn't involve me?"

"Then that's what I'll do," he replied crossly and left the room by the French window, not telling her he had already been in touch with a travel agent.

Charlene, who had heard the raised voices, met him as he came into the garden. "Charlene we've got to talk," he said taking her arm and walking over to a large jacaranda tree. "You know what they say about fish?"

She shook her head.

"It goes off after you keep it for a few days. I think that's what's happened here. Marjorie's obviously under a great strain. Might be a marital problem she doesn't want to discuss. But whatever it is we've got to get away for a few days."

He paused for a moment. "And there's another thing."

"What's that dear?"

"Absence makes the heart grow fonder."

"We should have noticed a rift was developing. I suppose we should take part of the blame," she said.

"It's fortunate, I've already phoned the travel agents about a five-day trip to the famous hotel at Victoria Falls. They've two cancellations for tomorrow. I was about to ask Marjorie if this would fit in with her plans, when she blew up. The woman at the travel agency said she'd hold the places while I talked it over with my daughter. Now that's done, I'll phone and confirm the booking."

"I'm in your hands, Roger. I hope five days away will be enough to clear the air again."

Charlene had taken some of their clothes from the cupboard and had laid them on the bed ready for packing when Roger reappeared. "I've confirmed our trip to Victoria Falls."

"When we've done the packing, we'll finish off the salad we left at lunchtime and get to our beds. We want to be fresh for tomorrow," said Charlene feeling more than a little tired.

"It's late and Marjorie hasn't returned yet," said Charlene. "We'll have to wait till tomorrow to let her know our plans."

"She's a big girl now. She knows what she's doing. Let's leave it up to her and get that rest we need."

Next day the alarm clock failed to ring. "Look at the time, Roger! When does the plane takes off?" Charlene was worried. If they missed their flight there would be no refund.

They dressed quickly in casual clothes and went downstairs intending to tell Marjorie what they had planned.

Unfortunately she had already left for an appointment with her dentist. She'd be away for at least an hour her note said.

"That means she won't be back before we leave," said Roger. "Charlene dear, phone for a taxi, while I write a note for Marjorie."

When they arrived at Harare airport they picked up their tickets at the desk and went straight through to the plane. "That's the queue going through the gate. We can make it if we put on a spurt," said Roger, encouraging Charlene by taking her arm.

"I'm so sorry Roger. I just don't seem to have the energy. My indigestion seems to be getting worse. Maybe if you hurry on ahead, they'll hold up the plane for me."

"I had hoped your health would improve on this holiday." He let go her arm and rushed over to join the queue. "Come on lass, you can make it," he called reassuringly.

When Charlene eventually joined him, she cheered him up. "We've made it, we've made it at last." She was pleased with her efforts, despite the discomfort she had been suffering. They were still short of breath when they went out on to the tarmac to board the plane.

"Can you hear something?" said Charlene, whose hearing was much keener than Roger's.

"They've started the engines. That's a good sign," he said flippantly.

"No, not the engines," she insisted. "I can hear someone shouting my name."

She turned round and looked towards the gate. It was Marjorie. She was waving and shouting to attract their attention. "She's telling us to have a nice trip. So everything must be fine again," said Charlene, smiling happily.

"I can hear her myself now," said Roger. "That's nice. She says she'll see us when we get back. Well, now we know we can go back."

They waved towards Marjorie until they had boarded the plane and disappeared inside. The doors were made fast as the pilot turned his aircraft towards the runway and accelerated the engines.

The time passed quickly as they thrilled to the wonderful scenery below them. They were able to recognise the safari park where they had been staying with Marjorie and very soon the outstanding cataracts of the Victoria Falls. "We're getting a bonus," said Roger, as they flew over the famous Falls. "But it's not as good as the small five-seater they use for The Flight of Angels trip."

There were few formalities as they went through Victoria Falls airport to the front entrance to look for a taxi.

"My friend," said a porter indicating a man beside a taxi. "He will take you on a tour of Victoria Falls before you go to the hotel."

"Are you feeling up to it?" Roger asked Charlene.

"I'd like to see the giant baobab tree. We might not get another chance," she replied gamely.

They tipped the porter, perhaps too generously, for his help, and agreed to go with his taxi friend. "I show you the Zambezi," the driver said at once and drove out towards the game park. He must have had some arrangement with the warden for he waved to the man on duty and used the private road, which ran, close to the great river.

"Isn't that a wonderful sight," exclaimed Roger, getting out of the car. "I've wanted to see the Zambezi ever since I was a small child. It was the missionary people showing their slides that did it. But it's all been worth while."

The taxi driver pointed to the river. "David Livingstone," he said.

"Yes," replied Roger. He did not wish to correct the man. "Dr Livingstone saw them from the other side," he explained to Charlene.

"We go now Zambezi Bridge. You get in please," said the driver politely. Roger had used up his time watching the river. They came to the magnificent bridge, which spanned the steep gorge and found themselves parked near it. "You walk to the centre and come back please."

"I don't think he wants us to waste any time. It's there and back," said Roger.

"There's a crowd of people looking over the bridge," said Charlene. "Let's find out what's happening."

On arrival they saw a young man standing on a girder with a rope tied to his legs.

"He's going to jump," exclaimed Charlene in alarm. "He's bound to be killed!"

"He's bungee jumping, Charlene. It's perfectly safe, much safer than white water rafting. So far no one's been killed jumping from the bridge."

Suddenly the crowd started counting down to zero. "Five, four, three, two, bungee."

On hearing the last word, the young man shouted in unison with the watchers as he plunged towards the river.

"He's still alive," Roger pointed out.

Charlene had covered her eyes. She just could not bear to watch.

"He's trying to catch a rope," Roger informed her. "Then it's into the boat and down the gorge to safety."

"Would you do that, Roger?" Charlene asked, innocently, when she had opened her eyes again.

"Most certainly not. It helps if you're insane - and of course I'm not. There isn't enough money you could pay me to do it. And to think the jumpers pay for the so-called pleasure."

"That's the driver shouting for us to come back," said Charlene, shaking Roger's arm.

"Not much time left." The driver cautioned his passengers. "Only enough for tree and hotel."

The tree was every bit as large as one would expect a tree to be that was at least a thousand years old. "Let's have a picture of ourselves taken beside it," said Roger and offered his camera to the driver.

"No. No. Not much time." The driver shook his head.

"Not even for a good tip?" Roger opened his wallet.

"Quickly, then please." The driver waved them over to the tree.

"We need you to take picture," said Roger pointing to his camera.

Reluctantly the driver pointed the camera as Roger and Charlene put their arms around one another and stood in front of the baobab tree. When they eventually arrived at the Victoria Falls Hotel it was beginning to get dark.

"Good evening sir," said the rotund head porter, wearing a deep red jacket and a top hat. He snapped his fingers and two porters came over to deal with their luggage. "If you will go to reception and book in, the porters will take your baggage." His voice was deep and reminded Roger of the black American singer, Paul Robeson. He was also fascinated by the head porter's waistcoat.

It must have been as heavy as chain mail, for it was covered all over with tiny badges. He looked more closely and saw they were from every part of the world. The man obviously realised that his hobby of collecting badges from foreign guests made him the centre of attention.

"Have you one from Scotland?" Roger asked him.

"Yes sir," he responded at once. "This one here's from Edinburgh." He proudly pointed at it so that Roger could verify the name.

Roger booked in at Reception, carrying their personal belongings, while Charlene looked at the windows of the nearby souvenir shops.

"We've time for a wash and a bit of a rest before dinner," said Roger as they followed the two porters carrying their luggage, upstairs to a room at the end of a long passage on the first floor.

The Buchanans were walking to the hotel reception when they saw the sign pointing to the outdoor buffet. "I'd like to go there, to the barbecue," said Charlene.

"You never know, we might meet someone interesting to talk to," said Roger.

Charlene looked at her husband in mock indignation. "Aren't I interesting to talk to?"

"Of course you are, dear," he apologised. "It was lovely being with you. It gave me another chance to admire you in that cream dress. I've always liked you in it so much. But then there aren't many women with your stunning figure. You could wear anything and make it look like "a million dollars"."

"Are you sure you weren't born in Ireland with that sweet tongue of yours and all that blarney?"

"I really mean it." Charlene smiled at Roger's remark in that happy way, which made the recipient, in this case Roger, feel so comfortable.

"You're just teasing me," he said. "You like it when I tell you how pretty you are. Don't you?"

She smiled. It was her way of agreeing with him when she would have thought saying "yes" to be conceited.

"I think we should go straight through to the back lawn," he suggested, offering her his arm as they made their way to the outdoor buffet.

"I can't get used to it being dark at seven o'clock," said Charlene. "But tonight is different, somehow, with the subdued lighting. It's just as if we were on our honeymoon once again. Imagine what it would have been like if we'd been able to afford to come here to Victoria Falls then."

"We're being very romantic tonight," he said. "Maybe the candlelit tables have something to do with it."

"Oh look! Roger," she exclaimed with obvious delight. "There's a chef cooking the meat on an open fire."

Roger looked around for a suitable table, but was unable to decide which to choose. Either the table had no candle or it was in some inconvenient place. Then he spotted a table, which met all his criteria. Two diners already occupied two of its four places.

"How about that one over there?" He drew Charlene's attention to the tree-sheltered table where a couple of about their own age were sitting already.

"I don't mind, if you don't," she replied. "It means we'll have company tonight. I think we should take a chance. At least we're the same generation."

The couple looked up and smiled, as Roger and Charlene approached them. "Why don't you join us?" said the man indicating the two empty places. "We'd very much like your company, if you don't mind ours." He spoke with an Afrikaans accent.

"Thank you. We'd love to join you," replied Roger. "It was so quiet last night. You could hear people at the far end of the dining room taking their soup."

He helped Charlene to her chair and then sat down opposite her. "I like to admire the view," he said grinning at Charlene.

"Philip, why don't you say nice things like that to me any more?" said his wife.

"We've been married too long. I would imagine these two have only been married a few years. They're still full of the delights for each other. By the way, I'm Philip and this is my wife Patricia."

"I'm Roger and this is Charlene."

Roger enquired when the waiter would come to attend to them.

"It's self-service here," said Philip. "The waiter will bring your cutlery, serve wine and take the dirty dishes away. We always eat in the buffet. You meet such nice people."

"I couldn't agree with you more," grinned Roger. "Have you flown over the Falls yet? We went up today. It was out of this world."

Philip and his wife had done so on other occasions and agreed that it was a thrilling experience. "Did you get a fright at the down draught when you went over the Devil's Fall?"

Roger admitted that part of the flight had scared him a little, since he had been concentrating on taking photographs and was unprepared for the sudden downward drop.

"Livingstone described the Falls as being like a flight of angels. Did you live near his home in Scotland?"

Roger had not only lived near David Livingstone's former home but he could lay claim to a distant relationship with the famous explorer. "I used to," he said briefly, knowing that Charlene had become bored with his frequent telling of his family history, especially his connection with the Livingstones.

"Have you been to see the giant baobab tree yet?" enquired Patricia.

"Yes we have. They say it's well over a thousand years old," said Roger. "It gives me a thrill to think it might have been here when Livingstone was around."

Charlene and Roger went to collect their main courses, and then concentrated on eating. When they had finished they looked at the sweet table. Charlene's eyes lit up.

"I've been waiting all evening to have a go at that." Charlene behaved like a child at a birthday party. "I simply must try everything."

There were at least fifty different tempting items on the table.

"I've had so much to eat already, I don't think I'm going to manage much more," said Roger. He took one small plate and asked the server for a small portion of each of three sweets he wanted to try. "That'll do me," he said and went back to the table.

Charlene always regarded other people's cooking as a challenge to her powers of observation. She wanted to know what was in it and was interested in how well the cook had succeeded or failed, to blend the ingredients together.

"I'm looking forward to this," she confided to the server as she walked back to the table with a very large plate; having selected seven sweets.

"Charlene!" Roger was appalled when he saw how much she had taken. "You'll be lucky if you can wear anything from your wardrobe after that."

She dug her spoon into a fruit and cream flan and was about to lift it to her mouth, when she called out. She dropped the spoon on her lap. "Oh my God! There's that pain again."

Roger went to her side and put his arm about her. "You shouldn't have been so greedy," he jested, trying to make light of her discomfort. "When you've had a lie down things should be all right."

The other couple looked on in embarrassment. "Is there anything we can do?" Philip asked.

"You never mentioned feeling this kind of pain before," said Roger. "Is it much worse than the discomfort you've talked about so often?"

"I'm afraid I pretended to myself that it wasn't bad." Charlene rubbed her abdomen. "I didn't want to upset anyone. In any case, I don't want to see a doctor for what is probably indigestion once again."

Charlene already had a disagreement with Marjorie when she suggested the houseboy's cooking had upset her stomach.

"Is it as bad as before?" asked Roger.

"No. It's very much worse. In fact I am feeling nauseated by everything." She pushed the plate disdainfully away from her and attempted to stand up.

Roger was still holding her when her legs suddenly gave way.

"I'm holding you," he said anxiously, his strong arms preventing her falling heavily to the ground."

"I think we should take Charlene to the hospital," suggested Philip. "It has the best possible facilities. Your wife might have developed appendicitis. If that's so, she'll need urgent surgery."

"Would you phone a taxi for me Philip?" Roger asked.

"I'll do better than that. My car's at the front of the hotel.

I'll drive there you myself. Patricia's a nurse. She'll be able to give some advice."

"I'm Jamie Kyle from Scotland," said the young doctor introducing himself. "Your wife's been telling me she's been having treatment for indigestion." He examined the tablets from her bag. "Does she normally eat a lot at meal times? From what I heard I'd say she's needing to rest her stomach for a while."

"Have you managed to deal with the pain?" asked Roger.

"Yes. I used an old remedy. Peppermint and warm water. We can deal with the pain. What's more difficult is to find out what's causing it. And in your wife's case it would appear her digestive system needs further examination. She can stay with us overnight while we carry out tests. It's likely you'll be able to continue with your stay in Victoria Falls the day after tomorrow."

Roger left the hospital with Philip and Patricia.

"You can count on our help any time you need it," said Philip. "We're in room 214, if you want to contact us."

By the time Roger had returned to his room, the bedspread had been pulled down. There's nothing lonelier than a double bed with only one person to occupy it, he thought. It was the first time he'd been separated from Charlene since their marriage. He was going to be very lonely.

Why hadn't Charlene told him she had been feeling unwell since they arrived? He saw a small white box on the pillow with the name of the hotel on it. It was a chocolate to wish them goodnight.

The ringing of the telephone abruptly ended his fragile sleep. He wondered who it was? Could it be Marjorie phoning to apologise for her behaviour? What the hell! He thought, looking at his watch, it's just after four in the morning.

Roger picked up the phone. "Yes!" he said gruffly.

"This is the desk at Victoria Falls hospital. Am I speaking to Mr Buchanan," said a woman's voice at the other end of the line.

"Yes."

"Is it possible for you to come right away and see Dr Henderson Kambe? He has examined your wife and would like to speak with you before he goes off duty in an hour's time. I'm sorry to ask you to come so early. The doctor will be away for a few days and felt he ought to have a word with you before he left."

"Tell Dr Kambe I'll be there as quickly as I can," replied Roger. "Thank him for letting me know."

The doctor had been trained in the medical school at Glasgow University, before returning to practice in Zimbabwe. He divided his time between the rich and the poor, the rich patients financing his work in the poorer tribal lands.

"I have to leave in less than an hour," he explained. "I wanted to tell you my diagnosis before I left."

It must be serious if the doctor had to tell him now, thought Roger. Doctor Kambe went into great detail about his examination of Charlene and his discussion with her on the nature of her illness.

"I would like your wife to have a scan to confirm what I already suspect. She tells me you're insured, so you don't need to worry about the cost."

"The money wouldn't enter into it, doctor. If my wife needs anything to help her get well then you can consider the cost will be met."

"From what your wife told me of the nature of the discomfort she's having and that tiny discharge of blood she experienced about a year ago, after she had reached the menopause, I am led to believe that your wife may have an ovarian tumour."

"But she never seemed to be in very great pain."

"That's the trouble with ovarian tumours. By the time the patient has significant symptoms, it is often too late for us to treat it." The doctor seemed to be offering no great hope for Charlene's recovery. "We call it the silent cancer for that reason."

Roger was unable to say anything. The news had been a complete surprise to him.

"You can't be completely sure of your diagnosis if you're asking for a scan," Roger said hopefully.

"Unfortunately, it's something I come across every day among my own people and I have come to recognise it. However, it's better for you to keep an open mind until the scan is done. Do I have your permission to make the arrangements?"

"Of course. I suppose you'll have asked my wife."

"Your wife is under sedation Mr Buchanan. We would like to set up the scan right away."

An attractive coloured nurse joined him.

"I'll leave you now with sister. She'll take over from here. You'll probably have to be prepared to spend most of the day waiting around before the consultant will commit himself to an opinion," said Dr Kambe, gathering his notes together.

"Thank you very much for taking the time to see me when you're so busy," Roger, said gratefully shaking the doctor's hand. "I hope you don't mind my asking, why are you called Henderson?"

"I'm often asked this question." He smiled. "Some people are rude enough to suggest one of my parents was Scottish. I'm named after a Scottish missionary whose name was Henderson. It has been given to the eldest son since the time of my great grandfather, who was befriended by the missionary."

"What a very interesting thing," said Roger. "I'm related to David Livingstone, myself."

"That's very interesting. I wish I wasn't in such a hurry. I'd like to hear about it." The truth was that so many people claimed, without foundation, to have a relationship with the missionary that it was an almost daily occurrence for someone to claim kinship.

\* \* \* \* \*

Roger found a comfortable chair in the waiting room and slept fitfully until a nurse awakened him. She showed him the canteen and the men's room. "By the time you've had a wash and something to eat, your wife will be ready to see you."

Charlene was sitting up when Roger arrived in the ward, her pink cheeks belying the serious nature of her illness.

"It looks as though the night's rest has helped," said Roger, hoping to hear some good news.

"The scan showed a large growth," she said at once.

Roger went forward immediately and, taking her in his arms hid his face in her hair.

"Was the consultant certain?" he asked, trying not to show his distress.

Charlene lifted his head from her shoulder. "We can't behave like the ostrich, Roger. We must accept what's happened to me." She wiped a tear from his eye.

"I have to be brave and fight it as I would any other illness. With God's help and your support we can win the battle."

This was very encouraging for Roger, who could not imagine life without his perfect companion.

"The consultant told me many new drugs were coming on the market and one of these might be successful. Let's give hope a chance. But if there's a possibility I might die soon, I'd like to go back to Scotland."

Roger felt helpless. He could look after her but the thing he'd like to do most of all was not in his power.

"I have to take the view that a dangerous road lies ahead of me. I'll arrange with my GP for another consultation when we get back to Glasgow. Would you telephone my sister and let her know the position? And I suppose you'll also let your daughter know."

Roger waited impatiently for his daughter to answer the phone and, just when he thought he'd have to leave without informing her, Marjorie answered the phone.

"When are you coming back?" she said, thinking her father had phoned for this purpose.

"That's not the reason. I have to tell you Charlene's indigestion is probably cancer."

Marjorie gasped. "Oh my God! Where's she just now?"

"In the hospital at Victoria Falls."

"That's one our finest hospitals. Charlene's sure of the best treatment. I'll try and get a flight right away."

"Charlene doesn't want to die in Africa. So we're leaving tonight," said her father. "I'll give you another call when I have more news."

"Tell Charlene I love her and I'll be praying for her recovery."

"Marjorie I wish things hadn't been so acrimonious on our last day with you ... " he stopped. "But this isn't the time to talk about our problems."

"Mr Buchanan," interrupted the nurse, "doctor wishes to speak to you."

"Someone's calling. I'll have to go. Bye."

"Goodbye, Dad. I'll keep in touch."

On their way to the airport, the ambulance stopped to pick up their luggage.

"I told Marjorie and she's devastated. I'll write to her when I get home."

"And did you manage to get through to my sister?"

"It was easier to phone Shirley in Glasgow than it was to get in touch with my daughter in Harare. Shirley said she would meet us at the airport. I told her you were ill but didn't say what had been discovered."

"I'm glad you kept that part to yourself. She's such a worrier. I'd have no peace."

\* \* \* \* \*

Charlene, who was feeling better than she had done for a while, was looking out for her sister in the crowd waiting at the barrier.

"There she is!" Roger pointed towards the back of the crowd.

The two girls embraced, as though they were seeing each other after years of separation, instead of just a few weeks.

"I don't know why Roger was trying to frighten me with talk of your being ill and having to come home early. You look so well," said Shirley. "However, I asked Peter to make up more of that mixture for you," She produced a half litre bottle from her basket. "This will get rid of that discomfort you've had for so long. He says he'll guarantee it won't return this time."

"When you see him, thank him from me. He's been very thoughtful and considerate." She turned her head away to hide her feelings as she and Roger followed Shirley to her car.

# Chapter 16

It was too late when they arrived home from the airport for Charlene to visit her own doctor. But, soon after they had gone to bed she started to complain that she was in pain again.

"I'm going to phone the emergency service," said Roger when he saw his wife in obvious discomfort.

"Please don't bring the doctor out at this time of night," she said, as she began to have second thoughts about Dr Kambe's diagnosis. "I'd like to try some of Peter's indigestion remedy. Would you please get it for me Roger?"

She swallowed two large spoonfuls. "That's better," she said.

Roger decided to let her have her own way until morning and see if things had improved by then. He had intended to keep an eye on his wife during the night but was so tired from their flight that he fell asleep.

"How are things now?" he asked when he woke without detecting any sign of improvement.

"I didn't get very much sleep last night. Maybe Henderson Kambe was right."

"I'm going to phone the surgery," he insisted.

"I don't want to be a nuisance, but if you feel I should, I'd rather do the phoning myself."

"Will it do tomorrow?" the receptionist asked, trying to ensure that only urgent calls were passed on to the doctor.

"Yes, I think so," replied Charlene.

"Then I'll get the doctor to call tomorrow morning, Mrs Buchanan." When Charlene had put the phone down, she tried to rise from the bed and get on with her daily chores.

"I think I'll lie in a bit yet." She put her hand on her brow to feel her temperature as she felt a dizzy spell coming on.

"What time can we expect the doctor?" Roger asked.

"Tomorrow morning," said Charlene. "I don't want to call him out, if there's nothing really wrong with me."

Roger did not often get angry with his wife but there were times when her lack of self-interest made him furious.

"How stupid can you get?" he said passionately. "You need an examination now. I'm going to get this matter settled once and for all."

He dialled the doctor's surgery. "I'm sorry Charlene, this is out of your hands. I'm dealing with the problem from now on."

"Can I help you?" said the quiet voice of the receptionist.

"Yes! You damn well can!" said Roger furiously. "My wife, Charlene Buchanan, phoned just now for a house call and you've convinced her to wait until tomorrow. I think she's very ill and needing hospital attention. I want her to have a visit at the earliest opportunity."

The startled receptionist apologised and explained that his wife had agreed the call was not an urgent one. "The doctor is in with a patient just now. I'll have him call on your wife when he's through."

"Mrs Buchanan," said Dr Preston reassuringly. "For the moment we've only the opinion of an African doctor that you're suffering from cancer. This letter you brought back with you merely indicates the possibility and suggests further scanning. I think we should wait until the specialist at the Central General sees you before we start becoming despondent. Even if you do have cancer, we have lots of weapons in our armoury and a lot of success."

Charlene smiled for the first time that morning. "I've had it a long time as you know. But it's been worse lately."

The doctor felt her abdomen. "I still can't find anything unusual. We'll get you into the Central General right away. They'll arrange for another scan. Can I use your phone? I want to call the surgeon on duty and inform the ambulance service to pick you up. Meanwhile your husband can pack a few things for you."

The ambulance service was busy with emergencies and would not be available for two hours. "I'm afraid that's all I can do for you just now," said Dr Preston. "If you need my help just tell the receptionist to pass on your message."

When Roger was seeing the doctor out, the Reverend Anthony Drinkwater was standing on the doorstep.

"Good morning, minister," said Roger. "Please come in. Charlene's in the back bedroom."

The minister had only been appointed to the parish a few years ago, but already he was very well liked by his parishioners. They were pleased with the spiritual nature of his sermons and the readiness with which he visited those parishioners who were in difficulties.

He was standing beside the bed, praying for Charlene's recovery when Roger returned to the bedroom.

"You're the second of my parishioners to be afflicted," he said when he had finished his prayer. "She seems to be responding to treatment and to my prayers on her behalf."

"I hope they're equally effective in my wife's case," said Roger.

"We pray to ask for God's intercession. It's not for us to demand His help."

"Thank you for coming so quickly," said Charlene. "When I'm feeling better, you and your wife will have to come and hear about our holiday. It was absolutely wonderful."

"You both seem to have enjoyed the visit to your daughter," said the minister. "If you'll excuse me now I've some other people to visit."

Roger saw Mr Drinkwater to the door and said goodbye. "I'll be visiting Charlene in the hospital later today. She'll probably be able to tell me more then," he said, as he saw the minister out.

"I feel so much happier now that the minister has been. May I have a cup of tea, Roger? I'll probably be asked to drink lots of water - that is, if I'm given another scan."

"I'll see to the tea, right away, dear. Would you like a biscuit with it?"

"No, thank you."

"I'm wondering if I should get in touch with Shirley. After all, she hasn't been told of Dr Kambe's diagnosis," said Charlene.

"Once we have confirmation from the Central General, I'll contact her if you like?" said Roger.

"I think I'll phone from the hospital myself," said Charlene, remembering her husband's short temper.

The doorbell rang once again.

"Ambulance," said the taller of the two men who had just arrived. "We've called for Mrs Buchanan."

"I didn't expect you for two hours," said Roger. "Thank heaven you've come so quickly."

The two men assisted Charlene onto the stretcher and covered her with a blanket before taking her outside to the ambulance. "Are you coming in your car, Sir?" enquired the senior ambulance man.

Roger shook his head. "I want to be with my wife if you don't mind. I can always get a taxi back home."

"Mrs Buchanan is ready to see you now," said Sister Bell to Roger, who had been waiting patiently in the adjoining corridor. "You can stay a few minutes and then she'll be undergoing a series of tests. If you leave visiting till the evening, you'll have longer with her, and we'll be able to tell you more about her illness."

Charlene was sitting up in bed in a small section of the ward, which catered for cancer patients. Alongside her were three other women, two of whom were asleep.

"This is Maisie Conroy," said Charlene, pointing to a younger woman in the bed next to her. "She's been in and out of here so often, they keep the same bed ready for her!"

"Pleased to meet you, Maisie. I'm Roger Buchanan. How're you feeling?"

"Not very well. I've just had a rib replaced with bone from somewhere else. They say it's my only chance. By the way you haven't said why you're in here?" she said turning Charlene.

"They're not sure yet. But I've had a scan which is supposed to show a tumour in my right ovary."

"That's nasty. I hope they've found it in time. I'll read my magazine and let you two talk."

Roger had only begun his conversation with Charlene when Sister Bell came over and said the doctors were on their way.

"I'll come and see you tonight, Charlene. Is there anything you want?" She needed toothbrush, toothpaste and dental floss as well as a cake of pure soap.

"I'll attend to that. And I'll bring anything else I think you may need." He kissed her goodbye and shouted "Cheerio" to Maisie Conroy.

Shirley was waiting when he came out of the lift.

"You didn't tell me my sister had been taken to hospital," she said crossly. "I had to find out from your neighbour. They saw the ambulance leave and I guessed she'd been taken here."

"There wasn't time to phone you. It was an emergency situation," said Roger. "You'll need to be quick if you want a word with her. She's just about to be examined by the doctors."

"We'll discuss this later, Roger," she said as if not satisfied with his explanation.

Next day Roger had a call from the hospital asking him to come and discuss Charlene's condition with Dr Stevenson. The doctor had found a massive tumour in her right ovary and there were other complications. She was going to need a lot of surgery. The specialist went on with full details.

Roger was shattered. Although he had feared the worst, he had been desperately hoping for a more favourable prognosis.

"When she recovers from the surgery we'll give her a course of chemotherapy. Hopefully this treatment will help her recovery. We'll be carrying out the operation later today."

Roger thanked him and returned home, buying a fish supper on the way. He went into the kitchen, made a pot of tea, buttered himself a slice of bread and smothered his chips in tomato sauce.

He was hoping to eat his meal before someone phoned him or called at the door; but his luck was out. "I'm doing a wee job in the district and thought you might want me to straighten up your squint slabs," said a well-built young man with an Irish accent.

"There's nothing wrong with my slabs," retorted Roger angrily. "That's the way they're supposed to be."

"Sorry guv'nor. I didn't mean any harm. Would you like your red chips replaced?" he said with a charming smile, as he walked back down the path.

It was only when Roger went to wash his greasy fingers that he saw the red ring of tomato sauce round his mouth, making him look like an alcoholic nymphomaniac, whose lipstick had been dragged round her lips by an unsteady hand.

Several times throughout the evening he rang the hospital to enquire about Charlene's condition and was told she was still in the operating theatre. "That's coming up to five hours," he conjectured. "I wonder what they've been doing all that time." He would have been even more worried had he known that a second surgical team had been brought in to assist with part of the operation.

It was nearly nine o'clock and still there had been no news of Charlene's condition. He decided to make a last phone call to the hospital.

"How is Mrs Buchanan?" he asked the night nurse.

He could hear a muffled discussion going on with someone else.

"Mr Buchanan, I'm going to put you through to intensive care. Dr Currie would like to have a word with you. Can you hold on a minute please?"

Dr Robert Currie came to the phone. "I'm looking after Mrs Buchanan, here in the intensive care ward. Your wife has had a very big operation and we decided to give her some special care."

"In that case there doesn't seem to be any point in my coming in," said Roger.

"On the contrary, the reason I asked to speak to you is that I would like you to come and see your wife tonight. I have something I'd like to say to you."

"I'll be there in half an hour," said Roger sensing an emergency.

Charlene lay on top of a high bed surrounded by all the gadgetry of modern medicine and with an oxygen mask.

One of the nurses handed him a plastic apron and a mask. "Put these on," she told him, " ... and wash your hands. We like to keep everything as sterile as possible in this ward."

The nurse told Dr Currie, who had been attending to a patient at the far end, of Roger's arrival. He came up and introduced himself. "I presume you're Mr Buchanan? My name is Robert Currie. I'll be looking after Mrs Buchanan until she's moved into one of the individual rooms. I wanted you to come in and see me because I won't be on duty tomorrow when you'll probably be visiting. We had to do major surgery on your wife."

"I suspected that much," said Roger.

"She's very comfortable now, a bit drowsy from the drugs, but she can speak to you." He took Roger over to Charlene's bed.

Roger had never seen Charlene looking so radiant. It was as if she were smiling all over. Her eyes sparkled in the single light above her head. He leaned over and kissed her firmly on the forehead. "How are you feeling dear?" he asked inanely.

Charlene mumbled something behind the plastic mask. But it didn't matter that her reply was unheard. He could see for himself that she was getting the best attention possible. She was obviously not in pain and plainly was in a happy frame of mind. Since conversation was impossible he simply held her hand and looked into her eyes, until it was time to go.

"I'll come and see you again tomorrow," he promised and kissed her hand before replacing it under the cover.

He kept looking back and waving to Charlene, as he walked along the passage, which connected the intensive care unit with the small waiting rooms.

Roger phoned the hospital next morning and was told that Charlene was out of intensive care. She had taken some milk for breakfast and was sitting up." Roger would be able to visit her. The nurse explained, "We have two visiting periods in this hospital, between three and four and seven till eight." He thanked the nurse and then went into the kitchen to make his own breakfast.

"Toothbrush, toothpaste, dental floss and pure soap," Roger intoned to himself as he put them in the holdall. Their next door neighbour had given him some magazines. I'll take these in and she can make her choice, he thought. And I know those so-called energy drinks do not impress her, but I think, I'll take her a bottle of lemonade and a packet of Rich Tea biscuits. That'll give her something to nibble and drink if she doesn't feel like eating the hospital food, he thought. And finally he cut a small bunch of flowers from the garden.

As usual, parking during the day was virtually impossible either in the hospital's car park or on the streets outside. Roger had to park the car some distance away and walk back to the hospital.

Charlene was much more alert than she had been the night before and she was no longer dependent on oxygen.

"This is real luxury," Roger said. "Your own TV and no one else to share your room. You don't even get this at home!"

"I'd much rather have some company. I'm not feeling like reading or watching the tele," Charlene countered.

Then she noticed the small bunch of flowers from the garden. "They're our own flowers, Roger. How nice to see them."

"Nice?" repeated Roger. "I thought that was a forbidden word?"

"All right, good then," said Charlene. "How good it is to see them. When I went in for the operation I wondered if I would see the next day. The problem was that the mass was embedded around the colon and it has not been completely solved yet. Did you have a good night's sleep without me, Roger?"

"Remarkably yes," he replied, taking her hand in his and squeezing it slightly. "Now for that kiss I didn't get last night."

"Last night, Roger? I didn't see you last night."

"I spoke to you in the intensive care unit and told you I would come back today. You had so many tubes connected to you, maybe you were dazed with the morphine drip."

"Yes, maybe that's what it was. Dr Stevenson came to see me today. He's the cancer specialist. He told me about the cancer and what he proposed to do about it. He'll give me a course of chemotherapy when I've recovered from the operation."

"How do you feel just now?" he asked solicitously.

"A lot better than I have for a long time. We're going to think positively in the future Roger. I'm going to do everything I can to beat the cancer."

"And I'm going to do everything I can to help you," he said, once more squeezing her hand.

\* \* \* \* \*

Charlene had spent most of her time in bed since she had come home from the Central General and was now anxious to start doing things for herself again.

"I'm going to get up and sit in the front room for a while," said Charlene when Roger came in to collect her breakfast tray.

He looked at the empty dishes. "I'm pleased to see you've finished your breakfast this morning. That's a good sign. I think it's about time we started some light walking."

Charlene pushed the tray towards him and gathered her pink bathrobe about her. "I want to weigh myself today." She inspected her arms, which were usually quite thin, for some indication that she was absorbing nourishment from what she was eating.

Roger stopped on his way to the door. "I'll put the dishes in the kitchen and light the fire in the sitting room before I come back."

He heard the letter-box clinking, and thought he might as well check the post.

Apart from the usual letters, offering to take your money and return it to you as a fortune, and several Get Well cards, there was an envelope printed Central General Hospital on the back.

"There's a letter from the hospital," he said passing it over to Charlene.

Anxiously, she tore it open and extracted a letter and appointment card. "They want me to start treatment in a month's time."

"I'm glad to hear it," said Roger, who had been preparing her medication, which was to be taken three times a day.

"I know you're not fond of this one." He gave her a small plastic cup with the unpleasant potion filling it.

"I want to be walking into the Central General without any help, when you take me there for my first chemotherapy." She swallowed the thick fluid in one gulp. "I'm going to start walking a little each day until I've recovered from the operation."

Roger pulled the sheets back from the double bed they had shared since their wedding night. "Swing your feet over the edge, dear, and see if you can stand by yourself."

Charlene, who was still in some pain from her operation, winced slightly as she turned her legs sideways. "There you are. How's that for a start?"

"Very good." He gave her a kiss of encouragement. "Now for that one big step for woman," he said, satirising Armstrong's landing on the moon.

Charlene smiled. "I feel just like a child trying to stand on my feet. Now I know how they suffer."

Roger hovered beside her with his hands ready to catch her should she fall, as she walked slowly step by step into the hall.

"I see you've got the scales ready for me." She stumbled slightly and grabbed a hold of his hand. "You're so good to me Roger." She squeezed it as if to confirm her words.

"Careful, dear. The scales are unsteady. Balance yourself on me when you stand on them."

He bent down to get a closer look at the dial itself. "You've put on half a pound since the last time."

"Good!" Charlene was delighted with her progress as she stepped down. "At that rate I should be up to my normal weight by the time I have my first chemotherapy."

He released her hands. "Now let's see how you manage the rest of the way to the front room."

"I think everything's going to be fine from now on," said Charlene positively.

"Is there anything else you'd like just now?"

"It's been some time since I looked at television in the morning. Could you switch it on for me?"

She snuggled down in Roger's green reclining chair as he wrapped a heavy tartan rug about her legs. "How's that?"

"Just perfect," smiled Charlene. "I'm happier now than I've been in a long time."

"I'm so glad to hear that," Roger said going over and switching on the television.

\* \* \* \* \*

The days passed slowly until at last there was just one more day to go before Charlene's appointment at the hospital.

"I phoned Maisie Conroy. She's had to go back in for more treatment," Charlene told him when they had finished their lunch. "I think I'll buy some flowers and take them to her tomorrow."

"Do you think you can walk that far to the florist on your own?" he asked. "I'll come with you if you like."

"It's only about five hundred yards. Surely I can manage that? After all I walked round the pond yesterday."

"My dear, I was thinking about your falling. We don't want any setbacks at this stage, do we?"

He took her coat down from the hook in the hall. "I'll come with you if you like." She shrugged her shoulders.

"I'll be fine by myself." She checked that she had her purse and left. Almost immediately she met Dorothy Dalrymple, who had been in her class at school.

"Charlene! I haven't seen you for some time," she said, as she emerged from her gate. "From your colour I'd say you've been ill."

"Yes I have. I've had a major operation, but everything's fine now."

"I'm glad to hear that. Did you get a letter about the Centenary Committee at our old school?"

"Yes, I did. I believe the Town Council is giving a function to commemorate it." Charlene hoped she would be well enough to attend.

"How about us going together?" Dorothy was excited with thoughts that went back to their schooldays.

"I'll need to think about it." Charlene was aware that she might not be well enough. "I do want to go, but I wouldn't want to disappoint you by not being able to take part." There's no sense in making idle plans, she thought.

"Our infant teacher Louise Harkness has been invited as a guest," Dorothy informed her friend.

"She must be about the oldest surviving teacher from our schooldays," said Charlene.

"She's also holding an informal party for her first infant class at her flat. She taught us when she transferred to the primary school. Let me phone her and tell her you'd like to come." Dorothy remembered their shared childhood, and eagerly wanted Charlene's company.

"I'd like that very much. When is it?"

"Next Saturday afternoon at her home. I'll give you the details after I've phoned her. See you later." She turned in the direction of the florist. "I'm going to buy some seeds ready for the spring."

Charlene raised her eyes in surprise. "That's a coincidence, so am I."

She bought a bunch of mixed flowers for Maisie Conroy, and went over to Dorothy, who was looking at the packets of seed on display. Charlene wanted to buy seeds as well. She might still be alive to see some of them in flower.

"What do you think of this variety?" Dorothy showed her friend a packet of runner beans.

"Canadian Wonder. Hmmm. It's not bad. But you ought to try the one I always grow." Charlene glanced over the display. "Here you are, Scarlet Emperor. You won't buy anything else, after you've eaten it." She handed her friend the packet, took another for herself and quickly selected several of the spring annuals she had sown over the years since her marriage.

"No wonder these plants are doing so well in here," remarked Dorothy. "It's like a hothouse."

"I'm going now. Mind and let me know if I've been invited next Saturday."

"I'll phone you tonight. I'm certain there will be no objection. And, by the way, we can take my car."

Charlene started to walk back home and had just turned the corner into the avenue, when a wave of debilitating tiredness suddenly came over her. "Oh my God!" she murmured. "I hope Roger won't be able to say, "I told you so"."

Fortunately, she had been near the low-lying wall of a neighbour's house when this distressing event took place. She'd sit for a bit, before returning home, and immediately began to worry about being seen in this condition. She hoped Dorothy didn't come round that corner before she left. She could pretend she was fixing her shoe. She removed the left one and examined the inside for an imaginary stone.

Charlene had just begun her subterfuge when Dorothy appeared, carrying a large plastic bag with her garden supplies. She saw Charlene deliberately turn the sole of the shoe upwards and shake it, as though she was dislodging an intruding, irritating particle.

"Having some trouble?" enquired Dorothy, as she came up to her friend.

"Yes," was Charlene's terse reply?

"You can't walk with a stone in your shoe, can you? It's just got to be removed."

Charlene nodded and stood up. "I think I'm all right now." She pressed on her left foot as if she were testing that the remedy had succeeded.

\* \* \* \* \*

Roger, who normally was awake very early in the morning shook Charlene's shoulder very gently. "This is the day."

She mumbled something about wanting to sleep. "It's far too early to get up," she grumbled.

"It's chemo day!" Roger called out. These seemed to be the magic words. Charlene threw the bedclothes off and sat upright. "It's my first day for chemotherapy." Her voice sounded full of hope. "What time is it?"

"It's seven o'clock and I know your appointment is for eleven, but I thought you would want to take things slowly, and you can have a rest before we set out for the hospital."

Charlene rubbed her eyes and stretched her arms above her head. "I'm going to have a shower before breakfast."

Roger knew it would take only half an hour to reach the Central General, but he also knew how difficult it would be to find parking space.

"We'll try and be ready to leave by ten o'clock. "We need some milk and bread. I'll go along to the wee shop and get them while you dress. Will you be all right by yourself?"

"I think so," replied Charlene. "You won't be long anyway."

As they drove up the hill, which led to the hospital, Roger spotted a spare parking place. "I'll let you off at the door and I'll come back when I've parked."

He made a U-turn and dashed back down the hill, only to find someone else manoeuvring into "his" parking space.

"Dammit!" he said to himself and went on up the hill, hoping to find another empty spot. It took two circuits of the hospital grounds before he finally found one.

He dashed back, expecting to find his wife waiting beside the door, but she was not to be seen. Probably she felt tired and went inside to sit down, he thought. After all he'd been away some time. As he approached the big doors, they opened automatically for him. It made one feel like Royalty, he thought. Charlene was waiting for him.

"I'm sorry you had to wait, dear. I had a job finding a place to park."

Charlene smiled. "That's all right, Roger," she said. "This lady helped me into the café. She's just had great news."

The sixty-year-old woman was bubbling all over with joy. "It's clear. The cancer's all cleared up," she cried joyfully.

"Isn't that good news, Roger?" said Charlene. "There's hope for me, after all. Some people can be cured."

Roger was optimistic. His Charlene was going to beat her cancer too.

"Would you like a coffee?"

"Not now Roger. I've just given a blood sample, and I'm waiting to be called by Dr Stevenson."

The elderly lady, whose cancer had been cured, was still beaming deliriously over her wonderful news. "That's my ambulance," she said, when she heard her name being called. She finished what was left of her coffee and said good bye.

"Charlene Buchanan!" called a young coloured nurse obviously at the beginning of her nursing career.

Charlene stood up and walked slowly towards her. "That's me!"

The nurse looked at the documents in her hand, as if by doing so they would provide the verification that the woman who had just replied was the correct person.

"Will you please follow me?" she said, incongruously in a Glasgow accent.

Roger had forgotten to bring a book to read while he was waiting, so he decided to read the notice board opposite. He had only read one or two items, concerning the need to keep appointments, and such things, when Charlene rejoined him.

"They've told me, they're not going to give it to me." She was almost crying.

Roger took her arm, as they went back into the café. "You should have some coffee now." He guided her gently to a seat near the window and bought two coffees.

"Dr Stevenson said my blood count was not high enough. When I suggested he might give me the chemotherapy nevertheless, he was appalled. Do you want me to kill you lass? We can't give it to you this time. Come back in a month's time and we'll try again, he said to me."

Roger was relieved. "Then it's merely a postponement. Meanwhile, you'll get yourself built up ready for him by then."

"My next appointment is for December the twenty-fourth," she replied unhappily. "But that is the same day as Marion's twenty-first birthday party."

"Surely the meal can be served after you've had your chemo?"

"That's the problem. It depends on how long they connect me to the drip. It could be up to six hours, or even much more, and that would almost certainly mean an evening dinner. Shirley might object to that."

"Shirley's not the one with the cancer," Roger retorted testily. "If she can't wait for you, then we had better make other arrangements. But we'll need to know right away."

"Shirley said she'd come to see me next week. I'll ask her then," said Charlene.

"That's the trouble with your sister. The timing must suit her. It doesn't matter if it's inconvenient to us," he complained.

"Could we make a quick visit to the ward and give Maisie the flowers?" Charlene, as usual, ignored the problem by pretending it did not exist, much to Roger's annoyance.

"All right. But just in and out, mind you."

# Chapter 17

Charlene, who had just returned from an appointment with Dr Preston, saw Dorothy Dalrymple coming to the door. Her GP had given her the good news that her blood count had improved, so she would be able to attend the reunion party after all.

"I thought we ought to take something with us even though she asked me not to," said Dorothy. "You can share my present. The card says it's from both of us."

"Only if you let me share the cost with you," insisted Charlene.

"Never mind that just now. You can pay me later."

The retired primary school teacher rented a two bed-roomed flat on the first floor of a red sandstone tenement building. Dorothy pressed the bell push and was surprised to hear the loud chimes of an electric gong.

"Maybe she's a bit hard of hearing." She moved behind Charlene to give the impression that she hadn't pressed the bell.

A buxom, young woman with blonde hair opened the door. "You're the last," she said. "We'll be able to eat now. Miss Harkness wouldn't start till everyone was here."

The door leading into the large front room, where all the guests had assembled, was open, so that the new arrivals could see at a glance who had shown up before them.

"Do you remember me?" said the young woman who had just opened the door.

"It was an unusual name, I can remember that," said Charlene. "Don't tell me."

Dorothy said she was no good at remembering names at all. "I've forgotten," she said casually.

"Hildegarde," said Charlene and searched desperately for the girl's second name. "Hildegarde ... Hildegarde ... I know now, Hildegarde Woodbine," she finished with some elation.

"It's not that now," said the blonde. "I changed it when I married. I'm Hildegarde Smith. However, I remember that rhyme about you. "Dorothy Dalrymple had a pimple on her bum"."

Dorothy blushed. "I hoped that had been forgotten."

Charlene spotted a small elderly lady sitting on the settee with two of her former charges.

"I'd recognise Charlene anywhere," said Miss Harkness, when the two girls approached her. "She hasn't changed a bit." They shook hands and wished each other well.

"I understand you've had an operation," said Miss Harkness. "I hope everything is all right?"

"For the time being," replied Charlene. "I've to have other treatment when I recover from the operation."

After Dorothy had given Miss Harkness the gift, she spotted another of her friends from childhood. "Will you excuse me?" she said and went into the other room for the buffet.

A heavy damask cloth had been laid over a long low table and covered, from one end to the other, with plates of scones, pancakes, cream cakes, plain cakes and cakes with icing, biscuits, oatcakes with cheese and sandwiches catering for every taste - chicken, egg, salmon, lettuce and tomato. Another table was covered with glasses and bottles of whisky, wine and sherry. Dorothy and her friend joined the small queue.

"Has Charlene been ill?" Frieda asked, as she handed a plate to her friend and took one for herself.

"She didn't say ... but I've heard she had a major operation," said Dorothy.

"Do you think it might be ...?" said Frieda, helping herself to a variety of sandwiches.

Dorothy screwed her eyes and looked over to Miss Harkness, who was sitting talking to Charlene. "If anyone knows, she will."

"I can't help noticing the strain you're under Charlene," said Miss Harkness kindly. "I hope you're not feeling unwell. I don't want to cause you any embarrassment, but I'm worried about you."

"I'm all right, Miss Harkness. Really I am." Charlene tried to avoid an explanation for her obvious tiredness.

"You can't fool me Charlene. I had breast cancer twenty years ago. Is this why you're ill?" The worried old lady was dealing with Charlene's problem, as if she were still a five-year-old pupil in her class. "You gave yourself away when you said you were going to have further treatment."

"I'm keeping it private and only telling close friends at the moment," confided Charlene. "I would be grateful if you'd keep it to yourself, for the time being. I've got ovarian cancer and had a major operation, but I'm recovering. My doctor told me this morning that I'm to be given the course of chemotherapy, which was delayed from last month."

"You sound cheerful enough," said Miss Harkness. "I'm not able to offer anything other than prayer. But if you want to talk to someone, I'll always be here to listen."

"That's very kind of you. It's lovely to see you and I'm looking forward to meeting my old classmates again."

"I am too. It's so strange seeing you all again as adults. Look after yourself."

"I'm doing better than that. I'm being looked after by my Roger."

"I missed you Charlene," said Roger when she returned home from the party. "It's very lonely when you're not here."

"Well, I'm back now and I'm feeling thirsty."

"Didn't you get anything to drink at the party?"

"There was plenty to drink, but it was all alcoholic, and I didn't want to complain, since I was the only one who wanted something else."

\* \* \* \* \*

When Charlene returned to the waiting room of the cancer department in the Central General, her husband looked anxiously at her. "What did the consultant say?"

Charlene looked ecstatic. "Dr Stevenson gave me a wonderful Christmas present, I had my chemotherapy after all."

"What did he say about your weight?"

Although Charlene had not recovered her original weight, it was nevertheless improving and had reached a reasonable nine and a half stone. "He said how well I was looking."

"Didn't he say how fat you were getting?" teased her husband.

"Of course not! Gentlemen don't pass remarks of that kind."

"When is your next appointment?"

"Exactly one month from now."

"That's good; you'll be even better when you see him next time. We'll need to get a move, on now if we are to be at Shirley's in time. We should be able to get there for dinner despite, the fact that it's four o'clock."

Shirley lived in a post-war house built at the end of a long lane.

"You'd think she would put some pebbles in these potholes," said Roger, annoyed that his wheels were bumping dangerously in numerous deep cavities. When they arrived at the bungalow it was in complete darkness.

"I hope this doesn't mean what I think it does?" said Roger. He told Charlene to wait in the car whilst he went to investigate. "Is anyone at home?" he shouted, loudly, through the letter-box, since he had failed to receive an answer to his ringing of the doorbell.

He went round to the back of the house to make sure the family was not eating in the kitchen. There were no lights there, either. Obviously they'd gone out for their meal and forgotten to tell Charlene where.

"They're definitely not at home," said Roger when he returned to the car. "We can say goodbye to dinner." Despondently, he started the car and put it into first gear. "Our only hope is that we might see a place to eat on the way home."

Unfortunately they did not see any restaurant where they wanted to eat and since it was Christmas time the choice was between rough cafés and overpriced restaurants. By the time they arrived home Roger and Charlene were not feeling very cheerful.

"It would be very easy for us to feel sorry for ourselves." Charlene's face showed her disappointment.

"But that isn't going to happen. We'll be a little longer in eating, but I'm going to make a gourmet meal for us," said Roger.

"There's no need to go to that trouble. A tin of soup and a pre-packaged meal will be good enough."

"I'm afraid that's what I meant by a gourmet meal." Roger gave his wife a gentle hug. "I was just trying to cheer you up. Meanwhile we'll have a cup of tea to be going on with."

After the meal they tried to settle down and watch television but there was nothing worth watching.

Charlene was about to ask for the Radio Times to look at the programmes, when the telephone rang. "I know who that'll be," she said, rising to answer it.

"What happened to you tonight?" Shirley asked.

"On the contrary, what happened to you? We came straight from the hospital and were at your door with plenty of time to spare."

"Why did you go to my home? The meal was in the Darlington Hotel. I told you to be there for five o'clock."

Charlene was puzzled. She couldn't recall having been told that before. "You did say the meal would be served precisely at five. But you didn't say where."

"Surely you didn't need me to tell you? We've been there ever since father died."

"Well that explains it. A case of bad communication," Charlene concluded.

"You know very well that the fault lies with you Charlene. If you wanted to share a meal with us you should have done your homework. It's not up to me to prepare your script." Shirley was angry with herself, but could not stop herself. Charlene didn't need more problems than she already had. "Besides wanting to know what happened to you, I have been phoning to find out what happened at the hospital."

"I had my chemotherapy today. Dr Stevenson thought I was improving."

"I am glad to hear that." Shirley sounded happier than she had done for some time. "Peter's very busy now. He's on duty next Sunday, but we'll try and see you soon. Next week sometime." Shirley was beginning to calm down. "Bye for now, Charlene."

"Goodbye Shirley," said Charlene and replaced the phone.

"What was that all about?" Roger asked.

"Shirley thought we would know the invitation to the birthday dinner was at the Darlington Hotel." She suddenly changed the subject and opened the Radio Times. "Have we seen the "Sound of Music"?" she asked light-heartedly.

"It's about time for bed anyway. We'll get up early tomorrow and go for a drive to the Kilpatrick Hills." He put his hand to his mouth and yawned.

* * * * *

Charlene ate well, slept well and put on weight as one month followed another. There had been no more postponed treatments, and she had begun to look forward to hearing that her cancer had been arrested on this her sixth treatment.

Dr Stevenson was never too keen to let his patients know exactly what the position was. If there was no hope, he had to leave his patient room for the possibility, and if there was a prospect of success he did not want to arouse false expectations.

"Is this my last treatment?" Charlene hoped Dr Stevenson would say "Yes" and tell her that her cancer was in recession.

"I'm sorry I can't tell you. Your blood count hasn't been making the kind of recovery I'd expect. What I mean is that the chemotherapy with this particular drug hasn't achieved the success I was hoping for."

"Does that mean there's no hope of a cure for me?"

"Not at all, lassie. I've still got a lot of other tricks up my sleeve to try out. I've got a new drug which has been known to be successful with your type of cancer."

"When will I know what further treatment I'm getting?"

"I'll be arranging for one of our specialist nurses to make a weekly call on you to monitor the position. As to further treatment ... we've still to see the result of today's chemotherapy and that will be in a month's time. Your local GP will take the usual blood sample. And, depending on what we find, we'll consider what action to take," he said sounding confident. "Don't worry if you don't hear for a while. I'm going on holiday just about the time your results will come in."

Charlene thanked him for everything he had done. "With God's help we can beat this," she said.

"Let's leave God out of it for the time being. Maybe after I retire I'll look at the role of God. In the meantime, lassie, we've got to put our faith in the drugs and let it go at that."

"I can't agree with you Dr Stevenson," Charlene replied quietly. "The strength of prayer can work miracles. Lots of people are praying on my behalf. If it is God's will ... " She left the sentence unfinished.

"I wish you well lassie. You're a very special person to me. I hope for nothing less than that you will get better. I'll do what I can, but I'm not God."

By the time they reached home, Roger asked why she had been so silent throughout the homeward journey.

"It's not over yet, and I thought I was doing so well." Charlene began to explain what had happened. "I'm now able to drive the car on my own, and I can walk a fair distance, thanks to the programme you helped me to carry out. I'm also worried that you'll have too much of my stuff to clear out, if I fail to get better. I'm going to give the nurse some of my clothes to take to the charity shop when she calls tomorrow."

"If that's what you want. But I would prefer it if you could keep up your positive approach."

"And how are we today, Charlene?" asked Sister Davidson, when she arrived next morning. "Still managing to do all your household chores?"

"My husband let's me do some of them, but he won't let me tire myself out."

The sister had finished bathing Charlene and her leaking wound when she asked the sister if she could take clothes and other things to the hospice charity shop.

"If you want me to, I can hand them in to the hospice, today, when I visit one of my patients," said Sister Davidson.

"I want you to take all those things off my dressing table," said Charlene sweeping a hand in that direction. "You'll find a large plastic bag in the wardrobe. Take the clothes as well."

Sister Davidson cleared the top of the dressing table, which mainly consisted of unused toilet preparations given to Charlene in hospital. Roger came into the bedroom, just in time to see the nurse removing Charlene's wedding dress from the wardrobe.

"What's happening here?" he asked as the sister began to stuff the dress into the bag.

"I'm sending some things to the charity shop." Charlene said. "I won't be using that dress again."

"Even if you aren't using it again, I want it to remain here."

"Put it back please, Sister. My husband wants to live in the past. Let's see if he'll let us get rid of something else."

The sister pulled out a pair of brown corduroy slacks and a blue anorak.

"Definitely not that," exclaimed Roger. "That's what you were wearing that day when we first met on Ben Calder. I don't mind what you do with your other old clothes, but I want these to stay here."

"All right, Sister, let's sort out something else."

The doorbell rang and Roger went to answer it.

The Reverend Drinkwater was making his customary call. "And how is Charlene today?" he enquired, showing some concern.

"Much the same as she was the last time you were here minister."

"Is she still in there?" the minister enquired as he walked towards the bedroom. Sister Davidson, who had stuffed the black plastic bag with as much as it would hold, was coming out of the room just as he was about to enter. They collided, slightly, without injury to each other.

"The patient has a lot of washing this week," teased the minister, as he looked at the oversize plastic bundle.

"No, reverend, this is just today's washing," scoffed the nurse. "I'll see you again tomorrow, Charlene." She left by the door, which Roger was already holding open.

"How are you keeping now?" asked the minister. "You were telling me last time that you would be coming to the end of your six treatments this week."

"I'm still feeling fine. But it seems that the medical people are not satisfied with my blood count."

"Never let us give way to our darker thoughts," the minister said, as he started to pray for Charlene's return to full health.

Just then the doorbell rang again, but this time it was by an impatient hand.

"All right, I'm coming," shouted Roger who been washing up in the kitchen.

"It took you long enough to open the door," said Shirley irritably as she stepped inside followed by her three grown-up children.

"I'm sorry, Shirley. I can't be in two places at the same time," Roger replied. "The minister's with your sister just now. Would you go into the front room and wait for a minute? He doesn't usually stay very long."

Roger could hear Mr Drinkwater saying farewell to Charlene. "That's him going now."

The minister passed through the hall so quickly he reached the door before he noticed Shirley. When he realised his bad manners, he stopped and said sheepishly. "I'm getting absent-minded. Good-day to you all." With that he opened the door and left.

Shirley immediately went into the bedroom. "Why are you in bed? You're looking the picture of health."

"It's makes things easier for the nurse. I was just getting up," said Charlene.

"You look as if you'd like me to take you for a walk. Where will we go?"

"I'd prefer to put out my lobelias," said Charlene.

"Just leave that to me," said Roger lifting a tray of bushy seedlings from the window. "You go ahead dear." He encouraged her. "It will do you good to get some fresh air. But put your coat on, it's not warm enough yet."

"I want you to plant them in the usual places, Roger. If you've any left over put them where you can." She turned to Shirley and her family.

"Come on Auntie," said her niece Marion. "Show us your paces."

Roger wondered, as he planted Charlene's seedlings, if she would survive to see them in flower. He hoped the Good Lord would allow her that at least. If that wretched sister of hers had not called, Charlene would have had the pleasure of doing this for herself.

He looked at the plant collection, and saw the Scarlet Emperor runner beans, which Charlene loved so much. There wasn't much room at the back of the garden though, and it would be late before they were ready for picking. Would she be around to enjoy the crop? He told himself to stop that line of thought.

By the time Roger had finished planting out the seedlings, he could hear voices coming up the garden path. They had returned from their walk and he thought, as he looked at his watch that was far too long for Charlene. She was still not strong enough.

He went down the path to meet them. "I think you may have overdone it," he said. Charlene was looking exhausted.

"Nonsense," said Shirley. "We walked to the pond and round it and back. If we keep this up we'll soon have you climbing Ben Calder again."

Roger was angry but tried not to show it. He had hoped Shirley had not undone the good work of months. He had been increasing the distance of their walks gradually. If they went uphill, he had reduced the distance. Charlene was not ready for the damn silly walk her sister had forced on her.

"We'll need to do that again," said Shirley, slapping her thigh with enthusiasm.

Not bloody likely, thought Roger. You've done enough harm.

"Come on children. Time to go home." Shirley began to walk towards her Mercedes. Charlene waited, until her sister had gone, before revealing she was unwell. "I needed a rest, but Shirley wouldn't hear of it and made me continue walking."

"If I'd known what you've just told me, she would have had the harsh side of my tongue! She's so conceited, she thinks she knows everything there is to be known."

"Isn't that the way I used to behave when I was a teacher?" Charlene asked her husband.

"It's a danger inherent in the job I suppose. If I'm being fair, you could say the same thing about most professional people, including lawyers."

"I'd like to go to bed now, Roger. It's probably a good thing I'm not seeing Dr Stevenson until next week."

"I'll bring you a hot water bottle and a cup of tea when you're settled in."

"You're so good to me," she said, giving him a kiss on the cheek.

\* \* \* \* \*

Roger and Charlene had always loved to entertain their friends; Roger with films of their holidays and Charlene with her gourmet cooking. But there had been no opportunity to do this for the last eight months because of Charlene's illness. Now that the treatment had made Charlene stronger, they had been able to accept an invitation to dinner from William and Mary Drumhills.

"I don't know how we're ever going to repay you." Charlene felt guilty that she'd been unable on this occasion to invite the Drumhills to their home. "I believed I could make it but when I thought about actually preparing a meal and all the cleaning up I'd have to do, I just capitulated. You know it's nearly a year since we last treated you to dinner."

William, the perfect host, took their coats and hung them up on the coat rack, while Mary walked with her guests into the front room.

"Dinner won't be long. I'm making something special this evening."

Charlene's sense of smell was usually good enough to enable her to analyse the various aromas emerging from the kitchen.

"I think I know what the main course is going to be." She grinned.

William came in with a tray of drinks and placed it on the table. "I've made up the drinks we used to have because this is a special visit. But you can have something else instead, if you would prefer," he said offering the tray to his guests. "If you'd rather?"

"I always like malt whiskey with a little water," said Roger. "If that's what you've served it will do me just fine."

"And that looks like red grape juice," said Charlene. "That will be perfect."

When everyone had taken up his or her glasses from the tray, William announced he would offer a toast.

"We're being very formal tonight," teased Roger.

"I'm being serious for once," said his host. "We've all been very happy with the way Charlene has been responding to her treatment over the last months. So my toast is ... let Charlene continue to get better and better until she's well enough to cook a meal for us."

"To Charlene," the three of them called out. William added - "I do hope things are now on the road to complete recovery."

Charlene hadn't revealed to anyone, even Roger, the shock she'd been given when she had seen the assistant consultant, Dr Michael Winchester. She could still hear the consultant's angry voice: "If you're not responding to the drug, as well as we'd like, then you can't expect us to go on treating you indefinitely," he had said, without any pretence of hope. But there had been hope. Dr Stevenson had told her about a new drug, which had been giving some success. She could still look forward to that.

"I think I should tell you all that Dr Stevenson was on holiday when I called for my appointment today," Charlene announced suddenly. "His deputy told me that my course of treatment had not been successful." She did not tell them how harshly he had revealed the distressing news to her.

"I thought you were being a bit evasive when you came out from the consultation," said Roger. "What about all those tricks up Dr Stevenson's sleeve?"

"I've got another appointment with Dr Stevenson when he returns from his holiday. He promised me an expensive new treatment which he thought could be successful in cases like mine."

"Thank God for that," said Mary. "That's the timer in the kitchen telling me the meat is ready. Let's go into the dining room."

On their way home Charlene said she would like to have the Drumhills back to their house for a meal. "I'm beginning to feel like a MacTak instead of a MacGie."

"If you had told me before what Dr Winchester said about the failure of your chemotherapy, perhaps we should have stayed at home tonight. How are feeling now?"

"I'm all right. Honestly I am. We couldn't have cancelled the invitation. Mary was looking forward to seeing us and Willie's so good at being a host."

# Chapter 18

"Charlene," whispered Roger as he gave his princess a good morning kiss. "It's so lovely outside. I think we should spend some time just sitting in the garden."

She stretched herself, as she always did when she woke. "That'll be most enjoyable." She stifled a yawn with her hand.

"Will you need any help?" he asked.

"No, thank you, Roger, I can manage by myself. I expect we're having breakfast in the porch to enjoy the sunshine."

"That's what I had in mind. I'll put the things out on the table while you get dressed."

After a while Roger began to think Charlene was taking far too long to get ready. But then she had refused his help. He had just decided to give her a few more minutes, when he heard her faint voice calling him.

"Roger. I'm not feeling very well."

He rushed through to the bedroom; Charlene was still in her nightclothes. "I suddenly felt unwell after you left," she disclosed. "And, I haven't been able to do much since then. I was hoping this funny spell would go away and then I'd get ready, but it hasn't. What am I going to do?"

"For a start you're going back to bed. And then you'll have a home visit from the doctor. I'm sure it has nothing to do with what you ate last night."

Charlene looked disappointed. "I had hoped I was getting better. I was feeling so good yesterday."

"We'll hear what the doctor has to say."

Doctor Preston came very soon after Roger had phoned the surgery. "What's the matter with you this time Mrs Buchanan?"

Charlene described how she had suddenly become so weak that it was not possible for her to dress. The doctor took her temperature and blood pressure and noted them in his wee, black book.

"If you lie on your back, we'll have a wee look at your operation." After a brief examination he said. "There's a slight infection of the wound." He then examined Charlene's abdomen by pressing it at the relevant places.

"You know that the surgeons couldn't remove all of the tumour," he reminded her. "They were hoping to clear up the remainder with chemotherapy but this hasn't happened. I think we should send you to the Central General for their opinion. It's possible you'll need further surgery."

Charlene was upset. She was only just beginning to recover from her previous operation and now she was being faced with another.

"May I use your phone?" Dr Preston asked as he went out to the hall to make arrangements with the hospital.

"The surgeon on duty has a bed for your wife. An ambulance will come some time today," he advised Roger. "Don't be too worried, Mrs Buchanan. Sometimes things get worse before they get better."

"I hope you're right, doctor." Roger went with him to the door.

"Let me know what happens. It's usually some time before I get a written report," said Dr Preston as he walked with Roger, along the path to his car.

When he returned to the bedroom, Roger assured Charlene that, although her condition was not an emergency one, Dr Preston had advised him to let her family and his daughter know about this new development. He would send an airmail to Marjorie as soon as possible and phone Shirley once he knew the ward number.

Roger was on the point of making a cup of tea for Charlene, when the doorbell rang.

"Sister Davidson couldn't come today. I'm Nurse Spellman, her assistant," she explained.

"Mrs Buchanan isn't too well. The doctor's just away. He's arranged for my wife to go to hospital," advised Roger.

When she heard about the infection, she suggested that Charlene should be given a bed bath and her wound dressed.

"That would be a good idea," agreed Roger as he showed her to the bedroom.

By the time the nurse had finished Roger had written an airmail to Marjorie and was about to contact Shirley when he saw an ambulance draw up. He had no alternative but to phone later. Very soon the paramedics came hurrying over to the door carrying a stretcher.

"Mrs Buchanan," asked the senior.

"Yes, through here," replied Roger, showing them into the bedroom.

Roger looked into her eyes and wondered what she was thinking as the ambulance men skilfully put her on the stretcher. He knew what he feared most of all.

Within minutes Charlene was in the ambulance.

"Best of luck," shouted old Kate McKenzie, their neighbour, looking into the ambulance. Charlene raised her head and waved back.

"Will you be following in your car?" asked the driver.

"Not unless I can't come with you," replied Roger.

He held Charlene's hand and squeezed it frequently with his message of love and reassurance. Even if the other paramedic had not been present, he would have found it difficult to say anything meaningful, but that did not matter, she was being comforted by his smile and the gentle touching of her hair. They were now, as they had always been, at one with each other. He dare not show his distress as he thought about her chances of surviving another operation.

Since it was not an emergency, the driver did not treat the journey as a race against the clock, yet somehow he managed to cover the distance faster than Roger would have done by car.

Suddenly the ambulance had arrived at the unloading bay of the Central General and Charlene was sitting in a wheelchair in the waiting room. The driver informed reception and left immediately to help at a major accident.

Roger wrapped the tartan rug about Charlene's legs and wheeled her over to the reception desk.

"We've been expecting you, Mrs Buchanan," said the nurse checking a list of names. "Do you think you can manage to take your wife up to ward five?" she asked. "The porters are getting things ready for our red alert." Roger knew the location of ward five. He had been there before.

Sister Bell, who was waiting at the entrance to the ward, remembered Charlene right away. "I'll take over now," she said sweetly as she began pushing Charlene to a bed near the door. She advised Roger to go home and phone later in the evening.

"Goodbye princess. See you later," he said and gave her a lingering kiss.

Once Roger had left, Sister Bell came over to take her details. "You've had a wee hiccup," she said pleasantly. "One of the doctors will be coming to examine you shortly."

She wrote down all the usual information and took Charlene's temperature, pulse and blood pressure. Dr Winchester appeared just as she was finishing the preliminaries.

"We're going to arrange for a scan, Mrs Buchanan. From what Dr Preston said over the phone it looks as if you might need another operation."

Within a few minutes one of the porters, already known to Charlene, arrived to take her to the scanner.

"You've come back in again, Lassie. That's too bad. What is it this time?" he said.

"I don't know." She shrugged her shoulders as she settled herself in the chair.

He tucked the tartan rug about her legs. "It'll be a bit draughty waiting in the corridor."

When she returned to the ward after the scan Dr Winchester came to tell her the bad news. There was another tumour in the area of her colon, and it needed surgery. "We'll get you ready for the theatre if you agree."

Charlene knew that these decisions were out of her hands. If an operation was required then it had to be done.

"My husband has gone home and will be worried about me," she told doctor. "I'd like to phone him and let him know."

"By all means ... Sister will bring you the ward phone."

Charlene lifted the handset and was soon in contact with Roger who had gone home by taxi.

"Roger, I've just been told I need more surgery to remove another tumour. They're getting me ready to operate later today. Remember to phone Shirley." She stopped when she had run out of breath.

"I'm sorry to hear that, dear. I was hoping it might have been the infection of your op. Is there anything you need?"

"As usual we rushed off without my toilet things. Would you bring them in when you come?"

"Yes, dear. Remember I'll be thinking about you, my love. I do so want you to get better. God bless you. I'll come and see you tonight."

"And I'll be thinking about you as well Roger. Goodbye for now." They blew each other a kiss over the phone.

Roger had arrived at the start of the evening visiting hour only to be told, by Sister Bell, that Charlene was still in the operating theatre. She was in the process of explaining the position, when Shirley and Peter and their family arrived at ward.

"This operation usually takes about four hours," she stopped to let them appreciate the situation. "And Mrs Buchanan has been in the theatre for two hours already, so she's unlikely to be able to see anyone tonight. It would be better for you go home and phone back for news. Give me a call soon after nine o'clock."

"Have you seen Charlene yet?" asked Shirley as she and her brood settled themselves in every available seat round Charlene's bed.

"No, she was in the theatre when I arrived," said Roger sadly

"What picture are they showing?" chuckled Gary, Charlene's young, medical nephew.

"That's not funny at all." Roger reprimanded him sharply. "As you heard Sister doesn't think there's any point in waiting."

"If she's round from the anaesthetic before ten o'clock," said Shirley, "I'll be able to speak to her tonight; but if not, you can give me a call and let me know what happened."

"I don't see why you can't ring the hospital yourself," Roger said tartly.

"If you're going to be difficult then I won't bother," Shirley replied and stomped off without another word.

When Charlene came out of the anaesthetic she had a tube projecting from her abdomen. "What is this for?" she asked the sister.

"Your operation isolated two tumours in your colon. Your main feeding will be through the tube for the time being. Nurse will connect it to the pump and you'll be fed with concentrated nourishment from a bottle like this." She was holding a 500-ml bottle. "There are several flavours to choose from. You can have vanilla, chicken and chocolate, as well." Even Charlene knew enough to appreciate that the flavour was irrelevant.

"Will I be seeing Dr Stevenson today?" Charlene asked her. "I'm wondering when I'm to have my chemotherapy."

"Dr Stevenson has already assessed your case, Mrs Buchanan and has decided to go ahead with the new drug in a few days. But we're going to give you a blood transfusion to boost your platelets. After that we'll connect you to the drip. You'll be on it for at least eight hours."

Charlene was happier now that there seemed to be some progress. "Thank you, Sister. I think I'll rest now."

Charlene had been gaining strength over the past few days and had improved sufficiently for her to be given a blood transfusion and her chemotherapy with the new drug.

"Would you like a pain killer?" enquired a nurse, noticing that Charlene was uncomfortable. "There's no need to suffer nowadays."

"I'm not really in pain, just a bit of discomfort." Charlene dismissed the offer.

Dr Stevenson came to see Charlene. "There were problems with the operation and the drug therapy," he explained. "We are unable to continue the chemotherapy."

"But I would like you to continue," insisted Charlene.

"Lassie," he said. "If we continue this treatment it might do you harm. I don't want that to happen, and I'm sure you don't either. We'll examine your case again in a fortnight and see how you are," he said. He turned and left Charlene wondering what the future would bring.

When Roger arrived for the afternoon visiting, Sister Bell met him in the corridor. "I think you should take your wife for a drive in the country. It will do her good and keep her mind off things. She's worried about not having the second treatment."

"I would have offered to take her out before, but I didn't think it was allowed," replied Roger. "I could be there and back long before it gets dark."

"I've got a surprise for you Charlene," Roger announced cheerily, as he walked to her bed next to the door. "I'm taking you for a drive. There's no need to change, since you won't be leaving the car. Just put on your brown cardigan and we'll take a blanket with us."

"I was hoping you would take me somewhere. Maisie Conroy went out with her husband yesterday. She loved it. Can you tell me where we're going?"

"I'd like to make it a surprise, if you'll let me," he replied gently.

"If that's the way you want it." She smiled as Roger lifted her legs over the edge of the bed.

They drove towards the north west of the city and after some time, Charlene said. "We seem to be going to Loch Arden." They had reached a signpost with Loch Arden and several other names on it.

"We could be. But there are many other places we could be going as well."

"There's no point in going to the Loch at this time of the year, the steamer only sails in the summer months," she said, trying to elicit if this was what Roger had been thinking of doing.

"I know that, Charlene. That's not what I had in mind."

After a further few miles, Roger drew into a lay-by and switched off the engine. "Look straight ahead of you. What do you see?"

"A tarmac road," she answered gloomily. "Nothing very inspiring in that, Roger."

"Is that all you can see?" he persisted. "What's above the road?"

Charlene lifted her eyes and searched the horizon for something unusual. Then she saw it, and understood why Roger had stopped at this spot. It was the only point on the road from which one could see the top of Ben Calder.

"It's our hill," she exclaimed with delight. "When I was lying in the ward, I was remembering about our first meeting, and I thought I'd never see Ben Calder again." She turned and kissed him on the cheek. "Thank you for being such an understanding husband."

"If you go on like this Charlene we'll both be needing our handkerchiefs." And at that Roger kissed his wife.

\* \* \* \* \*

Charlene had been waiting all morning to learn Dr Stevenson's final decision on her treatment with the new drug. If they had been going to give her dose number two, the nurse should have been here by now to set it up, she reflected, as she began to suspect the possibility of another delay.

She saw Sister Bell attending to Mrs Constantine. It shouldn't be that long before she came to her, Charlene thought She looked at herself in the mirror. Her hair was in a mess. If she'd lost it like the others on radiotherapy she'd be wearing a lovely wig now. She rather fancied the one Maisie Conroy had picked. Just like her to fall somewhere in between.

She took her brush and carefully stroked her prematurely greying hair, to cover the thinning area, which had developed at the front. Charlene scanned the back and sides of her head with a tiny mirror, pushing her hair into position where she thought the brush had failed to do its job properly.

Suddenly, there was a slight commotion as Doctors Winchester and Brown, who had been informed of an emergency, hurried into the ward and went immediately to Maisie Conroy's bed. "Sister!" called Dr Winchester. "Will you come here?" His voice was urgent.

Dr Brown had already started to pull the screen around Maisie's bed when the sister joined them.

Charlene had only been able to have a few words with her hospital friend but they were sufficient for her to realise something was seriously wrong. She had looked so fit when her husband had come to take her home a few days earlier. "I'm away home to make my family's tea. They're getting bored wi' fish suppers," she had joked cheerfully as she waved the other patients goodbye.

"Mrs Conroy," said Dr Winchester shaking her shoulder gently, "can you hear me?" Maisie mumbled a few words and started to groan.

Sister Bell filled a syringe with a pain-killing drug, which she handed to the doctor.

"I'm going to give you something special to ease the pain," he said, as he got rid of the surplus air from the syringe. "That should do for now." He sounded satisfied. "I'll be back, as soon as we've decided on the next stage of the treatment."

Hearing this comment made Charlene wonder about the next stage of her own treatment. What had been finally decided about her? The screens round Maisie were still in place when the consultant, Dr Stevenson, joined the two doctors. "Let her husband see her," he whispered, and opened up his notes.

"Doctor says you can see your husband now," the sister told Maisie. "Shall I bring him in?"

Although Charlene did not hear her reply she assumed Maisie had nodded her head in approval, when she heard the sister say "All right. I'll get him for you."

She wished she'd had chance to speak to Maisie, but things were going to be busy very soon now and she supposed she would just have to wait until Dr Stevenson dealt with this crisis before he could speak to her.

"Hullo there!" Charlene could hear the loud voice of Robert Conroy coming from behind the screen. "Maisie, what did the doctor say hen?"

There was no reply. Perhaps Maisie smiled at her husband as she had often done when he had asked about her illness. She was too weak to speak; yet her smile was all Bobby needed to reassure him. He was no stranger to the Central General Infirmary. This was her third year there for the treatment of her cancer, which had involved several operations. Although he knew her condition was serious, he took the view that Maisie had been in this position many times before. Each time the cancer returned, another treatment had extended her life a bit longer. Robert expected the doctors to perform the same miracle on his wife as they had done so many times before.

"Sister Bell was saying the doctors are discussing your case," said Bobby letting his wife know he knew a little about what was happening. "Isn't it a great thing to know you're in such safe hands?" Once again there was no reply. "Maisie dear," her worried husband muttered. "Is anything wrong?"

Maisie Conroy looked as if she had dropped off to sleep with her eyes open.

"Sister!" he shouted. "Something's wrong wi' ma wife."

The cancer ward sister, who had seen death so many times before, passed her hand over Maisie's eyes to eclipse their vacant stare. "Mrs Conroy is no longer with us," she whispered.

Charlene was very upset by this. She had looked on Maisie as a kind of talisman, whose continued survival had given her some hope. What chance did she have now that Maisie was gone?

Dr Brown went out to collect Roger from the waiting room, while Dr Stevenson and his senior assistant went over to visit his wife. Dr Winchester pulled the curtains around her bed and said, "I'm sorry you had to be present when Mrs Conroy died."

"When am I going to get my second treatment?" Charlene asked at once.

Dr Stevenson hesitated before replying. What he had to say to Charlene he had said to many hundreds of women, but today was different somehow. This time he found it very difficult for he had allowed himself to become emotionally involved with his patient.

Dr Brown pulled the curtain back and asked Roger to join his wife.

"I'm Dr Stevenson and this is Dr Winchester," said the consultant. Then he turned to the junior doctor and asked him to have a few words with Mr Conroy.

Roger put his arm comfortingly round Charlene and gave her a small hug.

"Mr Buchanan I waited until visiting hour because I wanted you to be present when I spoke to your wife about her condition," said Dr Stevenson. "As you probably know, her cancer reacted badly to the first dose of the new drug. We can't use it safely in her condition." He spoke abruptly trying to end the pain of his confrontation.

Roger gripped Charlene. This was not the news he had been expecting. She was in very little pain and had been eating very well.

Dr Stevenson tried to be clinical to hide the turmoil of his involvement with this woman, whose behaviour had impressed him so much, but he found her reactions hard to bear.

Charlene looked at Roger then back to the doctors. "Why is it not safe?" she asked, and went on to ask another without waiting for a reply to her first. "Is my blood count too low to stand up to chemotherapy?"

Dr Stevenson hated it when he had to wear the judge's black cap. It made him sound more like an executioner than a healer.

"Your response to the new drug makes it impossible for us to continue treatment."

"Surely there must be something else," Roger suggested desperately. Dr Stevenson shook his head. It was just as he suspected Charlene had reached the end of the line.

"Mr Buchanan, it would be far too dangerous to continue with this treatment," the consultant replied firmly, as he looked at Dr Winchester for his support. He felt so isolated at these times. This decision was his alone and he was the one who had to break the news to the patient.

"Mrs Buchanan I regret there is no further treatment I can give you." Dr Stevenson opened his arms.

Charlene stared at him in disbelief. No further treatment possible! Nothing more to be done! It could be dangerous! What could be more dangerous than not to be treated at all?

Roger was devastated by the news. His Charlene under the sentence of death. This must be a nightmare.

"Mrs Buchanan, did you hear what I said?" enquired Dr Stevenson.

She nodded and opened her mouth but said nothing for a while. Then as the horror of the news sank in, she said slowly, "My condition ... is terminal."

The consultant nodded his agreement and took her hand in his. "Mrs Buchanan, if there was anything I could do for you, I would not hesitate." He squeezed her hand soothingly. "You once said to me "with God's help you'll be able to cure me"." He stopped and looked at Dr Winchester, "I'm afraid God will be working on His own now."

Charlene had taken the opportunity to rehearse her own response to the disclosure of a terminal condition, and, because she had done so, she felt stronger and more able to deal with it. She was not feeling sorry for herself; but she didn't feel particularly brave either. It was somewhat like being a Lancer in the Light Brigade going courageously forward; knowing there was no way to change the outcome of what was happening.

Thankfully her faith would see her through this final stage, now that she knew the end was in sight. There were still all those good people who prayed every day for her. Surely such a volume of petitionary prayer must be successful? But even if it ended in failure, she was on the threshold of the great-unexplained mystery. Now she was to be given the chance to join her parents. She had missed them both so much.

"Charlene!" said Roger, worried by her long silence, "Is everything all right?"

"Feeling as well as expected, Roger. Isn't that the usual reply in such circumstances?" Charlene adopted a resolute voice, which betrayed little sign of the calamitous chaos, which was going on inside her mind. "How long have I got?"

Dr Stevenson, who had been examining her wound, looked into her eyes briefly and then to Dr Winchester, his senior assistant, as if he were looking for his strength to help him. "Two months ... more or less," he said strongly.

"Good God," cried Roger. "Surely not that little." Charlene patted him on the shoulder.

"That's it then," she said with determination. "The next step is to get my affairs in order as they say." Charlene had accepted the inevitable with equanimity. She turned to Roger, "I think I'd like to go home."

Dr Stevenson picked up his case notes and looked sympathetically at Charlene, for what he expected would be the last time. "What can anyone say at a time like this that will be of comfort to you?"

Charlene looked into his eyes, searching for the man inside the doctor. She had often wished that the behaviour of those who looked after her could have been less detached and more personal.

"I regret this is one area of medicine where I'm not qualified. I feel so helpless ... so frustrated ... at times like these." He turned to Dr Winchester and nodded.

"Dr Stevenson knows I am a believer in the God of the Israelites and will offer special prayers to Him for His intercession, but if this is not to be, I shall ask Him to give you the courage to bear this burden bravely," he reassured her. "I'll leave a prescription with the pharmacy," said Dr Winchester. "Remember to collect the medication before you leave. I'm prescribing a strong painkiller. There's no point in feeling pain needlessly. Take it when you need it."

Charlene's reputation as a person with consideration for others was well-known to every member of the ward staff. She smiled tremulously at the doctors and thanked them for the devoted way they had treated her. "I, too, will be praying to God asking Him to help all of us in this time of our affliction and to guide those who practice in these wards."

Roger kissed the top of her head and embraced her warmly.

There were many things Dr Stevenson wanted to say to Charlene but stopped short of saying them. Sometimes people's thoughts came out in a way, which was not intended. He had learned to remain silent when he found himself becoming emotionally involved.

"If you feel you want to ask me about anything, just phone my secretary," said Dr Stevenson. "Sister will give you the number. If I'm not available I'll ring you back as soon as I can." Dr Stevenson was using the only words of farewell, which seemed to ease his pained conscience.

Immediately he had finished, he departed for his office, to discuss Mrs Buchanan's case with his assistants before submitting the files to their final resting-place in the filing cabinet.

Sister Bell, who had been attending to the late Maisie Conroy, returned to have a few words with Charlene. "I'm sorry things didn't work out differently," she said, pulling back the screen. Charlene reflected how hard it must be for nurses opting to treat cancer patients. Their disappointment at times like this, when they were unable to halt the inevitable progression towards death, must have needed almost as much courage as the patient.

"You don't need to say anything, Sister Bell. I think I know how you feel when you have to admit the battle is lost. For my part, I have nothing but praise for the way you and the others have looked after me. I know that everything that could be done has been done. The rest is up to me now."

"Mrs Buchanan, it's so kind of you to say so. But we were only doing our duty." Charlene smiled bravely at this, which had the effect of helping the sister to relax. "And I'd like you to know it's been a great privilege for me to have known you. My life has been enriched by your passing my way." She adjusted Charlene's pillow and started to walk away. "I'll send a nurse to show your husband how to use the feeding machine."

Roger kissed Charlene on the lips, and whispered. "Princess … we're still going to fight this thing, together."

# Chapter 19

Charlene waited in the car, while Roger took her things inside and lit the fire in the large front room. When he returned, he draped the tartan rug over Charlene's shoulder and helped her on to the pavement.

"I want to walk by myself. The neighbours might be watching," Charlene murmured between clenched teeth. But after a few steps, he had to take her arm and support her, as she walked the rest of the way to the door of 4 Burleigh Avenue.

"Push the door by yourself," he suggested.

Charlene did as he asked and was greeted by a "Welcome Home Charlene" notice, which had been stretched across the hallway.

"What a lovely thing to do Roger," said Charlene as she walked inside. "You're so good to me." She smiled and turned her face towards him for a kiss.

"I wish I were able to do more," he said holding her arm and guiding her carefully to the green chair, which she liked so much. "The room's not cold, although you might think so after having been cooked in that ward."

"Those weeks in hospital seem to have taken the use of my legs," Charlene said, apologising for her heavy, struggling gait. "I'll need to try and get some walking done now that I'm home." She settled herself in a sitting position with her feet stretched out. "I'll leave my coat on, until I feel warmer, Roger. Would you pull the tartan rug around my legs?"

Affectionately he tucked it firmly about her thighs, lovingly patting her legs from time to time. "How's that?"

"Just perfect, Roger. How about that cup of tea you promised me?"

"The kettle's been on since we came in. It should be ready now ... I'd think. Would you like a biscuit with it?"

"No, thanks. Nothing but tea with a little milk."

He returned with two cups of tea on a tray and put them down on a small, teak table lying between their two chairs.

"I'm having a chocolate biscuit with mine. The cook's been away on holiday for a few weeks. I'm feeling a bit peckish."

Charlene smiled as she took the cup from Roger's hand. "It looks as if the cook will be away for a bit longer." A disturbing silence ensued, as each of them drank their tea without either of them referring to "how long"? She had married Roger in the first place because his calmness balanced her own tendency to panic in times of stress. But she was showing no suggestion of alarm at the moment.

They held hands in silence as each wondered how to deal with Dr Stevenson's news. Then Charlene, who had been slowly sipping her tea, suddenly put cup and saucer on the table and said, "Do you remember that time when I was feeling pretty low after mother died?" she reminded him. "You said, I'll give you a medicine that doesn't come out of a bottle."

"Yes I do remember that very well. You misunderstood me, and were angry when you thought I was asking you to drink something alcoholic."

"But all you wanted me to do was to forget myself," she interrupted, "and everyone will think I'm a calm person like you. At the moment I'm trying to forget myself, I'm trying very hard indeed," Charlene said. "Now I want you to apply the same medicine to yourself Roger."

"My old friend Rickie Lawson is inconsolable over his wife's death. He keeps telling me he never knew the house to be so empty," said Roger.

"It all depends on the person," said Charlene philosophically. "Some men never do get over their loss. What I want you to do is to apply your own medicine. Get married again. There's no reason why you should live by yourself." The sound of the doorbell interrupted her. "Just tell them I'm not ready to receive visitors yet," said Charlene apprehensively.

"I think I'll have to monitor your callers from now on," said Roger, as he got up and started for the door. "We don't want you being tired out, do we?"

Dr Preston, who had been asked by Dr Stevenson to call on his favourite patient and see her settled in at home, had been about to visit another patient living in the same area, when the call had come through from the Central General.

"Oh. It's you doctor," Roger was surprised to see him so soon.

"Yes, I happened to be in the district," said Dr Preston. "I'd like a word before I see Mrs Buchanan."

"Of course." Roger presumed, he was going to be told that the cancer was terminal.

"You may think my incorrect earlier diagnosis of indigestion aggravated your wife's present condition." Dr Preston came to the point immediately.

Roger shook his head. He had discussed the possibility of changing to another doctor at the time but when Charlene had learned that ovarian cancer was very difficult to detect in its early stages, she had said no. Dr Preston had been the Graham family doctor for a long time.

"To make matters worse, I was asked to examine yourself and Mrs Buchanan and then inoculate you both for your trip to Zimbabwe. This had to be done quickly due to your departure date. Later, when I took everything into consideration, I thought you'd done the right thing, going on holiday."

Roger nodded his head with understanding acceptance and led Dr Preston into the front room. "I wanted to see you today, rather than tomorrow, when I'll be very busy. I'll be on my own then," he explained.

"It's all right doctor," Charlene said with a smile. "I'm always happy to see you."

"I had a call from Dr Stevenson telling me what he told you, that all the tests show that the case is too far advanced for us to do anything more."

"But there must be something you can do." Roger was in great distress at hearing this confirmation that the end was near. "How about alternative medicine?"

Dr Preston shook his head and said, "I suppose all doctors wonder why they can't help patients a thousand times or more. We know only a fraction of what we need to know. Instead of using our intellect and natural resources trying to increase the well-being of the human race, we invest in things that make for an increase in our misery, and people like Charlene here are allowed to die from cancer."

Charlene smiled at him and nodded her agreement.

"Doctors are often accused of behaving like gods, except when they are unable to perform a miracle," Dr Preston said emphatically. "It's no use. We've done everything we possibly can. Your wife has accepted this." Doctor Preston had not intended to go on at such length. His own frustration at having to watch helpless to do anything, as life was being extinguished from another innocent, was becoming more than he could bear. "Forgive me. I didn't mean to give a lecture."

"What am I going to do, doctor?" Roger asked like a helpless child.

"Charlene has already told you she has about two months left. You can expect her to be active for only a short time while she is still on her feet."

"Only a short while," Roger repeated. "Then what?"

"You've been protected by the hospital staff," Dr Preston said sympathetically. "They gave you hope when you needed it. Now you must make the next few weeks possible for Charlene to bear."

"I'll do anything I can for my princess. She need only ask and, if it's within my power to do so, I'll do it for her," Roger said, gaining some comfort as he did so.

"Isn't it about time for your wife to be given her feed?" said the doctor looking at the clock.

"It's all this talking. I'll make it and connect her up as soon as you're through."

"I've finished but I want a word with your wife before I go." He turned back to Charlene. "Mrs Buchanan, you are being very brave about this, you know."

"No, I'm not," she replied strongly. "Once in a while, when I think of what lies ahead of me, I find myself getting frightened. But then, I appreciate that the real test of how fruitful my life has been will not be determined by the number of years I lived. What will matter at the end will be, how I used the time I was given."

Dr Preston was deeply moved. He took her hand as she continued. "There is a happy, extraordinary, curious feeling inside me that I can't explain. It's as if there's nothing more left for me to do. It's as if my life is complete and I have become freed from the bondage of my human existence. Do you think I'm speaking nonsense?"

"Far from it," he replied. "In fact it makes a great deal of sense to me. You are a very rare bird indeed," said the doctor.

Charlene smiled at him. "You're not the only person to have said that to me. My husband first used the phrase when we first met on Ben Calder."

"You're a valuable specimen to be treasured. I've never felt so helpless. The next time I need someone to comfort me, I'll call on you. I'll come and see you again soon. However, if you feel you need me earlier have Mr Buchanan call me and I'll come as soon as I can."

"Dr Preston I want to thank you for everything you've done," said Charlene. The doctor nodded his head, lifted his bag and left.

Now that they were alone again, Roger thought they should spend some time in the garden and enjoy the last of the summer display, which Charlene had prepared that Spring.

"I'll put out the deck chairs and we can sit and just enjoy the view ... your view Charlene ... the one you created."

She shook her head strongly. "No! No! Roger. I didn't create it. I simply set it out according to the creator's plan. I was given the opportunity to decide where I wanted the plants to grow, but it was God who gave them life, as he does all living things."

Roger helped her from the chair although his wife was still able to do this for herself. It made him feel that he was doing something useful.

"Shall I bring you a book?" he asked.

"No, thank you Roger. I just want to sit and enjoy our garden." she replied closing her eyes.

"I'll do some tidying up then," said Roger.

Charlene breathed a myriad of delicate perfumes as a gentle breeze wafted over her face. She wished time would stand still and let her enjoy this moment for all eternity.

A male blackbird disturbed her reverie as he snapped angrily at a sparrow cheekily trying to steal a pea-sized crumb and several bluetits chirped happily as they played leapfrog in the apple tree. She wondered what had happened to the friendly robin that had appeared in the garden about the same time as her first chemotherapy and had made friends with her. He had come readily to her hand when she offered him a mealworm. Where was he now?

Charlene opened her eyes and looked over their small garden. She marvelled how much they had managed to cram into such a small space. Her father's azalea from the allotment was covered in pink blossom. She had chosen plants providing colour and texture throughout the year, but her illness had denied her most opportunities to see some of her better floral displays. She closed her eyes and imagined the garden as it had looked earlier when the snowdrops and yellow witch hazel gave way to daffodils and purple daphne through to the tulips and zonal perlargonium.

Roger had made a good job of planting her lobelia seedlings. These deep blue flowers ran down the edge of the path like a thin stream.

Everywhere she saw plants grown from seeds collected during their holidays. Pink lavatera from the Sulimanya Mosque in Istanbul and striped white flower heads of osteospurnum from the Sahara desert. There were trees from China, Japan and the Himalayas. Their garden was a microcosm of the world about them.

"Have you had enough?" Roger interrupted her reverie. "It's becoming colder."

"Yes," she replied. "I want to go to our bedroom." Charlene got up and asked Roger to take her arm.

Once they were inside Charlene stumbled towards the bed and sat on the edge of it. "I'd like to sit here for a minute or two. I'm not used to walking yet." She stared into her husband's eyes. "I've got a lot of clearing up to do."

"But Charlene ... you're in no condition to do any heavy lifting, and besides, I want you to conserve what energy you have for what we know is our final attack on your cancer," he parried.

She had already told Roger how she wanted her personal things to be distributed. He had asked her to write a list saying what she wanted him to do with them, so that there was no doubt what she meant. But some things were of sentimental value to him as well; he would keep these until he had no need of them.

"What things are you thinking about?" Charlene broke in.

Roger hesitated to reply for he did not want to become involved in another discussion about the distribution of her belongings.

"We've talked about this before. Neither of us wants to leave the other with the burden of decision as to what is to happen to the other's possessions."

Charlene pointed to her side of the wardrobe. "Roger, please open it." He slid the door to one side revealing a collection of clothes dating from the early days of her marriage.

"I've kept them all," she said running her hand along the hangers. "It's about time they did some good for somebody." She turned to Roger and playfully tapped the pocket where he kept his wallet. "Isn't it about time you bought me some new things anyway?"

"You know there was never any question of you being forced to wear your old clothes," he defended himself. "You always seemed to like your old things best of all and in any case I loved seeing you in them." He pointed to one or two items, which had become his favourites. "We'll buy some new things, just to show how determined we are to beat this cancer."

"Who are you kidding, Roger? Certainly not me. You know how long I've got, and that's how long we've left for each other."

Charlene picked out one of her earliest purchases, a pale pink, taffeta dress she had worn once at a wedding. Roger lifted the hem, and rubbed it between his thumb and first finger. "Is it silk or rayon?"

Charlene pretended to look hurt, as she pulled the dress from his fingers. "You should know better than that. It still fits me," she said with a flourish. "However it's out of fashion now. I don't know why I've kept it so long. It's one of the things you never saw me wearing."

"Maybe one day. You look lovely in whatever you're wearing," he said, taking her in his arms for the first time in weeks and pressing her gently to him, without causing her any discomfort. "Do you remember how we watched Fred Astaire and Ginger Rogers on TV before you went into hospital?" He was remembering how well Charlene danced.

A smile crossed her face. She did remember the occasion.

"And do you remember this tune?" Roger immediately began to sing the theme song, and rocked from side to side, simulating a dance, which he knew, was now beyond his wife's stamina.

"Yes, I do. It was one of the things I liked about the film. It reminded me of two people in love. Just remember I want to give my clothes to the Charity Shop." Suddenly she gasped. "I'm out of breath. I need to lie down."

"I'm sorry dear. I should have known better."

"Haven't you forgotten something?" Charlene asked as she climbed into bed.

Roger pretended to think hard for an answer.

"Of course, I know what! I haven't done this yet." He bent over and kissed her softly on the lips.

"That's not what I meant," she replied, showing a little impatience with Roger for not having understood right away. "What about my liquid diet?"

"The machine's ready in the kitchen. I thought I'd connect you up for dinner, as we went through to the garden. It's going to take most of the evening to empty the food container."

Charlene gripped her husband's large, strong right hand in both of hers, and looked into his eyes. "I'm forgetting you said you were going to look after me. I should have known better than to think you'd overlook that." She squeezed his fingers and lifted his hand to her lips. "I'm depending on your help from now on."

"Nothing makes me happier than being able to do things for you," said Roger and kissed her again.

\* \* \* \* \*

"You slept very well last night," said Charlene, as she leant across the bed, pursing her lips for her good morning kiss.

Roger rubbed his eyes and shook himself completely awake. He felt so guilty at having had such a good sleep.

"How about you dear? Did you manage to make a date with Morpheus?"

"I'm afraid not, Roger." The reply was what he had expected. "I needed to go to the toilet a couple of times during the night."

"That's something I can't do for you dear." He smiled. "But remember, there's no reason why you should be uncomfortable. If you need assistance, and I'm asleep, don't hesitate to wake me up. Promise me you'll do that."

Sister Bell had forewarned him in the hospital, that Charlene would gradually become weaker and less able to do things for herself.

"I promise," said his wife. "But only if I really need your help."

"Charlene, I don't want you to decide the degree of urgency," he emphasised. "If you feel discomfort, just waken me. I'll decide what to do if it should be necessary."

"You're such a wonderful man, Roger. I was so lucky to meet you that day on Ben Calder."

Roger felt very humble. "On the contrary. I was the fortunate one, to have met such a caring person at a time when I had reached the nadir of my relationship with Edith."

"That will be enough of that. We don't want to become the only two members of the Buchanan Mutual Admiration Society, do we now?" she said. "How about something to eat? It's all very well feeding overnight. But I'm missing the pleasure of savouring food as I chew it," she told him.

Roger had already anticipated her wish to eat a normal diet, and had soaked some dried apricots to go with their porridge.

"It's a bit early ... but it's also impossible for me to go back to sleep again, now that I'm awake. We can have breakfast and I'll get on with other things while you try and get some more sleep."

"Will you sieve my porridge Roger?" she reminded him as he left for the kitchen.

Roger was in the middle of setting up a tray for his wife when Shirley rang.

"Is that you, Roger?"

"Yes," Roger replied without any warmth in his voice. He had learned not to give Shirley any opportunity to criticise any comment he might make about Charlene's health.

"That was a fine thing you did to me last night." Her angry voice attacked some imagined wrong-doing on his part.

"I've no idea what you mean!" he retorted.

"What I mean? Surely it's fairly obvious," she said hotly.

"I'm not a mind reader. Would you please get to the point?"

"Nobody bothered to let me know my sister came home from the hospital yesterday afternoon. I went there only to be told she'd gone home. I specially made an extra visit on my way to the Pharmaceutical Society dinner with Peter."

"That explains why I couldn't contact you yesterday. I waited until Charlene was comfortable in bed before I rang. Clearly you'd left by that time."

Roger overheard his sister-in-law grunting throughout his explanation.

"That's what I mean. No consideration for anyone but yourself."

"You should use that answering machine Charlene gave you for Christmas," he pointed out.

"Have you any idea how expensive it is to reply to everyone who phones when the answering machine is on?" she said, without expecting him to reply.

"Is that why you've stopped using it then?" Roger seized the opportunity to make the point. "What would you have said, if I had called when you had gone to bed?"

"Never mind about that," she countered. "I'm coming over to see my sister some time today." The criticisms of her own action seemed to have gone unnoticed.

"Can you give me some idea when that will be?" Roger enquired politely.

"Certainly not. I don't intend to make an appointment," she replied indignantly. "I'll be over when I can manage to fit it in."

"I only thought you might arrive at an inopportune moment," suggested Roger. "It was just to save you any inconvenience."

"I'll have to risk that." She put the phone down without further comment.

"I suppose that was my sister on the phone," Charlene said when he took her breakfast tray into the bedroom. "I could tell from your angry voice that it must be she."

Roger put a large towel on the duvet and balanced the tray on top of it, before replying. "Charlene, you know she doesn't like me. I've never been able to understand why. It's not because of anything I've done to hurt her. Perhaps she's just jealous of our happy marriage."

Charlene put some milk on her porridge, as if she were working out in her mind what she should say next. Finally she spoke, "I wouldn't think that's the reason." She had warned him before about her sister's strange ways. "You gave her the chance by being awfully silly sometimes. That didn't start you off well. You should have said nothing when you saw she was trying to goad you into an argument." Charlene put a large spoonful of porridge in her mouth. "Oh! That's good."

Part of Shirley's problem was that she never thought anything she said was wrong. Roger had not intended to cause Charlene any distress by reminding her of the unpleasant relationship, which had developed between himself and her sister.

"I hoped so much you'd fit in with my family, that you and Shirley could become good friends."

"That's not my fault, Charlene," he answered. "I've done everything I can to make for a good relationship but she seems determined to be irritating and bring out the worst in me."

"Won't you make a special effort, when you know my time is running out?" Charlene pleaded. "It would make me very happy."

Roger wondered how the Almighty could have made two children of the same parents so much the opposite of each other. Charlene was slim, kind, caring and generous with her time and material things whereas Shirley was overweight, through selfish lazy living, and had a limited capacity for loving.

"You know the kind of person she is, and yet you ask me to seek her friendship." He opened his arms wide in a gesture of despair.

"Please Roger, just try this one more time for me," she implored him. "It's possible that Shirley thinks you want all my time for yourself and is feeling frustrated by it all."

"All right Charlene, my dear. Because you've asked me, I'll try. But it's going to be infernally difficult; I'll have you know. I've never suggested Shirley is unwelcome in our home. If you think about her reaction before your illness you'll find most of the effort for contact come from this side. And I should remind you that sometimes I was omitted from her invitations."

"I'm not blind to my sister's failings. But she is my sister. You'd better take your porridge back to the kitchen. It'll be getting cold by now."

"I'll bring you in a cup of tea when you've finished," he called back from the hall. "And afterwards I suggest you sit in the garden and enjoy the sun."

Important among the criteria Roger and Charlene had used to select their home, was that it was on level ground near a group of shops which could supply their everyday needs. They had taken this conscious step, rather than wanting to live high up on the side of the small hills which surrounded them. Winter with its frost, ice and snow would be difficult enough, even for fit people to negotiate, without adding the disadvantage of advancing age and a steep slope as well.

Charlene took Roger's arm in hers, not only because she always did so, but to enjoy having him close to her and give her some support.

"I did appreciate my breakfast this morning. They're far too busy in the hospital to cater for everyone's needs."

"It's not that I cooked it any better, just that I paid more attention to the way you like it. I could never understand why it was necessary to have resident nutrition experts, when all they seemed to be able to provide was mass cooking attuned to the economical use of hospital facilities."

Charlene did not like to hear him being critical, even when it was obviously necessary if some change in the system were ever to be effected.

"I'm sure the dietician was trying as well as she could," Charlene defended the food expert. "She can tell the kitchen staff to prepare a particular diet, and then it's up to them."

"But that's the trouble Charlene," said Roger tensely. "Everyone blames everyone else for things going wrong."

"Going back to what I was saying, ... I had a chance to see just how little care was taken over the patients' nourishment when I looked at the trolley returning with the uneaten meals from that cancer ward. I'm particularly annoyed at food being wasted when so many people are dying from starvation."

Charlene understood what her husband was saying; yet she wanted to defend the attitude of the staff. "They can only work within the rules. The nurses have been very helpful in trying to influence the catering staff."

"That's the trouble with people, Charlene, so long as those in charge keep themselves as far away from the wards as possible, they'll be prompted to think everything's going well. My grandmother used to say, when we were ill. Give them good wholesome food and they'll soon be better."

"I heard my grandmother say the same thing," said Charlene with a wink. Charlene's thoughts had turned again to the mountains and the enjoyment of the memory of their first meeting. She wondered what path she would have taken had Roger not been there that day. It had been a very interesting day. They'd done so much together it seemed like a lifetime instead of just a few years.

"Penny for your thoughts, Charlene. You know you've been staring out into space for the past few minutes without saying anything."

She was startled from her reverie. "I ... I ... I was thinking about when we first met on Ben Calder. You looked like someone who had endured much, yet you said nothing, as you sat on that large boulder with your thoughts. I was wondering if, whether I had known the reason for your unhappiness, I would have become involved with you. After all, you were still a married man and I believed in the sanctity of marriage. "Those whom God hath joined together, no one should put asunder!"

"Haven't you enjoyed being married to me then?" he enquired teasingly.

"Of course I have, Roger," she replied immediately. "I was criticising myself for having had such a narrow-minded view at that time. I still believe marriage is for a lifetime. However, I can now accept the idea of a New Beginning, which I could not then."

Roger, on the other hand, had taken the view that, except when young children were involved, it was wrong to expect spouses with nothing in common any more to continue together.

"I'm glad your goodness came through as it always has and you took pity on a lonely man in his time of need. I never told you

243

how much you did to dispel my idea that women are monsters, waiting to trap men and destroy their lives. I was very low that particular day. I couldn't see the chance of a new beginning. But your kindness helped me on the road to recovery."

"Roger, I did what comes to me naturally. I likened myself as someone else in difficult circumstances."

"Burns said it before you, Charlene. But it's true. If we only stopped to think about what the other person is undergoing, we might be a lot less critical of them."

They had been admiring the view and talking for fully ten minutes, without appreciating the chill in the wind even though it was technically a summer day.

"I wish I'd put on my brown cardigan before I came out. I'm feeling quite cold. Do you think we could now go back inside?" said Charlene.

"Of course, dear." Roger touched her cold hands and felt guilty for not noticing her need. "I should have known; you were never given as good an internal central heating system as some of us."

He would need to remember this and see that Charlene was always well-wrapped up when they went out. Her illness had increased the problem of keeping warm.

# Chapter 20

Charlene and Roger had just gone inside after a spell in the garden when they saw that the nurse was just about to leave, having received no reply to her knock.

"Hold on!" shouted Roger. "We've been sitting in the garden. Be with you in a minute."

The nurse smiled obligingly. "I'm glad I was able to see you. I'm so busy. I wouldn't have been able to come back again today. I wasn't able to phone and let you know. I'm Sister Morrison," she said introducing herself. "And you'll be Mr and Mrs Buchanan?"

"You'll have come to see me, I expect," said Charlene.

"Come inside, Sister. I was just going to make a cup of tea for my wife. Shall I make one for you as well?"

"No, thank you," she said quickly. "I'm late already and I've still got many other patients to see."

"I expect Sister will want to examine you in the bedroom," he said guiding Charlene in the direction of the door on her right. "I'll pop off to the kitchen."

"Do you think I could wash my hands?" enquired Sister Morrison, holding her palms upwards as if she expected matron to examine them.

Charlene pointed to the frosted glass door opposite the bedroom. "You'll find a guest towel on the small rail to the side of the wash-hand basin. And there's a small cake of soap specially for visitors."

"Would you get into bed, Charlene? I'll be with you in a few moments. I want to look at your tube."

Roger listened to the sustained ringing of the doorbell. That would be Shirley, he thought. Trust her to choose a time, which was inconvenient.

"You took your time!" Shirley snapped at Roger. "You don't seem to realise how cold it is standing here in the wind."

Shirley stood empty-handed on the doorstep with her husband Peter on the footpath behind her.

"Please come in," said Roger, politely, in an effort to keep his promise to Charlene. "I'm sorry you've come when we're busy, but if you go in the front room," he said, opening the door leading to it, "and wait there, Charlene will be ready in a minute."

Shirley opened her mouth, as if to make some caustic remark, but closed it again like a fish surfacing to catch a fly.

"I'll see my sister when I want to," she said aggressively, as she strode towards the bedroom door, which was slightly ajar.

Upon hearing Charlene's voice coming from the room, she assumed this was an invitation to come in. "It's only me and Peter," she called sweetly and went inside. "I thought you were speaking to me," she said disappointedly when she saw the nurse. "Roger never said you had company." Charlene knew her sister well enough to know that Roger had probably not been given a chance to tell her. Without an apology either to her sister or the nurse Shirley continued. "I'm Mrs Anderson, the patient's sister."

She bent over and gave Charlene a formal kiss on the forehead. "What's this?" she said, peering for the first time at Charlene's exposed abdomen with its plastic feeding tube.

"What do you mean Shirley?" enquired Charlene.

"You'll not be able to wear your two-piece swimsuit? I didn't know they'd made such a mess of your stomach. Why?" said Shirley, distressed at the evidence of her recent operations? She turned to the nurse looking for an explanation.

Sister Morrison did not take up the challenge and continued to bathe Charlene's wound with antiseptic.

"One tube feeds me, the other removes the waste, Shirley. Without this surgery I wouldn't be here."

"That's me finished," said Sister Morrison, as she secured a fresh dressing over the wound with adhesive tape. "You're all tidied up again, Charlene," she said gently. "I'll be back tomorrow about the same time. However, sometimes things are a bit hectic, so you might get a visit from my colleague, instead. One or other of us will be coming to look at your dressing every day from now on." She turned to look at Shirley, as if she expected some further interference. "There's an important point I need to raise." She redirected her gaze to her patient. "Will Mr Buchanan be able to look after you? You know you'll probably need more help from now on, and at any hour of the day or night."

Charlene was about to reply that Roger had been doing a good job and she had every confidence in him.

"Roger's not qualified," Shirley interjected. "Charlene needs full-time professional help. Can you arrange for nurses to take over? I was very surprised when the hospital authorities chose to send her home in the first place."

Sister Morrison had a lot of experience in dealing with interfering relatives. "This is not a matter for me to arrange." She did not want to become involved in a family squabble. "Mrs Anderson, I would suggest you have a talk with your sister and her husband after I leave."

Charlene suddenly realised she had not yet informed Shirley about the consultant's prognosis.

"Shirley, I've something to tell you."

Sister Morrison closed her small black bag and put on her coat. "Remember to take the pain killers, Mrs Buchanan," she reminded Charlene, as she made for the door. "There's no point in making a martyr of yourself. I'll say goodbye now."

Shirley dumped her body on the side of the bed where Roger usually slept. "Come here Peter," she ordered. "Stand here beside me. Don't you think Charlene's looking so much better after her treatment?"

"Yes. Charlene might be benefiting from my bottle. I'll go and help Roger with the tea things," he said and followed Sister Morrison out of the room.

"Shirley, I know you're worried about me. Try not to sound as if others are to blame for my condition." Charlene looked intently at her sister, desperately trying to assess the situation. How was Shirley going to take the news? It wouldn't help her if she broke down. Roger had taken the news so calmly. He was so strong, able to say just enough to comfort her without the situation developing into an emotional disaster.

"You know I love you very much," said Shirley. "I don't mean to be rude or hurtful, but that's the way it comes out sometimes."

"I know, I know," said her sister. "I'm very fond of you too and your children as well. They are the family I never had. They mean so much to me." Charlene was close to tears, but held them back. "Though I'd like to have seen them more often than I have."

"The young ones are so busy with their lives," Shirley replied, excusing their apparent lack of interest in their Aunt's illness. "When they're not busy working for a living, they're busy doing other things. That doesn't give them much time for play or visiting. But I'll have a talk with them, and see what I can do. I know that Marion, despite her work and looking after her baby, said she wanted to come and see you soon. Carol has been doing a lot of overtime in the laboratory and, of course, Gary is on call night and day since he became the junior doctor in that practice over in the north of the city. I'll make a special effort to see that they all visit soon."

"It'll need to be very soon then," said Charlene. "I've been given two months or less."

"I'm sure they'll see you before that," assured her sister. "Are you going back in for further treatment then?"

"That's the reason why I left the hospital," Charlene said calmly. "I was told I'd come to the end of my treatment. They can no longer help me fight the cancer. I might only live another two months."

Shirley, devastated, seemed to realise at last the gravity of the situation. "Good God Charlene, no! Not you. Anything but that." She started to cry.

"There ... there ... Shirley." Charlene tearfully joined her sister in her misery, patting a comforting hand on her shoulder.

Upon hearing the distress coming from the bedroom, the two husbands rushed in to find out what was happening.

"Is anything wrong dear?" Peter asked as he looked around for some obvious sign of an accident.

"No! There's nothing wrong with me," Shirley said through her sobbing. "Charlene's just told me some bad news. Roger should have warned me."

"You didn't give me much of a chance," objected Roger. "Had you gone into the front room as I had asked, I would have prepared you. You thought you knew what was required without my help."

The flare-up between himself and Shirley had always been there waiting to happen. "I'm sorry, I shouldn't have said that." Roger was ashamed with himself for having been unable to keep his promise.

"Roger Buchanan, what you have to say to me matters very little. I tried to dissuade my sister from marrying you in the first place. I warned her it would come to no good."

Shirley was about to go further, when her sister interrupted. "Stop it! Stop it you two! Don't you appreciate what all this quarrelling is doing to me? I was so hoping that you two would make up your differences so that I could die peacefully."

Shirley started weeping again. "That's it, blame me for what happened. I only wanted to protect you, Charlene. But if it will make you feel any happier, I'll kiss Roger and make it up with him."

Charlene's eyes brightened and she gave a relieved smile. "It would make me the happiest person." She took Roger's hand in hers and pressed it to her chest. "Roger, will you ... will you do this for me?"

"I gave you my promise that I wanted it that way too, and I'll go on making every effort." He put his arms about Shirley and gave her a kiss on the cheek.

"Forgive me Charlene," Shirley looked suitably penitent. "I've been showing my resentment for so long, it's become a habit with me."

"Just try a bit harder. Roger is. I know he's trying very hard."

The trouble with Shirley had been a lack of confidence in herself. She had recognised the condition early on in her life and had overcome the problem by always getting her point of view over first in a way that allowed for no opposition. She had learned very quickly that the best form of defence for those less confident was to attack before the other person did, or so she thought.

Undoubtedly the two sisters loved each other greatly. Why was it not possible for them to share Roger's love as well? But Charlene was happier now that Roger and Shirley had kissed and promised to be on good behaviour in the future.

"What's on your mind, Charlie?" said Shirley using a family diminutive she hadn't used for years. "You looked both sad and happy just now."

"Don't worry Shirl," she responded. "Nothing for you to worry about. I've come to terms with things as they are. From now on each day is a bonus - to be lived through, as fully as my illness will allow."

"Charlie, I didn't know you had it in you. You're very brave. I don't how I would bear up in your place."

"I don't feel very brave at all, but then there isn't anything I can do about it except pray. But, even if my petition goes unanswered, I expect to join those who have gone before me. My death is far from being frightening. Even something to look forward to in some ways, although I'll be sorry to leave Roger and my family and friends behind me."

Roger gave Charlene a kiss on the forehead and suggested they have tea and biscuits. "That'll be lovely," she said.

Peter put the tray on the small table beside the women and likewise kissed Charlene on the forehead. "I'm sorry to hear the bad news," said Peter, offering to pour her a cup of tea. "What can I possibly say that'll be of any help?"

"There's no need Peter. I understand. You want me to get well and are hoping for a miracle."

Peter handed cups to his wife and Roger, while Roger in turn offered tea biscuits all round.

"Don't you have any chocolate biscuits?" asked Shirley. "I love those thick chocolate wafer biscuits being advertised on the telly."

It was obvious thought Roger looking at her chubby frame. "We haven't got round to trying them yet, Shirley. I'm sorry."

"Oh well! I'll make these do," she said lifting a handful.

Charlene spent the next half-hour telling her sister and Peter the details of the last consultation in the Central General until she became quite exhausted.

"Charlene's needing a rest now," said Roger, looking uneasily at his wife. Her deterioration was becoming obvious; soon she would be entirely dependent on the help of others.

"We'll be going soon," replied Peter, ignoring Roger's implied request for their departure. "There are some things to be discussed."

"I am tired," pleaded Charlene. "If you wouldn't mind."

"This might seem to a bit insensitive Charlene but shouldn't you be thinking about the Graham things and what's going to happen to them? There's your mother's engagement ring and those things from your grandfather's English home," said Peter tentatively.

Charlene had spoken to Roger about the disposal of her personal things on the way home from the hospital and he'd given her an assurance he would attend to her wishes when this was necessary. For the time being, he reminded her, she was still alive and there was still a chance of recovery. He felt that it was a bit ghoulish to be handing these things over, as it were, from her deathbed.

"Firstly, have you made your will? You know how important that is. There's all those things you inherited from your parents. You'll want to pass them on to Shirley and her family."

"Peter!" Roger said angrily. "How can you be so insensitive?"

"That's enough," interjected Charlene. "I made some plans when I was well."

Charlene had stored some things in the roof space, which were intended for the family. She had written small labels and stuck them appropriately on each item, naming its family source and for whom it was intended.

"Shirley, there are things in the loft. It would make me very happy if you'd take them with you."

Roger sat quietly considering his position. Charlene had forgotten how distressing the effect would be on him when he saw the wholesale removal of her personal artefacts from their home.

Shirley raised her ample girth from her seat and began to walk into the hall where a folding ladder gave access to the roof.

"Peter," she called out. "I'll never make it."

Her husband was on his way to the door when Roger called out sharply, "You're not going anywhere in this house without my approval. What happens to our property is something for Charlene and me to arrange. I already know my wife's wishes in respect to certain matters. That is all that needs to be ... "

Peter interrupted offensively. "Charlene, you own half of the house. What do you want me to do?"

"I know why Roger intervened. Just leave things for the time being," she said. She was now feeling very much weaker because of this confrontation. "We'll deal with them when I'm feeling a bit better."

Peter went over and stood before Roger like a spoiled child deprived of his favourite toy, and glared into his face for a minute or two without saying a word. "Maybe you want these things for yourself. Is that it?"

Roger sat and said nothing.

"Shirley, would you please go? I'm exhausted by all this," said Charlene, without apportioning blame. "I'll need a rest before I'm connected up to my feeding machine again."

Shirley went over and kissed her sister goodbye, "I'll be along to see you tomorrow. I'll bring Marion with me."

Ignoring Roger, Shirley and her husband walked quickly to the front door and left.

"I didn't like what you did there," Charlene said, without any bitterness in her voice. "You should have let my sister have her way."

"I'm very sorry, Charlene," he replied promptly. "That's what's been wrong with your sister for a very long time ... and the reason for her attitude towards me in the first place. We both gave in to her far too often. You and I should have told her long before now that we would make the decisions, which affected us. Now we're suffering from the result of not having done so."

As Roger assisted Charlene to settle for the night, he wondered what Marjorie was thinking about his phone call telling her Charlene had only two months to live. He didn't expect her to come all the way from Zimbabwe but he was hoping for a letter.

Later that evening Charlene, who had been connected to her feeding machine, sat in Roger's comfortable chair reading the local paper, which had just been delivered. It was the same old news. Drugs, violence, sex, she thought, as she looked quickly through the pages. Those who lived decent lives rarely made the headlines. Like me she could have added. There was always the crossword. She supposed she liked it because it was simple.

Charlene turned to the middle page where it was usually to be found. Feathered intruder ... six letters ... that was beyond her, she thought. When Roger returned from the kitchen Charlene had nearly completed the crossword. "I expect you've finished it, as usual, and left nothing for me to do."

"Not this time dear. I'm looking for a six-lettered word meaning feathered intruder."

252

"Have you got any letters?" asked Roger.

Charlene counted along the empty boxes. "Second letter is u and the last letter is o," she replied.

"The person who made that clue up must be cuckoo." Charlene's eyes brightened. "That's it," she announced.

"That's what?"

"Cuckoo. That's the answer," she said victoriously.

Roger looked puzzled. "Feathered intruder. I don't get it."

"The cuckoo lays her eggs in another bird's nest. The intruding cuckoo's egg won't be saying anything for a while," she smiled.

"All right. Clever me."

He tucked in the rug, making sure she was comfortable. "I took pictures of our garden all the time you were in hospital, so that you wouldn't miss seeing your plants in bloom," Roger handed her a large packet of prints. She took the bundle and looked for a long time at the first photograph of the dwarf azalea her mother had given her as a house-warming gift.

"Are you thinking of your mother again?"

Charlene wiped her eyes with a tissue and nodded her head. "I still miss her very much."

"Maybe you'd like to hear some music while you look at the rest of the pictures," he suggested.

She looked pensively at him. "You know I haven't heard any of my own records since you got the new hi-fi five years ago."

"That's not my fault, Charlene. I often tried to get you to play them but you said you didn't want to damage the new machine."

"You know I get confused with these complicated Japanese objects. My own player was so simple by comparison. Anyway I'd like to hear Menuhin playing Brandenburg four. It ends with a splendid fugue."

Roger held Charlene's free hand as she turned the photographs over with the other. They listened silently to the recording of the great artist playing with the Bath Festival Chamber Orchestra, just as if they were part of the audience in the Concert Hall.

When the record was about to continue with the next concerto, Charlene squeezed her husband's hand. "That's enough Roger. Now I'd like to hear the Pa-pa-pa duet between Papageno and

Papagena from the "Magic Flute". Do you remember? We heard it - the first time we went out in public together."

"I remember it well Charlene. You felt the eyes of the world were watching us that night," he said, as he searched for the record. "Here it is. That's some name singing Papageno- Dietrich Fischer-Dieskau."

Roger had to try several times before he found the right excerpt.

"That's it!" called out Charlene. "Now put it back to the beginning. I want to hear the whole thing."

This time Charlene could not restrain herself from singing Papagena's part. Clearly she was enjoying Mozart's music and the moment.

Once again when the duet had finished, she asked Roger to stop the record. "I've had enough music for tonight," she said firmly. "Maybe we were a little like them. Free and easy until Papageno the bird catcher."

Roger interrupted. "Just like us when I caught Papagena, my rare bird."

"... Until Papageno the bird catcher had the worldly happiness of marrying someone, who was like himself," she ended, before agreeing with her husband. "Just like us Roger. It's time for the news. Could you let me hear it? I'll just listen to the headlines."

Roger switched on the television set and left.

Charlene picked up her diary. She seemed to be filling up the empty spaces in it tonight. Doing the things she had missed. Was there any point in it, any point at all? After all, her illness was terminal Was Roger just wasting his time trying to dot the i's and cross the t's for her? And yet, weren't all our lives terminal? It's just a matter of how long each one of us could expect.

Roger gazed at his wife, his heart breaking. "You looked in a solemn mood when I came in. Were you thinking about things?" he said, meaning her cancer, but avoiding mention of the name.

"No. Nothing like that dear. I suppose I was being a bit philosophical about our time here on earth, if you want to know."

Charlene sipped her milk and nibbled a tea biscuit.

"I've got another surprise for you," he said provocatively. "I taped your favourite programmes. You told me the ward television was usually switched off at nine o'clock, and that very often you couldn't see the programmes you liked, because the other women insisted on looking at the soaps."

"I've often wondered whether, if I hadn't spoken to you when you were lying low like a hurt dog, you would have spoken to me, that day on Ben Calder? It was certainly my lucky day."

Roger gave her question a little consideration before replying. "Speculation of that kind is frustrating and inevitably useless. What does matter is that we did meet. And I bless the day we did."

"But would you have spoken to me?" she persisted, for she felt certain he was avoiding her question.

"You've got me in a corner, Charlene." he admitted. "I did think when I first saw you at the beginning of the climb that you were different from the other women. I didn't know in what way, but there was something about you I liked very much. I'm sure I would have spoken to you once I'd overcome my problems."

"That took you a long time to say," she giggled, taking his hand and gently kissing his fingers. "I love you so much Roger. I'm such a lucky woman."

"And I love you too, princess. I'm such a very fortunate man."

"What are you going to show me from your archives?" she enquired. "Do you have that one on the food programme?"

Roger selected one of the six tapes he had used to record the programmes Charlene had missed. "I think it's on this one."

He put the tape in the video recorder and switched it on. "There'll be just about enough time left tonight for this one programme," he warned his wife. "You can see the rest another time."

When the closing titles of the programme came up, Roger suggested it was time for bed.

"Yes, you're right, Today's been a full one and I'm feeling tired."

The feeding machine, with its near full load of liquid nourishment, was too heavy for Charlene to carry.

"Just give me a shout when you're ready to go to bed," he said, as he laid the heavy blue machine on the floor beside the wash-hand basin and left to give her that one little bit of privacy, which still remained.

He had just settled Charlene in bed when the doorbell rang urgently.

Who could be calling at this time of the night? he thought.

He looked through the frosted glass and saw the figure of a woman, carrying a large holdall.

The nurse wasn't due to come until nearer ten o'clock. He fumbled with the keys, trying to find the right one to unlock the door.

"Hurry up!" The voice of his impatient daughter called out anxiously.

Marjorie had managed to get a flight from Zimbabwe at short notice.

"I won't be a minute," he called out as he finally located the key and opened the door.

Marjorie dropped her bag and embraced her father warmly. "I'm sorry about the misunderstanding when you left. It was all my fault."

They held each other for a long time, without another word being said.

"I didn't expect to see you after I phoned you about Charlene's illness and you said you were sorry you couldn't spare time to come over."

"It's difficult to get time off when you're the wife of a government official," said Marjorie. "Later, when I thought about what you said to me. I knew I'd suffer guilt for the rest of my life if I didn't make a special effort to see my stepmother before she died. I decided to bring my letter instead of posting it."

"I'm glad you're here, Marjorie. It's not been easy for me, especially when I'm being visited by Charlene's inconsiderate sister."

"You mentioned this problem in your airmail. I felt very sorry for all three of you."

"I can understand your feeling sorry for Charlene and myself, but I can't see how you can feel sorry for Shirley." Roger was perplexed by Marjorie's attitude.

She patted her father on the shoulder, showing she wished him to release her from his tight embrace, which was becoming uncomfortable.

"Haven't you learned anything yet from Charlene?" she said firmly. "How do you think she would have behaved had the circumstances been reversed, with you the cancer victim and me treating her as Shirley is doing to you?"

Roger felt humiliated when he realised how much this discord between Shirley and himself must be hurting Charlene.

"I appreciate she's helpless to do anything about these disruptions. I promised her once I would try to ignore her sister's goading, but no matter how quiet I remain, her husband, Peter, manages to fire the barb to inflame the situation," he replied.

"You'll need to try harder," Marjorie said stubbornly. "The only person who matters at the moment is Charlene. I don't think she should be distressed any further."

"I've done everything I can to ensure her comfort and well-being. If I've failed sometimes it is understandable. I too, am under a strain. Trying to be all things to her, all of the time has been very hard. There have been many times when I would like to have shown her sister the door, especially when I saw her behaving without the slightest consideration for Charlene's condition. But I didn't, because it would have done more harm than good. Charlene wanted to see her sister and her family as often as she could. To have denied these visits, especially those of the children, would have been the most cruel thing I could have done to my dear wife." He looked near to tears.

Marjorie embraced him again. "There, there," she said comforting him, as he had done to her when she was a child. "I didn't mean to upset you. I know you must be under a great strain just now. What I was trying to show you was that Charlene expects so much more from you. She's depending on your strength at this time. Use it. Give her confidence, so she can depend on you as she's always done."

Roger had never heard his daughter speak with such strength and so philosophically before.

"I suppose we both know what Charlene expects from us," he said. "All I can say is that I'll continue to protect her from any distress or hurt as far as I can. But there are times when it requires the ability of the Good Lord."

He picked up her heavy holdall. "Let's go and see Charlene now. She must be wondering who's at the door. We'll put the things in your bedroom later."

When they reached the door of the sick room, he whispered, "Wait here a second while I prepare her for your appearance. It might otherwise be too big a shock."

"You were an awful long time talking to the nurse," said Charlene when he finally entered the room. "Where is she anyway?" She glanced towards the door, expecting to see the nurse waiting there.

He lifted Charlene higher up on the mountain of pillows and wrapped her cardigan about her shoulders before answering.

"Are you quite composed now? It wasn't the nurse I was talking to. It was Marjorie," he said proudly.

Charlene's eyes sparkled, as they had not done for some weeks now. Marjorie had come to see her after all. Wasn't it kind of her to come such a long way from Zimbabwe? "Don't keep me waiting any longer, Roger. Tell her to come in right away."

Marjorie had been listening to their conversation, partly to assess how well her stepmother was keeping. "I heard you Charlene," she called out and walked into the bedroom. "Let me hold you."

She went round to the other side of the bed and was about to lift Charlene when she saw her emaciated frame. The hug Marjorie had intended was replaced instead with a gentle touch of her shoulder.

"It's so different from the last time you saw me," said Charlene, appreciating her stepdaughter's consideration.

Marjorie wiped her eyes and kissed Charlene firmly on the forehead. "Tell me what has happened while father makes a cup of tea."

"If you don't mind Marjorie, I'm feeling rather full up from all this liquid food." She pointed to the half-empty bottle in her feeding machine. "But," she stopped and looked at Roger, "your Dad will bring you a cup while we talk. I've got so much to say to you."

As soon as Roger had gone into the kitchen Charlene, told her stepdaughter that she was not expected to survive for more than two months. "I've already had two weeks - I'm happy you've come."

"Mother," said Marjorie deliberately omitting the "step" part. "I wish I could say I'm happy to be here, for that would mean you were going to be well again. Let me say it another way." She stroked Charlene's brow to lift a few strands of loose hair away. "I would rather be here than anywhere else right now."

"You seem to have accepted that I'm not going to get better. This is not the case with your father. He denies that my cancer is terminal and thinks there's a chance I'll get better. And he's not thinking it'll take a miracle, either."

"What does he think will bring about this cure?" said the mystified Marjorie.

"It's very simple. He still believes I can overcome the cancer by eating the right foods. But even if it had once been imaginable, it's too late now. I live each day as it comes and thank God for making it possible for me."

"It's such a pity I didn't listen to my father and get to know you earlier. I've missed so much, not knowing the wonderful person you are."

"I only do what lots of others do," said Charlene resisting her daughter-in-law's praise.

"I wish I had done more for you when you visited us." Marjorie was feeling guilty about her lack of consideration when the holiday had been brought to an early end.

"You shouldn't blame yourself for anything that happened. Sometimes things can go wrong, even with the best of intentions. You know what Burns said about the best-made plans? Anyway, we had a lovely time when we visited you. It wasn't anybody's fault that it ended the way it did. Who could have done anything to avoid a fault in the telephone system? How was anyone to know that I'd already reached an advanced stage in my cancer, which made things so difficult for me."

"Let's put all that behind us now and enjoy every minute we can, while we can." Marjorie was firm. "The sun seems to have followed me all the way to Scotland."

# Chapter 21

Every day that passed saw Charlene getting weaker, making the task of caring for her more demanding. Although district nurses had been calling three times a day to attend to Charlene's needs, particularly the dressing of her wound, the bulk of the caring fell on Roger and Marjorie.

"We'll go for a stroll round the pond in Eastgate Park. You'd like that, wouldn't you," said Marjorie.

Eastgate House, now in ruins, had formerly been the home of a Victorian tobacco trader and, as the result of a very generous bequest to the city by his descendants, the grounds were now a public park and open to everyone.

As she grew weaker Charlene was becoming less enthusiastic for the outdoor activities she used to enjoy so much.

"We'll take the wheelchair with us and, if you fancy walking for a bit any time, you can just push it in front of you." Marjorie hoped to inspire her to go out into the fresh air.

"I'll go if you want me to," said Charlene reluctantly. "But I don't think I'll be walking."

Roger came in and announced that he had put the wheelchair in the boot and that, as far as he was concerned, they were ready to go.

"I'll wear my heavy tweed coat. It looks cold outside," said Charlene, pushing herself out of the recliner.

Because the day was cooler than normal, the car park was quite empty, which allowed Roger to park the car close to the path where they planned to walk. He brought the wheelchair over to Charlene, who was standing holding on to the door of the car and, with the help of Marjorie, eased her into the chair and made her comfortable and warm with a heavy tartan rug.

"I'll push Charlene first," said Marjorie. "It's downhill from here. You can bring her back."

"I'd like to go over to the old house," Charlene requested. "When I was a child I used to play there."

"They do say you go back to your childhood," said Roger.

"I have so many happy memories of doing things with my friends."

It was now autumn and it aroused recollections of collecting leaves into a heap and jumping on them without hurting oneself.

"Wouldn't this lot make good garden compost?" said Roger as, he kicked a heap of beech leaves.

"Why did we never come and collect them, I wonder?" Charlene was curious.

"We didn't have the time on our hands we have now, I suppose." Roger offered by way of explanation and then realised how inappropriate it was.

Marjorie had walked the wheelchair over to the ruin, the turning point where Roger was to take over.

"Where's the ruined mansion?" asked Marjorie.

Charlene pointed to a mound covered in self-sewn rowan and silver birch. "It used to be a huge, red sandstone mansion. If you go closer you can see some of the stones. My friends and I used to play at houses in the ruins."

"Charlene! Then you saw it before it was demolished as being unsafe," said Roger.

"It was probably unsafe even then," said Charlene.

"It's a bit nippy today. I think we should all have a warm drink. The tea-room's not far from here,"

"Not for me," reminded Charlene. "Though, I'd like to be in the warmth and see the decorations."

"There's an empty table near the door," said Marjorie, calling his attention to one that looked out onto the meadow of Eastgate Park.

Roger joined the small queue at the counter. It had become so cold that most of the strollers had come into the warmth of the café. "Two coffee's, one without milk." Roger asked the young waitress.

"We've only got African. Will that do?" She sounded like Billy Connolly.

"Yes. That'll suit us fine."

As he was returning to the others with the drinks he saw a woman sitting beside Charlene. Then he recognised Jane Faulds, his former friend from the Kelvin Hiking Club.

"Marjorie, I suppose you've been introduced to Jane," he said, setting the tray on the table. "How've you been keeping?"

"Quite well, actually," she said glibly. "And how have you been keeping Roger?"

"Just fine." He did not develop it any further. "Would you like anything? A cup of tea perhaps."

"No thank you. I've just finished. I was on my way out when I saw Charlene. We haven't seen each other for ages. We've just been talking about the old days."

Roger was embarrassed. "They're not all that old, or that long ago for that matter."

He might have married Jane but for her petulant streak, Roger recalled.

"Jane's still not married," said Charlene. "Still a catch for some eligible male."

"After Roger married you, I opted out of the marriage stakes, for you captured the best of the bunch," asserted Jane. "Don't give much thought to a husband nowadays. Sometimes, think they're more of a nuisance than they're worth."

Marjorie, who had said little up till now, protested. "I couldn't do without my husband. Each of us would do anything for the other."

"You can have your man," said Jane. "There's nobody around my home to tell me what to do. I'm my own mistress."

"Do you still go walking?" Charlene asked.

"Not as often as I used to. But I do make the occasional effort. Have you both hung up your boots? I never saw either of you out walking after you left the club."

"We had too many other diversions," said Charlene.

"I'm not keeping well just now but I would like Roger to take it up again. Do you think you could encourage him to go walking some Sunday?"

"Whenever he wants the company, just phone and let me know," replied Jane. "I've waited longer than I intended. I'll have to go now. I've got an appointment."

She got up and waved farewell, as she walked towards the door. "If you're thinking about going with the Club sometime, give me a ring."

"Charlene, I get the impression you were trying to make an assignation for me." Roger looked strangely at his wife.

"Surely you couldn't think I'd be doing something like that? I've had enough Roger. I'd like to go home."

Charlene was watching the television when the door bell rang. "Would you please answer it, please?" she said to Marjorie who had been watching the wild life programme with her.

"Of course," she replied.

"I'm Sister Murray." Charlene could hear her voice quite distinctly. "I've called to see Mrs Buchanan. Is it convenient? If not, I can come back later."

"Please come in," said Marjorie. "Mrs Buchanan's in here."

Marjorie realised the nurse had obviously come for some special reason. "I was about to have a cup of tea. Would you like me to bring you one?"

"No thank you," replied sister Murray. "I'd like to speak to Charlene on my own if you don't mind."

"I'll be in the kitchen if you want me," said Marjorie.

Charlene recalled their earlier discussion when Sister Murray had indicated what could happen during the last days of her illness.

"I know how well you are being looked after by your husband," the nurse began. "But as you get weaker," she did not want to say near the end, "it's my opinion your husband will be unable to cope with the special problems which can arise. Only those of us who have been trained in cancer nursing can deal with the patient then. It's because I think it will be too difficult for Mr Buchanan that I'm suggesting you come into the hospice very soon. Monday, in fact. We'll have a bed available for you if you want it."

"I know you're right, Sister. Would you make the necessary arrangements?"

"I can only deal with the matters relating to the hospice itself. You'll have to arrange with your husband to take you there," was the precise reply. "I'll have a word with Mr Buchanan before I leave."

Roger was waiting at the front door when Sister Murray was about to leave. "How are things progressing?" he asked expecting a favourable report to support his feelings of optimism.

"As one would expect at this time," she replied. "Your wife is very ill. Are you aware of that?"

"I thought she was getting better when I saw her enjoying strained chicken soup," said Roger.

"I'm afraid her body cannot be nourished that way, now that the cancer is in complete control," she said sadly. "I've had a long talk with her and she's agreed to come into the hospice on Monday. You'll have to bring her in." She walked smartly to her car and drove off.

Roger was very close to tears when he talked to Marjorie about this bombshell. They returned to the bedroom and stood one on either side of Charlene, wondering how to begin.

"Sister Murray asked me to come into the hospice for a few days, to give you a respite," said Charlene, using the excuse that it was to give Roger a rest after his long spell of twenty-four hour nursing. Charlene knew that this was being done to provide the expert help she needed in the last days of her illness.

She was concerned for Roger's well-being and wanted to spare him any unnecessary distress if she could do so. It had always been like that during her illness - and before that, too.

"Find someone to help you with the cleaning." She was anticipating the time when Roger would be on his own. "There's no need for you to stay in this big house. There are small one-bedroom flats not far from here."

This was one of the reasons he had been attracted to "The Rare Bird" as he had called Charlene the first time they had met on Ben Calder. She never put her own needs before those of others. Sometimes, he would get annoyed when this self-denial reached the stage of giving away something she really needed for herself.

Then the doorbell sounded and once again Marjorie went to answer it. It was Charlene's sister.

"My name's Shirley Anderson," she said. "I'm the patient's sister," she announced, thinking Marjorie had come to nurse Charlene.

"Mrs Anderson. I've heard about you from my father. I'm Marjorie Ralston," she said, correcting Shirley's misapprehension. "Won't you come in?"

265

Shirley was accompanied by Peter and by her son, Dr Gary Anderson. "We'd like to see Charlene right away," she said entering the bedroom where Charlene and Roger were talking.

Normally Roger would have left Charlene and her sister on their own to talk in private, but this time he decided he would remain to share his wife's company as long as possible. After all, if the doctor was right he didn't have much time left with his dear Charlene.

Gary sat at the top of the bed near his Aunt, whilst his mother flopped heavily at the foot of it. Peter stood aggressively beside Roger.

"You're looking well, Aunt," said Gary.

"Mother's going into the hospice tomorrow," said Marjorie, trying to relieve the awkward silence, which had followed Gary's stupid comment. "My father," she turned towards him, "is making all the arrangements."

"I've been to the hospice to see one of my patients," said Gary. "She was very well looked after. They have ways of keeping people from suffering," he said, being as helpful as he could.

"How are you going to get into the hospice?" asked Shirley.

"Roger'll take me there."

"What you need is an ambulance," interjected Peter.

"Why didn't you think of that, Roger?" smirked Shirley.

"What was that Sister's name? The one from the hospice," asked Peter.

"Sister Murray." Charlene wondered why he wanted to know.

"Then get on the phone and tell her you want an ambulance," said Peter.

"I've already made the arrangements," Roger said quietly trying to keep tempers cool. "That's not how ..."

"I'm not talking to you," Peter interrupted him and then continued speaking to Charlene as if Roger were not there. "Call Sister Murray at the hospice and get her to make arrangements."

"There's no point in contacting Sister Murray. Transportation has nothing to do with her," said Roger softly.

"Roger's right," repeated Charlene. "It's nothing to do with Sister Murray. She told me so when she was here."

"I don't know why you keep ignoring me," said Roger. "The only way to get an ambulance is through our general practitioner. I'll be phoning Dr Preston in the morning and he'll confirm with the ambulance people that Charlene's need is genuine."

Shirley was clearly distraught with the way events were moving towards the end of her sister's life and was finding it very difficult to accept the inevitable. As she herself had said things didn't always come out, the way she wanted them. "I'm only wanting to help. Why's everyone against me?"

"I'm not, dear!" shouted Peter, very much upset at seeing his wife in a distressed condition. Then he turned and glared at Roger. "I should've punched your nose for speaking to my wife and me the way you did last time. You don't know how close you were to having your head bashed in when you refused to let me collect those things from the attic."

"Peter! You made a wise decision." Roger was very much fitter and experienced in the art of self-defence.

"Would anyone like tea?" asked Marjorie as she came into the bedroom carrying a tray. She had heard the raised voices and hoped the tea would settle the situation.

"No thanks," said Shirley. "We're all leaving. But we'll come and see Charlene again in the hospice."

"Please don't go just yet, Shirl," said Charlene. "Don't you realise every minute is precious now?"

Roger knew how much Shirley's visit meant to Charlene. "I would appreciate it very much if you would stay with your sister for a while yet, Shirley. She's right. These moments are too precious to be wasted bickering," he pleaded. "Marjorie and I will go next door to give you freedom to discuss things in private."

\* \* \* \* \*

Dr Preston, who had arranged for an ambulance in response to Roger's phone call, came to see his patient at the same time as the district nurse was dressing Charlene's wound.

"Mrs Buchanan, how are you feeling today?"

"Uncomfortable."

"Are you in any pain then?" Dr Preston was concerned he'd been unable to do very much to help her.

"No pain. Just a lot of discomfort," Charlene repeated.

"I think I'd be calling your discomfort, pain. Please let me give you something to make you more comfortable," he pleaded.

"Really I don't need anything. I can cope," she replied, imitating her father's determination when he was terminally ill. The district nurse brought some warm water from the bathroom and stood between the doctor and his patient. "Mrs Buchanan is to have a bed bath before she leaves, doctor."

"Go ahead, nurse. You're not in my way." He brought out his prescription pad. "There's no point in being a martyr when you can avoid it." He felt guilty that he had been unable to save his patient's life and was frustrated by her refusal of his offer to relieve her pain.

Roger was also concerned by his wife's refusal of a painkiller. "Charlene, please let Dr Preston prescribe a painkiller for you. It would make us all feel that much better, including yourself."

When Roger added his support to the doctor, Charlene, who was aware that she was coming to the end of her life, agreed. Her resistance had represented her final effort to fight the cancer.

The doctor spoke carefully. "Mrs Buchanan, you're going into the hospice for a week of respite care to let your husband have a rest."

Charlene pointed out that she had never had better attention in her life. Nothing had been too much trouble for Roger. "He couldn't have looked after me better," she said admiringly.

"I have to go now Mrs Buchanan. I'll leave a prescription with your husband."

Roger saw him to the door and then went outside with him so as not to be overheard by Charlene.

"Has my wife the slightest chance of getting better?" asked Roger, who still naively believed that the proper treatment would effect a cure.

"I don't think you've accepted the truth yet about your wife's cancer. It's terminal. Everything that could be done has been done. She has been given a few extra months of useful life. Now that has come to an end." The doctor spoke with clinical precision.

"Are you telling me my wife is going to die?"

"Yes!"

"How long has she got?" Roger asked hoping to hear that she was going to be with him for a long time yet.

"A week to ten days at the most," estimated Dr Preston.

Roger was shattered. He had known that Charlene was seriously ill, but he had pretended to himself she would improve.

"A week to ten days," Roger repeated automatically. "Then she might die in the hospice!"

"Your wife is likely to end her life there. It is not a matter of chance that she was offered a bed this particular week. Sister Murray has been keeping an eye on her condition. It is she who had the task of judging when your wife would be in greatest need of the hospice facilities."

Roger thanked him for all his help and returned to Charlene.

It was going to be very difficult for him not to show Charlene what he was feeling at that moment. This was when he had to be at his most competent. He could not let Charlene down at a time of her greatest claim on him when she needed his strength. He'd been treating her illness all along as if there was hope and he mustn't change his behaviour as a result of today's news.

After the nurse had left, Roger, whose heart was breaking, took Charlene's hand and squeezed it as he had done thousands of times before with its cryptic message of love. "Hello there, princess. Would you like anything?"

"I don't think so Roger," she said quietly. "Maybe some cold water and a bowl to spit into, to moisten my tongue. After that I'd like to rest."

"Dr Preston has arranged for an ambulance to take you to the hospice. Marjorie and I will come with you."

"I'd like that," she said and closed her eyes.

Next day when they got to the hospice, they felt a wonderful air of peace. "It's hard to believe that many of those people sitting around looking so well are terminal cases," Roger whispered to Marjorie. "Charlene looked like this some weeks ago."

Roger pushed Charlene's wheelchair into the ward and was asked by the sister to take her to a bed by the window with a view of the river; it looked like a canal in Venice or Amsterdam. Just then the ward sister came over and began to take Charlene's details.

"Marjorie and I will say cheerio for now," said Roger. "But we'll be seeing you later tonight."

They kissed Charlene goodbye and left the Sister to get on with her job.

Father and daughter decided to share the visiting, so that he went about ten o'clock in the morning and she visited Charlene in the afternoon. This left the evening free for Shirley and her family.

During the first few days in the hospice Charlene had been quite alert and had been able to talk about various things. But latterly she had become so weak that Roger was finding it hard to make out what she was saying to him, and sometimes had to ask the nurse to interpret.

One morning when he came into the ward, Charlene was sitting up, supported by her pillows and looking out of the window which overlooked the river. She smiled with her eyes only. Her face, with its stretched skin, could no longer show her happiness at seeing Roger. He bent over and kissed her on the lips.

"Good to see you, princess," he said stroking her hair. He looked out of the window at the scene Charlene looked at every day.

"Doesn't it remind you of that holiday we spent in Amsterdam?" Roger was looking towards the iron bridge and tree-lined walkway. "It looks like the view from our hotel beside the canal," he said, trying to get a positive response.

"I'm not interested Roger," she replied quietly in a monotone, like someone who had come to terms with their imminent death. On another happier occasion she would have been enthusiastic and agreed with him that the similarity was remarkable.

Although Charlene was no longer interested in material things for herself, she was still concerned for Roger.

"Are you looking after yourself? Getting enough to eat," she enquired in a hoarse voice.

"I don't have anything else to do," replied Roger. "How I wish I could eat for both of us?"

Suddenly Charlene said very quietly, so quietly he had to put his ear close to her mouth and listen again.

"Take me home." It was as if she knew the end was near.

Roger would have done so, without question, had he not realised the distress it would cause her during the transfer, as well as the fact he did not have the facilities of a morphine drip. She could die on the way home. He tried to justify himself. He was in a terrible position. How could he say no and distress her even more?

One of the nurses happened to be near. "My wife is asking to go home," said Roger seeking her advice.

"Just leave it with me," she said.

"Is there anything you want to say to me Mrs Buchanan?" enquired the nurse.

Charlene replied weakly. "No. Nothing."

When Roger sat down beside his wife again no further mention was made of going home. It was as if Charlene had accepted that this was no longer an option. She had been speaking for a while now and had used a lot of the little energy she had to spare. She pointed to a plastic cup on the locker with her eyes.

"Do you want some water?" Roger asked as he brought the cup over to her.

Charlene nodded her head and eagerly took hold of his hand. Some of the water spilled down her chin and over the pretty blue and white dressing gown she had worn the night they were married. Roger took a couple of tissues and wiped the moist part of her gown to dry it off. She tried to smile, as she had often done before, but was unable to do more than make a grimace with her tight jaws.

"Did you like that?" Roger wiped her chin, which had also become wet from the spillage.

Charlene nodded her approval and began to speak so quietly Roger had difficulty hearing her. "I want to be cremated," said Charlene. "What will you do with my ashes?"

Roger turned away to hide his pain. "I was unhappy when you said you wished to be buried with your parents, because that would have meant the two of us being separated. Now I know what I would like. When I die I shall be cremated as well and our ashes scattered together," he declared.

"Will they be scattered on my parent's grave?" she asked almost inaudibly.

"There's only one place. Ben Calder, where I first met my rare bird."

"I'd like that," whispered Charlene.

She started licking her lips to indicate her mouth was dry. "The ice." She pointed once again to the small locker.

Roger saw a small beaker of ice cubes and a batch of gauze pads. He took a cube and wrapped it in the gauze in the same way as he had seen one of the nurse's do for another patient.

"Here you are, dear," he said pressing the gauze into her mouth.

When she had sucked enough water from the cube, she turned her head away. Once again Roger wiped her chin to dry the surplus water.

"I want to rest now," said Charlene, closing her eyes. "I'm feeling very tired."

Roger kissed her again and said, "I'll be back."

As he was going down the stair he met Sister Murray. "Are you not staying?" She retorted sharply. "Can't you see Charlene is not going to survive very much longer?"

"Sister Murray. It's very hard for me to watch the one I love best of all dying slowly in front of my eyes. I made up my mind to go home and collect my daughter and bring her back with me, because I can see the end is near. I'm sure we'll be back in time."

"Forgive me Mr Buchanan, I've been so inconsiderate. I should have been comforting you in this time of your distress, instead of adding to it. There is an explanation but I don't want to go into it just now." she said regretfully. "You should be able to be with Charlene if you're here by five o'clock."

Roger drove home and collected his daughter.

The receptionist who had been on duty when Roger had gone home earlier recognised him on his return. "Your sister has just gone out with her family to have something to eat. She was told your wife had only a few hours left."

"She's my wife's sister, not mine," Roger corrected her. "You said she knows about my wife's condition?"

"Oh yes." The woman behind the desk nodded. "She told me her sister had only a short while to live."

"What do think of that?" Roger asked his daughter when they

272

were on their way to the ward. "Shirley knows that Charlene has only a little while to live."

"You would think she would have considered it better to wait here than go out and eat," said Marjorie.

Charlene had her head turned towards the door. "She's looking for us to come back as I said we would." She managed one last smile as they walked towards her.

She looks so happy that we've come at last. As if we had arrived in answer to her prayers, thought Roger. He gave her a lingering kiss on the lips, as he stroked her hair. "Hello princess. I'm back."

She was plainly very happy to see them.

"Hello Mother." Marjorie kissed Charlene. "Is there anything I can do for you?"

Charlene could not reply. Her weakness had made speech nearly impossible. She indicated that she wanted her legs rubbed, by stroking the bedclothes with her hand. Roger took one leg and Marjorie took the other. Slowly and carefully they manipulated what flesh there was to ease Charlene's aching limbs.

"How's that?" Roger did not really expect his wife to reply.

They put the bedclothes back over her legs and looked for some other diversion.

"How about some more ice?" said Roger, putting a cube inside a piece of gauze.

His wife made no reply, but opened her mouth willingly to receive the cold pad. She might have lacked strength elsewhere but her teeth crunched the cube into fragments, as she sucked its refreshingly cold fluid.

"The tea-room doesn't open in the evening," Roger told his daughter. "If Shirley went out, she probably had advice about the expected end. We may have to spend the night here. I think we should get something to eat."

Marjorie agreed and started to tighten the belt of her coat. Roger gently raised his wife and held her in his arms.

"We're going to get something to eat, but we'll be back as soon as we can," he said quietly.

He kissed Charlene for a few seconds before setting her back on the high pillows. Something was wrong, he thought. Charlene was staring at him, her eyes wide open.

"Father, Charlene's gone." His daughter took his hand. "She died in your arms."

Roger had never seen someone die before. He called the nurse to examine his wife who briefly checked her pulse.

"Mrs Buchanan is dead," she advised him, as she closed Charlene's eyelids.

There were no tears. The shock of losing his beloved Charlene had dulled Roger's senses. Tears would be shed later in private.

Roger and Marjorie waited respectfully for a while beside Charlene's body, remembering her courage and valiant struggle.

"The world has lost an angel and a saint tonight," Roger said to his daughter. "She was indeed a rare bird. I'll never see her like again."

The nurse returned with some documents. "These will help you to do the things which have to be done when you are least able to do them. If you find you need counselling, there is a telephone number you can ring. And if you want to come and see us, at any time, we'll make you welcome. It's too late to contact the doctors. If you come in tomorrow you can collect the death certificate and Mrs Buchanan's things. Meanwhile, if you come next door to the small lounge I'll make you a cup of tea."

They were just leaving the ward when tear-stained Shirley arrived with Peter and her three children. She had not been in time to see her sister die. Nothing was said as the two groups passed one another.

Roger and Marjorie needed that cup of tea. "I still can't believe Charlene has gone," said Roger. "Everything is so unreal, like looking at a film or the television, as though it was happening to someone else and not me."

For the first time Marjorie referred to her own mother. "That's the way I felt when mum died. It was awful. She died of the same sort of cancer."

"Come this way Mrs Anderson," said the nurse taking her to join the other two in the lounge. "I'll bring you a cup. There's plenty of tea in the pot."

"So you had your way in the end," said Peter. "It must give you great satisfaction to be able to say Charlene died in your arms."

"I've always been an honest person. I believe Charlene waited for me to come back to see her. When she died in my arms, it must have been what she wanted. At that time I felt that I was the most privileged person in the universe. I would never have been able to accept the anticlimax of coming here to find, as you have done, that she died while I was away. I thank God for His blessing."

"Charlene told me she is to be cremated instead of being buried with her parents. Is that what you intend to do?" asked Shirley.

"Yes. The decision was made by Charlene herself."

"What is going to happen to my sister's ashes?"

"They are being retained by me in our home until that day when my time comes."

"And then what?"

"And then our ashes will be combined and scattered beside the boulder on Ben Calder where we first met each other."

# Chapter 22

Marjorie had prepared lunch and was just about to serve it when the doorbell rang. "It's probably a neighbour with a card," said Roger as he went to open the door. "It's yourself, Mr Drinkwater. Come into the front room."

"I was wondering how you were taking your wife's death," the minister began. "Are keeping all right?"

"I'm surviving, Mr Drinkwater. That's about all I can say." He asked the minister to sit down. "I'd like to thank you for your frequent visits to Charlene, both here and in the hospital, and your prayers for her recovery. I know how much she appreciated seeing you."

The minister brought out a small notebook and shuffled uneasily on the settee. He had known Charlene and her mother for a number of years but he had no exact knowledge of Charlene's interests outside the church. "Where did Charlene teach?" he said suddenly. The minister had come to learn more about Charlene for his eulogy at the cremation the following day.

"I'm sorry I can't give you much information about Charlene's teaching career - I didn't know her then. But I do know she was dedicated to her job. She was very well liked by everyone; parents, staff and pupils alike. She was the assistant head in the early years of the school. If you contact her friend Mary Drumhills she can tell you much more than I can."

"I may do that," said the minister. "How long was she a member of the church?"

"That I don't know either. Her parents were members from the day they were married. And that's a long time ago."

Roger went on to extol the virtues of his late wife for several minutes. "We were an ideal couple. Our views about almost everything matched. She was the finest person I ever met in my life." He would have said much more had he not been interrupted.

"Yes, yes," said the Reverend Drinkwater impatiently. "What you are saying is, that apart from idolising your late wife, you knew very little about her background."

"I suppose I have to plead guilty to that," said Roger. "If I'd known I would be expected to provide a synopsis of her life, I would have started thinking about it some time ago."

"That's a lovely smell coming from the kitchen," remarked the minister. "I expect your daughter has your lunch ready for you."

"Yes, she has." Roger nodded wearily.

"In that case I'll leave you to get on with it. I'll be at the crematorium before two o'clock to meet the cortege at the entrance to the chapel."

Roger confirmed the time and saw him to the front door. "By the way, minister I think I should let you know that my wife's family and I don't get on very well. So, if you see us behaving strangely, you'll know why."

"Thank you for warning me." The minister seemed to understand. "I would not like to say or do anything controversial."

\* \* \* \* \*

During the last week of her life Charlene had asked Roger to take her home; but he had been unable to do so. Now he intended to put that right. He had asked the undertaker to stop the hearse for a few minutes at Burleigh Avenue before going on to the crematorium. When Roger told his daughter she said, "That's the way it should be." They had just stopped talking, when she heard the sound of a vehicle drawing up in the street outside. "That's the hearse now," she said looking out of the window to confirm it.

A young man, dressed in a black frock coat and top hat, alighted from the vehicle and came to the door.

"Whenever you're ready sir," he said politely. "This is what you asked for." He handed Roger a small plastic packet with a curl of greying hair.

Roger felt uneasy at this desecration of his wife's body, as he took the treasured memento from the young man's hand.

"We're ready now."

He put the packet in his pocket and reminded his daughter to collect the wreath from the bathroom. The simple floral tribute, prepared by Marjorie herself, consisted of a circular base with thirty pink geraniums decorating the circumference. It had been Charlene's favourite flower. Roger glanced at the card on the wreath and added some words before following his daughter from the house.

> To the dearest step-mum and
> friend a daughter ever had.
> Love from Marjorie.
> I miss you very much.
> Goodbye Princess,
> your Little Prince.

The funeral director opened the back door of the hearse and Marjorie placed the single wreath on Charlene's coffin.

Then the procession started to drive slowly along Burleigh Avenue. The young man with the top hat, walked respectfully beside the hearse, until they came to the end of the Avenue where it joined the main road.

At this point the procession stopped briefly, whilst the young man deferentially doffed his top hat in the direction of the coffin and took his seat beside the driver of the hearse.

Because the hearse had arrived while another was standing beside the chapel, the driver stopped in a lay-by near the entrance gate of the crematorium. "I'm afraid this is happening far too often," said the driver of the hired car. "The previous service is over-running. It detracts from the solemnity of the occasion when one group of mourners is rushing to get away, whilst another group is waiting impatiently to enter the chapel. They should either allocate more time for the service or see that the minister finishes on time."

Roger looked up the hill that led to the small chapel. "I can see Shirley with her husband Peter and the children standing on the road beside the minister."

"Such a large crowd of mourners have turned up, I hope you booked enough places in the hotel for the reception," Marjorie pointed out.

"I'm certain all will go well," said Roger. "Look, we're starting up again."

The hearse moved slowly uphill until it reached the Reverend Anthony Drinkwater. Some of the mourners from the previous funeral rushed, like drivers in the Monte Carlo rally, to their parked cars and raced off down the hill.

Roger and his daughter went across and shook hands with the minister and Shirley, reminding her of the meal to come in the hotel.

The minister led the funeral party into the chapel to the sound of quiet organ music. When he reached the front row of pews he indicated that Roger and the family should be seated. Mr Drinkwater, dressed in his finest robes, then stepped on to a raised platform and walked over to stand behind the lectern. When everyone had entered the chapel, the crematorium caretaker asked them all to stand.

Roger wanted to cry as Charlene's coffin was brought in and placed on the catafalque, but he forced himself to be calm. He had chosen the two hymns himself. One was Charlene's favourite and the other was his. Neither was the traditional Twenty-third Psalm.

Charlene would have approved of the simple, light oak coffin, with its single floral tribute, Roger thought. She would not have wanted anything that was brashly ornate.

Memories flooded in as they sang, and all the time his gaze was fixed on Charlene's coffin. The hymn had hardly finished when the minister's voice broke through his reverie.

"During the last few months of Charlene's life, I visited her regularly in hospital," he began. "I know she appreciated the prayers I was saying on her behalf. She told me several times that they gave her comfort and strength to endure what she knew lay ahead of her."

It's Charlene we're remembering not you, thought Roger to himself.

"We use the Latin expression "rara avis" to describe an exceptional person; unique like a rare bird. Charlene Buchanan was such an individual. It's not often in our lives that we meet someone like her. One, who was so caring, so understanding, so kind and selfless as she was."

Isn't this what he was telling him yesterday? Only you called it idolising your wife then, mused Roger

"Charlene never put herself before anyone else. She was happy taking second place, if that meant improving someone else's enjoyment of life. That is not to say that she herself lacked that indefinable quality of life we call happiness. On the contrary, she derived greater pleasure knowing that her actions were helping others. She never said an unkind word against anyone, even when the temptation to do so must have been very great."

When was he going to mention the grieving relatives, thought Roger? He should not have told him about his conflict with Shirley. Clearly, he wanted to avoid embarrassment.

"And, when the end appeared on the horizon she displayed outstanding courage in this time of her tribulations. She did not blame God for her painful illness. She did not ask Lord, why have you afflicted me this way? Have I not carried out all your commandments? Charlene was not only a rare bird she was also a rare Christian. She accepted God's Will. She knew that it was part of His greater plan for her. Even if some us are ready to declare," he looked aggressively at Roger for a few seconds, "that they can see no meaning in her illness and death. She was certain she had nothing to fear at this time. She is ... an example ... to us all."

That's it, thought Roger. Nothing about her dedicated work with young children. He could have said something about the devoted attention that I gave Charlene these past few weeks.

After the mourners had sung the last hymn, the minister said a final prayer and left the dais. As he passed the four main mourners, Roger, Marjorie, Shirley and her husband, Peter, he gave them a signal to follow him to the door leading out of the chapel. Here they took up their places with Roger at the head and the minister at the rear.

It was going to take some time for all of the mourners, approximately two hundred of them, who had come to pay their last respects to Charlene, to have a word with the grieving relatives. Her former school colleagues, members from the Kelvin Hiking Club, family and friends were all there. Marion, Shirley's youngest child, was the first to come forward and speak to Roger.

"It's good to see you here." He gave Marion a warm embrace. "You're so much like your Aunt." He had to hold on a bit longer.

The tears were close and he did not want to meet the next mourner whilst he was crying.

He looked over Marion's shoulder and saw Carol and Gary, Shirley's other two children slip out of the queue and make their way up to their parents and the minister. Now he knew how they felt about him.

He recovered his composure and released Marion. Roger patted his eyes with his hand, clearing the tears. "I'll see you later," he said to her.

As each of the mourners reached him, he shook their hands and thanked them for attending the service. "It's very good of you to come," he said simply.

Because the caretaker had allowed an earlier cremation to over-run, he did not seem to appreciate that all the later cremations would also be running late.

Unfortunately there were so many mourners that merely to say, "Hello and goodbye" to each of them would have taken all of the time allocated without a service. He still had to see some fifty mourners when the caretaker came up and demanded that Roger hurry.

Had Roger not been fully conscious of the fact that it was Charlene's cremation, he would have lost his temper with this man's behaviour, but her memory was more important?

Where were all the church members today? Roger thought when he saw the elder and his wife approaching him? That's only four of them, if I include the minister.

What about the woman who had been cured of cancer? Could she not have shown her appreciation by attending?

He shook the elder's hand warmly.

"What can I say?" Mr Brown appeared embarrassed. Had he noticed that the huge congregation of Elmwood Parish Church could only manage a total of four mourners? "Charlene was such a lovely person. Mind you keep your pecker up!"

If it hadn't been customary for the elder to attend the funeral of the parishioner in his ward, would he have been here? Roger was disappointed that so few had given their time. He knew he shouldn't have been, but what did they have to do that was more important than saying farewell to an "angel"?

After the last mourner had been passed on to the minister, Roger and his daughter joined Shirley and her family.

"There's room in the car," Roger advised.

"We don't need a lift," said Peter. "We've got several cars with us."

"Do you know where to go?"

"Yes. I know where I'm going," said Peter.

Roger said cheerio and sat in the hire car. As he took his handkerchief from the top pocket to blow his nose, he felt the plastic envelope and his cousin's letter.

"What is it?" Marjorie asked, as she saw them in her father's hand.

"It's a lock of Charlene's hair. I asked the undertaker to get it for me as a reminder."

He held the piece of paper in his left hand and used his right hand to clear his nose with his handkerchief.

"My cousin sent this letter to Charlene just before she had her second big operation. It's another way of looking at pain." He began.

"When I am in torment I go to Jesus and place myself in His everlasting arms. He covers my agony with His, which is very reassuring for me. I know how extremely fatiguing life can become when unbearable pain closes over us like a prison, from which we cannot escape. It is at times like these we need all the help we can get."

Roger folded the paper and returned it to his breast pocket with Charlene's curl. "I think she would approve, don't you Marjorie?"

The Elmwood Court Hotel, where the meal had been booked, was not far from the crematorium; but it was not on a direct route and could pose a problem for strangers to the area.

"We've waited half an hour for Shirley and her family to get here. I think we should ask the mourners to start without any more delay," Roger said to his daughter.

"I agree. You can't ask the staff to wait any longer. Some people are asking if you've invited Charlene's family? What can I say to them?"

"Just tell the truth to anyone who asks. Shirley was informed about the meal and say you don't know why she hasn't come."

The guests took their places and the hotel staff began serving. Roger stood by the door, hoping Shirley would appear, even at the last minute. It was not easy to get to the hotel from the crematorium. He himself had often taken a wrong turning himself on these country roads. Once you had made a mistake it was never easy to correct it. Perhaps that was it. It was unthinkable that Shirley intended to show a blatant disregard for her in-laws and the other mourners.

"Mr Buchanan." The quiet voice of the minister interrupted Roger's musing. "I'm sorry I'm late."

"That's all right Mr Drinkwater," Roger reassured him. "I know it's difficult to find this place."

"I've been many times in my capacity as parish minister, sometimes on happier occasions, such as christenings or marriages, as you well know. I came to ask ... Goodness! What is that?" Several latecomers had arrived and pushed the door open against him.

"Forgive us being late," said one of them. "We lost our way."

"Don't give it another thought. Go and sit down with the others," he said.

"May I say how much I liked the service," said one of Charlene's friends, who had missed the chance to speak with the minister at the crematorium. "Everything was so apt. That was the Charlene we all knew and loved so well." Tears came into her eyes, as she shook his hand. "The words were so appropriate."

"Thank you for saying so." The minister smiled as she walked away with the others.

"When I heard the latecomers arriving, I thought it was my sister-in-law and her family," said Roger.

"That's what I was about to say, when we were interrupted," said Charlene's girlfriend. "I'm late because I was comforting Shirley. Peter said he had made other arrangements. I tried to dissuade him. I'm sorry you didn't know."

"Many of the mourners here will probably draw their own conclusions," said Roger. "I hope they don't see Shirley in a bad light."

"Nothing's wrong, I hope?" asked the minister, overhearing.
"No, minister," he said.
"I just came along to see how you were coping and ask if you would excuse me from joining you in the repast. I do have other things to get on with and the time I save will be useful."
"Not at all. You'll probably be thinking about your sermon, tomorrow."
"Something like that."

Roger thanked him for his tribute to Charlene during the service. But it was almost word for word how he had described Charlene when the minister had called to comfort him. There had been a number of important omissions, however. Were they due to a lack of time, or were they an oversight? These lapses had been mentioned to Roger by some of the mourners who had also noticed them. He was about to walk towards the seated mourners, when he realised the minister was still standing by the door, shuffling uneasily, as if his mission had not been successful. He was smiling awkwardly.

Why wasn't he leaving? There was nothing more to be said. Could he be looking for payment? Surely that could not be his reason for calling? To expect to be paid by a life-time member of the church for doing his ministerial duty?

"Are you expecting a fee?" Roger asked quietly.
"I ... wouldn't quite put it like that. I thought there might have been an omission on your part. Some people have the impression that the undertaker gives the minister a gratuity to avoid distressing the bereaved," he wheedled.

Nothing could have distressed Roger more. He had always believed the minister to be one of the sincerest he had heard over the years but this one selfish act had destroyed Roger's faith in him and probably the church as well.

"I ask you again Mr Drinkwater. Are you expecting a fee?"
"I would not call it a fee," said the minister. "But I am usually given something for my additional work."

Marjorie, who had been watching the discussion going on between them, suspected something was wrong. She excused herself and left the table to join her father at the door in time to hear him say. "I'm appalled that you are so thoughtless as to look for payment in the circumstances. I asked the undertaker, who is himself an elder in the church, about the position. He advised me that no charge is made for "additional duties", as you put it."

Now that a witness was present, the minister immediately took up a defensive attitude. "I don't know what has possessed you, Mr Buchanan. Surely you don't think I could ever think of asking for money for performing a service for dear Charlene? I can only put it down to your grief, and that you are unaware of what you are implying."

"It's clear you've forgotten Martin Luther and his views on those clergymen, like yourself, who seek payment for their services. I'm sure God doesn't expect you to levy a charge today."

"I forgive you for what you are saying," said the minister. "Perhaps in the fullness of time, you'll understand how badly you have behaved and ask God's forgiveness."

Roger could no longer trust himself not to abuse the minister in full view of the mourners.

"Marjorie, would you return and look after our friends?" He took her arm and gently turned her in their direction. "Mr Drinkwater and I have things to say to each other, and these are best said outside, don't you think?" Roger said turning to him. "I think we should clear up this matter," he replied. "You can see me down to my car. It will be less public, and warmer too, if we sit inside to discuss it."

Roger toyed with the idea of commenting on the minister's expensive new Mercedes, but decided against it. He recalled the consultant's warning about the charlatans who offer hope to cancer sufferers in return for a large fee. "Look at the kind of car they drive," he had said. "It won't be a knocked-about ten-year-old Ford like mine."

"There were a number of omissions in your tribute to Charlene," Roger began.

"I was not aware of them," Mr Drinkwater replied coldly.

"You omitted to mention the constant attention, given in love, by a grieving husband, or the suffering sister and her family. Did you say to yourself, I had better not say anything at all? I do not want to be seen to be taking sides in a family dispute?"

"How could you think such a thing? The thought never entered my mind for a moment. There is so little time allocated to each cremation. I know from my experience just how long is at my disposal, and use it as I think most important at the time."

"I'm sorry, Minister, I just don't believe you any more. You wanted to sit on the proverbial fence. You want to be liked by all ... to be all things to all men and women ... and God too," Roger said passionately.

"You can say what you like, Roger, but it won't alter what I've already told you. Our church," he said, meaning his congregation, "is full of love and understanding. You are doing the devil's work for him just now when you behave like this."

"A loving congregation!" exclaimed Roger. "Where were they today? Apart from you, and our elder and his wife, there was only one other member of the church present at Charlene's cremation. Thank God for our friends. It was particularly distressing for me to know that another woman in the congregation, who recovered from the same cancer as my wife, chose not to be present. Was she too ashamed to come? The living example of petitionary prayer, I think that's what you said during a recent service."

"I really don't know how you can say these things, Roger." The minister was genuinely horrified by his parishioner's outburst. "God works in mysterious ways, as we have often been told. We are not able to question the actions of our Loving Father. We must accept that, in all things, He is acting for our own good."

"Mr Drinkwater, you have dented my faith. It will be a long time before I can attend your services again, if I ever can, I would always be asking myself which interest you were serving in your sermons. Was it for your own personal gain when you asked the congregation to give more to the church funds, or were you just taking an ego trip? You no longer have that strong image of sincerity, which made you stand out from other churchmen."

The minister was beginning to regret the insensitive way he had handled his gratuity.

"I'm sorry you feel this way. Won't you believe me when I tell you I'm devastated that you think I would ask for money for our dear Charlene's service? You know that I didn't ask you for any. You opened the discussion, and I merely tried to explain my position."

"I put this in my pocket when I came out this morning," said Roger, putting his hand in his trouser pocket and taking out a twenty-pound note. "I wanted to give it to you, surreptitiously, as a gift for the way you visited Charlene throughout her long illness, and the undoubted comfort you had been to her. But you spoiled even that." He crumpled the note and threw it in the minister's face. "There's your twenty pieces of silver, Mr Drinkwater!" he exclaimed. "Maybe you can put it towards next year's new car." He got out of the Mercedes and walked quickly away, without looking where he was going, and collided with Marion and her husband, Alexander.

"I'm so sorry," he said, apologising for his carelessness. "I'm so upset. I'm not working on all four burners, as they say."

"Don't concern yourself so," said Marion. "You've got enough problems on your plate as it is."

"I've just been seeing the minister off," he commented, without any further elaboration. "He was telling me what happened to Shirley. I really didn't expect to see anyone after that."

"It was only when we arrived home that father said he was going to eat somewhere else. I was horrified. Alexander and I would like to join you here, if you will have us?"

"Of course. I wanted you to be with me today and I'd be happy if you'd come back home with me afterwards. There are some things belonging to your Aunt she wanted you to have."

"That's not the reason I came," Marion said gently. "You need comforting and I wanted to help."

Roger embraced her warmly. "I want you to know you mean a lot to me. You remind me so much of your Aunt."

"I'm not like her really," Marion protested. "Ask Alexander what he thinks of me!"

"You're like your Aunt. You wouldn't do anything to hurt or offend anyone. You've been gifted with the same compassion that she and your grandmother possessed." The three of them had now reached the side door, which gave access to the reception suite. "It's so good to see someone behaving like a true Christian. There's so much hypocrisy going around these days." He pulled open the door and held it to one side. "Go on upstairs. The rest of the guests are already eating."

"Thank you very much, sir!" said Marion in the jocular manner of her Aunt, as she and Alexander went through the door. "I'm sure you must be hungry after all your exertions. If we hurry upstairs we may still be in time."

After the meal at Elmwood Court, Roger invited his relatives and some close friends back to Burleigh Avenue. The front room of his home had been prepared with a few extra snacks and drinks, just in case there were visitors who had been unable to attend the reception.

"That's a nice photo of auntie," remarked Marion, as she looked at the framed enlargement on the bureau.

"I like it too," agreed Roger. "It reveals that sweet innocence, which everyone admired so much. I'll let you have a copy if you like."

"Oh would you, Uncle Roger?" She gave him a kiss on the cheek and his courtesy title for the first time.

"Have you noticed? You called me Uncle. No one in your family has ever done that before."

Marion was slightly embarrassed by it all. "I never used the word previously, because father warned me not to. He told me you were not really my uncle, only my Aunt's husband."

Roger smiled. "It's so much easier using the title when you're young. Your father's right, I am technically not your uncle. But it's nice to hear you call me that anyway. I'm giving Charlene's clothes to the hospice shop. You're about her size. If there's anything you'd like just let me know," Roger said quietly, as Marion looked at the other photographs on the bureau.

She playfully slapped Alexander on the shoulder, sending him over to the drink cabinet. "Remember you're driving. Stick to low alcohol beer." He smirked. "Don't I always?"

Marion and Roger went into the bedroom. Roger opened the doors of the huge double wardrobe in the bedroom to display his late wife's, collection of clothes. "She never threw anything away. The style is sure to come back, she always said, when I chided her."

Marion was clearly upset at being asked to take some of them. Marjorie, who had just come in to join them, intervened.

"I think you're embarrassing Marion. Give her a little while on her own."

"Before we go, there's something I want to give each of you." Roger took out two boxes from the dressing table drawer. "That's for you, Marjorie," he said, handing her a small red box. "And this is for you." He handed Marion another small box with a worn, blue cover.

The two women opened them almost together and looked sadly at their contents.

"It's Charlene's engagement ring. Did you mean to give it to me?" said Marjorie.

"Of course. Charlene told me to," her father said solemnly.

Meanwhile, Marion stared at the ring in her box. "It's my grandmother's engagement ring. I'll always treasure it, Uncle Roger. Thank you." She put it on her engagement finger, beside the one given to her by Alexander. "They look well together," she said, rotating her hand in the light.

"And I'll always wear Charlene's ring, too," said Marjorie.

Roger shrugged his shoulders. "That solves a problem for me. I've been worried that I might have a burglary with them in the house. Now you two have the problem of keeping them safe."

Marion and Marjorie admired the rings in the silence that followed.

"That's the doorbell. I'll attend to it, while you two think about what you want by way of clothes. Everything you leave behind will go to the charity shop." Roger went to open the door and was surprised to see Jane Faulds standing on the step with a letter in her hand.

"May I come in?" she enquired politely. "This letter concerns you Roger."

Apart from the brief meeting in Eastgate Park, Roger had not spoken to her since the time when Charlene and he had been members of the Kelvin Hiking Club. He wondered if Maureen was still behaving in her nasty ways.

"Come into the front room," he invited, showing her into the room on his left. "There are some guests in the other room. It will be more private in here."

"I saw you at the service, but couldn't manage to speak to you when the mourners left the crematorium at the end of the service. I only learned today that Charlene had died. Naturally, I am very upset. I'm fortunate I didn't miss the opportunity of paying my last respects to her."

Roger pointed to the document in her hand. "You said that the letter had something to do with me?"

"Let me say this, before I let you read it," she said, preparing the way. "I never stopped loving you, Roger. Even when you married Charlene, I kept the flame going on in my heart. If I were to be denied your love, then I would give mine to no one else. That's why I'm still unmarried. I couldn't find another to replace you."

She put her right hand forward. "Will you become my friend again Roger? I'd like that."

"Whilst we're both in a confessing mood, Jane. I had to make a difficult decision all those years ago. I liked both of you and, at that time, I suppose I would have been happy with either. But Charlene had the compassion you lacked. When she was told I had a wife, just as you were, she didn't condemn me as you did. She gave me her love. It was this which helped me to overcome the tragedy of Edith's death."

"I know I was wrong. I've paid for it ever since by being without your love."

"I know what you're trying to say," said Roger. "It's a bit early for me to know how I may feel in the future. I know I'll need a woman's companionship. It could be this was meant to be. I'll be taking up walking again. Perhaps we can walk and talk together, as we used to do?"

"I think you should read this now," she said, handing him the letter.

Roger recognised the writing immediately. "It's from ... "

"Yes," said Jane, "It's from Charlene. She enclosed it with another letter, asking me not to open it until her death."

"She never told me she'd written to you." He extracted the single page.

Dear Jane,

As you are aware, you will be reading this when I am dead. I have taken this unusual step in speaking from beyond the grave, because I know that Roger will need a good woman to look after him, as they say. I remember the acrimony in the club when I was accused of stealing your boyfriend, and how much it upset me.

I would never have done anything improper, and certainly not step in between two friends. If you had stood by him, during the terrible time of gossiping scandalmongers, instead of condemning him, you might have married him instead of me. I do believe there is love in your heart for him and that, given time, he will come to know you as he once did. It is my wish to see Roger settle down with his old friend. I want you to make this known to him, if you are still of the same mind. However, I cannot make people like each other. All I want you to know is that I would like it to happen. Then you might be given the chance to enjoy that love you once had for each other. God's blessing on you both.

Sincerely,
Charlene.

After Roger had read the letter, there was a shocked silence for some minutes. "What can I say, Jane? She told me to go back to the club but she never mentioned your name. "Maybe you'll find someone else to take my place," she had said to me. Clearly she was thinking about you. Charlene must have written this after that day when we met in the park."

"When I read the letter, that was the first time I knew what was in her mind."

"There's one thing certain, dear Jane." He paused wondering if he should say what was on his mind. "You could have destroyed the letter, without showing it to me. Does that mean you still have feelings for me?"

"I've always had them," she replied at once. "Do you think there's a chance for us at last?"

"Given the time for me to get over my devastating loss, I suppose we might come together again. I was fond of you, Jane."

Suddenly the door opened behind them. "This is where you are, father! We've been looking all over for you."

"Something urgent of a private nature came up," he explained. "You remember Jane. We had things to talk over. She knew Charlene when we all walked together. "

"Marion has to leave now and wants to say goodbye," said Marjorie.

Charlene's niece peeped round the door. "That's me away, Uncle Roger. Thanks again for the ring."

"What about the clothes?" he asked. "Did you find anything suitable or sentimental?"

"I've taken one or two small items as mementoes of her." She came over and kissed him farewell.

"Goodbye," Alexander called out. "We'll see ourselves to the door."

"And I'll away in and attend to the mourners," said Marjorie. "Don't you think Charlene's engagement ring is simply wonderful?" she said showing it off to Jane.

"I thought that the first time I saw Charlene wearing it on the night she and your father announced their engagement. Your father and I used to be very good friends." She stopped and looked wistfully at Roger. "Maybe some day we will be again."

THE END

# Epilogue.

Several weeks had passed since Charlene's funeral. Marjorie had returned to Zimbabwe and Roger's grief had become unbearable. He was sitting on the floor in the front room re-reading some of the cards and letters of sympathy from relatives, friends and former colleagues, offering their condolences and asking how they could help. When he had finished, he gathered them into a folder, thinking he must try to write to everyone who had written to him, especially those who had included a personal message of some kind. Those sympathisers, who had taken the time to write a note about their own involvement with Charlene, had all agreed that the world would be a poorer place without her. He had not only lost his wife; he had also lost his friend and companion. Although Roger had been devastated by Charlene's death, he knew she would have wanted him to show the calmness, which she had always expected, from him. Somehow, in a way he could not quite understand, he had been blessed with an inner strength which was enabling him to carry on

He would never forget the agony of watching her dying bit by bit, day by day, as her emaciated body could no longer take in nourishment. He had not been able to do anything to help her.

There was no relief when people told him they knew how he was feeling. How could they possibly know? They could only feel sorrow for the loss of a friend. Did they not realise that the sudden and permanent removal of the most important person in your life was something completely different?

How could anyone understand the importance Charlene and he had attached to such simple God-given pleasures as smelling the first flowers on the witch hazel, or watching the fledgling blue-tits make their first unsteady flight from the nest, or the delicious flavour of the first picking of scarlet runner beans? These things would still happen but they would not mean the same for him any more, for Charlene would not be there to enjoy them with him.

One lady, who had visited Charlene for the first and only time in the last weeks of her life, had told Roger she considered it a privilege to have been able to talk to her. Other people, many of whom had known her over a much longer period, said she was the finest person they had ever met, or that she was a nice person. Oh! How Charlene would have dismissed that description of herself. She neither liked the word nor its implications. "I'm just an ordinary person getting on with the job of living," she would have said. "There's nothing special about me."

Christmas cards had replaced the Get Well cards, but he had been unable to arouse any enthusiasm for Christmas. Charlene had been keen to make the dark nights of the winter festival happier by displaying her treasures: the small wooden camels from Beirut, the manger from Bethlehem and the imitation fir tree and coloured lights she had used with her young classes. He looked in the corner where it once stood and saw three packages. One was the one Marjorie had thoughtfully bought before going back to Africa. "Remember and don't open it until Christmas Day," she had warned him. The other two were from his mother, and his sister, Netta. Any from Shirley, Jane and Marion were prominent by their absence. No one had thought about his loneliness on Christmas Eve.

Charlene had been right about the need for them to tidy up their lives. They had hoarded so many things - most of which should have been consigned to the bin a long time ago. The effort of tidying up was very therapeutic and very sad at the same time, but it did not stop him thinking about her. Quite the reverse. Charlene's personal things awakened memories - happy memories, which sustained him throughout the day.

Today had been no different from any other since her death, except that he had been exceptionally busy trying to sort out her enormous collection of photographs to distribute among those who appeared in them, or those which were especially well taken. He was very tired, after what had been a long session, and was resting in his recliner reading a book, as he waited for the late night news on television. After a little while he fell asleep. Inevitably the book fell from his hands, and startled, he awoke. The woman announcer was speaking about Christmas, when suddenly he saw the figure of a woman standing to the right of the television set, holding a large package in her two hands, which she offered him with a smile.

She was wearing clothes similar to those worn by Charlene long before he knew her and which had been among the things he had given to the hospice.

The vision did not speak. But the smile was distinctive - this was the way she looked when she had been up to one of her "little surprises", as she called them. Roger got up from his chair. "Charlene!" he called out, as he went unsteadily towards her outstretched hands, seeking her loving embrace. But, before he had moved a couple of steps, the vision weakened and shot away from him out to infinity. The sound of the television, which had been strangely quiet throughout, now filled the room

Had he really seen Charlene? The apparition had not looked very much like the girl he'd known. Then he realised he might have been looking at her when she was a much younger woman. He picked up a box of slides taken by her about that time on an early holiday to Beirut, and looked quickly at each one until he found what he had been expecting. The slide showed Charlene, with dark brown hair and a fuller figure, dressed like the woman in the vision. His perfect companion was still looking after him.